I0831866

Hardcover ISBN: 9798992918298

Cover design by: Magdalena Pietrzak
(barn-swallow.carrd.co)
Published in Crab Orchard, Kentucky
Printed in the United States of America

Wickedly Immortal

Kayla Robinson

For all the readers out there who are fiercely independent, hide all your pain and trauma behind a mask, and might have found yourself in your "villain era" because you're finally working with those inner demons instead of against them. Welcome to your healing journey. I hope this finds you well. It can be a long and lonely journey, but it is all worth it in the end. I promise.

Pronunciation Guide:

Scáil - scayl
Deiric - derek (just the gaelic/irish spelling)
Mira - me-rah
Oíche - ee-ha
Aris - air-iss
Eimear - ee-mur

Chapter 1

Scáil

I had been trying to track the Wendigo for a couple of hours with little success, which was odd. I was lurking close to a road when I heard someone humming. Immediately, I assumed this was the bastard luring me into a trap, but then I heard footsteps.

The humming continued, then stopped abruptly. "No, no, that won't do." A male voice. The humming continued. I looked over to the road for a moment to see a man probably twenty yards from me, walking toward the village appearing seemingly out of nowhere. I didn't recognize him as one of the villagers I'd seen that day and he certainly didn't dress like them either. Under only the light of the moon, it was hard to fully grasp what he looked like, but I could see that he wore an intricately adorned tunic, rather sleek but somewhat formal pants and boots. He had a lute strung across his back, and short hair. A bard.

Moments later, I could hear a baby crying. *That* was the wendigo. It had found its mark and laid a trap. There was a small basket at the edge of the road between the bard and I. It was where the sound emanated from, but was not there moments ago. I looked around and scanned the woods ahead of me.

"What on earth?" I heard the bard say softly as he noticed the basket.

There it was, lurking in the shadows merely twenty feet from the edge of the woods, watching and waiting. The bard approached the basket slowly. The sounds of the crying echoed through the trees.

I made my way silently around and through the brush so that I would be approaching it from behind, and hopefully strike it before it launched for the unsuspecting bard.

"Who would leave a baby in the woods like this?" I heard the bard say as I stalked up on the creature. His footsteps were closer now. He had to be close to the basket. I was running out of time.

I saw the creature's muscles tense, it was about to go and claim its prey, the bard was close for sure. I took a silent deep breath, I was right behind it, and could take one step before launching myself onto it. Now, I realized, I had to move now, as it crouched to pounce.

I launched myself just as it started to launch itself. I stabbed it right in the back with my sword and it let out a screech of pain. I missed its heart because it had moved when I made my mark.

"Shit." I mumbled as we both tumbled to the ground. Just as it started to scramble to fight me off I withdrew my sword and stabbed again, and this time struck its heart, killing it instantly. I looked up to see the bard now standing wide eyed and horrified looking at us. He was standing *right* at the basket, which was empty. The crying had stopped.

"What the hell?!" He shouted.

I smiled and stood up as I withdrew my sword again. "You're welcome." I said flatly. I walked over to where the basket was sitting, and grabbed the blanket that was in it to wipe off my sword.

The bard stumbled back. I could see him better now. He had light brown short hair that was straight and parted to the side across his forehead. His tunic was red with gold embroidery. He also wore a black leather jacket which I hadn't noticed when I briefly glanced at him before. Everything about his appearance was elegant. His eyes were a brilliant emerald green, and he had a distinctly handsome face. "What the fuck was that thing?" He finally stammered, looking me up and down after he'd finally stopped staring at the Wendigo that lay dead not far from us.

"It's called a Wendigo." I started to explain. "And you were almost its next meal." I looked him up and down again before meeting his gaze. "I guess I should thank you. You made this easier than I expected it to be."

His face crinkled in a bit of disgust or distaste. "You used me as bait?"

"Well, technically I didn't *plan* to use you as bait, but when you approached anyway I wasn't about to jump in and stop you. It made killing it quick and easy for me."

He scoffed.

"Besides, if I hadn't been here you'd be dead anyway, so again, you're welcome." I smiled.

He looked me up and down once more, that same look of distaste still on his face for a moment. Then, I could see the idea as it struck him, because his face softened and looked a bit devious instead. "Perhaps I should get some of the coin you're collecting for killing it then, since I was such a great help?"

I huffed a laugh. "I'll reiterate bard, that you'd be dead if I hadn't been here, so I hardly think sharing my coin is worth it for me." I walked over to determine how I'd prove my kill. I opted for cutting off a hand. It would be less messy than a head.

"That is disgusting." The bard said, as I walked back over to him and tossed the hand on the road before bending over to grab the blanket and clean off my sword again.

I sheathed my sword, grabbed the hand and turned toward the town. "Disgusting, but it'll do." I said with a smirk. I started to walk away, but I saw him excitedly dart up next to me to follow me.

"Perhaps you could tell me some stories of your other conquests in exchange for helping you then?" He persisted, keeping pace with me as I walked toward the village.

I gave him a sideways glance, and after considering for a few moments, I finally asked. "What on earth are you doing out here at night anyway?"

He groaned, but explained. "I had finished playing at a party in Wrenwood, before I went to the local tavern. I offended some piece of shit by flirting with a beautiful woman I didn't realize belonged to him, so I thought it would be best to get on my way before he could come to find me. So I headed for Bramblebury."

I raised a brow. "Why is that not surprising to me?" I said sarcastically. A rhetorical question.

Again he scoffed. We reached where I'd hung my cloak, not far from the outskirts of the village. I grabbed it from the tree with my free hand. I sat the hand on the ground in front of me as I needed both hands to swing it around myself and clasp it at my neck. When I was bending over to pick up the hand again, he walked around so he blocked my path to the village.

"One story. Give me *one* story and I'll leave you alone." He locked eyes with me as I stood back up again.

"What makes you think I have other stories to share?" I narrowed my eyes at him and I went to step around him and continue on my way.

He stepped to block my path. That devious and excited look returned to his face. "You were in the woods *searching* for this beast. You wouldn't be doing that unless you do this regularly. Surely you've killed something more interesting than this, and under far more exciting circumstances." He was smirking, a brow raised in question.

I sighed. "Yes. I have killed other beasts that are probably more exciting than this story." I tried to step around him again, but he blocked my path.

"My name is Cedric." He smiled now. "Who is the beautiful lady of the night with the most incredible violet eyes?" He mused at me.

I raised a brow, nearly letting a smile find its way to my lips before I spoke, but stopped it just in time and pursed my lips into a tight line instead. "Scáil."

"A fitting name for someone who lurks in the shadows at night." He tipped his head to the side in a slight nod with a sly smile. "Perhaps I could buy you a drink and then you would be more willing to share your tales with me?"

I smirked, finally. The sun was starting to rise in the distance. "It's probably a bit early to start drinking."

He spun and waved his arm toward the village, the entire gesture dripping with a grandiosity I thought was absurd for the situation, but a bit charming nonetheless. "Ah, but it is never too early to start drinking. Especially in good company." He smiled and waited for me to start walking before he stepped back into pace with me at my side.

I rolled my eyes and we walked into the village together as some people slowly began to stir. "You don't have to follow me all the way to the Lord's house you know." I said with a tinge of annoyance in my voice.

"I'm fairly certain if I let you out of my sight you'll disappear before I get my story." He mused. "And you may not feel like you owe me but I did prevent you from having to battle it outright, so I feel like you owe me something."

I sighed. "Fine." I pointed to the building across from the Lord's home. "Wait over there."

He nodded his head again, and after a slight bow he walked over and stood where I instructed.

I turned and walked up to the house. Before I knocked, a woman answered the door. Her attire suggested she was a maid or servant of some kind. She smiled at me.

"Lord Kallius sent me to pay you." She handed me a small bag. "He appreciates your help, but did not wish to be bothered so early in the morning." With that she shut the door and disappeared within the house.

"Seems the lord is too busy for you this morning." Cedric had already walked up behind me.

I tossed the hand of the Wendigo onto the ground in front of the house. "I suppose I didn't even need proof." I commented, and turned to walk further into the village, back to the inn where I had a room waiting and had left my horse Draga for the evening.

"Where to now?" He asked.

I glanced at him as I walked along. “I need some sleep, and I’d like to check on my horse.” He kept pace right beside me as I walked. “I suppose you’re going to follow me there as well?”

“Well, I’ll need a place to stay myself, so why not follow you to the inn in this town?” He smiled.

I didn’t reply, but kept walking in silence until we’d come up to the inn. I could see Draga out in the field grazing, and she seemed content. Her red bay coat glistened in the morning sun.

“Which of these magnificent beasts is yours?” Cedric followed my gaze out to the fields.

“The red bay.” I looked over at him. “The inn is just up there.”

He stepped to the side, allowing me to walk in the direction I’d pointed, and followed less than a step behind me. When we reached the inn, we walked in and the innkeeper looked him up and down before sighing.

“We don’t have any other rooms open, bard.” He said plainly. He looked at me. “Unless he’s with you for the day?”

I scoffed, and rolled my eyes. “Of course there are no additional rooms.” I mumbled.

“Looks like you’re stuck with me.” He had a sultry grin on his face now. “I’ll split the cost of the room with you?” He offered.

I gave him a sideways glance.

“I could bring a cot to the room.” The innkeeper offered.

“Please.” I insisted.

He nodded and disappeared. I walked toward the room I’d secured the evening before with Cedric in toe.

"I'll take the cot." He said simply as we got to the room. Moments later, the innkeeper brought the cot in.

"Thank you," I said to him. He just nodded and headed back out to the front desk.

I took off my cloak and hung it on the hook on the back of the door, and Cedric did the same with his leather jacket. The room was small, hardly enough room for the bed, cot, and everything else. The bathing room off of it was also small. I unstrapped the band of knives from my waist, as well as my sword, untied my corset and tossed it onto the small bedside table.

"Ladies first." Cedric motioned to the bathing room.

I shot him a look and made my way in before shutting the door behind me. I began washing the blood and dirt off my hands, before fully undressing and bathing myself. When I'd cleaned up, I put my blouse and skirt back on and opened the door.

Cedric had removed his tunic, leaving him in just a white loosely fitted shirt, mostly unbuttoned. It revealed more of his chest and abdomen, which was surprisingly muscular given his chosen line of work. He'd also removed his boots.

"See something you like?" He said with a sultry smile as I met his gaze.

I narrowed my eyes at him and sneered. "You certainly wasted no time making yourself comfortable." I commented.

He huffed a laugh and rose from where he was sitting on the bed, before brushing past me to head into the bathing room himself.

I shut the window to make the room darker, and rummaged through my saddle bags in the corner by the bed to get something more comfortable to sleep in. I'd just finished changing when he re-emerged from the bathing room and began to rummage through his satchel, likely for the same reason.

The cot was laid out where it partially blocked the door, the only place with room for it. I climbed into the bed and rolled to face the closed window.

"Wake me when you're ready for that drink." Cedric mused, as I heard him also shuffling into the clothing he'd chosen to slip into before he lay down on the cot.

"Sure." I mumbled, and after a few minutes of silence I drifted off to sleep.

*

A few hours later, I woke up and rolled back over to look around the room for a moment. Cedric was sleeping soundly on the cot, completely blocking the door as he'd sprawled out far beyond the cot itself. He hadn't slipped into different clothing. He was sleeping in just his boxers.

I laughed a little, because he looked a bit ridiculous. The sound stirred him and he grumbled as he rubbed his face. "Oh come on. I barely got to sleep."

I rolled back toward the window and opened it, the light hitting him right in the face.

He winced and groaned as he squinted his eyes to look up at me. "You're a cruel woman, you know that?"

I merely smiled. "You're the insufferable bard who insisted on following me until I would give you some elaborate tale to write a song about."

He scoffed, and lay back again with his arm behind his head. "Does this mean you're ready for that drink?" His eyes were closed again, but he was smiling.

"I suppose I'll take that drink now." Based on the sunlight I guessed it was mid to late afternoon at this point.

He sighed and rose up to a sitting position, the sunlight highlighting his chest and abdomen now. He certainly was enticing. I met his eyes again, and he had that same sultry smile I'd seen earlier. "You do see something you like."

I smirked and chucked my pillow at him. "Get dressed." I snarled.

He was still smiling as he rose and went over to grab some clothes. He put on similar pants, but a slightly different tunic this time. It was navy with gold embroidery, just as intricate as the red one had been.

I rose from the bed and dug out a blouse and skirt. I pulled on one of my favorite plain black skirts with a long slit up the right side, allowing me to grab the knife I always concealed on my thigh. Then I pulled the long silk nightgown I'd been wearing up over my head before putting on my bra and a simple purple blouse.

I could feel his eyes on me as I did all of that. "You're a sorceress." He said softly from behind me. "You're not just a mercenary." He took a few steps closer to me. "And you must have some wild stories with some of those scars." His voice was gentle, almost caring rather than inquisitive.

I turned to face him as I grabbed the strap for my thigh and began to put it on. "I would appreciate it if you'd avoid sharing that tidbit of information when you write a song about one of my stories." He raised an eyebrow. "I don't use my magic, and surely if you recognized that symbol on my back you would understand why."

He nodded. “You’re wanted I assume?” A simple question, with a complicated answer.

I simply nodded. “You can leave that part out too.”

His face contorted with confusion. “They don’t just hunt your coven for no reason. May I ask what you did?”

I locked eyes with him just as I’d slipped my corset back on. “No, you may not.” I grumbled. “It isn’t important, and the less you know the better.”

His face was unreadable now. “Okay.”

“I’ll cover one more night here, and you can stay with me if you’d like, but then I’m moving on, and it is better if you do also, or you pretend you’ve never met me.”

He nodded slightly. I finished strapping on my various weapons and grabbed my cloak from the door just behind him.

“Shall we make our way to the tavern then?” I gave him a half smile.

He was a little bit reluctant now, but he returned the half smile and slid the cot out of the way before opening the door for me.

I walked out of the room and he followed, shutting the door behind him as we made our way to the front desk. I laid a silver piece on the counter. “We’ll be staying one more night.” I said plainly, and he nodded.

We headed out into the village, now bustling with activity due to the time of day. We rounded the corner after walking up the road we’d taken to get to the inn and then reached the small tavern in the center of the village. It was loud and bustling with activity more so than the areas around it. I could hear a bard playing inside already.

I glanced over my shoulder at Cedric, “Looks like there’s already a bard offering entertainment here. I hope you didn't come here to play at the tavern?" I knew he wasn't playing tonight, but he hadn't mentioned why he'd come to this village specifically.

He smiled. "I have a party here I've been requested to play for tomorrow evening."

I inclined my head slightly in acknowledgement as we walked into the tavern. We went to a table toward the back, and after a few moments a woman came over to greet us.

"Good evening. Could I get you something to drink?"

"A mether of mead please." Cedric said with a smile before I could interject.

I smiled. "I'll have whiskey."

Cedric raised a brow as he locked eyes with me for a moment. "And two turkey legs please." He added, then looked at the woman with a sultry smile.

She smiled down at him. "Certainly." Then she made her way back to the bar.

"Ordering for me?" I said sweetly.

He looked back at me again. "Surely you weren't going to go hungry were you? It's not a good idea to drink on an empty stomach." He had that same sultry smile on his face that he'd given the woman serving us.

"I did intend to eat, but I don't usually have someone order for me."

"Did you want something else?" He started to turn to wave the woman back to us and I grabbed his hand before he could.

"No."

He turned to me with an even bigger smile, and I released his hand.

"I don't need anything else."

"Alright then." He said matter of factly. "How about that story you owe me?" His eyes glittered with excitement.

I considered it for a moment. "Would you rather hear about a Gorgon, a Shapeshifter, or a Behemoth?"

He almost leapt with excitement, just as the woman returned with our drinks and a small bowl of bread. He looked at her with a sweet smile and thanked her, before turning his attention back to me. "A Gorgon sounds fascinating."

I smiled, and went into the story, only stopping for a few moments when the woman returned yet again with the turkey legs he'd asked for. I finished my whiskey as I finished the story and he was now taking notes on a piece of paper he'd pulled out of his pocket.

"This is incredible." He breathed. "I've never heard anything like it."

I smiled as the woman brought me another drink. "Thank you." I said to her and turned my attention back to him.

"Could you tell me more? Describe it in a bit more detail?"

"Well, I didn't get a good look at it."

He scoffed. "That's fine. I can add my own flair to it." He paused for a moment as I took another two sips of the whiskey. He grabbed the mead and finished it off, then waved to the woman for her to come fill it. "How about the Behemoth?" He was beaming. "Can you tell me about that?"

I raised a brow. The woman came over and filled the mether for him. After a moment, I grabbed it and drank some of it. It was quite sweet, but good for mead. "I only promised you one story." I finally said.

"How many *more* drinks do I have to get for you to tell me the other two?" His sultry smile grew wider, the excitement still glimmering in his eyes.

I smiled. I was starting to feel a little buzzed, and I looked down for a moment, considering. "One drink per story." I met his gaze again.

He nodded. I began to explain the tale of my battle with the Behemoth next. He intently took notes for this story, but as the evening went on and we both had many more drinks he stopped taking notes and merely listened intently. Eventually, we paid our bill and headed back to the inn, both decently drunk, shamelessly flirting with one another as we strode through the village.

When we got back to our room, he helped me remove all of my weapons, including the knife strapped to my upper thigh, letting his hands wander a bit as he pulled it free.

"Watch it, bard." I warned him, though I only half meant that warning.

His face was inches from mine, and that sultry smile returned. "Or what?"

I groaned and tossed my head back for a moment before I looked at him again and grabbed a fistful of his hair. "I may be drunk, but I could still kick your ass if I wanted to." I said as I leaned in closer to him, my lips less than an inch from his.

His eyes danced from mine to my lips and then back again. "I might actually enjoy that, I think." He whispered, his hand sliding up under my dress so he could play with the lace of my underwear.

I huffed a laugh. "You would *enjoy* getting your ass kicked?" I released his hair and leaned back so I could look at him.

"If it ended with me in bed with you then absolutely, I would enjoy it." He leaned in so his lips were almost touching mine as he switched from toying with the lace of my underwear to grabbing my ass and pulling me closer to him.

I closed the gap between our lips, pressing mine to his in a wildly passionate kiss as my arms went up around his neck. He pushed himself onto me, causing us to fall back onto the bed, but he caught himself with his free hand. He slid me up so my head was onto the pillows before lowering himself over top of me. My hands ripped at his tunic, which he eventually pulled off and tossed to the side, along with his shirt.

He kissed down my neck before pulling my blouse and bra off and tossing them away as well. He stood from the bed and removed his pants, then leaned down to kiss down my chest and my stomach until he reached the hem of my skirt, and pulled that and my underwear off in one quick sweep.

He climbed back on the bed and lowered himself over me as he went to kiss up and down my neck again, nipping lightly a little bit as he went. We rolled around, intertwined with one another for a long while. Until we were both exhausted, and had climaxed, several times. I was sure we'd driven the other patrons of the inn insane with the amount of noise we made, but no one dared to complain.

We lay panting and exhausted, staring at one another for a few moments. Cedric smiled. "A wild lady of the night, I think is how I'll sing it."

I smiled and let out a small laugh. "I wouldn't call myself wild when I'm taking down monsters."

He brushed some of my hair out of my face. “No, but certainly wild with other pursuits.” His eyes looked heavy, probably as heavy as mine. “I’m glad to have met you Scáil.”

I closed my eyes and sighed. “I’m glad to have saved you from certain death. I would’ve missed so much fun otherwise” I said with a small smile again.

He chuckled and slipped his arm around my waist. I drifted off to sleep a few moments later.

Chapter 2

Scáil

I woke up just as the light of the sunrise hit my face through the open window. I sighed and rubbed my face. I needed to get moving in order to make it to the next town before nightfall. I rolled to my back and looked over to see that Cedric hadn't woken yet. I quietly slipped out of bed and began dressing, doing my best not to wake him.

I finished tightening and tying my corset, then strapped on my knives, sword, and grabbed my satchel of coin that I'd been given for killing the wendigo the day before. I placed a few coins on the table next to the bed, as well as a brief note for him to find when he woke. Enough coin to cover the room for the day until he decided to move along as well.

I turned and left the room, making my way down the stairs to the front door of the inn. No one else seemed to be awake yet except the innkeeper who looked up at me as I walked past the counter.

"He'll pay for the room when he's ready to leave." I said flatly, and she nodded before going back to whatever bookkeeping she was working on. I had already paid her for keeping my horse.

I walked out into the brisk morning air and donned my cloak as I made my way over to the small storage shed by the pasture to collect my saddle and equipment. Draga stood patiently waiting for me at the gate as I approached. I rested the saddle on the fence and slipped in to start to tack her up. I brushed off some of the dirt she'd collected overnight, put on her saddle blanket, saddle, and girth.

I slipped on her bridle and walked her out of the gate before mounting and heading down the road to the east. It was a two day trek to the town I'd heard was seeking a mercenary to kill a Chimera. There was a small village in between this one and my destination where I planned to stop for the night before continuing on in the morning, and I should make it there by nightfall if I made no other stops.

I traveled for most of the day, stopping briefly here and there to offer my horse water from a stream as we passed, and to sit for a moment while I ate a few pieces of the jerky I got from the previous town's butcher shop. We passed through a few other travelers on our way, and then finally arrived into the village called Sablecroft just as the sun was setting, making better time than I'd anticipated.

I walked my horse over to what appeared to be the only tavern, dismounted, and tied her to the hitching post near the water trough so she could have a drink if she wanted. I loosened the girth some and headed in to find a spot at the bar.

I chose the seat closest to the door. The tavern was mostly empty aside from a handful of other patrons, mostly sitting toward the back at a table by a window, and two men sitting down the bar. I grabbed some coin from my satchel and sat it on the counter as the barkeep approached. He was an older man with long brown hair that fell to just beyond his shoulders, with a clean shaven face.

His brow furrowed as he took in my tattoos, and he looked me up and down for a brief moment. “I don’t want any trouble in here.”

I locked eyes with him as I pushed the coins over to him. “I’m not here for trouble. I’m here for a meal and a drink before I head over to the inn for the evening.”

His face didn’t change, he merely motioned to my arms. “Tattoos like that are typically a sign that you’re a sorceress with Oíche. I’m sure you understand my hesitation to serve your kind here.”

I moved my cloak to show my sword and knives. “I am a mercenary. I do not associate with the Oíche and I’m just here on my way to Ashbourne. I hear they have a Chimera and are seeking a mercenary to kill it for them.”

There was a chuckle from one of the men down the bar. “A female mercenary that is going to kill a Chimera? You clearly have a death wish, or think that you can lie your way out of what you are.”

I held eye contact with the barkeep. “I just need a meal and then I’ll be on my way. Please.”

He looked me up and down again, then took the coin I’d laid down and nodded. “I’ll be right back.”

I turned to look at the man who had spoken up from down the bar. He was bald, his head cleanly shaved, but a short beard that was such a dark brown you could argue it might be black. It was rather rough and not terribly well kept. He wore a mixture of armor and regular garb, so was likely a part of the local militia.

"I am actually going to kill the Chimera. I don't have a death wish, but I could certainly use the coin they're offering for its head." I said coldly.

He huffed a laugh again. He covered his mouth for a moment with one hand while the other stayed resting on the bar. He stroked his hand down his beard and revealed a cocky grin on his face. "Perhaps you'd like some help? Surely you can't handle that on your own."

I rolled my eyes, and looked back as the barkeep approached with a plate holding a turkey leg and a bowl of stew. "I work alone." I grumbled.

The barkeep sat the plate on the bar in front of me, and then placed a cup next to it which he filled with water from a pitcher he had on the counter behind him.

"Thank you." I said softly.

He nodded, looked at me and then at the other man, and then back again. "I wish you luck in your quest." He said quietly. "Don't mind him."

The man down the bar scoffed. "I'd pay good money to see the fight." Then he quieted down and went back to drinking.

I ate the turkey and stew in silence and then when I'd finished, left a few copper pieces as a tip to the barkeep. As I stood from the stool to head back outside to my horse the man turned and spoke again.

"You sure you don't want an extra hand." I glanced over to see a small grin appear on his face again. "We could split the coin."

I scowled. "I told you I work alone." I turned and walked out to untie my horse and walk to the inn. The sun was beginning to set as I led her down the small dirt road to the inn at the other edge of the village. I glanced back once to see he'd followed me out and was watching as we walked off. The moment he met my glare he turned and walked in the other direction.

I walked up to the woman tending to the horses at the inn. She looked me up and down for a moment, looked at Draga, and then met my gaze.

"How long are you planning to stay?" She asked somewhat coldly.

"Just for the night. I'll be gone shortly after sunrise." I replied.

"Fifteen copper pieces." She said plainly.

I nodded, rummaged through my bag and paid her. She took my reins from me and turned to lead Draga to a field. "Your equipment will be in the shed in the morning." I grabbed my saddlebags before she walked off with her.

I turned and walked toward the door to the inn. When I walked inside there was a man at the front desk. He looked up as I walked in. "Last door on the left." He said plainly. He must've seen me pay the woman through the window.

I just nodded and headed where I was directed to. I undressed, used the small washroom off of the bedroom I'd been given to clean myself up a bit before slipping into the bed and drifting off to sleep.

The next morning I woke and dressed just before sunrise. I headed out to once again catch Draga, tack her up, and get on my way.

We set out this time at a much faster pace. I wanted to get to Ashbourne before dark. The Chimera would be more active at night, and if I didn't want to risk Draga on the way in, I'd need to get there and get her somewhere safe in town first.

We stopped only as much as we absolutely needed to, and arrived just before sundown. I went to an inn in the middle of the town this time, with a small barn alongside it. There was a man tending to the horse that was already there when I arrived.

"I'd like a stall for the evening, and part of the day tomorrow." I said as I approached. He turned and looked at me a bit surprised. "I will also need a room for the evening, when I return, and through part of the day tomorrow."

He raised a brow. "Through part of the day as well?"

"I'm here to kill the Chimera. I plan to hunt it through the night, so I will need to rest during the day tomorrow." I looked beyond him at the two open stalls. "I trust she'll be safe here and well cared for?" I asked as I motioned toward her.

"Yes." He still looked surprised. "She is safer here than the inn on the edge of the village." He reached for her reins. "Two silver pieces."

I pulled the coins out of my satchel and handed them to him with her reins. "Where do I find the Lord who put the price on the beast's head?" I asked.

He pointed behind me. "He lives close to the edge of the village, two buildings down from the tavern." He turned to walk Draga to a stall. "You'll take the last room on the right when you go in the inn. It is the quietest I can offer if you're seeking to rest during the day."

I nodded. "Thank you."

He'd placed Draga in a stall and started to untack her for me before he peeked out of the stall. "What should I do with her if you don't return?" He asked cautiously.

I turned back to him, having already walked a few steps away. “There is enough in her saddle bags to pay for her care for a few days. After that, I trust that you’ll find someone to take care of her, but I am not concerned about that. I’ll be back before the morning.”

The look on his face suggested he didn’t believe me, but he nodded and took to untacking her.

I turned again and walked in the direction he had pointed. It was slightly different from the way I’d entered the town. I finally came up to a rather large manor right where he’d described it would be. I knocked on the door and after a few moments the Lord answered himself.

He was tall and slender, dressed modestly in a simple shirt and pants. His auburn hair was short and slightly curly, falling to just above his eyebrows. He was young, probably in his late twenties, so he must've inherited his wealth from his parents.

“Yes?” He stared at me blankly.

“I’m here to take on the Chimera. I was directed to you.” I explained.

He looked me up and down. “You’re going to kill a Chimera?” His voice was dripping with doubt and disdain.

“I usually ask for some coin up front, but clearly everyone here thinks I’ll fail, so in this case I’ll accept the full bounty afterward. What would you like as proof that I’ve slain the beast?” My voice was cold. I didn’t want to waste any time deliberating whether or not he felt I was capable of the task.

“Bring me its head and I will give you the bounty.” He didn’t specify which one, but I guessed it didn’t matter.

I nodded. “I’ll be back at sunrise.”

He scoffed, but I didn't give him a moment to speak before I turned and wandered off toward the edge of town.

I took off my cloak after I made it out of town and hung it on a tree branch before I continued further into the woods. I didn't need anyone to see the rest of my tattoos, which would reveal that I was in fact a part of the Oíche coven, so I had to make sure it *didn't* get shredded in this fight.

I wandered for what felt like hours, with no sign of the beast. I started to wonder if it had moved on when I heard a low growl behind me. I drew my sword and turned to find the beast crouched in the brush less than twenty feet away.

I lowered myself into a fighting stance, just as it launched itself toward me in a full blown run. I dodged its advance, and swung at it as I spun away from it. I managed to slice its massive lion head.

It snarled in response and its goat head turned to watch me. I unsheathed and threw a knife from my belt just as the goat head turned to face me and took out one of its eyes.

Another growl in pain and frustration, and the tail flicked toward me, slamming into me before I could react and throwing me backward, rolling through the brush.

In one swift motion it was on top of me, and I was pinned down by its large taloned foot. It had my right arm, with my sword, pinned as well. I swore and just as it was about to snap at my face with its lion head I put my left hand up and hit it with a blast of shadow magic to obscure its vision and throw it backward.

As soon as it released me and stumbled back, I launched to my feet and ran at it, slicing its leg as I slid underneath it to stab it in the heart while it was distracted.

It had started a growl that was silenced almost as soon as my blade pierced its heart, and it dropped over beside me. I pulled out my sword and dropped to a knee for a moment to catch my breath. Now I'd need to make sure I move on tonight, as soon as I could..

"Bastard." I spat at the beast as I finally stood again and looked it over. I usually had two days before they caught up with me when I used magic, so I could still rest for part of the day. I considered for a moment which head I'd deliver to the lord, and opted for the goat head because it was smaller and would be easier to carry.

I walked around it, beheaded it, and carried the goat head by a horn as I made my way back to the village. The sun was just barely rising when I came up to the tree where I'd hung my cloak.

The blood on my skirt and blouse had mostly dried, as well as the blood on my hands, so I swung it over my shoulders, fastened it, and then picked up the head again to continue on my way to the Lord's manor.

Very few people were awake just yet, but those that were stopped to stare at me as I walked through, the goat head almost dragging on the ground beside me. Excitement filled their faces as they realized what this meant. I walked up to the Lord's door, knocked, and stepped back slightly.

After a few moments he opened the door, and I guessed he had just woken up because his eyes were still glossy with sleep. I tossed the goat head right at the edge of the door.

"As promised." I mumbled.

He jumped back a step, taking in the goat head as he woke up fully and then looked up to face me. “How?” He said in disbelief.

“I told you, I’d kill it. I don’t need to explain *how.*” I paused for a moment and he looked me over, still processing. “I’d like the coin that was promised.”

He nodded, “just a moment.” Then he closed the door and disappeared. More people were coming out of their homes now, staring at me and the head on their Lord’s doorstep. A few minutes passed and he returned to the door with a satchel in his hands. “Thank you.” He said as he handed me the bag.

I nodded. “Pleasure doing business with you.” Then I turned and walked back in the direction of the inn. It was hard not to smile as I met the gazes of several of the people who now flooded the dirt road, some not even dressed in anything other than their nightgowns or pajamas.

The excitement on their faces, and gratitude for the fact that they no longer had to live in fear was almost payment in itself if I didn’t need the money to keep myself going. When I finally made it to the inn, the man who ran it was feeding the horses.

He looked at me in disbelief. “Did you kill it?”

“I did.” I said nonchalantly.

“Thank you.” He said as he stepped out of the stall Draga was in. “I’ve placed your equipment in the room you’ll be staying in. Please let me know if you need anything else.”

I looked him up and down for a moment. “I just need to clean my clothes and clean myself up a bit.”

“There is a wash basin in there for you to use.”

I nodded. “Thank you.”

I turned and walked into the inn, to the last room on the right as he'd directed me last evening. I found the basin he'd mentioned and washed myself first, then carefully washed my clothes and hung them on a chair where the sun streamed in the window to dry them.

I climbed into the bed and slept as much as I was able with all the noise and light in the room. I finally gave up on sleeping as the sun was starting to set.

I checked on my clothes, which were still a bit damp, but dry enough to wear. I got dressed quietly and grabbed the satchel the Lord had given me, as well as all of my usual equipment and headed out to get Draga.

I nodded to the innkeeper as I passed him and then tacked Draga up and went on my way, heading toward the tavern before I left town to get something to eat. By now, the sun had set completely.

I tied Draga outside of the tavern and walked in. It was a busy night it seemed. Some of what I guessed to be the regulars of the tavern were lingering about outside as I walked through the door.

I scanned the tavern. There were a handful of people at the bar, but it was far from crowded. The men that did linger there raised their glasses to me as I walked past, I guessed it was their silent thanks for killing the Chimera that several of their local warriors tried to take out before I'd come through town. I gave them a nod and scanned the rest of the tavern before I finally went to the bar.

There were some townsfolk at the tables, nothing out of the ordinary. There were two men in the corner that caught my eye. They both wore black leather armor of some kind. It vaguely reminded me of the armor I'd seen my father wear, but I pushed that thought away. One of them was more lean, while the other was more muscular and well built.

The lean one had bland hazel eyes, and brown hair that was pulled half up in a bun on the back of his head, and the rest hung to just below his shoulders. They didn't seem to notice me as I carefully evaluated them on the way to the bar. The more well built one had shorter black hair that hung to just below his eyebrows and the most piercing blue eyes I'd ever seen. Both men had swords, and a few knives in a strap across their chest, similar to what I wore beneath my cloak.

Before I turned to face the bar, the blue eyed one locked eyes with me briefly. I pretended to be glancing around the room as if I hadn't been staring at them, and at last turned to face the bar. The woman behind the bar smiled as she approached me, a steaming bowl of stew in her hands as well as a cup of mead.

"This is on the house, for finally ridding the town of that beast."

"I-" I tried to cut in, but barely got a single word out before she sat it down in front of me.

"I won't take no for an answer." She said, and turned to walk back to the other end of the bar.

I sighed, removed my cloak and laid it over the barstool before I sat down to eat. My hair hung in a thick braid down my back to cover the tattoo I didn't want anyone to see. I sat and ate in silence, listening to the bard playing across the room for a few minutes before someone walked up behind me and stood at the bar to my left, far too close to me for my liking.

"What's a fine lady like yourself doing here alone this evening?" The man drawled.

I took another sip of my mead and without even looking in his direction said, "Trying to enjoy a drink and a hot meal."

"Just a meal and a drink?"

I sighed and turned to look at him. It was the tall and lean one who I'd seen sitting with the other man in the corner. "Yes. Can I help you?"

"I just thought you might like to have a little company." He said, trying very hard to be seductive, but it wasn't working for him at all.

I looked him up and down for a moment. "No thanks." I turned to go back to my meal and drink, but he grabbed my elbow.

In one swift motion I was up off my barstool, had a knife in my right hand, and held it right up to his throat. "I don't recall giving you permission to touch me."

He removed his hand from my elbow and put both hands up where I could see them. "Relax. I was just trying to be nice. It looked like you could use some company tonight." His pupils seemed to dilate and relax as he spoke.

I scowled. "If I wanted company, I'd have said so." I looked him up and down again. "Touch me again, and I'll slit your throat without a second thought."

His eyes got wide, but he backed off. "Sorry for the trouble." Then he wandered back over to the corner he'd come from.

I sat on the barstool once more and went back to eating, finished the stew after a moment or two, and then finished my mead. I waved the barkeep down.

"Thank you for the drink and the food. Could I get whiskey, neat, please?"

She smiled and nodded. "Absolutely."

"Thank you." I smiled. She walked away and returned a moment later with the glass. I gave her the coin she requested, tossed back the whiskey and sat some copper pieces on the counter as a tip before I put my cloak back on and headed for the door.

I untied my horse, mounted, and set her off at a steady walk until we reached the edge of the village, where we finally picked up a trot. I made it about a mile out of town when I started to get a bit dazed. Odd, considering I had only had two drinks and I tended to handle my alcohol pretty well.

I pressed on, shaking my head as though I could shake off the buzz and move past it. There was a rustling in the brush to my right, and I immediately halted my mare. I dismounted, grabbed the hilt of my sword, and turned to face the direction in which I heard the movement. Everything was eerily still, too quiet.

I wandered off the road into the brush, my head getting foggier with each step, but didn't want to continue without determining the cause of the noise. It was too large to have just been a normal animal lurking in the woods. A rustle again, but to my left this time. I shifted quickly and lost my balance a bit, swaying. *This makes no sense*, I thought to myself. *Two drinks would never do this to me.* I scanned the woods ahead of me and saw nothing.

Then it hit me like a slap to the face. My eyes were heavy and the world began spinning, as though I'd finished an entire bottle on my own on an empty stomach. I swayed. *Someone had to have slipped something in my drink while I had my back turned. This made no sense otherwise...* I couldn't feel my magic at all, couldn't muster up anything as I finally lost balance entirely and collapsed into the brush, still faintly clutching my sword, preparing to draw it as though that would really help me.

A figure rose from the brush where I'd heard the rustling and began coming toward me as I lost my grip on my consciousness.

*

My eyes fluttered open briefly as I felt myself lifted up and carried over someone's shoulder. The world was spinning and I fought to cling to the small shred of consciousness that had come to me to no avail, and within moments my world went dark again.

Chapter 3

Deiric

We had just settled in at a table in the corner of the tavern when I felt a shift in the room that I couldn't place. Alaster sat next to me, watching the patrons mill about. We were here to work on teaching him how to use compulsion, so we needed to find a good mark for him.

"What exactly are we going to have me compel them to do?" He asked me, his voice had a tinge of excitement in it.

I turned to look at him, instead of the edge of the bar I'd been staring at for a moment while I tried to place whatever that shift was that I felt. "Well, that will depend on who you choose to compel. You have to start small and make it something they won't be too bothered by if it doesn't work."

His lips curled in distaste and he shuffled a bit in his seat. His eyes danced around the room at the people he could pick.

"Choose someone who isn't with a group. Someone *alone*." I specified.

"This looks promising." He observed, and his gaze shifted to me.

A scent hit me suddenly, and something tugged at me to turn and look. It was the same energy that caused the shift in the room that I felt. It reminded me of a summer breeze. I turned and almost immediately locked eyes with the most breathtaking woman I think I'd ever seen. Her violet eyes sparkled in the dim light of the tavern.

The moment our eyes met hers darted away, acting as though she'd been casually glancing around the room, but I could tell she'd been staring for a few moments before I met her gaze. She settled at a seat toward the end of the bar, and was almost immediately greeted and served by the barkeep.

I considered for a moment that maybe she was a regular, but then I heard the barkeep say, "This is on the house, for finally ridding the town of that beast," with a smile.

She removed her cloak and sat on the barstool. She had intricate tattoos that laced down her arms, and long jet black hair that was braided and hung down the middle of her back. She wore a plain blouse, corset, and skirt. She had a strap of knives around her waist, and a sword sheathed at her hip.

She wasn't a regular. She was a mercenary.

"She seems like she's alone, and an easy enough mark." Alaster commented.

I huffed a bit, and shrugged. "If you think so." I looked at him. "What are you going to try to say to her?"

"Perhaps I could convince her she'd like some company for the evening?" He had a sultry smile on his face.

Something about what he said made a rage boil in me that I couldn't place. I didn't even know her. I had no reason to feel that way. "Give it a shot then." I said boredly.

I watched as he sulked over to her. I could see the muscles in her shoulders tense when she felt his presence next to her.

He tried to casually start a conversation, which she seemed entirely uninterested in. When he touched her elbow she shot to her feet and held a knife to his throat.

I stifled a laugh, and realized that he was finally trying to compel her. At that same moment, I saw a cloaked man wander over and drop something in her drink. She seemed too distracted with Alaster to notice.

His attempt failed, and when she finally retracted her knife he quickly retreated back to our table. She sat back down as though nothing had happened and went back to eating and drinking in silence.

"Okay, I didn't think I was *that* awful at it." He commented when he was starting to sit down.

"You did everything right." I smirked and then continued to stare at her for a moment. "I'm not sure why it didn't work." I was genuinely surprised.

"I didn't think anyone was immune to compulsion." Alaster commented.

"No one is supposed to be." I said, but my gaze stayed on her. She asked for a glass of whiskey, an interesting choice.

"Well, if she were one of us we'd know about her wouldn't we? There aren't any rogues out there just turning whoever they come across."

"No, she's definitely not one of us." I watched as she threw back the drink, left some coin on the counter and quietly left. "I'd like to follow her, and see if I can figure out why it didn't work."

A lie, but he didn't need to know that. Something was pulling me to follow her, and I didn't understand why. It was like an invisible tether that snapped into place the moment I locked eyes with her.

I looked at him at last. "Go back to the manor. We'll revisit this another day."

He scoffed. "Silas won't be pleased."

"Silas will get over it." I growled and stood up to follow her.

I waited until she'd left the village so I wasn't following too closely, but I stayed close to her so I could still try to read her thoughts.

Someone else was following her. The man who'd slipped something into her drink was ahead of me, flanking her on the right side.

I heard her begin to realize that she was not feeling right, just moments before the cloaked man made too much noise while creeping through the woods and caught her attention.

She dismounted and grabbed her sword, stalking into the woods in the direction of him. I could hear her mind racing. She spun toward another rustle in the bushes before she dropped to the ground.

The man who drugged her stood from the brush and stalked toward her. He pulled shackles from beneath his cloak and put them on her wrists, then tossed her over his shoulder. He walked to her horse, tossed her over it and then climbed up on it himself.

I followed, that tether still drawing me along with her. It drove me nuts, but I had to find out who she was and why I was so drawn to her.

He continued down that road for miles until he took a small path to the right. At the end of it was a little shack, which he tossed her into and locked the door.

He stalked off further into the woods, out of sight. This was my chance.

I ran over to the shack, swiftly broke the lock on the door, and then lifted her up over my shoulder. I thought I felt her stir for a moment, but she was limp again by the time I ran off with her.

I ran until I reached a cave I often used when I was out scouting closer to Silas' territory. It was far enough off the beaten path that we wouldn't be disturbed until she came to.

I laid her down gently on one side of the cave and removed her weapons. Even the one she concealed on her thigh. I settled against the wall on the other side. She looked so much different than she had in that tavern. Her face was calm and peaceful, rather than looking miserable and fierce, like a mercenary should.

I needed to know why compulsion hadn't worked. I needed to try that for myself somehow when she woke up. I also needed to figure out why the hell every part of me was telling me to stay near her.

I left the shackles on. I didn't know how she'd react when she woke up, and I certainly didn't need her running off before I had the chance to figure anything out.

Chapter 4

Scáil

My head was throbbing, and as I reached up to rub my face with my eyes still closed I felt them. Heavy, metal shackles at my wrists. "Fuck," I mumbled, and the sound of my own voice rattled in my ears making that throbbing in my head a bit worse. I blinked open my eyes at last to evaluate the area around me. It was quiet.

I looked straight up and out ahead of me I realized I was in some sort of cave along the edge of the woods. I couldn't tell if they were the same woods I'd been walking through or if they were vastly different. *How long have I been unconscious?* I knew I couldn't even attempt to break free of these shackles, but maybe I could muster the energy to run. The shackles didn't appear to be chained to anything.

I started to move my head to look around the room before I tried to rise or move any other part of me. I froze when I caught a glimpse of a man leaning against the cave wall across from me, obscured by shadows. What I could see of him was that he wore mostly black. It looked like armor but had this casualness about it that made me blink and really try to stare it down for a moment.

I looked up at his face. It was calm, unblinking. He had medium length jet black hair that was a bit shaggy. A few strands of it hung down over his forehead, almost reaching his eyes. Those eyes. That man that had been sitting in the corner of the bar. He just stared at me as I slowly woke up, not moving, not making a sound.

I pushed myself back toward the cave wall that I'd realized was behind me and tried to bring myself to a sitting position. I swayed a bit. Whatever I'd been drugged with was still gnawing at me, but I fought it. I looked at the shackles and quietly mumbled a spell to unlock them, but nothing happened.

I frowned, repeated the spell and I felt nothing. Finally, I held one hand out, palm up, to summon a small flame, thinking maybe I was delirious and forgot the right words to the spell. Nothing appeared in my hand. I scowled.

"What did you do to me?" I hissed at the man standing across from me. He merely stared back blankly in response.

"Why can't I use my magic?" I pressed. "What do you want with me?"

His face remained blank and unreadable, but his head cocked to one side. "Your magic?" He muttered, little more than a whisper.

"Are these shackles enchanted somehow, or did you dose me with something to block my magic?" I questioned again.

"Hmm" He took a few steps toward me and crouched down in front of me. I could see now that he was further out of the shadows that he had a sword strapped across his back and knives tucked into a strap across his chest just like he'd had in the tavern earlier.

"Answer me." I persisted.

He reached out a hand to touch me and I pulled away. He sighed. "I didn't do anything to your magic." He met my stare. "I'm not the one who drugged you in the first place." He said plainly. "You're a witch of some kind I take it?"

I blinked, and stared at him in silence.

"I saw someone slip something into your drink while my- acquaintance was trying to talk to you." He said simply. "I left him at the tavern and followed you to make sure you weren't harmed. I thought perhaps he was just trying to fuck you. My original plan was to simply catch up with him and kill him before he completed the act and just leave you be until you woke up, but when he put you in shackles and locked you in that shack I changed my plan."

"I snuck in to get you out when his guard was down." He stood up again, looking down at me he added, "I guess he figured you'd be out for hours and he didn't need to keep a close eye on you. You should be thanking me, I suppose. I could've just let you rot in there." He turned and started to walk back to where he had been standing by the other side of the cave.

"If your friend hadn't distracted me he likely wouldn't have had the chance to drug me." I scowled. "So you rescue me from whomever that was and bring me here only to leave me shackled?"

He spun around at that, locking eyes with me. "I left you shackled because I didn't know what state you'd be in when you woke up. Wouldn't want you to try to run and harm yourself when you're still half drunk."

He came back over to me, knelt down in front of me again and grabbed my hands with such swiftness that I didn't have the chance to react before he'd broken both cuffs and chucked them to the other side of the cave.

I gasped, glanced at my hands, up at him, and he smiled slightly. The speed and strength he'd just shown was utterly inhuman. A vampire then. He had to be. There wasn't any other being I could think of that would look so human and have those abilities.

"Clever little witch." He mused, as he held my gaze.

Fantastic. I was right and he must be capable of hearing thoughts or reading minds.

I tried to bring myself up to standing but the dizziness I still felt from whatever I'd been drugged with left me no further than getting to my knees before I risked toppling over.

"Rest." He mumbled. "I may not be your favorite type of company but I will at least make sure no one disturbs you while you sleep it off. Regardless of what you may feel about me or my kind, it would be cruel of me to leave you so helpless out here." He waved his hand at me as he walked back over to the other side of the cave and sat down against the wall.

I didn't really have any better option, so I laid myself back down on the cave floor, wrapped my cloak closer around me and laid down. I had no intention of sleeping. However, after what felt like hours, I couldn't keep my eyes open and I drifted off to sleep. The exhaustion was inescapable.

*

I woke when the early afternoon light was peaking into the cave. I quietly brought myself up to my knees so I could look around at the cave once more. He was sitting against the wall still in shadow, one knee bent with his arm resting on it and the other leg straight out in front of him. He appeared to be sleeping with his head leaning back against the wall.

I attempted to stand, and realized that all of my weapons were close to him by the edge of the cave. *Great.* I thought to myself. I wasn't dizzy now at least. I could tell my magic was still far out of my reach though.

I crept over to my weapons as quietly as I could and I pulled them away from where he was sitting. When I was sure he hadn't moved I began to strap them all back on. I looked up again and he still sat in the same place, unmoved.

Now was my chance to get away. He couldn't follow me into the sun unless he had a daylight ring. A risk I could take, I suppose, because few of them were lucky enough to possess them.

I began to make my way toward the edge of the cave and had almost reached where there was direct sunlight when he caught me from behind.

He had his left arm wrapped up around my shoulder, his hand held my head to the side to expose my neck. His right arm had wrapped around my waist. He could have simply killed me right then, but for some reason he hesitated. My right hand rested on the hilt of my sword.

"Leaving so soon." He whispered into my ear.

I stood as still as possible, despite the fact that his hot breath on that part of my neck sent shivers down my spine.

"Most people would be shaking in their boots right now. You don't seem to be concerned that I could kill you before you could even cry out for help." He whispered against my neck, his lips brushed that sensitive spot on the back of my neck as he spoke.

I squirmed a bit, heat rushing to my cheeks. I desperately tried to hide the reaction that touch got from my body. I gripped the hilt of my sword more tightly and gritted my teeth.

"What do you want from me?" I spat.

"All business." He paused, but I could feel his smile against my neck.

I tried to elbow him with my left arm while I moved to draw my sword. Before I could get very far he'd spun me around and backed me against the cave wall behind us, pinning my arms over my head so I couldn't fight him.

"You're quite fun to torment." He was smiling wickedly. "Tell me, what other interesting things excite you?" His pupils moved similarly to the man who had walked up to me in the tavern.

He was trying to compel me, I realized. How I missed that in the tavern I didn't know. I decided to play along for a moment. That had never worked on me.

I let my face relax a little as I said, "I really like," then I scowled and kicked at him as I said, "when you get to the point and then leave me alone."

He dodged my kick and snarled at me. His eyes were black as night and his fangs were out now.

I just stared at him. "If you're going to feed on me or kill me just get it over with."

He stared at me for a few moments, before his eyes returned to that beautiful blue and his fangs disappeared. "You really don't care if you live or die, do you?" His voice was quiet now, contemplative.

"I've been on the run for years. They clearly have gotten better at tracking me when I use my magic or I wouldn't be in this situation. It would likely be quicker and less painful to die here and now than to face whatever they had prepared for me." I said flatly.

I meant it. I had been running for so long, alone for so long, that I was tired. The only thing that kept me going was the fact that a death at their hands would likely involve torture first. My only options were to keep running and either finally get bested by one of the beasts I sought to kill or to end it myself, but a small shred of me hoped that one day they'd lose interest and I wouldn't have to run anymore.

He released my hands and just continued to stare at me for a moment. "I don't intend to kill you. I do, however, have a need for a sorceress. I could offer you a safe place to lay low for a while in exchange for eventually doing a spell for me."

I crossed my arms. "What sort of spell?" The idea of not having to run for a little while was enticing, although I doubted he truly had somewhere they couldn't track me to.

"I need daylight rings for myself and a handful of my death dealers."

"That spell has been forbidden by Solas."

"You're already on their shit list, aren't you?" He raised a brow at me. "Or is it someone else who is hunting you?"

I sighed. "How many rings?"

"Six in total."

"That is going to take a hell of a lot of power to do all at once."

"Can you do it?"

I looked him up and down for a moment, while I considered. "I might be able to do it." A slight lie, but it wasn't something I was eager to do. That amount of power would bring the Solas mercenaries and assassins right to me. "How can you be so sure they won't track me to wherever it is that you claim is safe to lay low?"

"You'll just have to trust me that it is a well hidden and protected place."

I rolled my eyes. "And what makes you think I won't just kill *you* when I have full use of my magic again?"

He just smirked. "Didn't you already point out that they track you with your magic? You wouldn't risk being tracked just to kill me."

I scowled and glanced out of the opening of the cave. He wasn't wrong. "How am I to trust that your death dealers won't kill me?"

"They'll be given an order that you're off limits. They have plenty of other ways to find a meal for themselves."

"Fine."

He smirked. "There's a small stream that runs through the cave down around the corner back there. It's a little dark, but you can use that to get a drink and wash up if you'd like." He pointed further back in the cave, then wandered back to what I guessed was his favorite spot a moment later. Likely the only place toward the mouth of the cave that was safe at all times from the sunlight.

*

I finished cleaning myself up and walked back into where there was more natural light to put my corset and cloak back on so I could see what I was doing with the laces. My hair now hung damp and loose all the way to my hips. He stood leaning against the wall, looking out at the woods. I loosened the laces on my corset more and pulled it on. When I'd spun it around to tighten and tie it, he appeared behind me in the blink of an eye. I flinched, but he just took the laces from me, tightened it, and tied it.

"Thank you." I said over my shoulder and watched him walk back to his side of the cave.

"You're welcome. Seemed better than watching you struggle with it."

I gave him a scowl. "I do this all the time, you know."

He merely smiled. "I can leave you to it yourself next time if that'll make you feel better." He leaned back against the wall and crossed his arms. "My name is Deiric, by the way."

"Scáil." I mumbled and wrapped my cloak around my shoulders.

He glanced toward the woods. "When the sun is fully set we'll start to make the trek toward the manor. We're about a two day hike, at your speed."

I nodded.

*

We sat in silence for about an hour until it was dark enough. Neither of us had anything else to say to one another, but I noticed he kept staring at me, evaluating. I was sure it was driving him a bit crazy that I hadn't been able to be compelled. As soon as it was dark enough he pushed off the cave wall and motioned for me to follow him.

We made our way out into the woods in silence. I followed him quietly through the trees for a long while, until my stomach began to growl with hunger.

He glanced back over his shoulder at me for a moment, then stopped. “There’s a small clearing up ahead.” He said, glancing back at me again. “Gather some wood for a fire and meet me there.” Then he was gone.

I sighed, but proceeded to do as he requested, gathering twigs, branches, and whatever else I could find to burn. By this point I could feel some of my power, however small it was, coming back, but I didn’t want to waste that bit of magic to start the fire.

When he finally returned, he dropped a small doe on the other side of the pile of sticks and leaves I’d thrown together to make the fire. It was drained entirely of blood. I was still working on using some rocks to spark the fire. After a few more tries I finally had sparked a small flame and blew on it to help it along.

With that I stood and walked over to the doe he’d brought. “Thank you,” was all I muttered as I drew my knife and began to work on carving out a sliver of meat to cook on the fire. He remained silent. He walked over to sit on a downed tree by the edge of the clearing.

When I’d finished cooking and eating and the fire burned down to a low smolder we continued on.

The sky began to light up as the sun threatened to peak over the horizon when he finally spoke again. “There’s a cave up ahead. We’ll camp there for the day and continue on again tonight.”

I nodded and followed him into that cave.

Chapter 5

Scáil

I woke when the light of the sun as it set finally reached where I was laying in the cave. When I raised myself to a sitting position I noticed he'd taken up a spot on the wall where the sun's rays likely never touched. I assumed he must prowl these woods regularly, since he was so familiar with them. He appeared to still be sleeping. Since I didn't have to wait till nightfall to leave the cave, I decided to wander out and see if I could find something to eat on my own, and maybe find a stream suitable to have a drink from.

I made note of where I was heading to make sure I could get back to the cave to meet up with him. I found a stream before the sun set, and finally found a nice raspberry bush shortly after dark. I started to make my way back to meet up with him at the cave when there was a rustle in the bushes to my left. I paused, listening, and then spun around with my sword drawn, the edge of the blade stopping right at the throat of another vampire.

He had a murderous smile on his face. His fangs were out and his eyes were black. He was a bit taller than Deiric, with golden brown hair that was long enough to tie back into a small bun on the back of his head. He was also far more muscular and broad shouldered, but he wore similar clothing to what Deiric had on. I considered that he might be someone Deiric knew, but he clearly was more of a kill first, ask questions later type.

In the blink of an eye he had pushed my sword out of the way, blasted me back and now held me by my throat against a tree. The shock and swift motion of it all caused me to drop my sword, leaving me to just my knives.

I grabbed his arm with my left hand and went to make a move for my knife at my thigh with my right hand but he caught my wrist before I could get ahold of it.

"Don't even try it." He growled, his smile widened, fully exposing his fangs. I was gasping a bit for air in his grip. Not entirely suffocated but not able to breathe well as I continued to claw at his arm with my left hand.

"What's a pretty little thing like you doing so far out in the woods at night?" He paused, looking me over for a moment. "Hasn't anyone told you it's not safe to be out here alone?"

I kicked and thrashed to try and get him to release either my throat or my hand but he held firm. His grip tightened as I struggled, and I was getting a bit lightheaded as it got harder to breathe.

I started to consider summoning whatever magic I could muster to at least get free of his grip when I saw a flash of movement out of the corner of my eye, and an instant later he was gone, sent flying off to my right while I collapsed to my hands and knees. I coughed and gasped, finally able to breathe normally again and looked over to where they'd gone.

Deiric had him pinned down. "Hands off, Zane." He snarled.

"Oh come on. She was an easy meal, and she had enough sense in her to fight. What's the issue?" I heard Zane grumble.

Deiric stood up, releasing him, and ran back to where I was still hunched over catching my breath. He held out his hand to help me up. I took it, and he pulled me to my feet.

I was still rubbing my throat when Zane stood and walked over to us, stopping a few feet away. "This your new pet?" He said, looking me up and down again.

"I'm no one's pet." I spat at him.

"She's a sorceress." Deiric said, still watching me, trying to determine if I was hurt at all.

"Bloody hell." Zane snarled. "Are you out of your mind?"

"We have a bargain." Deiric said curtly. "You and the others are not allowed to harm her, and she won't harm you." He glanced at Zane as he said that last part. "She's going to make us daylight rings."

Zane rolled his eyes, scowled a bit, and crossed his arms. "And how exactly did you get her to agree to that?" He was entirely unimpressed. Likely because he knew that any witch, or sorceress, in their right mind would just kill them both and say no. Even if the spell had not been outlawed, most of us simply hated their kind, and would've taken pleasure in killing them regardless of whether one of them had saved their lives or not.

"I saved her ass when someone drugged her and took her prisoner." Deiric stared at Zane now returning his scowl.

"She owes me." He went on. "And at the moment she's hardly a threat. Whatever he drugged her with has blocked her from using her magic temporarily. However, she must have gotten at least some of it back because I heard her contemplating using it to get you to back off." He smirked.

"Would you stay out of my head for fuck's sake?" I spat.

Zane half laughed, his posture softening a bit. "Fine, I guess you're not a complete moron then." He looked from Deiric over to me. "Still, probably a bit stupid of you to let her wander off on her own out here."

"She did that on her own because she thought I was asleep." He looked over at me as he said that. "In her defense, she did leave the cave when the sun was still up, but didn't come back before dark. That idiocy is on her."

I scowled at him. "You said we were a two day hike away."

"I lied." He shrugged. "Tell the others I'll be arriving shortly with a sorceress and to be on their best behavior."

Zane sighed, nodded, and then he was gone.

"You're completely insane." Deiric said at last.

I walked over to retrieve my sword and put it back in its sheath at my side. "I've faced many beasts far more terrifying than him." I mumbled as I turned to face him again.

"Completely insane." He repeated, with a raised brow and then gestured for me to follow him as he headed in the direction of where Zane had run off to moments earlier.

Chapter 6

Scáil

We arrived at a rather large manor deep in the woods, with nothing at all around it. No roads, no pathways, just a manor by the base of a mountain. Odd, but also somewhat comforting. It would be far off the beaten path and we likely wouldn't be tracked here. A small wave of relief washed over me at that.

We walked up the front steps and through the door into a large and open foyer. There was an archway on either side leading to a dining and kitchen area on the left and a large den on the right. I could hear people in the dining and kitchen area to the left, which is where Deiric headed.

The entire space was lit only by a handful of candles and a small fire in the hearth where a woman with her back to us was cooking. The dim light made it hard to really discern any details of what the place looked like, but it seemed very simple and plain. I looked around the rest of the room and found Zane sitting on a stool in the corner of the dining area.

"Where is everyone else?" Deiric asked.

"Out hunting." Zane mumbled. "They'll be back in a few hours."

While they continued speaking for a few moments, I studied the woman who was cooking, going back and forth between the counter and the hearth without looking over her shoulder at us. She had light brown hair, which was intricately tied up into a bun on her head with a braid holding it in place. She was about my height.

I noted that she had a tattoo on the back of her neck. Upon closer inspection, it was clearly the mark of the Oíche Coven and had the insignia underneath to denote her place in the coven. She was a witch.

I interrupted whatever conversation Deiric and Zane were having abruptly when I asked, still staring at the woman, "what do you need me for if you've already got a witch here?"

Zane stiffened, I could see him out of the corner of my eye. Deiric didn't seem to move, but I could feel his eyes on me.

"She's not a witch. Not anymore." Zane mumbled and I finally turned my gaze to him with one of my eyebrows raised in question.

"We had to turn her, years ago, when I found her barely alive." He paused, glancing over at the woman still cooking without really taking a moment to glance back at us at all. "She's lived with us ever since."

There was a moment of silence as he studied me, and I surveyed him, for any indication of where, when or how that might've occurred. The Solas Coven had succeeded in turning all the people against the Oíche coven for their tendency to include vampires in their ranks, claiming that they were evil, so it made sense that they'd attempt to kill one of their members, but it seemed odd that they wouldn't have succeeded and left her to be found by them.

"How did you know she was a witch?" Zane asked me, his eyes now narrowing in suspicion and curiosity.

"She's got the mark of the Oíche Coven on her neck." I replied simply.

His face didn't change, he didn't react, although he did shift a bit in his seat, so I could tell he was a bit surprised that I recognized it. "And how did you figure out her rank from that? Only members of the coven know what the different markings mean"

"She's a part of it as well." Deiric said before I could respond.

I spun around and shot him a look - there was no hiding that I was surprised by that comment. He smirked. "Your mark wasn't covered by your cloak or your hair when I helped you tie up your corset yesterday."

I scowled. He didn't help me because he thought I needed it. He helped me so he could get a better look.

His smirk changed to a sly smile.

"Would you stop that?" I snapped.

Zane chuckled. "He never has been good at staying out of anyone's head."

I looked over at him again and the smirk he had vanished when he saw my face, a mixture of rage and frustration. I didn't appreciate the lying, or perhaps lack of communication that they seemed to have with me. I understood their lack of trust, but it still pissed me off.

"You've already met Zane," Deiric mumbled, changing the subject. "That is Liala." The name sounded vaguely familiar to me. "Liala and Zane, this is Scáil."

With that the woman at the hearth finally turned her attention to us and turned around. I looked over at the same moment and her face went ghostly pale. She froze and just stared at me like she'd seen a ghost.

It took me a moment, but it finally clicked as to why that name was familiar, and I stumbled back a step, just as shocked as she was to see me. She hadn't aged a day.

"Mira." She breathed.

Zane stood up and took a step toward Liala as if he planned to jump in front of her to protect her from me, but he just stared at me.

"My name is Scáil." I almost whispered.

She cocked her head and confusion washed over her face as the color slowly came back. "You look just like…" Her voice trailed off and she took a few steps closer to me, looking me up and down and examining my face for any sign that I might falter in my insistence that she was wrong in who she thought I was. "Mira, you look just like your mother."

Zane's face went ghostly white now as he looked at me a little closer than he had before. He put together how we knew each other now, or maybe knew who I really was.

"My name is Scáil." I repeated and tried to retreat another step but I was blocked by Deiric.

"You can deny it as much as you'd like, but I could never forget your face." She said, her lips in a tight line. "Even if it has changed some as you've gotten older. And your eyes are unmistakable."

I wasn't going to be able to get myself out of this. I wanted to run and not turn back, abandon the deal I'd made with Deiric, but I was stuck. I hadn't spoken to anyone from the coven since the day of the attacks, and that is not a time I liked to remember.

"I didn't know you made it out. It all happened so fast." Liala said. "How did you get out? Where have you been all this time?" Relief had washed over her face now and she walked closer now like she was trying to reach out and hug me, but I shrunk away from her. We weren't close then, but she lived with us for years. She was my mother's closest friend.

I backed further into Deiric, despite that I didn't really want to be that close to him either. She stopped, noticing that I wanted nothing to do with being hugged, or being so close to her.

Deiric spoke for me. "She's a mercenary. I am assuming that she took on the alias Scáil to avoid being tracked but clearly that didn't help."

"It worked for a few years." I snapped, stepping to my right to move away from him now.

"How did you get out?" Liala asked again.

I looked at her blankly for a few moments. I didn't want to talk about it. They all just stared at me now, patiently waiting for my explanation. I finally, reluctantly started to speak.

"My mother was hit from behind with a stake. They had crossbows that were modified to shoot stakes instead of arrows and were aiming to shoot one at me when Aris grabbed me and yanked me out of the way. She screamed at him to get me out, and he took off running before I could get away from him to run back to her."

"We got less than a hundred yards into the woods before he also got hit with a stake and we both went down." I was looking at the floor now. "He held me under him for a few moments until he was sure that no one was coming for us, then he rolled me away and ordered me to get as far away as I could. At that point I realized I couldn't run, so I shifted myself farther away and found somewhere to hide until I could figure out what to do next."

"That's when you decided to change your name and become a mercenary?" Liala asked gently.

"No. After a few days I went home, everyone was gone, but there was still blood everywhere. It was a mess. I grabbed some clothes and supplies, decided on that alias, and then I left and never looked back. I learned enough lurking through a few towns, and figured out that there was money to be made in bounty hunting and being a mercenary."

They all just stood there silently for a few moments.

Deiric finally broke the silence. "You're the Dhampir?" He asked.

"Yes." I replied.

"The entire coven thought you were dead." He sat down at the table to our left. "We all gave up because we thought they had killed you, and we lost half of our ranks that day." He put his head in his hands. "All this time you've been doing *our* job."

"We need to get word to the remaining magisters." Zane finally said.

"No." Deiric said coldly.

"They need to know." Zane persisted.

Deiric stood up now, cold and threatening. "We don't tell anyone that we've found her." He paused, locked eyes with me for a moment and then looked back at Zane. "For now, the less people that know she's alive the better. Solas already knows, or they wouldn't be hunting her. She'll lay low here for a while, help us get the daylight rings we were supposed to be getting that day, and *then* we'll call a meeting to notify them."

"They will be pissed if they know we've got her here and don't tell anyone." Zane said.

"Let them be pissed. No one even *tried* to look for her, and I am sure that someone noticed she wasn't among those that were found dead. Yet they let all of us think she was dead, and that we would all stand down, go into hiding, and let Solas take over or we'd be executed." His tone was riddled with rage.

Zane dropped the idea at that point and we all just sat in awkward silence for a few moments. Then, I guess eager to break the silence he finally said, "So your sword and weapons aren't just for show then?" He smirked a bit, an attempt to somewhat change the subject.

"No, they're not just for show. I learned how to fight before all of that, and then just continued to grow my skills over the years as I fought new and different beasts."

"Huh." He half laughed, surprised. "Too bad that didn't help you with me earlier." A sly smile returned to his face.

"I don't generally go up against vampires." I snapped. "However when I am backed into a corner and forced to use my magic, that's always when those bastards have caught up with me."

"Have you ever hurt or killed a vampire for catching you like that?" He asked, almost too quietly.

"No. I haven't run into any vampires at all actually." Not surprising to me, as I tended to avoid areas I suspected they lurked, but either way.

Deiric finally snapped his attention back to me. He'd been staring at the ground for a while, appearing deep in thought. "Perhaps Mira could show us a few moves. It wouldn't be a bad idea for us to train with a blade again."

Zane's eyes snapped to Deiric, a mixture of surprise and maybe confusion flashed across his face.

"Once we've got our daylight rings we'll have to fit into the crowds and society as though we aren't vampires. Being able to fight like a human might be something we could use to our advantage to keep suspicion away from us." He smiled a bit.

Zane's eyes narrowed as he studied Deiric, though he likely couldn't decipher much with Deiric still facing me and having his back to Zane.

"Tomorrow, let's gather everyone and have Mira give us a sparring lesson." He finally spun around to Zane. "Tonight, we'll get her settled in and worry about figuring out when and how we'll create the daylight rings later." And with that, he walked back out into the foyer and up the stairs to the second floor.

Zane sighed, looked me up and down and walked out as well, but he went back outside.

Liala and I were now alone in the dining room.

"I made you some soup." She said quietly as she turned and grabbed a bowl from the counter to ladle the soup into. After a few moments she brought it over to the table and gestured for me to sit down.

"It is probably not the best, because all I had were the herbs that I grow in my small garden, but sit and eat." She stepped away and returned to the kitchen. "We can catch up some other time."

Chapter 7

Mira

A few hours later I was directed upstairs to the first door on the right. When I walked up and walked into the room I found Deiric preparing a cot on the floor.

He looked up at me. “You can take the bed.” I raised a brow, before he continued. “We don’t have any other rooms set up for someone to sleep in at the moment, and given that the others haven’t fully been caught up on your arrival yet, I thought my room would be the best place for you in the meantime.”

I walked over to the bed and ran my hands along the soft blankets on it. It had been a while since I’d slept in anything other than a seedy tavern or inn’s less than ideal accommodations, or even a cave or forest floor for that matter. “Are you sure?” I looked over at him. “I don’t mind taking the cot on the floor.” I paused, and glanced down at the bed again. “I’m used to it.”

He sighed. “You can take the bed. I’m sure you could use a more restful night of sleep.” He threw the blanket he was holding out over the cot. "Besides, if I sleep by the door I can stop you if you just decide to run off in the middle of the day." He gave me a sly smile.

I just sighed, and pulled back the blankets on the bed.

"The wash room is just through that door." He motioned to the door behind him. "There's a nightgown laid out in there for you thanks to Liala."

I nodded and walked around the bed and into the room he motioned to, so I could take a real bath finally and get changed. When I'd finished and came back out, he was already undressed and laying on the cot. I quietly climbed in bed and it didn't take long for me to finally drift off to sleep.

*

I was frantically running to the house. I thought maybe if I got there fast enough I could save them. I arrived to find everyone dead. Bodies and blood everywhere. I was screaming, running, and checking each of them to see if anyone had survived. My mother, laying in the center-

"Mira."

Someone was grabbing my shoulders and shaking me.

"Mira!"

My eyes snapped open.

"It was a nightmare. It was just a nightmare." Deiric panted, straddled over me and holding my shoulders gently.

I was still breathing heavily, but looked up at him, looked around and realized I'd thrashed the blankets all over the place. He was just in his boxers.

"Breathe." He whispered. "You're safe." He finally released my shoulders and shifted to sit down next to me.

"I'm sorry." I mumbled, shifting backward to lift myself up to a sitting position. My hands were shaking.

"Do you want to talk about it?"

I looked over at him. His blue eyes filled with a concern I didn't think he was capable of possessing. "I-" I looked away. "No, I'd rather not."

He reached over and gently squeezed my shoulder. "Are you okay?"

"Honestly, no." I said, way too fast. I pulled my knees to my chest and held them tightly. "I haven't thought about that day, about what happened, or what I saw in years." I shuddered at the thought. "I'm sorry for waking you."

He wrapped his arm around me and gently pulled me closer to him so that my head was resting on his shoulder. "I'm sorry."

I should've been uncomfortable, being so close to someone I'd only just met, but in a weird way I'd never felt more safe and secure. I hadn't been around anyone who actually knew who I was since that day I left. I hadn't been around anyone who I knew with certainty *didn't* wish to kill me. I relaxed a bit, released my knees and leaned into him.

He shifted so he could lay back against my pillows, pulling me down with him. "You are safe here." He whispered. "We had some wards in place before everything fell apart. No one can get in without being invited. This was one of our training and safe houses." He paused for a moment.

"You were at one of the main locations for coven gatherings at that time. We had too many people coming and going from those sorts of places to ward them like this." He explained.

"Thank you." I said softly.

He glanced down at me. "For what?"

"For being willing to comfort a complete stranger." I glanced up at him finally. "For allowing me to stay here and have a few nights where I don't have to sleep with one eye open."

He squeezed my shoulder. "Get some rest," and he rose from the bed to return to his cot by the door

I lay staring at the ceiling for a long while before I was finally tired enough to drift back off to sleep. The room was surprisingly dark in the middle of the day thanks to the shutters and dark curtains. You would've thought it was the middle of the night. I turned on my side, closed my eyes and slowly drifted off to sleep again.

*

The next evening, I woke up just before sunset. Before Deiric. To my surprise though, after I lit a few candles, I found clothes sitting out on the dresser that I hadn't seen the night before. Either he got them out before he fell back asleep or Liala had stopped in with them before I woke up.

I'd only managed to get my underwear, bra, and skirt on before I heard him stirring behind me.

"Morning." He mumbled, as he sat up, rubbing his face and locked eyes with me in the mirror.

"Technically it is the evening." I pointed out as I pulled my blouse over my head.

"Well, it's morning to me." He said as he stood up and turned to the dresser next to the door to grab a pair of pants. I watched him for a few moments in the mirror. I hadn't noticed the tattoos he had because his clothing had covered them. It had been so dark last night that I'd barely noticed them then either.

He had two intricate dragon tattoos, spiraling up each of his arms with their heads likely just over the tops of his shoulders on his clavicle on either side. On the back of his neck, and just between his shoulder blades he had the moon and lotus, the mark of the coven, and below it two crossed swords and a skull, indicating he was not only a death dealer but also an elder.

"See something you like?" He said with a sultry smile over his shoulder.

I jumped, and looked back at the corset I was idly loosening in my hands. "No." I said quickly.

"Interesting, I could've sworn I heard you admiring my tattoos. You were also too busy staring at my back in the mirror to notice I'd glanced around to look at you."

"You know, it's not very polite to invade people's thoughts all the time." I said as I pulled the corset over my head and finished lacing it before I spun it around to tighten it.

He appeared behind me in the blink of an eye and yanked the laces tighter around my waist. I jumped and gasped, the breath practically knocked out of me by how quickly he'd pulled it.

"How did you get all those scars?" He asked gently, meeting my gaze in the mirror.

I turned around when he'd finished tying the laces of the corset and leaned back against the dresser to put some space between us. "I didn't get away from all of my battles completely unscathed."

He pursed his lips, looking me up and down for a moment. "You didn't heal yourself?"

"Well, once I figured out how they tracked me, no. It wasn't worth the risk. I only use magic when I can't see any other way out during a fight. I had to use it to stop the Chimera before it killed me. They found me a lot faster that time than they ever had before."

"You killed a Chimera, and you walked away without a scratch?" His brows were raised, and eyes wide.

"Yes."

"Hmm." He turned and went back to dressing himself. "Most of the guys have had some formal training with combat, but have never had to use it. They were all still rather new when shit hit the fan years ago." Once he'd gotten his shirt on he spun around to face me again. "I can't wait to see how this goes today." He had a small smirk that told me that I was in for a long night.

It was my turn to smirk and taunt him. "I'll take pleasure in kicking every single one of their asses." I walked up to him until I was just a few inches from him, stood a bit on my toes so I could look him dead in the eye as I added. "Especially yours."

He scoffed. "Sure, we'll see how it goes." He patted my left shoulder as he turned to walk past me out of the room.

I grabbed his hand and twisted it around behind his back before he had the chance to brace himself or react. Then I stood on my tip toes and whispered against his neck. "Are you afraid I'll embarrass you in front of your men?"

He spun us both back around in the blink of an eye and had me pinned against the dresser behind me. One hand rested on either side of me on the dresser, the weight of his body holding me in place. "I'm just concerned you won't have the energy to go up against me after you've schooled each of them today."

I raised a brow. "We'll see how it goes." I mused back at him, and I pushed him back off of me before I wandered out the door to go downstairs. Two could play the teasing and taunting game, and I still had to get back at him for what he did in that cave.

Chapter 8

Mira

Just after sunset we all made our way to the open area in front of the house. I met the others now. There was Leo, Xander, and Renwick. We skipped the pleasantries, other than exchanging names and hellos.

Zane was the first to set foot in the "ring" with me, which was just the area between the stairs and the fire we had started to give us some light. Everyone who wasn't sparring was sitting on the steps or leaning against the columns that supported the roof watching.

Zane chuckled. "You're going to fight me in that?" He motioned to my skirt, corset, and blouse.

"What, are you afraid to get your ass kicked by a pretty lady in a skirt?" I teased, sinking into a fighting stance. I had my knives strapped across my waist, and my favorite knife tucked away on my thigh like I always did.

Zane sunk into a fighting stance now. "Hardly." He said, a wicked smile coming to his face. "I'm just worried I'll cut up that skirt of yours and leave you exposed."

I smiled and motioned for him to make the first move. "The only rule is, you can't use your superhuman speed or strength."

He made his first move, and it took all the self control I had not to cackle at the face he made in shock when I blocked it and sent him flying back.

"Is that all you've got?" I quipped. "Pity, I expected this to be a little harder."

He snarled and charged at me again. We went back and forth for almost an hour, where he would think he'd get me and I'd send him back. He finally managed to break my stance at one point, causing me to fall back and catch myself with my free hand. He paused with his sword pointed at my throat, a pleased smile on his face.

I just smiled right back and my eyes moved to where my sword now pointed before glancing back up at him. His face contorted with shock and confusion as he glanced down. My sword was pointed right at his stomach, and held a gentle pressure there.

"I may be dead, but you're gutted too." I chuckled as he stood up straight and lowered his sword.

"Alright, you're pretty good." He mumbled as he walked over to sit down on the steps, a bit winded. I still hadn't broken a sweat.

"Who's next?" I challenged them.

Xander stood up and made his way down the steps. He was a bit shorter than Zane, just as bulky and muscular with dark brown hair that was also tied back into a small bun on the back of his head. He, unlike Zane, was clean shaven, and had an undercut. He spun his sword casually as he settled into a fighting stance.

I motioned for him to make the first move again, and we went back and forth for nearly 45 minutes before I spun his sword out of his grip and he yielded.

Leo stood up next. He was tall and slender, with blond hair that was cut very short on the sides, but longer on top. He didn't look like much of a fighter to me. This time, he motioned for me to make the first move.

We went blade to blade for almost an hour before we both finally gave in, equally matched and likely not to end in a victory for either of us. Though admittedly I didn't try as hard as I could've.

Renwick was next, practically shoved into the ring with me by Deiric as he smirked. It was pretty obvious based on the stance he took that he'd had no formal training with a sword, or any form of combat.

I tried to take it easy on him, but it was quite sad actually. I realized he'd been thrown in more for their entertainment, so I stopped and critiqued his stance and worked with him for several minutes until he could at least block my advances.

"That's getting better." I said after another much more successful block. Then I stopped and turned to the stairs. "Don't think I've forgotten you." I said, pointing my sword at Deiric.

Deiric smirked, stood up and walked down the stairs, a blade I hadn't seen this whole time in his hands. "Are you sure you want to do this?" He asked, a smug confidence in his voice.

"Are *you* sure?" I retorted as I spun my sword and took a sturdy stance.

He merely put on that same sultry smile he'd had this morning. "On with it then."

I nodded, and we charged one another. Blade for blade, I would strike and he would block, then he would strike and I would block. Faster than any of the others, we went back and forth until we were both starting to get a bit winded.

He pulled a maneuver he hadn't done yet and managed to get me spun around with my back against him for a moment.

I thought he was going to try to hold his blade to my throat and went to block accordingly, so I didn't notice when he shifted slightly to bring his face into the crook of my neck and gently nip that same sensitive spot he'd discovered sent shivers down my spine in the cave a few nights ago.

He thought it would distract me for the split second it took him to grab my braid and spin me again, this time succeeding in sticking his blade to my throat as he held my head back by my hair. His face was inches from mine.

For a few seconds, we were staring into each other's eyes, that blade paused right at my throat, a wicked smile on his face believing he'd won this battle.

I merely huffed a laugh smiling more wickedly than he had at the beginning, and glanced down, then met his gaze again. He couldn't hide his confusion for a moment, and he finally glanced down as well. I held my blade right above his crown jewels.

Zane was howling with laughter when they all also realized where we'd ended up. The others who were trying to hold back a laugh joined in moments later and were rolling on the stairs.

"You cheated." I muttered as we both lowered our swords.

He scoffed. "*I* cheated." He raised a brow. "I'm not the one going for the cheap shots."

"I wouldn't have had to go for the cheap shot if you hadn't tried to win this by getting me all hot and bothered." I crossed my arms. "Besides, how is grabbing my hair *not* a cheap shot?"

He grabbed my braid again and pulled me close to him. His face was less than an inch from mine. "Because in a real fight, no one plays fair." His eyes danced from mine to my lips and back again. "This braid is as good as a death sentence."

I just stared at him keeping my face as stone cold as I could as I said, "funny. It's never been a problem before."

The guys were quietly watching us now, I realized. Deiric, it seems, realized it at the same moment as me, because he looked over and snarled at them. "Don't you have somewhere else to be?" Then he released my braid and stepped back. They all quickly dispersed, to where though, I wasn't sure.

I smiled and wandered toward the steps. "Just admit it - I'm a little better at this than you'd expected." I said as I sat down and leaned back on the steps, stretching my arms a bit. "Or, you're a lot more rusty than you thought." I jabbed.

He huffed a bit, and walked over to sit next to me. "Fine. I'll admit that you're better than I thought you'd be." He paused for a moment as he looked out toward the fire. "I am probably a bit rusty too." He half smiled.

I gently jabbed him with my elbow. "Maybe next time you can beat me fair and square. I'll make sure I've got my braid out of the way at least."

He just smiled and gave me a sideways glance as he stood and sheathed his sword, then sauntered off toward the tree line to do whatever he would normally do for the day.

Chapter 9

Mira

I spent the rest of the night in the den, browsing through books of herbs and poisons they had on the shelves there trying to figure out what might've been put in my drink that had blocked out my magic for so long.

About an hour after I'd settled onto the couch I started to realize how many places were now sore from where I had collided with everyone repeatedly earlier. I tried to ignore it as I read through a handful of the books I'd grabbed, but decided a nice hot bath might help to ease the discomfort.

Liala helped me draw a bath after dinner, and had given me some bath salts and oils that not only smelled delightful, but that she assured me would help with some of the soreness. The guys had not returned yet from whatever it was they had run off to do so I left my pile of books on the bed and undressed before slipping into the steaming tub off of Deiric's bedroom.

The oils and salts she'd given me were incredible, they'd left a thin layer of bubbles across the top of the water, and the smells were enough to make me almost fall asleep laying there. I don't know how long I had been in the tub before I jumped when I heard someone clearing their throat.

I lifted my head and opened my eyes to find Deiric leaning against the door frame, arms crossed, smirking, still wearing the same leather armor he'd been wearing when we'd been sparring a few hours ago. "You know, at some point I'd like to get cleaned up as well."

I half frowned, resting my head back on the edge of the tub again. "I'll be out of your way in a few minutes."

He chuckled, "Oh sure, if you don't fall asleep in there." I could practically hear that smile still on his lips as he spoke. "Liala mentioned you were a little sore. Did we go too hard for you today?"

I lifted my head again, narrowly opening my eyes so I could glare at him. "I am just fine, thank you." I paused for a moment to wipe the bubbles off of my neck.as I sat up a bit further, but not far enough to reveal more than my shoulders beyond what remained of the bubbles. "I don't generally train or fight for several hours at a time, that's all."

He just raised a brow, but I could see his gaze lowering from my eyes to my shoulders, and eventually the water as if he could see past the bubbles and foam on the surface.

"You're insufferable, you know." I muttered. "Are you like this with every woman you meet or has it just been so long since you've been around a woman other than Liala that you can't help yourself?"

He scowled and finally pushed himself off of the door frame then turned to walk back into the bedroom.

When he was out of sight I stood from the tub, wrung out my hair, and dried myself some with the towel before I wrapped it around me and walked into the bedroom. I found him sprawled on the bed, without a shirt, propped on his elbow as he flipped through one of the books I'd left laying there.

"Are you trying to find some way to poison us?" He mused, not looking up from the book.

I walked over and snapped the book shut before I took it from him. "No, I'm trying to figure out what herbs he used to block my magic. My mother knew many herbs but never mentioned or taught me anything that might do that."

He looked up at me, meeting my eyes. "I doubt you're going to find it in those books. I don't think anyone has ever mentioned it, so I would imagine it is a new discovery from the Solas Coven's archmages."

I shrugged and turned to walk around the bed to the dresser. "It's possible, but it doesn't mean I can't try." I looked in the mirror at him as I sat the book down on the dresser. "These books contain all of the known plants and their attributes, at least at the time they were written. There must be something in here that hinted toward that sort of effect for them to try it and find it."

He hadn't moved, and was still facing away from me as he said, "I can reach out to some of the other Elders and see if they've heard of anything."

"Are there other elders still out there?" I asked. A genuine question because I didn't know how many were left. That attack on my family and that house we'd been living in was just the start. There were many others.

He sighed. "Not as many as there should be, but there are some who managed to stay under the radar, in similar warded houses like this one." He rose from the bed and headed to the bathing room. "I'll send Leo out tomorrow to ask around." Then he went into the bathing room and shut the door.

Before he finished and came back to the bedroom I'd climbed into bed. He quietly slipped into his cot by the door, and after a few minutes I slowly drifted off to sleep.

Chapter 10

Deiric

I woke early, before anyone else. I realized after we had all done some sparring that I'd let that slide for far too long. We should have been training all this time like we did years ago, but I had given up on the idea of ever being able to rally the coven again. At the chance to get out of hiding away in this manor.

I sighed and finally quietly got up to get dressed. She didn't stir, and continued to sleep soundly in my bed.

I suppose I should make an effort to prepare one of the other rooms for her at some point. She didn't seem like she'd be likely to make a run for it, but on the off chance that they *did* track her here, I'd rather be closer to her.

I quietly rummaged through my drawers to get some clothes, got dressed, and then headed downstairs. Zane sat at the table, to my surprise, awake already.

"You're up early." I grumbled, as I walked in and sat down a few feet from him on the opposite side of the table.

He sighed. "I woke up and couldn't go back to sleep. After a while I gave up and just came down here." He had a book laying open on the table in front of him. It looked like a book I'd seen him with before.

"Haven't you already read that one?" I asked.

He glanced up at me. "Several times." He said plainly. "It isn't like we often get *new* books."

I sighed and rested my elbow on the table, leaning into it. "We should probably keep training at least a little bit everyday." My voice was flat. I expected he'd push back a little, but it wasn't like we had a whole lot of other things to do anyway.

He scowled a bit, and closed the book. "You don't seriously think that she's going to help us bring everyone back together do you?" He was looking over at me again, studying how I sat against the table.

"I think that if the rest of the coven finds out she's alive it will make a difference, yes. They may have let us believe she was dead because they thought she'd been captured instead and knew they couldn't get her out." I paused for a moment, studying his reaction just as he studied me. "I'm sure at some point they began to assume she was dead as well. She certainly seems to have a knack for keeping herself hidden from *everyone*."

Zane rolled his eyes a bit. "If you thought that you would reach out to the others."

I glared at him. "If we contact them now they'll come and just take her. Something tells me she wouldn't take kindly to that." I heard some of the others moving around upstairs now. "Besides, if they came and took her, we still wouldn't get daylight rings. Do you really want to jeopardize that?"

Zane was silent now, his face had softened some. "I suppose not." He looked over when we heard someone making their way down the stairs. He lowered his voice. "Do you think she'll stay here with us after she's made the rings?"

I met his gaze. I could tell it wasn't her. The footsteps were too heavy. "Only time will tell."

Xander appeared in the doorway now. "I guess we all couldn't sleep."

"Deiric has decided that we're going to train more often." Zane said flatly.

Xander scoffed and leaned against the threshold. "Of course he has."

Zane snarled at him slightly. "Watch your tone. He's not wrong. We should be."

I looked at Xander fully now, just in time to see him roll his eyes. "We can include Mira in the training, just to keep it interesting." I offered a small smile. I doubted she wanted to join today given how sore she seemed after yesterday, but perhaps that challenge might motivate them more.

Xander just scowled in response. "I know I'm *new* but last I checked we didn't train or turn women. Why should we include her?"

I snarled at him now. "She was clearly trained at some point. That's an old and unspoken rule. There's no reason to *exclude* her if she wishes to train with us now."

There were light footsteps coming down the stairs now, which could have been Liala or Mira. We all went quiet.

Mira wandered past Xander and over to the kitchen. "Am I interrupting something?" She asked, but I suspected she already knew the answer. She had put on another skirt, blouse, and her corset. It seemed to be the only thing she ever wanted to wear I guessed. It was all she had asked Liala for yesterday when she offered to go out and get her more clothes.

Zane spoke up. "Deiric would like us to train more regularly. Would you like to join us this evening?"

She was busy preparing a small fire now, so she could make herself some tea. "Are you going to give me a real challenge this time?" Her voice had a somewhat playful tone to it.

I couldn't stop the smile as it found its way to my lips. She was certainly good at getting under everyone's skin.

Xander was entirely unimpressed and huffed a bit at her question.

She turned to face him once she had the kettle over the fire. "Just because it seems to bother *him*, I'll join you this evening."

Her gaze shifted to me and I quickly tried to hide the smile I'd let creep onto my face. She saw it though and gave me a small glare for just a moment.

Zane broke the silence that had settled over all of us. "Great. We'll go out just after sunset and pair up."

The others were shuffling in now. Mira made her tea in silence, and Liala took a cup as well when she finally came down. When the sun set they started to build a fire so we had more light, and then we all shuffled outside.

I planned to just observe and cut in as necessary to correct anyone's stances or general form.

She paired up with Leo. I watched each group, but couldn't help myself from lingering and watching Leo and Mira more than the others.

The way she fought was so fluid and so smooth I started to wonder if she had been taught to wield a blade from the moment she learned how to walk. No matter how much you train some, it takes them years to become as fluid as she was with that sword. An elder's blade, I'd noted.

She'd be better suited to a smaller blade, but she wielded it well. Like it was made for her.

She caught my gaze for a moment, but didn't let it distract her from Leo's advance, which she used to disarm him.

He scoffed. "Lucky shot."

She smirked. "It wasn't luck. You left yourself wide open when you thought I was distracted." She looked over at me again. "You haven't taken your eyes off me for a while. Why?" She raised a brow and pointed her sword in my direction.

I approached her while Leo sauntered off to retrieve his sword. I grabbed the edge of the blade carefully and turned it so I could look at it more closely.

"This is an elder's blade." I said softly. "Where did you get it?"

She looked me up and down for a moment and her expression softened some. "I hadn't noticed there was a difference." She said softly. "It was my father's."

That answered my question, I suppose. It wasn't made *for* her. She probably was trained the moment she could walk, and he'd let her use his blade because he couldn't have one made for her.

"Interesting." Was all I finally managed to say. In some small way it almost made me sad. She was probably trained in both magic and combat, her entire life. Likely whether she wanted to be or not. This was all she knew. It explained why she traveled alone, and why she chose that line of work. She didn't know how to blend in any other way.

Leo appeared next to us. “If you’re quite finished admiring her blade and her skills, I’d like to get back to sparring now.” There was feigned annoyance in his voice.

I stepped aside and let them get back to it. They were all mildly annoyed with how I had changed in her presence. I still couldn’t understand *why* she was so intriguing to me, and why I couldn’t just treat her like any other sorceress I’d encountered over the last 600 years. Something about her was just *different* and I couldn’t place it.

Chapter 11

Mira

After we finished sparring, I decided I was going to continue my research on what they might've dosed me with to nullify my magic. I didn't move from the couch much after I piled books on the table next to me to pick through. I had a few pages marked with shreds of the paper I'd also been taking notes on all night.

I heard someone enter the house, pause at the entryway for a moment and then head in my direction. I didn't even bother to look up from the book when they picked up my legs, which were resting on the arm of the couch, and sat down, sitting my legs back on the arm of the couch over top of them.

"That book must be super interesting for you to not even flinch."

Zane. I would've guessed it was Deiric. I put another sliver of the torn up paper in the book and sat it down on my stomach so I could look at him. His hair was pulled up into a small bun on the back of his head, likely to keep it out of the way while we were training earlier, though this seemed to be his chosen hairstyle regardless. He had a mildly amused look on his face. I put one arm behind my head, propping myself up so I could look at him without straining my neck.

"Deiric didn't tell you that I'm trying to figure out what they dosed me with?"

He shrugged. "Contrary to what you might believe he doesn't tell me much actually." He looked at the stack of books on the table, scribbled pieces of paper and my empty cup of tea. "You've been quite busy though I see."

"I have some suspicions on what they used to block my magic but I won't be able to say for sure without experimenting, so I'm marking the books and taking notes as I go to narrow it down to a few likely culprits." I gestured to the papers. "Those are my guesses so far."

He leaned over toward me to reach for the papers. I picked them up and handed them to him, because they were slightly out of his reach. He began to sift through them slowly.

"Vervain." He muttered, slightly scowling, and looked over at me. "That is believed to repel vampires."

"It is also believed to repel witches according to one of the books in that pile." I motioned toward the stack of books I had pieces of paper sticking out of.

"Repel is a bit different from entirely incapacitating." He mumbled as he flipped through a few more pages.

"Have you ever encountered vervain?" I watched him pick through the remaining pages and then sit them down.

"No, but I have heard that vampires, when they consume too much of it, do become completely incapacitated." He looked over at me. "I have no idea what it would do to a Dhampir."

I raised an eyebrow for a moment as I spoke. "Vervain is at the top of my list, given that it could be used against vampires and witches, but Agrimony is a close second."

"I've never even heard of Agrimony." Zane mumbled, and looked over into the fireplace.

"I hadn't either until I found it in the books. My mother never mentioned it." My voice trailed off a bit as I thought back to some of the lessons I had with her, concocting poisons, potions, and all sorts of herbal salves. "She did mention vervain, but we never used it. She also certainly didn't mention that it supposedly repelled witches."

The front door opened and I heard several sets of footsteps entering the house and making their way upstairs or into the kitchen. Moments later Deiric appeared in the doorway. "Any luck?" He jerked his chin toward the stack of books, and papers. "I see Zane has made himself comfortable."

"That's my cue to leave I guess." He gave me a sideways glance and a small smirk before he patted my knee and I moved my legs to allow him to get up and go anywhere but this room.

I sat myself up and crossed my legs on the couch, giving Deiric the space to take the seat that Zane had just been sitting in. "Well?" He asked.

I frowned, placing the book I had on my stomach with the stack on the table. "I have a handful of ideas, but the two that stick out to me the most are Vervain and Agrimony."

I could've sworn he shuddered at that, before he picked up my notes. "Vervain?"

"Yes. I knew it was said to repel vampires, but one of these books also suggests it repels witches and protects against witchcraft." I grabbed for the book I believed had that note in it and opened it to where I bookmarked. "Here." I passed him the book and pointed to the paragraph that explained it.

He sat silently for a few moments, reading. "That seems most likely, especially since you fit into both of those categories." He read beyond just the paragraph I'd indicated for a few more moments. "What about Agrimony? Was there anything detailed about that?"

I rooted through the other books, flipped one open to the bookmark and passed that to him. "Here." I again pointed to the small section on that herb.

"Hmm." He tapped his chin and looked deep in thought for a moment, staring at the book. "What if they've combined them?"

I raised both eyebrows. I hadn't considered that. "I suppose that's possible." I sat in silence and thought through everything I'd read. I remembered that the book mentioned Agrimony was thought to be a sleep aid, and Zane had said that vervain could knock out a vampire if consumed in high enough quantities.

Deiric looked at me at the moment that I'd finished that thought. "You wouldn't have been able to taste the vervain. I can't speak for Agrimony as far as taste is concerned, but if that is a sleep aid then the combination would've definitely knocked you on your ass even in small quantities. I think even vervain, consumed in high enough quantities, can knock out a human as well as a vampire."

"How do you know I wouldn't have been able to taste the vervain?" I didn't bother questioning its potency.

"Because it isn't the first time they've tried to use it on us, and I couldn't taste it when they spiked our drinks at the Magister's meeting many, many years ago." His face had a hint of rage or frustration as he spoke. "We'll need to get the word out to everyone, even the sorcerers and magisters. If they've figured out it can also block magic, we're in deep shit."

With that he rose from the couch and walked over to the cabinet next to the books. I watched as he pulled out a fancy glass decanter and two glasses.

"You know, I doubted that you'd find anything in those books, but I'm actually impressed. I'm also a little bit annoyed with myself that I hadn't even considered vervain as an option, but regardless."

He sat back down next to me and poured two glasses of the amber liquid in the decanter. "If this all goes to shit, I have a feeling they'll wipe us all out this time, so there's no sense in keeping this whiskey locked away and never taking the time to enjoy it."

He had a very odd smile on his face, that didn't meet his eyes. His eyes were distant, almost vacant. I didn't dare ask what happened that day that he had experienced the effects of vervain himself, or what followed. That vacant look and broken smile told me enough. He handed me a glass.

I took the glass and sniffed it to find it was the most rich, but sweet smelling whiskey I think I'd ever had. I looked back up at him. He clinked his glass with mine and took a sip. I sipped mine as well and it was indeed a very rich and somewhat sweet whiskey.

Chapter 12

Mira

I was jolted awake the following morning by Zane banging on the bedroom door. "It's unlike you to sleep so late Deiric, are you alive in there?"

It took me a moment to realize that Deiric was already awake and lying right next to me. His arm was pinned underneath me and he had a sly smile on his face. I went to sit up and pull back pretty quickly, but the throbbing that started in my head at that movement stopped me in my tracks. I groaned and rubbed my face.

"I'll be out in a few minutes." He called to Zane, the sound of his voice grating against the pain in my head. "Good morning sunshine." He mocked quietly after Zane had walked away.

"How are you not hungover, and what on earth are you doing *here?"* I grumbled, motioning to where he was laying in the bed.

He motioned to the empty glasses behind me on the bedside table, and the empty decanter. "I am not hungover because unlike you, *I* am immortal and it takes a hell of a lot more liquor than that. You handle your liquor pretty well, surprisingly, but I had a feeling you'd regret that today."

I sighed and rubbed my face again. His arm was still pinned under me and he didn't try to move. I glanced down at him. He had his pants on, but no shirt. I glanced down at myself and I was still clothed, at least. "You didn't answer my second question."

His sly smile just widened a bit. "I am here, because this is *my* bedroom."

"You know that's not what I meant."

He reached over and gently brushed the hair out of my face. "You don't remember, do you?"

I could remember most of the evening, or I guess you could say the early morning. We'd brought the glasses and decanter up here shortly after we'd both finished our first drinks and sat here drinking and talking until after the sun had risen outside. After that, I didn't really recall much.

"I know that you still had your shirt on and we were talking, but I don't recall much after that." I finally said after a few moments.

"You were buzzed, or maybe actually drunk after a little while. Drunk enough that you finally openly admitted you'd noticed and admired my tattoos that first evening you saw me without my shirt and asked me about them. Why I'd gotten them, or what they were for, so I had taken my shirt off to give you a closer look and explain." He flicked my nose and I flinched.

"Then you fell asleep before I was halfway through explaining the story behind the dragons. You either hadn't noticed or didn't care that you were laying on my arm and I didn't want to disturb you, so I laid here for a while thinking you'd eventually roll over or wake up so I could move."

He gently tugged on his arm and I lifted myself up just far enough for him to finally get free. "You didn't move though. Or rather, I should say you didn't move *away* from me. You just snuggled closer, so despite the fact that I figured you'd wake up and punch me I just gave up and slept here."

I made a face and gave him the most pathetic jab to the ribs as I propped myself up on my elbow. "You could've taken your arm back at any time you know and I wouldn't have been upset."

That sly smile faded into something a bit more genuine. "I know, but you looked so calm and peaceful it hardly seemed right to disturb you." He paused for a moment, brushing another piece of hair back behind my ear. "Besides, I imagine you haven't really had many super restful or peaceful nights. I figured the least I could do was lay here and let you drool all over me while you slept off your buzz."

I jabbed him a lot harder this time and he flinched away. "You're going to make me barf. Who knew the alluring and audacious elder vampire had it in him to be so mushy and cute sometimes."

That wicked grin returned as he leaned down closer to my face. "You think I'm attractive?" He mused.

I laid my hand on his chest for a moment and leaned in a little bit closer, acting like I'd move for a kiss. I could see that excitement dancing in his eyes. "I think you're a little too full of yourself is more like it." I snapped, glancing from his eyes to his lips and then back up again. Then I pushed him away.

He scoffed, placed one hand on his chest and acted a bit offended. "You're the one who called me an alluring and audacious elder, I'm just reiterating *your* opinion." He glanced back at me with a teasing look as he stood from the bed and fished a fresh shirt from out of his drawers.

"You're not going to wash up first?" I called after him as he walked to the door, still carrying the shirt in his hand.

"I've already laid in bed, and for all the rest of them know, overslept by at least two hours. I need to get moving or they'll get the wrong idea." He looked me up and down before he turned to open the door. "You, on the other hand, look like hell and should probably take your time getting up if you have any hope of getting rid of that hangover." And with that, he slipped out and started walking toward the stairs.

Zane must not have wandered far, because I could hear him in the hallway. "I'm sorry, was I interrupting something?"

"No." Deiric hissed.

"Your lack of a shirt would say otherwise." Zane jabbed.

"You'd do well to mind your business Zane." I heard him growl before both of them made their way downstairs.

I sighed and rolled over onto my back. "Super smart Mira. Drink with the Elder until you practically black out." I muttered to myself as I again rubbed my face. I could've sworn though, that I'd only had two glasses. Whatever that whiskey was, it must've packed a hell of a punch.

A few moments later I heard footsteps coming upstairs and Liala walked in with a plate and small steaming mug. "Deiric mentioned you had a bit too much to drink last night and likely wouldn't be coming downstairs for a while. I figured I could at least bring you something to snack on and some hot tea to ease the hangover."

She smiled at me as she sat the plate and mug down on the same side table as the decanter and glasses sat on. "You know, he's never shared his personal stash of whiskey with anyone. It's nice to see him relax a little." She sat on the bed by my knees.

"His stash must be one hell of an expensive collection of whiskey to get me that drunk with just two glasses." I finally shifted myself up into a sitting position and grabbed the mug, the smell of the brilliant earthy tea already helping a bit. I took a few sips.

"Well, dear, vampires usually tend to drink the stronger liquors. Your average tavern whiskey doesn't even give us a buzz unless we finish an entire bottle."

"That bastard." I mumbled, and she laughed. "He didn't even warn me."

"Of course he didn't warn you. He also hasn't drank with a human in ages, and probably forgot how potent his whiskey actually is."

I smiled and shook my head. "Thank you for bringing this up to me."

She nodded, and started to turn to leave before I gently grabbed her arm.

"You were close with my mother, weren't you?" I knew the answer, but it was my way in.

She hesitated and tried to offer a small smile as she nodded. "I was for many, many years, yes."

"Would you tell me about her?" I asked quietly. "Before me, I mean. She never really told me much about herself before she had me. Like how she met my father, or what made them decide to have me despite how dangerous it might be."

She rested her hand on my knee. "Sure."

I sat and listened for hours as she shared some stories, and I occasionally asked questions. For those few hours, I felt normal again, or as normal as I could be I guess.

I felt like I was back in that house from my childhood, just enjoying time with an old friend. There would be plenty of time to worry about the Solas coven, and plenty of time for planning and scheming, but I didn't want to miss out on having a few normal days. When Deiric mentioned he'd rather not save up all his good whiskey only to never get to enjoy it if this all did in fact go to shit, that reminded me too that I should take in all these moments of normalcy before we delved into this messy potential war we were headed for.

Chapter 13

Mira

Later that evening, I was preparing my own dinner for once. The house was quiet except for the crackle in the hearth. I was by the counter, cutting up an apple, when I felt someone right behind me. I switched the knife to my left hand and swung before I even registered what I was doing - a hazard of being on my own for so long I guess.

Deiric caught my wrist right before the knife made contact with his throat. "Easy killer." He said with a stifled laugh. "Remind me to never get on your bad side, or sneak up on you again." He just smirked. His right hand was resting on the counter beside mine.

"Sorry-" I gasped. "It's a reflex. I thought I was alone." I heard Zane chuckle from somewhere behind us.

"You're lucky you've got good reflexes, Deiric, or I'd have one hell of a mess to clean up."

Deiric was still holding my wrist, gentle, but firm. He let go of it and I sat the knife down before I turned to face him. There was almost no space between us and I leaned back against the counter to create at least a bit of a gap so I could look at him.

"I see that you've managed to drag yourself out of bed." That familiar smirk on his face. "How are you feeling?"

"Fine, no thanks to you." I didn't try to keep the edge from my voice. "You could've warned me that the whiskey you gave me would be stronger than what I'm used to." I managed to cross my arms, despite that there was barely enough space between us to allow me to do that without leaning further back over the counter and straining my back.

He huffed another little laugh. "You handled it just fine." He was not hiding that he was more focused on looking at my lips than meeting my eyes.

"Wait a minute, you won't let any of us drink that shit, but you drank it with her last night?" Zane's voice had a tinge of jealousy in it.

Deiric's other hand brushed my braided hair back over my right shoulder and then continued to trace down my shoulder and arm. "You'd have been welcome to have a drink as well if you hadn't gone off to bed so early." He replied sort of mindlessly to Zane, more focused on me.

"Besides, you lot would just drink until you were shitfaced and waste it. That whiskey is meant to be sipped and enjoyed slowly, in good company." He added.

I glanced over Deiric's shoulder at Zane, who merely scowled and stood silently evaluating whether he should stay or go. When I shifted my gaze back to Deiric his eyes met mine and the intensity in them made my breath hitch for a moment.

"How exactly did you manage to sneak in here so quietly just now anyway?" I asked, trying to change the subject before the others who were now filing into the dining room and kitchen could get offended at not being offered anything to drink last night.

A wicked smile found its way to his lips. "Years of practice."

"Would you get a room already?" Xander snapped from where he was now sitting at the table.

Deiric was about to speak, but it was me who responded with, "Jealousy isn't a good look on you Xander. Do I need to find you a woman to give you a little bit of attention?" I smiled.

Zane was practically on the ground, doubled over in laughter and unable to breathe. Leo was too shocked to speak, Renwick was trying desperately not to completely lose it, and Xander just sat in stunned silence.

"I like her." Was all Renwick finally managed to say before he finally broke and was howling with laughter with Zane.

I think the only reason Deiric didn't join them in laughter was because he was too focused on me, and that sly smile had transitioned to a wide and wild grin. His eyes practically sparkled as he stared into mine. His left hand was slowly and casually wrapping around my right hip and pulling me off the counter, into him. My still crossed arms kept some space between our faces though. After a moment he leaned in to whisper in my left ear.

"Who's the insufferable one now?"

I rolled my eyes, huffed a small laugh, and pushed him off so I could go back to putting my dinner together. It was hardly a fancy meal, but I ladled some of the soup I'd reheated from lunch into a bowl, set the bowl onto the plate where I'd put the apple slices and some of the raspberries Liala had picked last evening.

Deiric hadn't moved from where he stood beside me until I walked over and sat down at the table next to Renwick.

Renwick nudged me. "Care to come out and spar with us tomorrow evening? I'd like to think I stand a chance against you now. Or at least that I won't make a fool out of myself again."

I had a few spoonfuls of my soup before I replied. "*You* didn't make a fool of yourself. These pricks made a fool out of you for sending you to spar with someone without any formal training."

There were a few disapproving grunts and groans from around the table. Deiric was now leaning against the wall on the other side of the entryway from Zane.

"But sure, I'll come out tomorrow." I said softly.

"We've scouted out an area far from here that would be the perfect place to do the spell to create the daylight rings." Leo reported. "I have made the rounds to some of the other groups of us within a day or two's journey of here and they are not aware of anything that could've been used to block your magic, but they are sending the word out, discreetly, to get ahold of the higher ranking members of the coven if they're willing to meet with us."

I stared at him blankly. I was only told he would research what I'd been drugged with. I didn't know anything about meeting with the rest of the coven.

Deiric pushed off the wall and stepped in, noting the look on my face and likely hearing me curse about them keeping me in the dark again. "I hadn't told her about that plan just yet." He mumbled, and sat at the head of the table next to me.

I shot him a small glare, then he continued. "She's hell bent on making us our rings and then moving on as far as I can tell, but I'm hoping we can convince her to stay and work with us."

Leo locked eyes with me. "Some of my sources say that the people have grown quite tired of the Solas coven and their ridiculous taxes. They're seeing that the bastards aren't holding up their bargain to protect them." He paused for a moment. I just went back to eating my soup. "It wouldn't take much to convince them to switch their allegiance, and the other Elders believe that the Magisters will be willing to discuss things with us, for once."

"And you've told them about me?" I stared at my plate as I started to pick at the fruit.

"No. They don't know why I'm asking about the herbs. They seem to have been considering trying to band together again for a while now anyway." Leo continued. "But- they may already have put together that you escaped that day."

I looked up again, my face cold and blank.

"The other Elders have seen your wanted posters and they don't understand why the Solas coven is hunting the only mercenary they know they can count on to hunt the beasts terrorizing the villages."

"No one will say anything though, about what or who they think you are." Deiric finished that thought for him.

I sighed. "Surely I'm not the only mercenary out there that's taking on these beasts. I've bumped into many others on all my travels."

"You are the only one who comes back consistently, alive, bearing pieces of the monsters you've claimed to kill as proof they've been taken care of." Zane said, his voice was cold and flat. I looked up and met his eyes, which told me all I needed to know, but he continued anyway. "You may not think much of yourself, but you are significantly stronger and faster than any other mercenary for a reason, and it has nothing to do with your magic."

"And if you hadn't stumbled across me by accident, do you think that this would all be falling into place anyway?" I pressed, looking at each of them as I spoke. "Do you think that if I were captured or killed that they would still gather and attempt to overthrow those bastards now?"

"I do." Deiric said, almost too quietly to hear. "But you're safe here."

"We'll be provoking them, taunting them almost when I make your rings. Summoning that much power will quickly give away my location to them."

"We've planned for that and are choosing a location accordingly." Deiric said.

"We could always just continue without the rings." Renwick suggested, seeing the point I was trying to make.

"We need to be able to move regardless of the time of day if we hold any chance at getting this going. No one else seems to care enough to get the ball rolling on this effort. Considering banding together and actually making moves to do it are entirely different things. The Magisters will not want to meet us in the middle of the night. And we certainly won't be able to convince any other sorcerer or sorceress to do this for us." Deiric said plainly.

He had a point. I wouldn't even be on this schedule if it weren't that *everyone* in this house followed it.

"We have a few days until the next full moon." I finally said. "Do you have the rings you'd like me to enchant?"

Leo nodded, and pulled a handful of silver rings with various different cuts of small stones on them. I picked them up and examined them carefully. "These will do." I set them back down. "If this goes poorly, and they show up to take me, you're going to stand down and let them."

"Absolutely not." Zane snapped before Deiric could say a word, though I saw him open his mouth to snarl the same thing.

I locked eyes with Zane. "*IF* they come for me, they are there for me and no one else. They won't come after you, and you can get out and save yourselves. If you truly believe that everyone will come together regardless of whether or not I am here, then you will stand down." I insisted.

Deiric opened his mouth to insist otherwise and I continued. "I can handle myself, as you well know. They clearly don't intend to kill me right away, which would give you the chance to swoop in and play savior again if needed, but if you intervene when they come to take me, you'll surely all be killed."

Deiric scowled and looked down at the table. He knew I was right, even though it seemed to make him want to scream.

"I suspect they want to try and convince me to join them, or they'd have just killed me that day they drugged me. If I can't get away on my own in transit to wherever it is they'd take me, when the coven finds out I'm alive you'll have the resources you'd need to get me out." I paused, looking around at them all again, their faces a bit grave as they were processing what I was saying. "Even if the Oíche coven doesn't deem saving me worth it, they sure as hell wouldn't want me working with the Solas coven and would likely agree to get me out just so they aren't threatened by me."

"Fine." Deiric finally grumbled. "If it goes poorly we will leave you to it. If we can do so discreetly one of us will try to follow to keep tabs on where they're taking you."

"I can live with that." I mumbled, before standing up to head upstairs. I laid my hand on Renwick's shoulder. "I'll see you in the morning." I gave him a half smile and walked my plate and bowl to the sink before I headed up to the bedroom.

*

I was just finishing in the bathing room when Deiric finally also came upstairs, likely discussing plans long after I'd walked away. He didn't say a word as I walked out in my towel and he went in to wash up.

When he finished and came back out I was standing in front of the dresser in the nightgown Liala had given me and braiding my hair. I watched him through the mirror for a moment. He had his towel wrapped around his waist and rummaged through his drawers.

"Still can't keep your eyes off of me I take it?" He didn't look up, but the attempt at teasing me must have been his way of apologizing for keeping me out of the loop of their plans.

I quickly looked down and pretended my braid was the most interesting thing in the room as I finished the very last part and tied it off with a small leather strap. I didn't notice he walked up behind me again. He'd managed to slip on a loose pair of pants before he made his way over to me.

He gently traced one of the scars on my back that was visible above the nightgown. "You asked me about my tattoos, but I didn't get to ask you about all of these scars." He said softly. I met his eyes in the mirror. "Which beast is responsible for this one?"

I offered a half smile, flinching a little bit at the memory though. "That was a Gorgon."

His brows raised. "You faced a Gorgon?"

I spun around to face him. "Is that so unbelievable?"

"Honestly, it is pretty impressive." His fingers now lightly traced my jawline. "How did you manage to get out of that without being turned to stone?" A genuine question, but his eyes were asking a different question as they traveled to other places.

"I had to fight it blindfolded." I said, my voice barely a whisper as I also let my eyes wander a bit.

"Huh," he lifted my chin gently and his eyes met mine for a moment. "I could think of much more fun things to do blindfolded than fighting a Gorgon."

Those blue eyes were shimmering in the candlelight, a quiet hunger lingered in them. I decided to play into his little game, and glanced from his lips to his eyes as I said, "Like what?"

His right hand slipped around my waist to the small of my back and he leaned his head in closer to me until our lips were almost touching. "I'm sure you could take a few guesses."

I reached up and let my right hand slide up his neck and into his hair, "I could think of a few things." I let my lips graze his, just for a moment and then locked eyes with him again as I twirled my fingers in his hair.

That was it, that broke the tether he had on himself and he pressed me back into the dresser. His left hand traveled up to my hair and he pulled me into a kiss with such passion and ferocity that I gasped against his lips and wrapped both arms around his neck, my right hand grabbing a handful of his hair and gently tugging while his hands slid down my back. Those hands found their way past my ass, grabbed the back of my thighs, and he lifted my legs up around his waist.

His lips didn't leave mine while he spun around and laid me down on the bed, his right arm behind my back and his left hand tracing the curve of my side before sweeping up under my nightgown to gently caress my breasts. His right arm followed moments later, and I put my arms over my head so he could slip my nightgown up over my head.

His arms wrapped around me again as he lifted me up and climbed onto the bed with me, laying me down with my head on the pillows. He traced my neck with his lips, kissing up and down my neck twice before moving lower. Licking his way down my body until he reached my breasts, where he paused for a moment before traveling lower, until he reached my underwear.

He looked up at me and smiled wickedly as he tugged at them gently with his teeth for a moment before sliding them off. He kissed down the inside of my thigh, pausing for a moment and nipping at that sensitive area right at the top of my thighs. My entire body shuttered for a moment before he lowered himself between my legs, shifting me so my legs were over his shoulders.

I moaned at the first stroke of his tongue, and I swore I could feel him smile against me while his tongue continued moving in long strokes. My hands found their way to his hair. He didn't stop feasting on me until my legs were shaking, I was moaning, and I came completely unglued as release cascaded over me.

He rose from the bed long enough to remove his pants before climbing back on top of me. He kissed his way up my stomach, stopping for a moment at my breasts. He licked, sucked and nipped at my nipples gently, before he continued up to my neck. He kissed his way up to the crook of my neck. He paused just for a moment and my right hand lazily played in his hair. He kissed my neck one more time gently before he bit me, hard. But there were no fangs. I moaned and arched my body up against him. He bit me again, a little softer this time and I pulled gently on his hair while my other hand traced down his back.

He nipped his way up my neck until his lips at last found mine again when he thrust himself into me. I gasped and moaned and moved my hips in time with his as he retreated and thrust again and again.

I twisted and shoved him over so that I was on top of him. He stared up at me, his eyes a mixture of excitement and surprise. I leaned down to kiss him and I took over, lifting and lowering myself on him so torturously slow.

"Fuck, Mira," he said softly into my lips. I started to kiss down his neck now, nipping gently occasionally, still grinding on him until I reached that same spot on his neck and bit him just as hard as he'd bit me. He let out what sounded like a growl mixed with a moan and flipped us back over, his eyes black and fangs out.

I smiled up at him and arched my neck so it was available to him. He kissed down my neck and bit me with his fangs this time, just above my shoulder. I gasped and arched up into him. He sucked on my shoulder for a few moments and then his lips found mine again. I could still taste my blood on his lips. He thrust deeper, and faster until we both found release and his body shuttered into mine.

He stayed over me, in me for a few moments, while we both were panting- out of breath, until he pulled himself out and lay down next to me, staring into my eyes while he gently ran his fingers through my hair.

I rolled to my side, gently caressed the side of his face, and kissed him. I felt a small trickle of blood sliding across my neck. He leaned in and licked it, tracing it back to where he'd bit me and kissed my shoulder again.

"I'm sorry," he whispered as he leaned back again so he could look at me.

I just smiled. "What are you sorry for? I let you bite me. I could've said no."

He traced my cheek with his fingers again and then traced down that same shoulder gently. "Yes, but I could've had better control of myself."

I huffed a laugh, my breath finally steadying. "I bit your neck. I knew exactly what I was doing."

He smirked now. "You did that on purpose?" He raised an eyebrow.

"I might have." I glanced up toward the ceiling and tried to look a little innocent for a moment.

He flicked my nose and chuckled. "You're insane."

"I'm pretty sure you knew that the moment you had to rescue me from Zane because I wandered off on my own."

He rolled his eyes, but smiled and leaned in to kiss me again. “You don’t have to keep proving me right.”

I took a deep breath. “You’re insufferable, you know that?” I whispered into his lips with a smile.

“I know.” He kissed my forehead and rolled onto his back. He shifted to put his arm around my head and shoulders and pulled me over to lay my head on his chest.

“Are you going to finish that story about your dragon tattoos?” I asked, as I closed my eyes and hooked my arm around his waist then snuggled against him.

His fingers traced lazy circles on my back. “Are you going to fall asleep halfway through again?”

“Maybe.” I whispered, my eyes already a little bit heavy.

“Another time then.” He leaned down and kissed my head and we lay there for a few minutes before I drifted off to sleep.

Chapter 14

Mira

We woke the next evening still wrapped in each other's arms, utterly naked. At some point one of us had pulled the blanket up over us.

"Good morning," I whispered and traced the lines of his tattoo with my left hand.

He kissed my head again, squeezed my shoulder and whispered, "Good morning sunshine."

I lifted my head and shimmied myself up so I could kiss him. He rolled to his side and his left hand slid down to my left leg. He pulled it up and around his hip. He leaned in and deepened the kiss, his tongue grazing my lips. My hands slid up into his hair. I shifted myself a little closer to him and his hand slid back up to grab my ass.

There was a quick knock before the door swung open and Zane started to say, "Rise and shine we've got trai-" He stopped abruptly, undoubtedly just realizing what he was interrupting and I heard him shift around so he was no longer looking into the room. "Fuck's sake Deiric, have you ever heard of hanging something on the door so no one just blindly walks in?"

Deiric hadn't stopped kissing me, despite the interruption, but pulled back to speak now.

I cut in instead. "Haven't you ever heard of waiting to be acknowledged after you knock before just barging in?"

Deiric huffed a little laugh and then leaned in to kiss me again, his lips trailing down my neck.

"We'll be down eventually." I tried to keep my voice from wavering while his fingers traced up my side, tickling a little as they made their way to my breast.

I heard the door close and Zane walked away rather quickly.

I pulled back and Deiric stopped.

He frowned at me.

"As much as I would enjoy laying here all day with you, we probably should get up and get down there." I said.

"We've got time. The sun hasn't even set yet." He whispered. His lips returned to my neck and he made his way back up my neck then to my lips, where he bit my lower lip.

I groaned and arched myself into him.

"You know you want to." He whispered into my ear as he rolled me onto my back and positioned himself over me.

I didn't reply, but instead slid my hands into his hair and lifted my head to meet his lips again.

He smiled against my lips and he kissed his way down my body again, slipping under the blankets until he was between my legs. He wasted no time, and had me gasping his name and clutching the sheets. He held my hips with one hand, and thrust two fingers into me with the other, licking and sucking until my legs were trembling and I could hardly breathe.

He kissed his way back up to my lips, thrusting himself in me before I had the chance to stop trembling or catch my breath.

I clawed at his back as he gradually went harder, and faster.

His hand knotted in my hair and he pulled my head to the left kissing his way down my neck, the side he hadn't fed on last night, until he reached my other shoulder. He bit me and sucked gently, no fangs this time. I groaned and arched up into him as we both found our release together again. He collapsed slightly onto me, breathing hard into my neck. He stayed there again for a few moments, until he stopped twitching and then pulled out and lay on his back next to me, breathing still uneven.

In between jagged breaths, he whispered, "you call out my name like that when I'm inside you and I think that would be enough to undo me." He rolled to his side and kissed my cheek before he rolled back over to the edge of the bed then started to get up to get ready.

I was still breathing a bit heavy. I sat up and propped myself on my elbows to watch him rummage through his drawers for a moment, completely naked. His muscular back glistened a bit with sweat in the dim light of the room.

"I'll have to remember that next time." I said and he glanced back at me as he pulled on his underwear, then his pants. He had that same wicked grin on his face I realized I'd started to admire.

"You should get up and get ready. I'm sure they probably heard you this time and are down there squirming about it." He said and he pulled on his shirt.

I slid out of bed and headed past him to the bathing room. "I think we know who's to blame for that." I raised a brow at him as I went through the door to clean myself up before I got dressed.

He appeared in the door just as I was finishing up. "Is that a bad thing?" He leaned against the threshold and crossed his arms.

"I didn't say it was." I stopped and smiled before I walked past him. "They might though." I went over to the other dresser and pulled out a skirt and blouse, as well as some fresh undergarments. Once I had my skirt and blouse on he came over and helped me with my corset before we both headed downstairs to get prepared to do some training with the rest of the guys.

When we reached the bottom of the stairs Zane was leaning against the threshold to the dining room and kitchen just shaking his head. "Please hang a sock on the door next time, or something."

Deiric walked by him into the dining room without saying anything, but I intentionally bumped into him and said, "you live with a woman already and you don't understand that you shouldn't enter without being acknowledged?"

"Okay, in my defense, that *is* Deiric's bedroom. You just happen to be staying in it with him right now. I've never had to worry about what I might… walk in on." Zane retorted. He turned toward where I was now walking to get some of the tea Liala had made.

"Wait a minute, you two-" Leo, completely flabbergasted, looked over at Deiric who was now leaning against the far wall of the dining room, then looked over to me where I leaned against the counter with my mug in my hands. His eyes landed on my shoulder. "That's a little irresponsible, don't you think?" He looked at Deiric.

Deiric just shrugged. "It's only irresponsible in the sense that I shouldn't feed on her the day before a big spell, ritual, or battle, but all we're doing is sparring today. She'll be fine."

He scowled, but didn't say anything else.

Liala walked over and examined my shoulder for a moment. "It's nearly healed." She commented. "You must have inherited some speedy healing too."

I glanced over to my shoulder briefly. "I suppose so. I've never really paid attention or had anything to compare it to."

"See, she's fine." Deiric jabbed at Leo again, who just quietly waited for me to finish my tea.

"Well, are we going to go out and fight or not?" I walked over to the table, and half smiled at Renwick, who stood and followed me outside.

*

Renwick had actually improved substantially since our last attempt at sparring, but he didn't manage to get in a successful jab at me yet. After about an hour or two of sparring and training they went off to do some hunting.

I stayed back at the house to research to see if by chance I could find something that might counteract the vervain and agrimony. I went through every book in their den, and still didn't find anything useful. Liala even helped me when she returned and we both came up empty.

I had wandered upstairs before Deiric had gotten back to soak in the bath for a few minutes, a bit sore again from sparring that morning, but not as bad as the first time.

He walked in while I was braiding my hair and walked up behind me, kissing the back of my neck gently, right in that spot he knew would send shivers down my spine. I was still only wearing my towel. His hands slipped right up underneath it to my hips.

He spun me around and hoisted me up so I was sitting on the dresser. "Did you find anything exciting in your research efforts today?" His hands now rested on my thighs.

"Nothing useful." I frowned a bit. "I'll have to keep looking."

He reached to tug at the towel, but I held it in place.

"*You* need to clean yourself up before you get too carried away." I scolded him.

He huffed a slight sigh and kissed my cheek. "Fine." He walked off toward the bathing room.

I hopped off the dresser and walked over to the bathing room to hang my towel on a hook by the door. Then I climbed into bed.

He came back out a few minutes later, naked, and crawled into bed next to me. Apparently, we both had the same idea. He gave me a look.

"No nightgown?" His face was both amused and excited.

"I don't *usually* sleep in a nightgown." I said with feigned annoyance. "I just had to because we were sharing a room and *weren't* being intimate." I looked him up and down. "No boxers?"

"I normally sleep naked, but wore them in case you decided to wake up in the middle of the day and I *wasn't* under the blankets." He smirked.

"Who's to say I didn't plan on making you sleep on the cot again?" I said with feigned annoyance.

He scoffed now. "This is *my* bed. If you planned to fuck me in it, *twice* and then didn't expect me to sleep with you tonight then I think it is your turn to take the cot."

I raised a brow. He just gave me a sultry smile, whispered, "come here," and slipped his arm around me to pull me into a kiss.

I slipped one hand up to his neck and the other around him and kissed him for a few moments before I finally pulled back and said, "what if I just wanted to sleep?"

He practically purred, "and do you? Just want to sleep?" into my neck as he kissed down it. His hands had started to wander, and the light trace of his fingers down my back caused me to arch into him.

I didn't just want to sleep.

Chapter 15

Mira

I took my tea into the den and settled onto the couch to review a grimoire I'd found on the shelves when I was looking for herbal resources. I had loved looking through my mother's grimoire before the attacks, seeing all the spells she'd crafted, and memorizing some of them for future use. I somewhat regretted not taking that with me all those years ago, but it would've been cumbersome to lug that around with everything else. I was sitting on the couch for less than thirty minutes when I heard talking outside and then several sets of footsteps coming through the front door.

It wasn't unusual for them all to come in at once, but it was rather early for them to be getting back from whatever it is they usually did. They had only left a few minutes before. Then, a voice I didn't recognize was speaking.

"I thought it was about time I checked in personally, your lackey has been asking some interesting questions of my men lately." There was a slight pause, and just as I was sitting the grimoire down to turn to look he was standing in front of me, looking down at me. "You've got a pet I see?" He leaned down and his face was inches from mine. He had white hair, and looked slightly older than Deiric, but age for them is relative. He was more slender than muscular, but well built. His white hair was short and cut in a fade with it slightly longer on top and a bit ruffled. His hazel eyes were piercing and cold as he studied me.

"I am not his pet." I spat.

He ignored me, grabbed my arm and lifted me to my feet in front of him. "Care to share Deiric?"

Deiric circled the couch and blasted him into the wall across the room in a flash, where he now held him with his forearm braced across the top of his chest, almost at his throat. "Do not lay a single hand on her Silas." Deiric snarled.

Silas had a vile grin on his face. "Oh, touchy. You really fancy this one don't you."

"I'm not kidding. Touch her again, and I'll kill you." Deiric pressed him harder into the wall, and Silas just rolled his eyes.

"Fine." He finally grumbled and Deiric released him.

"She's a sorceress. Leo was asking those questions because when I found her someone had drugged her with something that blocked her ability to use her magic." Deiric explained.

Silas brushed invisible dirt off of his chest where Deiric had held him to the wall. "It seems a little overkill to ask around about that for one sorceress. If she's here now you have nothing to worry about. Is there some other reason this concerns you?"

"Considering the fact that it could be an issue for the others when they're outside of our warded manors, yes."

Deiric glanced back at me for a moment. “I’d hate to see other coven members in the same situation because of whatever this is.”

“How noble of you.” Silas mocked. “My sources tell me they’ve been aware of something being used during the attacks years ago that blocked the use of magic, which is why the attacks were so deadly. We didn’t ever determine what it was, though.” Silas looked at me again and sized me up once more. He took a few steps toward me, despite Deiric’s warning snarl. His eyes got wide for a moment, and he glanced back at Deiric.

“Is that all you came here for?” Deiric finally asked after a few moments of uncomfortable silence where Silas looked at him questioningly and he merely glared back in response.

“For the most part, yes. I also came because I hadn’t seen this place since it was built. You’ve kept it at least from falling to ruin.” Silas smiled and his face relaxed some. “And you seem to have found your own sorceress. Perhaps she’ll become your archmage one day.”

I scowled at him.

“I’ll see you soon brother.” Silas half smiled at Deiric and then he ran out.

“That went well.” Zane commented from behind me.

“Brother?” I asked. They looked nothing alike.

Deiric turned to face all of us now. “We were once like brothers. We transitioned at the same time, trained together, and fought together for almost five hundred years. Eventually we were both assigned to be elders of separate manors. Silas took over for someone else in a well-established manor. I was sent here and an archmage was supposed to be assigned before all hell broke loose ten years ago. After that, they never sent one."

"He seems like a cocky bastard." I commented.

Zane laughed. "Oh he is. He usually summons Deiric when he needs newer vampires to learn how to control their ability to read minds or how to compel people."

"They're still creating new death dealers?" I looked at Zane now.

"They haven't since the attacks, but some of them take years to get their shit together before they can be trusted to go out in the villages to learn some of those things."

I nodded and then sat back down on the couch to flip through the grimoire again. "I have a feeling I'll never like him." I said flatly.

"None of us do." Leo commented from somewhere out in the entryway behind Zane.

Deiric walked back over to them. "Let's get moving." And with that, they all shuffled back out the front door.

Chapter 16

Mira

We woke up extra early the evening we planned to do the ritual. Deiric helped me put on my usual skirts, blouse, and corset. He strapped me in a few extra knives before we headed down to prepare with the others.

When we walked into the dining room Xander spoke up, "You're down here earlier than we expected you." He sounded generally surprised. "You didn't want another pre-ritual roll in the sheets?"

Deiric snarled at him, probably more aggressive than I'd ever seen him act. I just continued on over to meet Liala by the counter to get a cup of tea.

"What? We all know the risks of this little outing. Makes sense to do it again just in case."

"Xander." Zane snapped before Deiric could say anything. "We have no reason to expect this to go poorly."

"If it does, we still have the backup plan." I mumbled. It was the first time I mentioned it since that night when we'd all argued about it.

Deiric locked eyes with me for a moment, his face a mixture of rage, understanding, and sadness - so conflicted.

"We'll stand down if someone intervenes and I will follow." Zane said. "Deiric and the others will return here, and I'll see if there's anything I can do."

Deiric opened his mouth to speak but Leo cut him off. "We discussed it before you came downstairs. You're too close to her. Zane will know when it is appropriate to step in without risking himself and making the situation worse." He said, glancing at me for approval and I merely nodded. "Besides, we need our Elder here to deal with whatever else may come up in the meantime."

Deiric looked over at me again. "Fine."

"I'll be fine." I said as I walked over and put a hand on his shoulder. "I've survived this long on my own." I tried to add a smile to be more convincing but it didn't work.

"The sun is about to set." Renwick mumbled from where he was sitting at the window. "We should get going. We can stay in the shade of the trees at first, and that will give us more time to get there." He looked back at us. "Deiric, you'll have to carry her, so we can run there."

Deiric nodded. "Let's go then."

They all put on their weapons and we walked out the front door. Liala had decided to stay back, one of them would bring her ring to her afterward.

"Ready?" Deiric asked me.

I nodded and he scooped me into his arms. "Do you have the rings?"

Leo nodded.

"Let's do this." I said, and with that, they each ran to the spot we'd decided on. Deiric hesitated for a moment.

"I love you." He whispered into my ear, and kissed my cheek, before he ran after them without giving me the chance to reply. Before I could even register where we were going or any of the landmarks that were flying past me we were there, and he sat me down in the middle of a small clearing. Leo handed me the rings he'd shown me before.

"Alright." I said softly. "Everyone take up your positions around the edges of the clearing. As soon as I get setup, I'll run through the enchantment as quickly as I can. If *anything* goes wrong, do *not* forget the plan." They all nodded, and with one final concerned look from Deiric, they disappeared to their spots in the trees.

I set the rings out into the places I knew they'd taken up around the edges so they could all run to grab theirs quickly if needed. I got down to my knees and took a few steadying and grounding breaths. I needed to draw on the power of the moon for this spell.

Once I was grounded and ready, I began to focus on the power of the moon, and drew in as much of it as I could handle. Physically, my tattoos began to glow with the energy I was summoning.

I recited the spell once, twice, and then three times with my hand hovering over the rings. When I felt everything click into place, I sent the energy down into the rings. A flash of light went from my hands to the rings as the energy I'd summoned transferred the enchantment to them.

At the moment that the spell was completed, an arrow pierced me right in the stomach. I was caught breathless, and screamed in pain. But I sent out a shield around me, blocking all of them out. I felt Deiric slam into it.

A wave of my hand sent the rings to each of them, and then I sent out a silent message to them as I looked up at my assailant. *Get out of here. They want me, not you.*

I yanked the arrow out of my stomach and tossed it to the side as the archer who'd shot me stepped out of the trees. I shot a blast of flames directly at his head, which he somehow managed to dodge. The shield faltered for a moment.

"Shit." I gasped and fought to stay upright with my stomach on fire with pain and a steady stream of blood dripping from the wound. The arrow head must've been laced with the same poison I'd been drugged with weeks ago that nullified my magic. This didn't work as quickly though. I saw Zane reach Deiric out of the corner of my eye and grab his arm. *Get out of here. NOW.* I sent out the mental message to them again. *They won't come after you, they're here for me*"

With that, I summoned shadow to fill the clearing, hoping it would obscure his sightline enough that he couldn't hit me with another arrow as I drew my sword and used it to help me rise to my feet, my entire body screaming at the pain blasting out from the wound. I turned and took off, fighting that pain every step of the way. I couldn't shift. I had to lead him away from them.

Another arrow hit my shoulder and I cried out in pain. It was useless, he clearly could see me well enough to know where I was anyway. I kept pushing on, running as fast as I could. I dropped the shield as I neared the edge of it.

A stabbing pain hit my left thigh as an arrow struck there and I slammed to the ground, at least not hitting face first. Every move I made sent pain shooting through my body at this point. I reached around and yanked the arrow from my shoulder just as the man who'd shot them caught up to me. I lashed out at him and sliced his leg with the tip of the arrow.

"Bitch." He snapped and kicked me in the stomach.

I saw stars for a moment. If he was going to kill me, I wasn't going down without a fight. I shot another small blast of fire up at him as he reached down to grab me and he hissed as it burned his hand. At that same moment, I yanked the other arrow out of my left leg and lashed out at him with it.

Before I could make contact with the arrow he kicked me in the stomach again. This time I blacked out from the pain, or the blood loss, or both.

*

I blinked and squinted against the light. Every movement sent a wave of pain through my entire body. I realized I was laying over the back of the horse. My injuries had been bandaged, and I could tell that they'd at least stopped bleeding but were still quite tender. I quietly looked around, finding it to be just me, the horse I was on, and the man who had attacked on his horse. There were no restraints on me except a small shackle that more closely resembled a simple bracelet with a pale green gem on it. I attempted to unlock it with magic and that seemed to make it glow.

It was enchanted, and prevented me from using magic. Fantastic. I looked ahead to where we were going and we weren't far from a small village. I gritted my teeth against the pain that still shot through me with each step. Surely when we reached the village I'd have the chance to escape.

After what felt like an eternity, we stopped somewhere within the village. I could tell because I heard people and other horses bustling around us. I listened, keeping my eyes closed, as he dismounted and tied both horses. He walked back to evaluate me. He poked my shoulder, where he'd shot me to see if I would react and verify that I was still unconscious.

Every fiber of my being wanted me to react and scream out in pain but I fought against it to be as limp and still as possible. When he was satisfied at my lack of reaction, he turned and walked away. I waited a few moments before opening my eyes and trying to look around cautiously. I saw the door close just as he slipped inside of the building in front of where he'd tied the horses.

I lifted my head to look around me and saw no one. This was my chance. I quietly lifted myself and lowered off the horse, wincing at the pain but trying to be as stealthy as possible. Then I quietly, but quickly limped away. Each step sent a flash of pain up through my body, but I had more important things to worry about.

Once I was far enough that I trusted running I took off at a sprint, trying to stay away from main roads and duck between buildings. Grinding my teeth against the stabbing pain in my leg that throbbed with each step. When I caught sight of people I slowed to a walk and tried to appear as though I was meant to be there. No one so much as batted an eye.

I glanced behind me briefly to make sure I wasn't followed and when I turned my head back around I collided with a woman in a beautiful sparkling black cloak.

Her bright green eyes were wide as she looked me up and down.

"I'm sorry." I stammered. "I wasn't paying attention to where I was walking."

She just stared for a moment, and then I heard a commotion in the distance. I assumed that it was him realizing I'd escaped. The look on my face must've conveyed my concern and fear, because she stepped to the side and gestured over her shoulder. "Go" she mouthed to me.

Before I took off, her hand gently clasped my injured shoulder, and a small flash of white light filled the space between us. She'd tried to heal me, but didn't realize it was more than just my shoulder that was injured. That small amount of healing did at least numb some of the pain, as I sprinted in the direction she suggested.

I don't know how far or how long I ran for. I ran until I couldn't see the town behind me anymore, and then continued to run until I couldn't catch my breath. The adrenaline kept the pain at bay for the moment. I finally stopped when I reached an area where the rock jutted out overhead and gave me some shelter so I could hide. I collapsed to my knees and was gasping and coughing, trying to catch my breath and slow my thundering heartbeat. I crawled under the rock as far as I could get before I didn't have the energy to push myself any further.

My leg and my stomach had started to bleed again, likely ripped back open in my crazy run to this spot.

I don't know how long I was laying there before movement in front of me caught my eye and made me look up. There, standing by the edge of the rock that stuck out over me was the woman I'd run into in the village.

I crawled backwards for a moment. She'd helped me in the village but I didn't know if she was here to turn me in or what her motives were.

She ducked under the rock, which was low enough that you couldn't stand up completely and kneeled in front of me. "Are you alright?" She asked quietly.

I was still a bit out of breath, but managed to gasp. "I am a little bit better now. Thanks to you, but I reopened the wounds on my leg and my stomach."

She nodded. "May I?" She asked as she reached over to touch my left shoulder.

I relaxed some and let her begin removing the bandage around my shoulder. When she'd got it off, she frowned. "What did they do to you?"

"He shot me with three arrows, each laced with what I believe was vervain or agrimony or a combination of the two to block my magic."

"You're a part of the Oíche coven." She said plainly, seeing the tattoos that were exposed by my torn and tattered clothing.

"Is that a problem?" I asked, a bit hesitant.

"No."

Just as she was about to lay her hand on my shoulder to try to fully heal it, I heard a familiar voice behind me.

"Mira?" Zane came down around the side of the rock and made it halfway to me before he stopped. "Eimear?"

The woman helping me stopped and looked up at him. "Zane." She said plainly. Before anyone could say anything else she'd mumbled something and that same light flashed between us.

I let out a relieved breath. My shoulder was as good as new, I could move my arm without it feeling like it was on fire again. "You two know each other?" I should've been relieved to have Zane there, but I was too exhausted to really react.

She met my gaze again, and motioned to my stomach. I nodded, and I tried to move so that she could get my dress out of the way to get to that bandaging.

"We'll have to take it off completely I think." She said quietly. "Or possibly lift it up high enough that I can get under it."

The adrenaline had started to wear off at this point and while it was no longer a striking pain it still throbbed every time I tried to move. I winced as I tried to wiggle to where I could easily remove my dress.

"You should probably do her leg first." Zane was now right next to me, kneeling as well. He reached over and slipped his arm under my shoulders to pull me toward my right side and lift me gently to untangle my skirts from my legs. I yelped. "I'm sorry." He mumbled once he finally got my left leg free.

Eimear reached over and began carefully removing that bandage as well. A few moments later she'd finished healing my leg. "I'm impressed you managed to run this far with all of this." She locked eyes with me for a moment as I laid back into Zane to allow her to lift my dress and remove the bandage from my last remaining wound.

"I wasn't going down without a fight." I finally mumbled.

Zane chuckled. "And a hell of a fight at that."

I managed a half smile as I glanced up at him.

"It took you long enough to catch up with me." I mumbled.

"Well, I didn't see you run. I didn't even know you'd escaped until I heard all kinds of commotion and saw him taking off on his horse." He paused and watched Eimear carefully for a moment before continuing. "Someone sent him the wrong way."

Eimear finally finished unwrapping my stomach and healed that as well.

"Thank you." I said finally, and shuffled my dress and skirts back down around myself as Zane helped me sit up onto my knees.

"So, how do you two know each other?" Eimear asked, looking between Zane and I.

"Deiric found her a few weeks ago, saved her from someone who drugged her." He smiled a bit. "Clearly she's got a knack for being captured."

I rolled my eyes.

"I'm surprised to see you in the daylight." Eimear finally said.

Zane met her gaze. "Before they took her down, literally." He glanced at me with a small smile again. "She had made us all daylight rings. After they attacked and took her, I followed her to keep track of her whereabouts until we could find a way to get her out without getting ourselves killed." He paused for a moment. "How did you end up with her?" He looked at Eimear again.

"We bumped into each other in the village as she was running away from someone." She looked at me and we locked eyes again. "I didn't ask any questions, but helped her get away. Then figured I should make sure she'd made it far enough away and didn't reopen her injuries."

"Thank you for helping me." I said softly.

"I'm a part of the Oíche coven also, but I haven't been in contact with anyone else from it since the attacks all those years ago. I heard they killed everyone at the manors and houses they attacked."

"Not everyone." Zane nudged me.

"You escaped?" She raised a brow.

"Barely." I looked at the ground. "I was the reason for the attack."

Her face paled. "The Dhampir."

"Yes."

"I heard about you. I thought it was a rumor though. I was heading there to find out for myself, but when I arrived it was nothing but a blood bath." She finally said.

"Well, now that you've run into us, would you like to come back with us and help us figure out our next steps?" Zane asked. "We need to figure out a way to reconvene the coven and take the fight to them."

Eimear scoffed. "Are you mad?" She glanced between us. "They'll kill us all."

"Is running and hiding any better?" He challenged.

A small scowl found its way to her face. "Well, I don't really tend to run and hide. I just don't advertise my abilities." She considered it for a moment. "I suppose it would be nice not to have to hide my ties to the Oíche. I'll consider helping, but I'd like to speak with Deiric and find out how many of you there already are first. No sense in signing up for a suicide mission if you can't recruit enough help."

"Alright." He looked at me. "Are you up for traveling now?"

They both were looking at me. "I am not sure how far I'll make it right this moment, but I don't think we can stay here much longer anyway."

Zane nodded. "When you can't get any further I can carry you until we reach somewhere safe to camp for the night."

"Wait-" I realized the bracelet, or rather, the small shackle was still on my wrist. "We should probably get rid of this first, just in case it is also charmed in a way they could track it."

Zane snapped the lock and chucked it off into the woods. "Let's get moving."

I clung to Zane as we walked. I was fully healed but I was completely exhausted. It didn't take long before he ended up just carrying me.

Chapter 17

Mira

We traveled the rest of the day, only stopping finally because we all were exhausted. We opted not to make a fire, to avoid detection. Zane took the first watch, Eimear took the second. We set off the next morning as soon as the sun was up. About halfway through the day we'd finally reached somewhat familiar woods.

"I'm going to run ahead and let them know we're coming." Zane said, when we stopped for a moment. "You two just wait here for a few minutes." He hesitated a bit before he continued. "I just want to make sure that we won't run into any surprises."

My stomach whirled at that thought, but I tried not to think about it too much. He was gone in the blink of an eye and we waited in silence. Several minutes passed, and then Deiric appeared a few feet from us.

"Mira?" He took a step toward us, and I cleared the gap before he got any further. I wrapped my arms around his neck and his arms wrapped around my waist, squeezing me tightly to him and lifting me off the ground for a brief moment. "I am so glad you're okay."

"You can thank Eimear for that." I mumbled and finally released him so I could look at him. I don't think he could fathom how relieved I was that they hadn't actually followed them and killed them for being anywhere near me.

Deiric looked up over my shoulder. "It's been years." He released me and stepped around me to give her a hug as well.

She only half returned the hug. I could tell she was still a little bit reluctant to fully join the cause. "You haven't aged a day," was all she said to him before stepping back again to look at both of us. "Lead the way."

Deiric just nodded and started to lead us back to the house, grabbing my hand as he passed me and pulled me along with him. Eimear kept pace with us just a few steps behind.

"Is everyone else alright?" I asked a bit hesitantly. I wasn't sure if any of the others had been caught or harmed that night. Deiric and Zane were the only ones I could see before I had to shift my focus entirely to that archer.

"They're all okay." He said, but kept looking ahead. "Whoever that was only wanted you. He didn't even make an attempt to come after us, but certainly noticed we were there." He paused for a few moments as he led us down a narrow path between two boulders. "I don't believe he was a warlock. He didn't use any magic, only those arrows."

"Zane mentioned something about taking the fight to them. What are your plans exactly?" Eimear jumped in.

"We're working on getting in touch with any of the connections we used to have within the Oíche Coven. Most of them went underground, but I did maintain some contact with a handful of the other legions who stuck together after that. We're getting the word out as quietly as possible." He glanced back at us. "We haven't met with any warlocks or other witches yet. Perhaps you can help with that?"

"I know of a few. Some of them may have a way of contacting Garrick."

"Garrick?" I glanced back at her.

"He's one of the four remaining magisters of the coven at the moment." She explained.

"Great. He'll be our best bet to continue to gather our forces." Deiric ducked around a branch ahead of us, I could see the house now, we were closer than I thought. "Silas may be able to get in contact with him too, but I'm hesitant to pull that string right now."

"There aren't as many of us anymore you know. A lot of the lower ranking members simply disbanded completely. After those attacks, most of them were terrified they'd be next."

"I figured it would not be as many as we'd hoped, but maybe we can inspire them to come back." Deiric stopped just beyond the tree line. "Hopefully knowing that Mira made it out will give them incentive to help."

Eimear scowled a bit. "I don't think that is going to help your case. There are wanted posters and mercenaries all over the place looking for her. They don't exactly call her what she is, but those who knew her would likely recognize the likeness."

"Well, we'll make due with what we can round up anyway. I don't see how we have any other choice." Deiric said, with a tinge of anger in his voice. He looked at me again. "Let's get you inside and get you into something that isn't ripped to shreds." His half smile didn't reach his eyes, which were still shaded in a small veil of relief but hopeless exhaustion also plagued them like he hadn't slept since I'd been taken.

*

Once I'd cleaned myself up and redressed I headed downstairs. I couldn't tell what was being discussed, but their voices were tense, and it was clear that they were arguing amongst themselves. When I rounded the corner I noticed there was another man I had yet to meet standing with them around the dining room table. It was weird to see the house lit up with sunlight. I had never noticed how beautiful the dining table was, or how much space the room really had in it.

Deiric met my gaze and the discussion immediately stopped. They had all stopped to look at me, I realized.

"Ah yes, the Dhampir Deiric led me to believe was just a sorceress." Silas mocked.

"My name is Mira." I snapped, probably a little too coldly. He merely raised an eyebrow in response.

"Watch your tone with me *Mira*." He said my name like it disgusted him. "I'm still irritated that you went along with the lie."

"I think you should take your own advice" I crossed my arms now, one eyebrow raised as I stepped up to the table. Some of them were standing, others were sitting around it. I could tell I walked into what I suppose you could call a war meeting, discussing the gathering of all of the resources they'd casually mentioned earlier.

He glared at me, but didn't push any further. "My name is Silas." He held out his hand and offered a sinister smile. "We haven't been properly acquainted.

I gave him another once over before giving him my hand. He kissed the back of my hand and bowed slightly. "It is a pleasure to meet you." He gave a sideways glance to Deiric, before continuing. "I am the Elder, or Master Death Dealer, depending on who you speak to for another group within the Oíche Coven."

"I've been well informed of who you are." I glanced at the other male that was standing to the right of Deiric. He had longer golden brown hair which was pulled partially up into a braid that hung down the back of his head. He was more slender and refined in his posture. He dressed as though he were more of a mage or warlock.

As though my gaze landing on him prompted him to speak, he finally broke his silence. "Elias." He said plainly. His arms remained crossed. "If we're going by our official titles, I am an archmage." He lacked pleasantries and seemed a bit annoyed to be there at the moment. "I work with Silas, most of the time."

I nodded.

"We were discussing the safest place for all of us to meet to discuss the matter of pulling the coven back together more officially." Deiric cut in.

I finally looked down at the table, where a map of the entire world had now been laid out.

"This house is one of the few remaining locations that are entirely outside of a town or other major area. I think this is our best option." Deiric said finally.

"We need to ward and shield it better though." Elias commented. "There's hardly anything protecting you right now at all."

"Well, until we found Mira, we didn't have anyone with the proper abilities to even put something like that together." Deiric paused as he glanced in my direction again for just a brief moment. "She can't create the wards for us. They are tracking whatever energy signature that she emits when she uses her magic, so I'd need you to help with that."

Elias took in a deep breath and sighed. "If we'd like a strong set of wards and shields it would take more than just me." He considered it for a moment. "Eimear could help, but we'd need at least two other more powerful and higher ranking members for it to really be effective. Have you been able to contact Killian or Lazarus yet?"

"Not yet. I've sent Leo out to try and track them down." Deiric explained. "Do either of you know how to get in touch with Garrick?" Deiric finally asked.

Silas sighed. "We haven't heard from him in ages, but I believe some of our contacts will know. I'll spread the word."

"Be sure you don't give them a meeting place. Just let them know that we're seeking an audience with them. We won't bring them here until they're aware of the situation." Elias said as he glanced at me again, entirely unimpressed.

I snorted. "I may appear insignificant to you, but you'd better watch the tone of that look on your face. If I didn't need to avoid using magic to stay hidden you'd have a vastly different opinion of me quite quickly."

Silas howled with laughter. "Oh you were absolutely correct about her attitude and I quite like her if she's got the balls to stand up to Elias and his bullshit."

"Don't test me." I glanced at Silas now. He raised his hands at me in what I might've thought was defeat until he kept talking.

"My apologies, little wicked one." Silas mocked.

If looks could kill, he'd have been dead on the spot.

Deiric chuckled. "Alright, that's enough. As much as I'd enjoy watching her rip the two of you to shreds I think we should focus our energy on working to get this all arranged instead." He looked over to Silas, who was now eyeing me up like his next meal. "Silas, I've already warned you what will happen if you lay a hand on her again. Do not test me."

"All I was doing was looking at her. Relax, brother. I remember the warning." He glanced at Elias. "Elias, let's get a message back to the crew at home. We'll need them to get the ball rolling sooner than later." And with that, he and Elias headed out into the den, leaving Deiric, myself and Eimear in the dining room.

Deiric walked into the kitchen. "Liala will be in shortly to finish cooking everyone dinner." He paused. "Feel free to make yourself at home, Eimear. We're working on moving things around to make accommodations for you to have somewhere to stay here at least for tonight."

Eimear sighed and took a seat at the table, rolling the map and moving it out of the way.

I joined her at the table, and Deiric headed out into the den with Silas and Elias.

"So, what are you thinking?" I asked gently.

"I am not sure. I've kept a low profile and never had any trouble, so I don't really have a *reason* to get involved." She said, staring at the table.

"Well, you know we could stand to have more of a female presence around here. Maybe you'd at least be interested in staying here so that Liala and I are not so outnumbered?" I smiled, and she finally looked up to meet my gaze.

"I'll think about it."

Liala walked in then and started working in the kitchen. I got up from the table and walked over to her. "Can I help?"

She looked over and smiled. "Sure." She motioned with her chin over to the cutting board. "You can cut the vegetables."

I nodded and got to work. Eimear just sat at the table in silence and watched us for a few moments before she finally came over and started to help as well.

Chapter 18

Mira

We were all in the dining room, discussing where we'd managed to locate some of the other groups within the coven, when Deiric seemed to notice some movement outside. It was likely Leo finally got back from his travels, albeit a day early, but if he'd found something important he would've come straight back.

Deiric was out on the front porch in the blink of an eye.

"You were told not to bring anyone here without consulting me first." I heard Deiric snarl at him, and before Zane could move to block me I was already out the door on the porch.

There, standing a few paces from the bottom of the steps was Leo, and next him stood a tall slender man. He looked up at me, and despite that he looked ragged and unkempt, I realized it was Aris. He had a small beard now, which was not very well groomed, and his eyes and face looked tired and weary. His black hair was messy, long enough to cover his eyes if it were actually brushed, but it fell to just above his eyebrows. His gray eyes softened when they met mine, filling with a small amount of relief.

"Aris?" I asked, as if I couldn't believe my eyes. I made my way down the stairs to stand just behind Deiric, who stepped to the right to block me and glanced back at me for a brief moment. Aris still stared at me, now looking me up and down and evaluating me as if he also couldn't believe his eyes. "I thought you were dead." I said plainly.

"I came close," He said with a half smile.

I put my hand on Deiric's arm, which was slightly raised to block my path, and glanced over at him. *It's okay.* I said in my mind, knowing he could hear me. *He's who got me out during the attack, remember?*. He lowered his arm, a bit reluctantly, and allowed me to step around him.

"How?" I just stared at him in disbelief.

"They never came to verify that they actually killed me." He said, his voice rough. "I laid there until all of the screaming and fighting stopped, as still as I could, and continued lying there for quite a while afterward expecting them to come check. When I was sure they'd all gone and weren't coming to check on me I removed the stake. It was laced with vervain, so it took me forever to heal." He paused for a moment, glancing at Deiric, then back to me.

"As soon as I was able, I tried to search for you, but you knew how to disappear." He smiled and had a glimmer of pride on his face. "I saw a wanted poster a few years ago, and recognized you instantly, but I could never seem to find you or catch up with you, despite all the stories I'd heard of your travels and victories. There are a handful of bards who have written songs about some of them."

I almost laughed out loud at that, and smiled. I knew precisely which bards he was talking about, but didn't ever imagine they'd have written the songs after I encouraged them not to ever mention they knew me.

"Teron would be quite proud of the work you've been doing all these years." He gently put his hand on my shoulder.

I shrugged off his hand and hugged him. I saw Leo smiling as I looked over Aris' shoulder.

"I found him in the tavern of one of the towns I was scouting out. Two men had approached me to ask if I'd be interested in hunting the beast that was killing their livestock. I declined, and said I didn't do that. One of them grumbled that they needed to wait for Scáil to come through town. Then Aris grumbled from the bar that he'd heard she was dead, killed by a Solas assassin, so they should keep trying to find someone else."

"They wrote him off as the town drunk, but I caught up with him when he left. He said that someone told him they'd seen you slung over the back of a horse in another village nearby, and they thought you were dead. I figured out who he was, and thought he might like to see that you *weren't* dead. And you might feel the same way about him." Leo explained.

I released him from the hug, then turned so I was looking at Deiric, Aris, and Leo. "He was my father, Teron's, right hand man. I guess you could call him the second in command." I finally commented. "He taught me most of what I know, with a sword and knives anyway."

"That would make you an Elder now." Deiric observed.

Aris stiffened, his face switched to a cold expression as he met Deiric's gaze. "That is not a title I'm eager to hold." He said coldly.

"You're the one who trained her?" Zane had appeared on the porch behind us, or maybe had been there the entire time.

He looked up to Zane. "Eventually yes, we trained for years before the attacks. Her father *started* her training. I took over later. She seems to have learned much more on her own though." He looked back at Deiric. "I'd be glad to serve under you, if you'd have me. It is the least I could do as a thank you for finding her and helping her when I couldn't." He bowed his head slightly to Deiric.

"We'll discuss it." Deiric's voice was cold and flat.

"We could use all the help we can get, and he is certainly someone I would trust." I gave Deiric a sort of stern but pleading look.

Deiric just sighed, slipped his right arm around my waist, and turned to swing his free hand toward the house. "Come inside. We can introduce you to the rest of my crew, and the others who are staying with us at the moment."

Aris nodded, and followed Leo into the house. Deiric held me back for a moment. "Are you sure you still feel he's trustworthy?" His eyes scanned my face for any doubts, as he gently cupped the side of my face.

"He risked his life to save me all those years ago. I have no doubt if he'd actually caught up with me he'd have done it again to keep me from getting drugged or captured that night you found me. He was probably one of the most honorable and trustworthy death dealers I'd ever met before you found me."

Deiric smiled. "Alright then."

We walked up the stairs and into the house together just as they were all exchanging introductions in the den.

*

Later that evening, while I was getting ready to climb into bed Deiric came out of the bathing room and said, "I didn't forget what Aris said about the bards that sang songs about your greatest moments, by the way."

Heat rushed to my cheeks. I was finishing tying off my braid, but turned to face him. "Is there a question behind that statement, or are you just pointing out that you want to hear the bard's songs?" I asked with a smile, and then climbed into bed.

He slipped under the blankets next to me and propped himself on his elbow to look at me where I sat on the bed. "How exactly did these bards learn about these stories that they wrote songs about?"

"I told them the stories." I laid on my side so I was facing him, also propping myself up on an elbow.

"I've seen how you react to someone trying to speak to you in a tavern." Deiric flicked my nose.

"No, you've seen how I react to someone I don't *want* to speak to in a tavern." I smiled. "There's a very distinct difference."

He raised a brow. "You *wanted* to talk to someone?"

I scoffed. "You know, some of those bards are quite attractive. So yes, I *wanted* to talk to them. Do you think you're the only person I've slept with in the last ten years?"

His jaw practically hit the floor, but he snapped it shut just as fast. "You slept with a bard?"

"Several, actually. Some of them were quite fun." I smiled as I thought about one of them. "They asked me to tell them stories, so I obliged. I didn't think they'd actually write songs about them."

"How many?" He asked, his hand traced my side.

"How many stories or how many bards?"

He pulled me closer to him. "How many bards?"

"What, are you going to go find them all and hunt them down?" I mused.

"No. I have a little more control than that. You didn't know me then." He met my gaze finally. He'd been letting his eyes wander. "I am just curious about your life before me."

"Three men, two women." I said, very matter of factly, as I let my own eyes wander a little bit.

"Two women?" I met his gaze and his eyes glimmered with intrigue.

"Is that so surprising?"

"Am I going to have to compete with women too?" He sort of whined. His hand traced my side again.

"No." I traced circles on his bare chest. "I mean, I might look, but you won't be competing with them by any means."

"Good." He smiled. "I am not good at sharing what's mine." That hand now wandered to my leg and pulled it over his hip. "Unless of course you'd like someone else to join us at some point."

I met his gaze again, admiring those beautiful blue eyes. "Absolutely not. You're all mine and *I* am not good at sharing either."

His eyes traveled to my lips then back to my eyes for a moment. "Good." He leaned in and kissed me slowly, pulling me in closer to him as he did so. He stopped abruptly, and pulled back slightly. “But, you’ve never told me your stories. How did these bards get you to tell them your favorite tales?” His eyes met mine again.

“They asked.” I kissed him, and stared into his eyes again. “You’ve never asked.”

“Hmm.” He grumbled as he leaned in and kissed me again, this time pushing me back onto the pillow and letting the hand that was on my leg wander up to my hair, pulling gently as he kissed down my neck. “After this, I’d like to hear at least one of your favorite stories.” He whispered as he kissed down my chest and then my stomach, until he reached my navel. “Then, when all of this is over, we’re going out to find these bards so I can hear them sing your stories.” He smiled up at me, before kissing his way farther down my body.

Chapter 19

Mira

The next morning I found Eimear in the dining room staring off into space with a cup of tea. Deiric had sent some of the guys out on various errands, and he went out to spar with Zane and Renwick. I poured myself a cup of tea and sat down with her, which startled her for a moment.

"I'm sorry, I didn't mean to startle you." I said softly, and took a sip of my tea. "What are you thinking about, if it is okay that I ask?"

She sighed. "A lot of things, and nothing all at once." She stared into her tea now. "I lost a lot of friends back then. I don't really want to get involved in this mess, but there's also a part of me that wants to get revenge for their death. I also didn't realize how used to being completely alone I was until I came here with you and have seen how you all interact. I miss that."

I stared into my own tea for a few moments before I looked up at her again. "You're welcome to stay here with us even if you don't want to be involved within the coven again."

She looked up and met my gaze. "I don't want to impose."

"Not everyone who lives here has to serve a purpose to us. It may not be *my* house, but I am sure Deiric would not turn you away. I told you yesterday that we could use more of a feminine influence around here." I gave her a small smile. "You can help me make this less like a dreary old vampire cave and more like a nice manor that's welcoming to other people."

She half smiled. "I guess it is sort of dreary looking in here." She glanced around. The walls were mostly empty, no artwork, no decoration, just empty except the furniture that was necessary. "I'm surprised, with Liala, that they didn't do anything to spruce the place up a bit."

"To be fair, until recently they were all only active at night, so you couldn't see just how dreary it was by candlelight."

"Good point." She took a sip of her tea. "Well, where should we start?" She had a real smile now.

"We could start by digging around to see if there *is* any artwork anywhere that we can hang. Then we can see if we can find any plants to bring in here."

"What on earth would we put them in?"

I considered that for a moment. "I'm sure we could find some material to make pots to put plants in, or we could just use some of the dishes and bowls." I chuckled. "It's not like there's many people here to *use* them anyway. I'd say we could go to a nearby town to shop for things but I don't think I should be wandering beyond the wards."

"No, you shouldn't set a single foot outside of the wards right now beyond what you absolutely have to do." She finished her tea and stood from the table. "Let's see what we can find."

I followed suit, and we set off down the hall beyond the stairs, the den, and the kitchen to see what other rooms there were and what sort of things we could find.

There were a lot of rooms back beyond the stairs I'd never paid attention to. Most of them were empty, and I wondered what they were intended for. We finally came into a larger room at the back of the house where we found all kinds of things. I remembered Deiric mentioning that a mage was supposed to be assigned to this house, so I guessed this was where they'd have done the training for young mages, similar to what was at the house I grew up in. There were pots for plants, small cauldrons, tools for working with herbs and natural magic, among other things. There was also some artwork toward the very back of the room, that I guessed was brought here to be put up one day by the mage, but hadn't ever been touched.

"Jackpot!" Eimear said as she started to pull some of the pieces out.

"They're beautiful." I breathed as I took some of them in when she pulled them out. They varied in size from something the size of a large piece of paper to larger paintings that were half as tall as me. Some were of landscapes, and others were portraits of sorcerers or archmages using their magic.

I shifted my focus to some of the magical tools and other furniture that was strewn about the room. I drug a cauldron the size of a large soup pot out.

"What on earth are you getting that out for?" Eimear asked when she finally finished looking through the art and turned to see me admiring the cauldron.

"Just in case I have time and want to mix up some potions or elixirs." I smiled. "It's been years since I've done anything like that. My mother made all sorts of interesting things."

She walked over and evaluated it for a moment before blowing some of the dust off. "Maybe you can show me some of them some other time?" She smiled. "For now, let's figure out where to put all the artwork and tapestries."

"Tapestries?" I glanced back over to where she'd been, and sure enough there were tapestries on the floor behind the paintings. I walked over, picked one up, and gently unrolled it. It was of Crann Bethadh, and it was beautiful. "Before we can figure out where to put all of this, we'll need to find a hammer and some nails."

I turned to face her and she already had them in her hands. "Where did you find that?" She gestured over to the pile of tools by the door.

"It is like they got all of this here and then just forgot about it." She commented.

"Deiric mentioned that they were sent here and an archmage was supposed to follow eventually, but that never happened. They were supposed to get their daylight rings shortly before that happened, but they obviously didn't get those either." I walked over and took one of the hammers from her and a handful of nails. "Let's see what we can do." I smiled and we walked out to the foyer first to start planning and figuring out where things would fit.

After a few hours we were covered in dust from the paintings, but we'd managed to find places for almost all of them. I hung the tapestry I found in the foyer. It was the only wall space large enough to fit it. I had just climbed down from hanging another painting when Deiric, Zane, and Renwick walked in the front door.

"You've been busy." Deiric commented as he looked around. There were several paintings on the walls now leading up the stairs, down the hallway, and a handful in the sitting area.

"We found them in the room down the hall." I motioned back to the hallway behind me, where Eimear was now running excitedly out of.

"I found several grimoires back there." She practically yelled with excitement, then she stopped and looked at Deiric, Zane, and Renwick who were staring blankly around at the work we'd done. "What, you don't like it?" She asked, her voice a little defeated.

Zane raised his eyebrows. "I've never seen so much on the walls. It's not that I don't like it, I just wasn't expecting it."

"It looks nice," Renwick said with a soft smile at Eimear.

"It was Mira's idea." Eimear said and shrugged.

Deiric smiled at me. "I didn't realize that you enjoyed decorating so much."

"I don't really *enjoy* it, but it was sort of fun to go snooping around and then put up what we found." I glanced at Eimear, who smiled again and lifted the grimoires a bit from where she held them. "Let's take them to the den." I smiled. "We can look through them after we get something to eat."

She walked them into the den and then headed for the kitchen. I followed, realizing we'd completely skipped breakfast and lunch and I was starving.

*

Renwick stayed back with us after we ate while Deiric and Zane went out to go hunting. Eimear had wandered off to poke around some more in that room where she'd found the grimoires while I cleaned up. Renwick walked over and leaned against the counter.

"I heard you have a thing for bards." He said casually.

I smiled over at him, but rolled my eyes a little. "Aris mentions one time that a couple of bards sing about me and suddenly everyone thinks I've got a thing for bards?"

I saw him smile out of the corner of my eye. "I wanted to be a bard once." I stopped drying the plate I had in my hands and looked at him. "A *long* time ago. Before I was chosen and transitioned to be a death dealer."

"Did you actually play any instruments?"

"I did. I still do sometimes, but not nearly very often anymore for obvious reasons." He looked at the floor.

"Do the guys know?" I sat the plate down and turned to face him completely now.

"Oh hell no. They'd never let me hear the end of it."

Eimear came around the corner now, holding a couple of glass bottles. "I found mead!"

I jumped and turned to look at her. "I hope that isn't from Deiric's stash. He doesn't like to share." I crossed my arms and smiled.

"Deiric doesn't drink much mead, so I doubt it was from his stash." Renwick commented. "Where did you find it?"

"It was in one of the other rooms that we'd looked in earlier in a cabinet on the wall." Eimear explained. "I don't know how long it's been sitting there, but I vote we try it." She was smiling, and seemed genuinely excited, such a drastic difference from how she acted this morning.

Renwick had turned and reached up to grab some glasses. "Why not? I don't have anything important to do tomorrow."

I just gave him a sideways glance. He smirked and winked at me. Eimear I guess didn't need to know that he likely wouldn't even have a buzz.

We all walked into the den. I lit a few candles, because the sun would be setting soon and I settled into a seat on the couch as Eimear sat down also and began opening one of the bottles to pour us each some.

"Did I hear you say you wanted to be a bard?" Eimear looked at Renwick as she poured. He sat in the chair to the left of the couch.

"You might have heard that, yes." Renwick replied, sniffing his glass of mead. "Might be raspberry. It smells like it's still okay."

Eimear took a sip of hers and smiled. "It's perfect."

I also sniffed mine, a little hesitant, and then finally took a sip. "It is pretty good."

She turned to me now. "That wasn't very convincing."

I just gave her a half smile. "I usually drink whiskey, but I learned my lesson about drinking *their* whiskey. I think we're safe with this." I took another sip. "It is nice and sweet."

Renwick took a sip of his finally and nodded slightly in agreement.

"You should play for us." Eimear looked at him again, with a huge smile on her face.

"I haven't played in a long time, I'm sure it is out of tune and would sound awful." Renwick commented and took another sip of his mead.

"We promise not to mock you for eternity if you're awful at it." Eimear teased, taking a few more sips of her mead.

Renwick swirled the mead in his glass while he thought it over. "Fine." He took another sip and sat his glass on the table. "But you had better not mock me if I'm a little rusty." Then he stood and walked to the stairs. "I'll be right back."

I was leaning back into the couch and just watching as she smiled after him for a few moments. Then she turned and took another sip of her mead before grabbing the bottle and topping off her glass.

"You like him, don't you?" I asked quietly.

She turned and the smile on her face said I wasn't wrong. "No. I just like teasing him."

I raised an eyebrow and sipped my mead.

"Oh don't look at me like that. Are you the only one that's allowed to get a little too close with a vampire?" She reached over and filled my glass back up before I could wave her off. "Relax. *We* don't have anything to do tomorrow either. Have a few drinks with me."

"So does this mean you're going to stay with us?" I asked as I heard Renwick heading back toward the stairs.

"I think I'd like that, but if I'm going to stay here, we're going to need to find more to do than just rearrange and decorate. This place needs more fun and excitement."

I realized then that she probably spent most of her time in taverns, dancing and listening to bards, much like I would when I knew I had enough of a lead on them that I could relax a little and not worry about being caught. That's really the only place us loners tended to fit in.

"It's not as out of tune as I would've thought. I think I've got it now." Renwick said as he sat down with a lute. "I had a couple songs of my own, but I've also learned some of the songs from local bards." He glanced up at me from where he sat. "I may have also heard one of the ones about you too."

I raised my eyebrows. "Oh don't tell me you learned that one too?"

He laughed. "No, I only heard that one once and didn't pay enough attention to play it myself, but I can play some of the others I learned."

"I want to hear a Renwick original." Eimear mused, leaning toward him while she took another sip or two of her mead.

He smiled at her as he began to play a sweet and light melody. She sat staring and smiling at him, sipping occasionally as he played and eventually began to sing. He was pretty good, and certainly could have pursued a life as a bard if he hadn't become a death dealer. He likely still *could* be a bard if he wanted to do both.

We all drank, and he played and sang for us for a while. I started to lose track of time and realized that was because Eimear would refill my glass when I wasn't paying attention. We began to dance along to Renwick's songs, and the songs that he'd learned from other bards. We were twirling and giggling, dancing around him at some moments while we drank.

We were so enthralled in the music and dancing that we didn't notice that everyone else had gotten home already. They were standing in the foyer and quietly watching for I'm not sure how long before Deiric finally came in and jumped in to dance with me when I stopped to sip my mead.

Liala joined in as well, dancing with Eimear before she noticed that I stepped away. I was a little bit surprised Renwick didn't stop playing when we noticed everyone else.

"I see you got him to play." Deiric whispered to me as he spun me into him.

"You knew he *could* play?" I glanced up at him.

He just smiled. "I've heard him playing the lute occasionally when I got home earlier than he probably expected me to. I never let him know I heard him, and he never noticed I'd arrived."

He spun me away again so I was facing him. "It was Eimear that convinced him." I laughed as I swayed a little bit with our next movement because I was starting to feel a little drunk. "And found the mead."

He chuckled. "I didn't even know we *had* mead anywhere, so it must've been sitting somewhere for years."

"It's still pretty good." I smiled and reached to grab my glass. Before I got it to my lips Deiric took it from me and tried a sip.

"It's not bad." He smiled a little. "I think you've probably had enough though."

I scoffed and snatched it back from him, managing to stay steady on my feet even though he tried to move to make it so I couldn't reach it. "I know my limits." I snapped, and finished the glass.

He just raised his eyebrows and pulled me in close to him, his eyes dancing from my eyes to my lips and back again. "Really? I seem to recall you having a pretty wicked hangover that night we drank together."

I scowled. "That was because it was whiskey and *someone* forgot to mention it is stronger than your average whiskey."

"Oh yes, let's blame me." He teased, and leaned in to kiss my neck.

"Get a room would you?" Zane snapped from the doorway.

"Well, we have a room but that doesn't stop you from walking in so what's the difference?" I retorted.

He just stared at me, mouth hanging open, completely stunned and speechless.

Deiric almost doubled over laughing. After a moment Zane just rolled his eyes and his head back a little in annoyance and wandered off.

Aris smiled faintly from where he stood leaning against the threshold. Xander and Leo both shook their heads and headed upstairs.

"Join us. Have a drink!" I held out my glass to Aris.

He slowly pushed himself off the threshold and walked over to take the glass from me and pour himself some mead, then walked over to Liala and Eimear to join them in dancing around Renwick. It was a half hearted attempt though, as he didn't seem fully into the dancing, but it made me happy to see him at least *try* to be happy and lighten up some. I could tell the last ten years still weighed heavily on him.

"He'll be alright." Deiric whispered, just holding me now.

"How can you be so sure?" I also whispered.

"He's been around a while. He'll move past it, but it will take some time. We've all lost people, but it is harder when we lose one of our own, and he lost many."

I understood what he meant. You expect humans to die eventually. You don't expect your fellow immortals to die unless it is in battle.

"We were having fun. Let's get back to dancing." Deiric smiled just as Renwick started a new song. A song about me.

I practically shoved Deiric to the side and stared at Renwick stunned. "I thought you said you didn't learn the one about me."

He just had this sly smile on his face as he kept playing and singing.

Deiric grabbed my hand and spun me around. I smiled. "I guess I have one less bard to track down now." He laughed and we started to dance again.

Chapter 20

Mira

I was not hung over at all the next morning, thankfully, and was up before Deiric. I made my way down to the kitchen after I'd gotten dressed and got to work on a herbal mixture that I knew would help Eimear with her hangover. She had *far* more to drink than I did.

I was busy grinding some peppermint leaves using the mortar and pestle I found in one of the cabinets when Deiric walked in and came up behind me. He kissed my neck as he leaned in over my shoulder. "What are you making?"

"Something to help Eimear with her hangover." I said softly as I poured the peppermint into the bowl with the ginger I'd also ground up. I poured in some honey and started to mix it all together into a thick paste.

"That looks awful." He said after a few moments.

I chuckled. "I didn't say it would be *good*, I just said it would help."

"She certainly went a little extra wild last night." He commented softly. His hands rested on my hips and he gently kissed my neck again. “You snuck out extra early this morning, what do you have planned today?”

I finished mixing the paste together and turned around to face him. “I wanted to train some with you all before you go out, and then I was going to see how Eimear was feeling.” I crossed my arms and smiled. “I figured if I *didn't* sneak out early you’d try to convince me to stay in bed and I wouldn’t get to make this until she was already up and feeling too miserable to even consider trying this.” His sultry smile told me I wasn’t wrong. “So I’d like to get this up to her room *before* she gets too miserable.”

He nodded and stepped to the side so I could move past him. I grabbed the bowl and the spoon and made my way out of the kitchen, up the stairs, and down to her bedroom. I knocked gently on the door and got no answer. I peeked in quietly and she was still sound asleep in bed. I walked over and sat the bowl on the bedside table, then pulled the note I had in my pocket out to put it with the bowl.

When I turned to leave she stirred some, her eyes were glassy and she made a face. “What time is it?” She asked sleepily.

“It’s still early. I left a paste on the bedside table for you that’ll help with some of the hangover I’m sure you’ll feel when you get up. I’ll be downstairs if you need anything. Go back to sleep.”

She sighed, rolled over and settled again.

I made my way back downstairs after making sure she had some water as well. By the time I reached the kitchen everyone else had gathered there already. I got myself a cup of tea and sat quietly while they talked over their plans for the day. We would all spar together, and then some of them who hadn’t gone hunting yesterday would go hunting while the others would make rounds to some of the local villages. I gave them a list of things that we needed so they could grab it while they were out.

I paired up with Aris for a change, and we sparred for about an hour before we all switched around and I ended up with Renwick. Renwick had improved significantly since the last time we'd trained together. He seemed to get much better each time, and more fluid in his movements.

At some point, Eimear had made her way out to watch us, and was sitting on the steps when Renwick and I took a short break.

"How are you feeling?" I asked her cautiously. She looked like she wasn't as bad as I thought she'd be.

"I still have a slight headache, but thanks to that god awful paste you left for me I don't feel like I'll puke at least." She gave me a small smile.

"Good." I smiled. "You can stay in bed if you want to, you know. You don't have to come out here with us."

"I don't like laying in bed all day." She shrugged. "Besides, watching you all train is actually quite interesting."

"It probably wouldn't be a bad idea for you to learn as well." Renwick said gently.

Eimear shot him a look. I hadn't paid attention to what they'd done after Deiric and I had run off to bed last night. "I am in no condition for *that* today. Perhaps another time when I haven't practically drunk my weight in mead."

He laughed. "Another time then."

I looked back at him. "You still need to successfully disarm me, you know." I jabbed him with an elbow.

He turned and took up a solid stance, then waved for me to make a move. I lunged for him, and he blocked me again, then we both went blade for blade for several more minutes before he almost managed to land a good blow. I stopped his blade less than an inch from my face with the flat side of my own and held it with my forearm.

"Maybe don't go for *my* face while we're practicing, but nice shot." I said, and I couldn't hide my shock at how close he came before I managed to block him.

"Sorry." He said, genuinely as he stepped back and paused for a moment.

I looked behind me to see Deiric glaring at him from across the clearing. "Never mind him. I blocked it, so you're fine."

"That look suggests I am *not* fine, but I'll take your word for that." He said simply and we went back to going blade for blade against each other until he finally managed to disarm me.

"Nicely done." I said with a smile and collected my sword and then sat down next to Eimear to watch the others for a few minutes. "That's enough for today I think."

"Don't tell me you're a little hungover too." He mocked, raising a brow.

"No, I'm fine. I told you you needed to disarm me and you did." I insisted and looked over to watch Deiric and Aris.

Zane and Xander came over to get Renwick, and they all went off to the towns they'd decided to visit today. Renwick had my list of supplies we needed. A few minutes later, Aris, Leo, and Deiric went out to go hunting for themselves and for Eimear and I.

"What do you think about learning how to throw knives?" I asked Eimear. She was laying back farther on the stairs now, watching the birds flutter around the treetops.

She lifted her head and met my gaze. “Throwing knives?” She asked.

“Yes. You said you don’t feel good enough to spar, and throwing knives isn’t very challenging but is a useful skill if you’d ever need it.” I looked her up and down. She seemed to be fine enough for something like that, if she didn’t want to just lay in bed all day.

She shrugged. “I suppose I can handle that.”

“I’ll be right back.” I got up and wandered into the house to collect my knives. When I came back outside she was still in the same spot, staring up at the trees. “Come on.” I said, and motioned my head over to the edge of the clearing where there was a nice large tree that we could use as a target.

She reluctantly rose to her feet and followed me. I stopped about twenty feet from the tree and showed her how to hold one if she intended to throw it. Then I demonstrated a throw, and the knife landed in the center of the tree.

“You try.” I handed her a knife and stood off to the side, so that if she did mess it up at all, I at least wouldn’t get stabbed. Her first attempt stabbed the ground not far in front of us.

She frowned. “You made it look so easy.”

I smiled. “I’ve been doing this for a very long time. It takes a lot of practice.” I handed her another knife. “Try again.”

She tried until we’d run out of knives. I collected them all and had her keep trying. She was getting a lot closer each time.

“Try with your other hand now.” I instructed.

“I haven’t even gotten it with my dominant hand.” She started.

"Yes, but you need to be able to use both hands, so practice with both."

She sighed, but obliged. She went back and forth between hands and kept trying until she'd gotten at least one. A few times I stopped and showed her again. She was determined to get as close to the center of the tree as I had done, but I reminded her, hitting the tree at all was still an accomplishment.

After a little more than an hour, I heard movement behind us that had me drawing my sword and spinning around ready for a fight. I was staring directly at Silas, Elias, and three other men who I presumed to be sorcerers behind them.

"Easy little wicked one." Silas mocked. "We've come to set up stronger wards for you, and I also have things to share with Deiric. Where is he?"

"He's out right now." I said coolly, but only relaxed a little bit and did not sheath my sword.

"Hmm." Silas walked over closer to me.

"Eimear, would you be able to assist?" Elias asked.

Eimear frowned, but nodded and walked over to Elias and his men. They talked quietly for a few moments before heading out to set up the wards.

"When do you expect Deiric to return?" Silas asked. He was circling me now, while evaluating me carefully.

"I'm not sure. He's hunting."

"Hmm." Silas said again, considering for a moment. In a movement so swift I barely saw it and couldn't react to it, he'd stolen my sword from my grip and was now holding it to look it over more closely.

"Give that back." I stepped toward him, reaching for it and he merely stepped back and turned so it was still out of my reach.

"This is interesting." He said, somewhat softly. "This is an elder's blade, but it is clearly not Deiric's." He continued looking it over, spinning it carefully in his hands. "Where did you get this?"

I walked over and snatched it back from him at last. "It was my fathers." I said simply.

"It's a little large and heavy for you. You should likely have one of your own made. I'm surprised Deiric hasn't offered that to you yet."

I scowled at him. "I handle this just fine."

"Sure you do." He mocked, and then stalked toward the house for a few steps. "We could have one made for you."

"If you don't believe me, I'd be glad to demonstrate." I seethed.

He spun on his heel and took a few steps back toward me. "Surely you don't think I'm stupid enough to fight Deiric's mate?"

I raised a brow, "mate?"

"Yes. If I accept your invitation for a fight, I'd be challenging or threatening you and he'd gladly have my head." Silas said with a hint of annoyance. He seemed to ignore the fact that the term *mate* had surprised me.

"Are you just saying that because you're afraid I'll kick your ass?" I was baiting, hoping he'd take me up on the challenge. Even if I *didn't* kick his ass, if what he said was true I'd take great pleasure in seeing Deiric kick his ass.

He scoffed. "If I take you up on your little challenge, you had better step in and say that it was *you* who provoked this."

I smiled. "The only rule is you can't use your speed or strength. It has to be a fair fight."

He rolled his eyes, but drew his sword and motioned for me to make a move. "Fine."

I launched myself at him, but he blocked me. He lunged for me, and I blocked it and then spun out of the way. We went back and forth for several minutes. Eventually Eimear, Elias, and the other three sorcerers gathered and just watched. A few more minutes after that I managed to fling Silas' sword across the clearing. It skittered to a stop right in front of Deiric, who I hadn't noticed was now standing and also watching, leaning against the tree Eimear and I had used as a target for the knives.

Deiric was smiling. "I have to say it will never get old watching you get your ass kicked, Silas."

Silas merely scowled at him. I smiled, sheathed my sword and put my hand on my hip. "And *you* were worried he'd be bothered." Silas glared at me now.

Deiric came over and slipped his arm around my waist. "I assume you're here with them because you have news?"

Silas brushed himself off, walked over to retrieve his sword and came back to stand in front of us. "Yes. We were able to get in touch with Garrick." He said flatly, his face expressionless now. "He's agreed to meet here in two days."

"That's a little sooner than we thought." Deiric commented.

"Yes, well he was surprisingly eager to chat with us. We came today to set up the wards and let you know." He paused and glanced at me. "You're better with that sword than I thought." His gaze shifted back to Deiric. "We'll notify Killian and Lazarus." He didn't wait for Deiric to respond before walking back over to Elias.

Elias locked eyes with me. "You will be able to use some magic, within reason, and the wards and shields will mask it. Don't do anything large or crazy and you'll be just fine." And then, in a wall of shadow, they shifted away, leaving Eimear standing by herself close to where they had been.

I turned to Deiric. "What's this about me being your *mate?"* I asked, my hand remained on my hip and I raised a brow.

He raised his brows and seemed genuinely surprised. "Who said that?"

I simply waved my hand over to where Silas had been standing shortly before they shifted away. I could see out of the corner of my eye that Eimear now turned to walk into the house, likely not wanting to be present for this particular conversation.

Deiric sighed. "You don't have to call yourself my *mate* if you don't like the term, but he said that because he can smell it on you." He paused and his eyes danced around my face, studying every movement I made, every expression. "You've been around vampires your entire life and you never overheard anything about mates?" He asked quietly.

"I haven't."

"It is *very* rare to find your mate, but when you do, you just know." He stepped closer to me and took my face in his hands. "When I saw you that night in the tavern and locked eyes with you just for that brief moment, something told me to follow you, and it wasn't just because I saw someone drug you. I wouldn't have intervened for just anyone. I followed that instinct, followed you, and I couldn't stop staring at you once I'd gotten you free of that mercenary. I couldn't understand why. I'd never been so captivated by anyone before." His thumb gently rubbed my cheek. I just stared at him, studied his eyes, unsure of what to say.

"You drove me absolutely mad. The rest of them saw it before I did. I couldn't stay away from you, and I don't know how I didn't see it then, but when you brushed your lips against mine that night it hit me like a stake through the heart. It was like the moment you made an advance on me, however slight it was, it opened the floodgates and snapped that bond into place in a way I couldn't deny it any longer.

"I could no longer chalk it up to just some weird attraction to a woman who finally saw me for who I was rather than the monster most people *think* our kind are. I was so desperately in love with you, so absolutely hungry for you I couldn't hold myself back. That's why I couldn't control myself when you bit me. It absolutely unraveled me in a way I can't even explain to you."

He paused, still searching my face for any reaction, but I just stared back at him, blankly. "Leo didn't say it was irresponsible because I'd fed on you or even that we'd had sex. He said it was irresponsible because they could smell that on you, on both of us, after that night. That you were my mate."

"When a vampire finds their mate they become so incredibly possessive and protective. He knew that after that I'd go absolutely feral if anyone touched you or tried to harm you. I would have felt that way anyway though, I think. Even if I didn't know for sure." He paused and sighed again. "I love you Mira."

I gently put my hands over his, where he held my face. I was still just staring into his eyes in silence. I pulled his hands away from my face.

His face sank for just a moment, until I had released his hands and slid my arms up around his neck, my hands tangling in his hair. I pulled him down into a kiss and his hands slipped around my waist. Then I pulled away to step up on my toes and whisper, "I love you too," into his ear.

He let out a sigh of relief, like he didn't believe that I returned those feelings, and pulled me in tightly to him. I realized I hadn't actually *said* I loved him, even though I knew I felt that before I created their rings. I was going to say it that night, but he didn't give me the chance before he ran to get us to the location they'd picked for it.

"I'm sorry that I didn't tell you, but I wanted you to decide how you felt about me without that weighing on your mind." He pulled away enough to look at me. "It absolutely *kills* me to be away from you, and when you had asked me not to intervene it took all the control I had not to follow you anyway that night you were attacked. The only reason I obeyed was because you were right. Zane would intervene when it was safe and I would intervene no matter what because I was blinded with rage and the need to protect you."

"I'm sure you know I'm perfectly capable of protecting myself." I said softly.

He just smiled. "You are very good at protecting yourself but even you can't protect yourself from everything. Not right now anyway."

I wasn't sure for a moment if he meant because I couldn't use my magic without risking being tracked or because I was still human.

"Both." He smiled.

"I hate it when you do that." I snapped.

He kissed me gently. "I can't help it."

Liala yelled from the porch. "Mira, I've made some lunch for you and Eimear if you're hungry." I realized I hadn't seen her all day, and wondered what she'd been up to earlier in the morning. "Oh- I'm sorry Deiric I didn't realize you were here."

I smiled up at him. "Did you come back because you were actually *done* hunting, or did you come back because you heard me sparring with Silas?"

"I don't wander very far when I'm hunting so I can try to pay attention to what's going on around here, so truthfully I came back because I heard the clanging of swords. I was worried someone had found this place, and then when I saw it was Silas I just sat back and watched." His smile widened. "I did really enjoy seeing him get his ass handed to him by you. He's not as good with a blade as he should be."

"Then I guess you should get back to hunting and I'll go see what Liala made for Eimear and I." I kissed him on the cheek and turned to walk away.

I hadn't made it more than a single step before he'd taken off back into the woods again. I walked over to Liala who just smiled at me and motioned for me to head inside.

Chapter 21

Deiric

I woke up the next morning and Mira was not in bed with me, which was unusual. Usually, I woke before her. I wondered if she'd woken up early to see Eimear off, and listened for any sign of her downstairs.

The house was eerily quiet. I had a sinking feeling in my gut, but tried to brush it off. I quietly got out of bed, got myself dressed and then headed downstairs. The kitchen, dining room, and den were all empty. There wasn't *any* sound of anyone. I grabbed my sword and headed outside.

I was trying to think through everywhere she might go. They had explored the house but I suspected if she were in there I would've at least heard her. In the dim gray light of the morning I didn't see any sign of her until I went around to the side of the house, where a small stream ran down off of the mountain past the house.

She sat on the ground, facing the stream and almost looked like she might be meditating, but she was surrounded by shadow. It sprawled out from her like smoke from a smoldering fire.

I approached slowly and mostly silently. I didn't want to disturb her if she *was* meditating, but she hadn't done anything like that since she came here.

Suddenly, I couldn't move my feet anymore, and a shadow sword showed up in front of my face.

"Mira?" I finally said softly, a little bit of fear in my voice. She must've heard me approaching.

She jumped, like she hadn't heard me approaching. The sword disappeared and I could move again. Slowly the shadows and darkness that seemed to be emanating from her dissipated.

She turned her head and looked at me with a small smile. "Good morning." Her reaction to me didn't suggest that she had any idea she'd just stopped me and threatened me with a shadow sword.

"What on earth was that?" I couldn't stop myself from asking.

"Elias said I could do some small magic. I was just meditating, but I put up a small shield in case anyone disturbed me." She rose from where she was sitting and turned to completely face me. She must've read the look on my face, because hers contorted with a bit of concern and confusion. "Is something wrong?"

"Well, I didn't expect to end up with a shadow sword in my face this early in the morning." I tried to offer half a smile.

"I'm sorry. I'm a little out of practice. It wasn't meant to keep *you* away." She walked over to me and put her hand on mine, which I hadn't even noticed was still resting on the hilt of my sword. "Eimear left a little while ago, so I took advantage of the quiet to practice a bit."

I relaxed finally, and nodded. The sun was finally peaking over the horizon and filling the clearing with a soft pinkish yellow glow.

"Do we have any specific plans today?" She asked, a small smile still lingering on her lips. I almost didn't hear her question though, because I'd gotten too distracted admiring how her eyes seemed to glow in the morning light. I never noticed it, but we usually weren't out so early.

I blinked and shook my head as if to snap myself back into focus. "Not anything specific, no." I looked back toward the house briefly, then back at her. "We'll probably sit down and discuss what we'll say tomorrow, but I'm sure that discussion will bore you."

Her expression was a bit unreadable, and her thoughts gave nothing away. "I may not have been in any major meetings, but I eavesdropped on many years ago. They're certainly not all that thrilling. I do want to be involved though."

I frowned. "They don't typically include women in these meetings, unless they're an archmage that is necessary for one reason or another." A bit of rage flickered in those violet eyes. "I'm not saying that I won't include you. I'm just telling you that they might be uncomfortable with that tomorrow."

"Then they can be uncomfortable." Her rage didn't rise to her voice or her face. It stayed contained in her eyes.

"You really are going to rock the boat aren't you." I said with a small smirk.

The rage shifted to something brighter. "Well, if I'm going to be around *forever* they're going to have to consider changing a few rules around here." A smile rose to her lips again.

That was the first time she'd made reference to eventually transitioning. I didn't think she'd even thought about it. "I can't wait to see what chaos you cause." I smiled back at her. "Let's go inside. Have you had any breakfast or tea yet?"

She started to step around me to walk inside and shook her head. "Eimear left without having breakfast. I haven't gotten around to making anything for myself yet."

*

Around lunch time, everyone who *was* going to be in tomorrow's meeting had gathered in the dining room. Aris, Zane, and Mira, by her request.

"You know they're going to have a cow if we have Mira in there?" Zane said. His inflection made it sound like a question, but it was more of a statement.

"We're going to have the archmage that Eimear is bringing also, and I'm going to ask Eimear to attend." I responded.

Zane scowled. "That's not going to make a good first impression."

Aris was watching Mira as we both spoke. She sat to my immediate left. I didn't see any reaction from her out of the corner of my eye. "They aren't going to be talking, but will be here if we need anything from any of them." I explained.

That got me a look from Mira, though I couldn't see it fully. Aris smirked.

Zane glanced at Mira, and scowled. "Women are *never* allowed in these sorts of meetings. You should feel lucky he's even willing to include you."

She snarled. "If I'm going to be used as a weapon then I damn well should be included in these meetings."

Aris looked away when she said that, off to the corner of the room and away from all of us. There was history there that neither of them seemed willing to share or explain.

"Regardless of your power or overall purpose they will not be thrilled." Zane snapped right back at her. "In their eyes, women do not belong in war meetings, or *war* for that matter."

Shadows rippled through the room. I could *feel* her rage.

Aris finally looked back at us, at me. "She's right." He looked at Zane. "She shouldn't be excluded anymore. She has a right to know what *all* of the plans are."

There it was. A small drop of whatever the history was. She had eavesdropped because she wasn't allowed in the meetings. She sat outside while they discussed what to *do* with her.

"She'll be included, and if needed she will speak up, but to try to keep them from completely exploding about it, she will stay quiet unless she's needed." I glanced over at her. She didn't look at me, and didn't react. I suppose that was as close to an agreement I'd get from her.

"We'll explain how we came to find her, and then have Aris explain what happened the day of the attacks. Then we will share our plans to sway the opinion of the people while we band back together to rebalance the power between the covens like it *should* be."

"Should I mention the vervain soaked stakes?" Aris asked.

"Yes. We will bring up that we believe Vervain and, or Agrimony are being used to block magic as well and advise they begin training the sorcerers and sorceresses in hand to hand combat so they can defend themselves if they are left without magic." I looked around at each of them. "It is ludicrous to me that they're not at least trained in *some* combat just for the sake of knowing simple defense."

"They have no idea how to defend themselves at all without magic. They aren't even taught the full extent of the limits of their magic either." Mira said, her voice was solemn. "They know it comes at a cost, but they all think their magic will protect them to the end." Her gaze shifted to the table. "In some ways I pity them, but am also a bit jealous of their naivety. They didn't have to learn the hard way."

Zane's face and general demeanor softened now as the weight of her words hung heavy over all of us at the table. "Surely they'll understand the importance once we've explained that they *did* have something that blocked magic all along." He tried to say.

"Have you ever been involved in a meeting like this with a magister?" She asked coldly. Her gaze rose to Zane again.

"No." He said softly.

"They are not going to change their methods of training or their ways just because we've brought this to their attention. For all we know, they already *knew* about it and kept it a secret." She paused, glanced at me for a moment, and then back at Zane. "We'll see how it goes tomorrow, but I've never found them to be very open to new ideas."

Aris shifted in his seat again. One day, I needed to find out the history there. If either of them ever cared to share it all. It seemed that the tensions around her specifically were far worse than we thought, which explained her insistence that this wasn't going to work all those weeks ago.

Mira rose from the table and wandered into the den.

I looked at Aris. "I can tell there's something that neither of you are sharing. Would you care to elaborate?"

He met my gaze, glanced to where Mira had walked off to, and then looked back at me. "There were a lot of plans for her. None of which she was ever involved in deciding. Honestly, neither were her parents, despite that her father and myself were always in the meetings." He looked back toward where she'd walked off to again.

"She was not supposed to know what she was, and she was not supposed to be trained with a blade in addition to magic. They trained her anyway. *I* trained her anyway, when no one was around." He paused for a moment and locked eyes with me again. "She's going to have a hard time staying quiet tomorrow, I hope you know. I hope that Garrick is different from the Magisters we usually dealt with." He rose from the table to walk away. "For his sake anyway."

Chapter 22

Mira

I woke to the sun in my eyes. Deiric was still sleeping soundly next to me, facing away from the window. The sun had only just barely crept over the horizon but managed to slap me right in the face first thing in the morning.

I quietly got up and got dressed. I put on my black corset, one I hadn't worn often, with a plain black sleeveless blouse and deep purple skirt. I put my hair into a tight braid down my back, simple, but proper enough for the meeting today.

Deiric began to stir and rubbed his hand across his face as he rolled onto his side and looked over at me. "You're up early."

I leaned back against the dresser and crossed my arms. "I could say you're up late." He tended to be awake before me most mornings, even if he didn't get out of bed.

"I see you've opted for showing more skin than usual." He smirked as he started to sit up and move toward the edge of the bed. "Hoping to charm Garrick into helping us with your looks?"

I scoffed. "The only difference compared to my usual attire is that this blouse doesn't have sleeves." I knew that they couldn't be charmed anyway, but I guessed this was his way of making light of my feelings about the Magisters in general.

He walked over and slipped his hand into the slit of my skirt, gently caressing my thigh. "You sure about that? I could've sworn your other skirts aren't slit up quite this high?" His hand traveled just an inch higher and he toyed with the lace of my underwear.

"Only *you* would notice that." I teased. "You should get dressed. We need to make sure everyone is ready and on time. The last thing we need is for him to disagree over tardiness."

Deiric sighed and walked over to his dresser.

I walked out to head downstairs and have some tea. When I reached the dining room and kitchen Silas, Elias, and Aris were already sitting at the table. Liala stood in the kitchen, readying some small plates of fruit and cured meats to serve to those attending since we'd planned it for noon.

"I see you've already made yourselves at home." I said as I walked over to grab a mug and pour myself some tea before joining them at the table.

Silas smirked and patted the seat next to him. "We thought we'd get here extra early, just to make sure things were all set up. How have you been, little wicked one?"

I scowled and took the seat across from him next to Aris instead. "If you're going to keep calling me that, you'd be advised to sleep with one eye open lest you wake up without certain body parts."

Elias, for the first time I'd ever seen actually laughed.

"You are sworn not to harm us." Silas had a wicked grin on his face now.

"I am sworn not to harm you unless provoked." I smirked. "You seem to enjoy provoking me."

"I'd probably choose a different nickname for her if I were you." Aris smiled and jabbed me gently with his elbow. "Good to know that you haven't lost your sense of humor."

Deiric walked in then, with one of his maps in his hand to lay out on the table.

"Who else are we expecting today?" Elias asked. "Other than Garrick, Killian and Lazarus of course."

"Eimear will be joining us with an archmage named Celeste that she managed to track down on her own." Deiric said, as he smoothed the map out and put it close to the head of the table where he'd be sitting.

"I brought some of my death dealers who did have rings to stand guard around the perimeter of the shields." Silas said. "They're waiting outside for their orders."

"Thank you. Leo and the others will go out shortly and direct them." Deiric glanced over to Aris. "Aris is going to go over everything that he remembers from the attack, including the vervain soaked stakes."

Silas' face paled. "They had what?"

Aris looked at the table, his jaw tense. "They had crossbows fitted to hold wooden stakes, which they'd soaked in vervain."

Silas rested his elbows on the table, pressing his hands together deep in thought for a moment. "They're far more prepared than I would have thought. That was one of our best kept secrets." He paused for a moment, his eyes were distant. "This is going to be a bloody war."

"Not if we can convince the people to shift their allegiance to us." I added quietly. Silas and Elias both looked at me. "If we win over the people, we'll have a lot more manpower to go after them. We can arm them and do precisely what Solas did all those years ago."

Silas and Elias were just staring at me a bit surprised. "We're taking the fight to them, we might as well fight as dirty as they did." I added, before standing from the table to take my now empty cup over to the kitchen.

"She's right." Elias said. "The people are very disgruntled having had to live under their rule for these past few years. We could sway them by offering them freedom, a chance to rule themselves again if we can balance things out."

"It looks like Killian is here." Deiric interrupted, looking beyond Elias and out the window.

"I'll go out to greet him." I said and I made my way toward the front door. Zane appeared at the bottom of the stairs at the same moment as I walked past it and walked with me outside, almost as though he overheard and knew Killian likely wouldn't have any idea who I was.

We met Killian when he was halfway to the house from the edge of the woods. He appeared to have come alone, which was a surprise to me. He was about my height, he had black hair which was pulled neatly back into a bun on the back of his head, and he wore a navy tunic with silver trim and small intricate designs around the edges of it. He had a plain pair of black leather pants and a single sword sheathed at his side. He was exactly what you would expect of a leader of an army in more fancy dress.

He looked at Zane first. "Zane." he nodded his head, and then his focus shifted to me. He looked me up and down, pausing for a moment to evaluate my tattoos. His eyebrow raised, but he bowed slightly, hinging at his waist and waiving his arm a bit elegantly. "You must be the Dhampir." He said as he met my gaze.

I raised my eyebrows. I didn't think they'd told anyone yet, except those who had been here before. "Mira." I said plainly and nodded my head.

"It's a pleasure to meet you. They didn't mention that you'd be here." He said with a sly smile. "They didn't mention you at all actually, but I knew they had to be hiding something important when they requested I come here."

"How did you guess who she was?" Zane asked, immediately a bit suspicious.

Killian scoffed. "You think I didn't notice the wanted posters for a mercenary with violet eyes and black hair?" He looked me up and down again. "There's no reason for the Solas coven to put a bounty on the head of a normal mercenary, and there's certainly no incentive for the people not to try to turn her in knowing the bounty they'd receive unless she were important to them somehow." His small sly smile now turned into a much wider grin. "I had a feeling you'd escaped all those years ago, but I didn't believe it until I heard the stories of your conquests."

"I doubt the people know what I am." I spoke before I even realized what I was saying.

"No, they certainly don't know *what* you are, but they know *who* you are. A savior in the night who took over when they crippled the Oíche coven and we stopped saving them from the monsters they thought we'd created."

I rolled my eyes a bit at that. "I didn't do that for *them.* I did that for myself. They paid quite well."

"That may be true, but you're more than just a mercenary to them, Scáil." He chuckled. "I quite like the alias you created by the way." He looked back to Zane, whose face was a mixture of confusion and shock. "Take me to Deiric."

Zane nodded and we all headed back for the house. We'd almost reached the steps when someone appeared in front of me and stopped me in my tracks, stopping Zane and Killian also because they were just one step behind me. I stumbled back a step and bumped into Zane.

In front of me now stood a man who was a bit taller than even Zane. His golden eyes were piercing and it almost felt like they were staring directly into my soul. He had fiery red hair which had a slight wave to it and fell to his shoulders. He was dressed in a tunic that was a beautiful gold fabric with a black trim, and had similar black leather pants to Killian.

"So the rumors are true?" He hissed. "Deiric does have the Dhampir here."

Zane didn't move from behind me. It was Killian who walked around us and stood next to him, casually glancing at me for a moment before he turned and stood to face this man. "Honestly Lazarus are you that surprised?" He quipped. "They had to have something up their sleeve if they asked us both here."

"That would've been an important detail to mention, considering she was the reason for the attacks years ago." He seemed pissed, and I had a moment where I genuinely considered shouting for Deiric.

"Those attacks were *not* her fault." Zane said calmly from beside me. "They would have happened regardless."

Lazarus glared at him. "They were *absolutely* her fault, or more precisely Teron's fault for daring to try to create another Dhampir." He looked back at me now. "I'm not interested in protecting her and likely getting myself and any more of my men killed in the process."

That comment set me on fire, and I snapped. I stood as tall as I could make myself and got right up into his face. "I don't need your protection. You've been called here to help us bring the coven back together and right the wrongs that were done years ago. If you'd rather sit idly by while they continue to track down and kill the remaining members of the coven then so be it. You can leave right now."

He merely raised his eyebrows. "You'd do well to learn your place. You have no right to disrespect an Elder."

"You have no right to blame me for the attacks years ago. Now you can put your anger aside and work with us, or you can leave and go simmer in your rage for the rest of your miserable life. Until the Solas assassins catch up with you anyway." I never broke eye contact.

"Back off, Lazarus." Deiric was standing at the top of the stairs now, his voice more like a growl. I saw Silas out of the corner of my eye over to my left, and Elias stood on the porch next to Deiric.

"Control your pet Deiric. She's got an attitude problem." Lazarus snapped and turned to face Deiric.

Killian just rolled his eyes and turned around to look at Deiric as well.

"She is not my pet." Deiric snarled. "And she isn't wrong with what she said to you. If you don't want to work with us you can leave now."

Lazarus huffed, glanced over his shoulder at me, and then looked back to Deiric. "Pet, mate, it's all the same to me. I'll stay and listen, but I won't make any promises. You could've at least been a little more open about what the purpose of this meeting was."

"We didn't lie to you. This is to reconvene the coven, to take the fight to the bastards who slaughtered half of our ranks years ago." Deiric snapped.

"Yes, but you didn't mention that the Dhampir was in fact still alive and was *here*."

"Would knowing she was here have changed your opinion as to whether you'd attend?"

"It may have. I don't want to meet the same fate some of my men did years ago." Lazarus said flatly. "Get on with it then. What are we here to discuss?"

"Inside. We have a lot to discuss and we're still waiting on Garrick." Deiric turned and motioned to the door. Everyone filed past him into the house.

Silas brushed past me and smiled as he glanced back. "You continue to impress me, little wicked one."

I gave him another look that could've killed him if I wanted it to and he just shrugged and continued in the house.

Deiric blocked my path as I got to the top of the stairs. "You may have been right, but you should probably avoid challenging the elders. Lazarus especially is.. Sensitive." He smirked.

I shrugged. "Someone needs to put him in his place. He's an asshole."

He just chuckled a bit and lowered his arm to allow me to keep walking into the house and followed behind me.

Garrick finally arrived about an hour later, with two sorcerers alongside him. Eimear had arrived right before him with Celeste. The table was quite crowded, so Garrick's sorcerers stood back against the wall behind where he sat at the table. Zane stood by the door, and I took up a place along the front wall sitting by the window. I sat staring out the window and casually listening as I was instructed.

Deiric explained how he found me, and that I knew they tracked me when I used magic, but left out the part about the herbs that blocked my magic. Aris explained what had happened the day of the attacks, including the vervain soaked stakes. Eimear and Zane explained how I'd escaped and made my way back here before this meeting.

Then Deiric went into his plans for how we could work to turn the tables on the Solas coven and rebuild ourselves by building an alliance with the people again. He pointed out that I already had a reputation as the mercenary who has been working to hunt down the beasts that our coven once hunted for them for free.

He explained that I would go back out as a mercenary under my alias, but take death dealers with me. Rather than accepting their coin for my help, I would request that they help us rewrite the narrative about the coven and seek their support and alliance. I was someone they trusted, and never turned in for my bounty because I *always* killed their monsters. If I wasn't enough by myself, we already knew they were frustrated with the taxes they had to pay Solas for their protection from us as well as these beasts. A protection that they never actually received. We could always make a play on that for their support instead.

Finally, Deiric circled back to the night I was drugged and mentioned that they'd figured out a concoction of herbs to block magic.

"There are no known herbs that can block us from using magic. We had suspicions during the attacks years ago but couldn't ever prove it." Garrick insisted.

"I'm telling you that they succeeded in finding a concoction that works. When I found Mira, she hadn't just been knocked out. She couldn't use her magic for days." Deiric persisted.

"That's not possible." Celeste muttered and glanced in my direction. I had finally turned to look at them rather than out the window. "They've enchanted shackles and other items before to block magic but there aren't any herbs that do that, that we know of."

"Vervain and Agrimony do." I pointed out, forgetting that I was supposed to stay quiet unless they *needed* me to jump in. But Celeste made a comment, so that ship had sailed.

The entire table turned to me.

"We already know that Vervain can impair a vampire. Based on my research it also can be used against witches. Combine that with Agrimony, which is not only poisonous in large quantities, but also blocks magic, and you've got a potent concoction to disable any magical or supernatural enemy." I locked eyes with Garrick, who seemed the most unwilling to even consider it.

"Given that they can block your magic, we're recommending that all witches, sorceresses, warlocks, and sorcerers be trained in the same kind of hand to hand combat that we are, so they can fight even if their magic is useless." Deiric added for me.

Garrick scoffed. "We have no use for hand to hand combat. You said she was drugged in a drink. They wouldn't be in situations where they would be drugged and have to worry about that."

I realized that when they went through the story of how I was attacked in the woods, they didn't mention that those arrows were tipped with the same poison that they'd dosed me with. I hadn't told them that.

"They are also dipping their arrows and other weapons in it too, just like the stakes years ago." I said, and once again the entire table shifted to look at me. Even Deiric was a bit surprised. We all knew about the stakes, but I don't think anyone put it together that they could do that with anything.

Garrick had a scowl on his face. "We shield ourselves with magic. There's no point."

Rage flared inside me and I left my post by the window to walk up to the table. I stepped in between Silas and Aris and slammed my hand on the table.

"Have you *ever* had to fight in hand to hand combat a single day in your life?" His brows raised, but the scowl didn't shift. "Vervain and Agrimony nullify magic. If they shoot your shield with it, it will go right through it and *into* you." When he rolled his eyes that rage boiled more in me than it ever had. How could he write off training his people to defend themselves when their magic might be useless?

"When I was shot with that first arrow, I was still able to put up a shield to keep Deiric and the rest of them out so I could draw him away. I shot fire at him, despite the poison from that first arrow. I filled the space with shadow so I could obscure his vision enough that he couldn't shoot at me again. Then I ran to try to draw him away from Deiric and the others. He shot me again anyway. I let the shield drop so I could conserve what magic I still had. I only went down because the third arrow hit me in the thigh. With the little bit of magic I still had left I threw fire at him again and swung at him with the arrows I'd pulled out of my shoulder and leg."

I paused for a moment. He had started to lean back in his chair and his sorcerers stepped closer to him. "I am the most powerful sorceress on this planet, so I was still able to use some magic after three arrows. You will likely have nothing after just one. That is, assuming that you can even still stand to fight when your entire body is screaming in pain." I seethed.

The entire table was speechless, their faces somewhat pale. Even Deiric was looking at me with a bit of fear in his eyes.

I looked down and realized there was a pale glow coming from my tattoos, and I had singed the table without even realizing it. I flinched backward, lifting my hand and looking at it as I'd never summoned power like that before. In that moment, it all flickered out.

"Well, you certainly proved your point, in more ways than one." Garrick finally stammered. "Thankfully the wards cloaked your little display, or you'd have drawn them right to us."

I was still examining my hand, unsure where any of that had come from.

"It seems that the legends were true in the regard that you're the most powerful sorceress to walk the earth. If what you said is true," I glared at him, and he quickly added, "and I am not doubting it, then I will notify everyone to begin some training for hand to hand combat."

"Stronger emotions, like rage, will draw more power than you are used to handling." He explained. "You'll need to try to keep your emotions under control so that doesn't happen again." He gestured to the table where my handprint was now signed into the corner of the table.

I retreated and took my place back by the window. They continued chatting about our next steps, who would work to gather intelligence and how we would win over the people. I was too distracted by the power I'd just summoned to pay much attention. The rage that had sparked inside me was foreign to me too. I wasn't sure where that even came from. I did generally loathe the magisters because of my history with them, but this was well beyond that. I could keep that rage under control. This was very different.

*

After the meeting Garrick approached me and held out his hand. I took it, and he shook my hand. "It was a pleasure to meet you, Alesmira." He smiled. "I do apologize for questioning or doubting you, and I am sorry that we were not better prepared to have protected you or your family all those years ago. I believe if we had different leadership back then, we might've been able to prevent some of this."

I raised a brow at that comment, and wondered if the magisters I'd overheard meetings with were among those we'd lost at that time.

He looked out at the setting sun through the window. "When this is all over, you'd be welcome to take a position as a Magister for the Oíche coven. It would only be right given how powerful you are, and that I suspect you'll be around much longer than any of the rest of us." He was clearly alluding to the fact that I could become immortal, likely would have to at one point or another.

He headed out with his two sorcerers in toe, who did not take their eyes off me until they'd left the room.

Silas approached me next. "I suppose I *should* find another nickname for you, so you just kill me in my sleep one night." He smiled. "It will be an honor to fight with you." He bowed his head as he also walked out.

Lazarus approached now, but kept a safe distance. "I would like to apologize for how I spoke to you earlier. I lost a lot of men that day, but realize that you lost a lot more than that. I've been around far too long, and my history with this coven put a very bad taste in my mouth when I heard there was another Dhampir of this variation specifically."

I couldn't stop my face from contorting in confusion at that comment. He ignored my confusion, and carried on with what he had to say.

"Still, you would do well to learn your place in the coven and *not* challenge elders."

I held his gaze firmly now, unwilling to ask the question I meant to simply to push my point further. "I am ranked above you in the coven as a whole. I don't make a habit of challenging Elders, but I also haven't had an Elder speak to me that way. You had no right to show up here and talk down to me like that. Respect goes both ways."

He smirked, nodded, and headed for the door as well.

I rose from the window to walk over to Deiric, who was chatting with Killian still at the head of the table and looking at the map. When I came up beside him, he moved so I could also see what they were pointing to. They had been marking where the other groups were, and where any or all of our allies might be. After a few moments I glanced up because they'd both stopped talking and were just looking at me.

"That was quite the impressive display earlier. I'm excited to see what havoc you cause when you're one of us."

Killian smiled, something wicked in his eyes told me that he'd have taken great pleasure if I'd singed Garrick instead of the table. "It will also be nice to have one of us at the highest level of authority in this coven."

I cocked my head. "What is that supposed to mean?"

He jerked his chin over to the window. "I heard what Garrick said. You're getting a promotion."

I rolled my eyes. "Let's not get ahead of ourselves." I mumbled, looking back down at the map. "We have a long way to go before that could happen."

"Have you given any thought to when you'd like to be turned?" Killian asked, and when I looked up his face had softened some, like he actually *cared* and wasn't trying to be a smartass.

"No. I hadn't ever considered it, if I'm honest." I looked over to Deiric whose face was curious and contemplative. I had only made a vague mention of it to him yesterday, but hadn't thought about it too much beyond that.

"You'd be better off to do it sooner than later. You know, the gift of being young and beautiful forever." He added. I glanced over and he now had a seductive look and sly smile on his face.

"I'll think about it." I looked at Deiric again with a slight smile.

"You just tell me when *you* are ready." He said softly, and brushed a small piece of my hair that had fallen from my braid back behind my ear. "You have plenty of time to think and decide on that."

"When you get bored of him, just let me know." Killian mocked.

I glared over at him and that sly smile had turned into a wicked grin. "I don't think I'll ever get bored of him, but thank you for the offer."

His eyebrows raised in a mixture of shock and amusement before he walked around us and saw himself out.

"Remind me again to never piss you off." Deiric chuckled. "I thought you were going to kill him for a moment. You were glowing."

I looked down at my arms, my hand, and my tattoos. "I don't know where that came from."

"Your eyes, I've never seen anything like it. It was like white smoke or flames were rising from them. You were basically a human candle. It was both impressive and terrifying. I didn't know if I should try to intervene or just stay out of your way."

I met his eyes for a moment. "I think if that ever happens again it's best to just stay out of the way. I've never felt rage like that before."

"You're probably summoning the rage of the gods, for this bullshit that the Solas followers are unleashing on the world." He joked, but something told me that he wasn't far from the truth there. "I'm thankful we reinforced the wards though. You'll need to be a little more careful with that."

I nodded. "I'll work on it."

Chapter 23

Mira

I spent the following day reading until I could hardly see straight. Deiric's comment about the rage of the gods, as well as the fact that they'd shielded this *place* had me on a mission to find a way to shield myself so they couldn't track me.

I knew that the Oíche coven had originally primarily worshiped Hecate, but most didn't have altars or offerings to deities anymore. It was an old practice. I wondered what gods or goddesses I *might* be channeling some rage from. Or what gods or goddesses I may be able to work with to aid me, aid us with this conflict.

Eimear wandered into where I was now laying on the floor, papers, books, and notes in chaos around me.

"Are you looking for something specific?" She asked as she knelt down and picked up one of my note pages. "The Morrigan." She read off of that page. "What are you up to?"

I looked up from the book I was looking through. "Just research." I said quickly, and returned my focus to the book. I heard her ruffling through the pages that were sprawled out around me, but I was on the verge of something with shielding and didn't want to lose my train of thought.

"These are all gods and goddesses outside of Hecate. Not many worship them. Most people are too afraid of some of them, or afraid to offend them." She mumbled. Clearly she wasn't going to let this go.

"I can help you, you know, I just need to know what you're looking for or thinking." She added, after I ignored her for a few more minutes and continued reading.

I sighed, scribbled another note on the paper next to me so I didn't forget where I was with that thought. "I am researching other gods and goddesses because something Deiric said made me think that perhaps I'm channeling powers or feelings that aren't my own."

I looked up at her, and she was now sitting cross legged with one of the other books in her lap. "That book," I pointed to the one in her hands, "I grabbed because I'm also researching shields and wards. I want to see if there's a way for me to mask or shield my magic so they can't keep using it to track me."

"I'll help you with the shielding research at least." She mumbled, thumbing through the book. "I've never heard of someone shielding just themselves in any way other than preventing magical or spiritual attacks."

"That doesn't mean it *isn't* possible though. If we can shield against attacks why can't we shield our own energy from being traceable?" I stared off in the distance for a moment, considering. "We have this place shielded and warded such that no one can see what's going on here unless they've been invited in. If you walked up to this place now and weren't on the approved list you'd just see a mountain and turn around without knowing why."

"You are onto something there." She mumbled as she looked closer in the book. "We just need to figure out how."

"I've got it." The idea fell into my head out of seemingly nowhere. Like it was placed there by something outside of my mind. I shot to my feet in such a swift motion that I blew some of the papers around.

Eimear jumped and looked up at me. "What?"

"I need to speak with the Morrigan."

She raised her eyebrows. "Okay, now you've completely lost it." She looked back at the book she had in her hands, entirely dismissing the idea.

"No. I'm not." I insisted. "Very few people worship her, but she is the goddess of death. The phantom queen. She surely has more knowledge on this subject than any of us do."

Eimear looked up again, and I could tell she thought I had gone entirely insane. "Yes, but no one just *talks* to her."

"There's nothing written that says that you *can't* channel her and talk to her though." My mind raced now, and I was pacing while I tried to gather my thoughts. "I know exactly what I need to do to talk to her."

"Did you break into Deiric's liquor cabinet or something? You've got to be fucking with me right now." Eimear finally closed the book and stood up.

"I don't know how I know, but I am telling you that I am fairly certain I *can* channel her, and it doesn't hurt to try it." I scrambled for my notes on the Morrigan. When I finally found that page I almost jumped with excitement.

"Oh you are far too giddy about this. You must be drunk." Eimear looked around for a glass, but when she came up empty she just stared at me with her mouth gaping. I was stone cold sober, and I'd never been thinking more clearly. "How do you know what to do?" She finally asked, as she came over and looked over my shoulder.

"Honestly, I don't know how I know what to do." I scanned the paper I'd made notes on again. "I didn't get all of this from the books. Some of this just came to me while I was reading. I told you it was like something just dropped into my mind."

"I need to gather offerings for her, and I'll need somewhere quiet and safe to do this, because I'm not sure if I'll still be able to tell what's going on around me while I do it." I held the notes so she could see them. "This is a list of all of the things we know about her, likes and dislikes. This is also a list of the things that just came to mind while I was researching her specifically."

"Honeysuckle, dragon's blood, bloodstone, mead, red meat, willow" She listed off some of the items as she read them over my shoulder. "Okay. Say that I don't think you're nuts. How can I help?"

"You could help me gather a few supplies, and I'll need someone who can watch over me while I do this. It shouldn't require any actual magic, but I won't be aware of my surroundings."

I looked over and saw Eimear had grabbed a new piece of paper and sat down so she could lean on the table. "Tell me exactly what you need."

"We need fresh honeysuckle, fresh red meat, mead - cherry is best, willow bark, and a bloodstone." I paused, thinking for a moment. "I also need three candles. We'll need all of this before the next waning moon."

She raised her brow at that. “This is very specific. None of this was in your notes.”

“Not all of this was in the notes, because some of it is to help me channel her. I never thought the herbal lessons I got from my mother would come in handy, but some of this I learned years ago.” I explained.

The front door opened and several sets of footsteps wandered into the house. Zane was the first one to appear in the doorway, then Deiric came in and stopped right next to him, both of them gaping at the mess on the floor around me.

“What on earth is going on in here?” Zane asked.

“She’s had an idea, and as much as I think she’s crazy it is actually a pretty good one.” Eimear said, finishing scribbling what I’d told her I needed on the paper she had.

“I also need mugwort, lemongrass, and bloodroot.” I added.

Eimear glanced at me again, her eyes suspicious but thinking it through as she wrote it down. “For a tea?”

“Yes.”

She nodded.

“Okay, now you’re concerning me a bit.” Deiric crossed his arms and looked at me. I met his gaze and crossed my arms as well.

“What is concerning about it?” I asked.

“You are listing off a laundry list of random herbs and Eimear seems to think it’s somewhat crazy. What are you up to?” Deiric leaned back against the doorway.

“I’m going to channel the Morrigan. I have questions, and I think she’s got the answers.”

Zane, Deiric, and all of the rest of them were now peeking their heads in with their jaws on the floor.

“She’s joking right?” Zane finally asked.

"No, she's stone cold serious, and honestly with how specific her requirements are I'm starting to think she must be onto something." Eimear said, finishing her notes. She looked up at me again. "You need all of this before the next waning moon?" That was more of a question than a statement. "Is this because you plan to *do* this on the next waning moon?"

"Yes." I replied. "You burn willow bark and sandalwood on a waning moon to summon spirits. The mugwort, lemon grass, and bloodroot is for tea for me. The meat and mead are for her. The honeysuckle is because that is a plant that is associated with her and rubbing the crushed flowers on your forehead increases psychic abilities. The three candles are because she is typically associated with the number three. The bloodstone is also associated with her, so I would like it as an offering."

"You got all of this from those books?" Deiric asked, trying to hide his shock and slight concern.

"Not entirely. The herbal knowledge I have always had, but some of what I mentioned was in those books, and some of it just popped into my head as I was working through all of this." I knelt down and fumbled with the papers and books on the ground to organize them a bit. "You are who inspired me to even look into this."

"Me?" He scoffed. "How on earth did I start this?"

"You," I said as I finished piling up the books and my notes, "mentioned that it seemed like I was channeling the rage of the gods." I looked up at him and his lips were in a very tight line, his arms still crossed. "Something about that just hit me in a way that I can't explain. We know that a Dhampir is rare, and more so for a Dhampir that is a sorceress. It would be possible that the creation of one is blessed by the gods. Given that, it is entirely possible that I am in fact summoning a rage that goes beyond what I have on my own."

"Okay, but I was joking." He tried to say.

"That may very well be, but I think you joked your way into uncovering something that no one had ever considered." I began putting the books back on the shelf, but kept them separate from the others so I could remember what I'd been through already. "We'll keep this between us until I know more, just in case this whole thing doesn't work."

They all nodded simultaneously, although it was very hesitant.

Eimear stood up and folded the paper with the list of items to stuff into her pocket. "I can gather all of these over the next day or so. Once we have them, we can plan an evening for you to do this where I'll be available and one or two of them will be available as well." She said, before wandering out to the hall. "Right now, I'm going to go upstairs and get some sleep. You should probably get something to eat and then do the same."

I nodded as she walked away, and everyone but Deiric followed her.

"Are you sure this is a good idea?" He asked, walking over to me and tracing my shoulder gently with his fingers.

"I've never been more sure of something in my life." I said quietly. "I can't explain to you why, but this all just makes sense."

He nodded and kissed my cheek. "Then I'll help you in whatever way I can. Right now, that means insisting you go eat something. You look like you haven't moved from this room all day."

I smiled slightly, because he wasn't wrong. "I haven't left this room today." I admitted.

"Come on. I'll get Liala to get something together for you." He wrapped his arm around my shoulders and walked me into the kitchen.

Chapter 24

Mira

The next morning Deiric had already gotten up and left before I woke. I took my time getting dressed and got downstairs midmorning to find Deiric, Aris, and Leo sitting at the table looking at a map again.

I sighed and walked over to heat some water to make tea. "Isn't it a little early for that already?"

"We need to figure out where you're going to go first." Deiric mumbled, I could tell by how his voice sounded he hadn't looked up from the map. I hung the teapot over the fire still smoldering in the hearth, poked it and added a log, before I turned to walk over and look at the map with them.

"Why not the town that Leo found Aris in?" I skimmed the map as though I had any idea where that actually was.

"That's probably not a bad place to start." Aris commented, dragging his hand over the map to point to it so I knew how far it was. "It's a pretty decent trek from here though. But they did have a Chupacabra lurking around that was killing their livestock and some of the people that wandered too far from the town."

"And the mercenaries aren't willing to take care of it?" I commented, looking up at him.

"It's an easy enough mark, but no. A few did try and it bested them, or they just ran off with the coin they were given." He met my gaze. "They stopped offering coin up front after the second one never returned."

I considered it for a moment. "Are we aware of anything closer?"

"We've heard some reports of other creatures in these towns." Leo pointed to a few other places on the map. "But we don't know what those are yet. Silas has his people looking as well. His second should be coming here with an update in a few days."

I nodded, looking down at the map again. "That seems like our best lead for now then." I turned to go remove the kettle from the fire as it started to scream that it was boiling. I poured myself a cup and put a tea ball in it to steep for a few minutes. "I'd prefer to wait until *after* I channel the Morrigan."

I saw Deiric stiffen a little bit at the mention of that. "Eimear left early this morning to gather the items you requested. She should be back by midday tomorrow." He paused and turned to look at me. "The waning moon is the following day."

Aris peeked around him. "No one has tried to work with any of the gods or goddesses in hundreds of years. Not even the self proclaimed psychics who like to do bone scrying or read cards. Are you *sure* you want to do that?"

"I don't see what harm could come of it. I'm certainly not going to demand anything of her, and I'll be giving her several offerings that she'd be inclined to like." I glanced at Deiric, then looked back at Aris again. "The worst thing that can happen is it *doesn't* work. The best thing that can happen is she gives me some answers or helps us in some way."

Aris just looked back at the map again. "We'll plan to head to Valla the day after you do that then."

Deiric cut him off. "Aris and Leo will be accompanying you, just in case there would be any trouble."

"It will look a bit suspicious if the solitary mercenary that they all have grown so fond of suddenly shows up with two attack dogs behind her." I commented, raising a brow and meeting Deiric's gaze, a slight challenge.

"They found you and swore fealty to you, or at least that is what you will tell anyone if you're asked." He said flatly. "I don't want you going out alone when we know they're still hunting you and there's a hefty bounty on your head. *Especially* since we also know they're using vervain or agrimony to block magic."

I huffed, and turned to grab my tea and take a sip. "Fine." I grumbled, blowing on my tea for a few moments. "I'll take on the Chupacabra myself though, and they'll only intervene if they have to. I don't want to get rusty just because you've sent me with helpers."

Leo came around the table and leaned against the door frame, with his arms crossed and a cocky grin on his face. "Have to keep all the glory for yourself?"

I took a sip of my tea and scowled at him. "You can carry whatever we take back as proof that we've handled the problem if you'd like. But yes, I'd prefer to handle these myself. I work better alone."

"I will be jumping in if things even so much as appear to be taking a turn for the worst though." Aris cut in coldly. I locked eyes with him. "I was sworn to protect you a long time ago, and I didn't get to uphold that order like I should have, but I *will* now."

"You won't need to, but I'll accept that." I said, holding his gaze long enough to really push that issue with him.

I looked over at Deiric, who was now leaning back against the table with his arms crossed. "You are just as insufferable as me, but for entirely different reasons." He had a small smirk on his lips. "And stubborn as hell."

I smirked, cocked my head to one side and gave him a bow with my arms wide, but held his gaze. "Would you expect anything less from the people's favorite monster hunter?"

Leo scoffed and shook his head, before heading out of the room. "I'm going to go find the others and tell them our plans." Was all he said as he walked away.

Deiric just chuckled, walked over to me and leaned against the counter next to me. "I wouldn't expect anything less, but I *would* appreciate it if you'd be a little less stubborn sometimes." His expression got a bit more serious. "I don't want to lose you again, and I'll personally gut anyone who even so much as lays a hand on you."

I looped my fingers into his belt and yanked him closer to me. "As fun as that sounds like it might be to watch, I make it a point to not let anyone even get close to me without my permission."

Those blue eyes sparkled with amusement for a moment. "So you wanted me to catch you that night?"

The first night I met him.

Aris cleared his throat. "I'm - uh.. I'm going to go see if Leo needs any help." I heard him hurry out a moment later. I'd completely forgotten he was still in the room.

Deiric huffed a laugh. "Well?"

"You did catch me by surprise." I finally whispered. "But every time after that I *was* okay with you pushing my limits." I smiled. "I'm sure you could imagine what I would've done otherwise when you saw me hold the knife to his throat." I let my eyes drift to his lips, and then back up to meet his again.

He pressed me back into the counter, bracing a hand on the counter on either side of me. His lips grazed mine for a moment before they trailed down my neck, leaving gentle kisses as they went. I slipped my hands up around his neck, into his hair.

"If I knew we wouldn't be interrupted, I'd have you right here." He whispered into my neck as he made his way back up to my lips again.

"I don't think they'll be back for a couple hours." I whispered against his lips.

He loosed a breath and one of his hands slid onto the small of my back. "Don't tempt me Mira." He paused, pulling back a little bit. "I do actually have things to do today."

"Other than me?" I looked up to him coyly, with a wicked grin on my lips.

His hands slipped down to my thighs and he lifted me up wrapping my legs around his waist. "You're insufferable."

I laughed. "Gee, I've never heard that before." I said, and leaned in for another kiss.

His tongue danced across my lips, and he spun around and started to walk toward the entryway, then up the stairs. His hands firmly around my waist, holding me close to him as he made his way to our room. He kicked the door shut behind him.

I kissed him and bit his lower lip.

He let out a soft groan and sat me on the dresser so his hands could wander. He began to untie my corset as he kissed down my neck again.

My hands found their way to the bottom of his tunic, ripping it up to his chest and over his head.

He raised his arms over his head for me so I could pull off his tunic and shirt. He tossed my corset to the floor while my hands wandered to his belt. I ripped it off and tossed it to the side.

He pulled off my top and then picked me up again, this time with his face in my chest. One hand pulled at my skirts while the other held me tightly against him. He turned around and crawled onto the bed, laying me down with my head among the pillows.

His lips traced their way down my body and he pulled my skirt and underwear off before removing his own pants and positioning himself between my legs.

His hand found its way between my legs, caressing me for a few moments before he plunged himself into me in one smooth thrust. I gasped against his lips. He stilled for just a moment, and then retreated and thrust in again so slowly that it was torture. I could feel him smile against my lips as he slowly retreated and thrust in again.

"Oh, Deiric." I whispered.

Again, he moved so slowly. I wrapped my legs around him and arched up into him. "Deiric," I gasped again as he plunged in so slowly it was killing me.

He let out a small and devious laugh.

I clawed at his back. “Please,” I breathed as he thrust slowly again.

He smiled and flipped me over, pulling my hips back into him as he thrust his entire length into me and I gasped and clawed at the pillows, my face buried in them, stifling any noises I was making.

He sped up now, finally, his hands firmly on my hips. He kept going until I shuttered as release washed over me and I called out his name into the pillow as release found him just a moment later.

He gently kissed down my back before he pulled out of me and lay down next to me just as I collapsed into the bed. He chuckled and lazily traced circles on my back with his fingers.

“It’s quite fun to torture you and make you beg.” He whispered in my ear.

I rolled to my side so I was facing him and rolled my eyes. “And you want to call *me* insufferable.”

We laid there for several minutes, until both of us had returned to breathing normally. “I really should get moving.” He finally whispered as he kissed my head.

I sighed. “You actually *do* have things to do today?” I asked and looked up at him. His blue eyes still had a little shimmer to them.

“Unfortunately, yes. Otherwise I’d never leave this bed and we’d spend the day tied up together.”

I just let out another sigh, and wiggled my way up so I could give him a short and gentle kiss. “I love you.” I whispered into his lips and my eyes met his again.

His eyes were sparkling now. “I love you too” He whispered into my lips and kissed me again, before he sat up and got off the bed to redress himself.

"Liala should be back soon with some fresh food from the town to the east. She'll prepare some lunch for you."

I didn't move from the bed and just watched as he dressed for a few moments. "Do you need me to help with anything today?" I asked quietly.

He looked back as he was heading out the door. "No. You don't need to do anything at all until you're ready to head out and get back to your second favorite activity." He smirked.

Monster hunting. "That's not my second favorite activity." I smiled at him and he raised a brow. "I wouldn't even classify that in my top *ten* favorite activities if I were to really choose. I just refuse to let anyone fight for me."

His smirk widened into a real smile. "I know." He said as he turned and left, leaving me alone for the rest of the day to do as I pleased. It was so odd for me to have so much time to myself. I decided I'd return to my research through enchantments and wards.

Chapter 25

Mira

Eimear finally returned midday the day of the waning moon with everything I requested except the fresh meat, which Deiric promised to get and bring to me before sunset.

I spent the afternoon grinding up the willow bark and sandalwood to fashion it into some incense to burn, mixed the perfect portion of tea for myself, and carefully selected the goblet I would put the mead in. I also cleaned my sword, polished the bloodstone, and inscribed some symbols that correlated to the Morrigan into them.

By the time I'd finished preparing everything, Deiric had come back with a doe for us to butcher to prepare fresh meat for the Morrigan and to preserve for Eimear and I over the next few days.

I began setting everything up as the sun was setting. I placed the candles first, the goblet of mead in the middle of them, an extra empty goblet next to it, and a small plate with the piece of meat I planned to give as an offering. I sat my sword and the bloodstone down in front of me, between me and the offerings.

Eimear brought me my tea and looked over everything I'd laid out. "Are you sure about all this?" She said quietly while I sipped the tea and watched the sun set over the mountains in the distance.

"Yes. There's no sense in backing out now." I looked over everything again, the honeysuckle was in my mortar and pestle to my right. I set to grinding that up while she walked back to the house with the empty mug. I took the honeysuckle and rubbed it on my forehead.

I sat on my knees. "I will bow to her if she appears to me. That is how you will know it's working." I glanced back at them. Deiric stood on the front steps, leaning against one of the posts supporting the roof. Zane, Leo, and Aris sat along the edges of the porch. Eimear sat on the steps and nodded.

I turned back to face everything laid out in front of me, lit a match and used that to light the candles and incense. I took a few deep breaths, settling into a quiet meditative state. After a few moments I called out to her in my mind.

"Morrigan, Lady of War, Goddess of Death, Nightmare Queen, I beseech thee, stand with me and grant me your guidance." As I said that, I took my sword, sliced my palm and let the blood drip into the empty goblet I'd brought out. "Lady Morrigan, hear my call. Grant me your wisdom."

The air around me became heavy, thick, and in my mind's eye, I saw her appear before me, beautiful, despite being mostly hidden in shadow by her dark cloak.

I bowed, so low that my forehead touched the ground, but kept my hands outstretched before me and palms up and open to her.

"I've been expecting you." Her voice was smooth as silk, but almost deafening and otherworldly. "You may rise, child."

I rose from where I bowed before her. "I seek your wisdom to protect my family, my coven, and the people. Many were slaughtered by another coven, and we are still hunted."

She stood silently, watching as I spoke.

"I seek to know how I might shield myself so that I may use my magic to protect them, and tip the tides in our favor, so we can regain balance and practice openly."

"This coven tracks you by your magic." She said simply.

I nodded.

"I can grant you invisibility, shield you from their eyes and others. They would no longer be able to track you."

She paused, but before I could speak she continued.

"You are preparing for a war." She said flatly. "I can grant you other forms of assistance, but it will come at a price."

I bowed again as I said. "What is it you would like in return, Lady Morrigan?"

"When the conflict is resolved, you will erect a temple in my honor. Beginning now, and after that temple is created you will leave me offerings on each dark moon."

I looked up at her again, and her eyes were practically glowing.

"I prefer blood, but I see that you've included many other offerings here. Any of these will do as well." She continued.

I nodded.

"You must recite this invocation while I cloak you." As she said that, a small scroll appeared in front of her.

She stepped toward me, her cloak wrapping around me until I was completely consumed in darkness. I recited what she'd shown me.

"Dark lady, phantom queen, shield me, keep me unseen. Hide me from all prying eyes, cloak me with your dark disguise. Keep all enemies away from me. So it is, and so it shall be."

As I finished reciting that, a gust of wind blew around, felt like it blew through me, and she was gone. I opened my eyes and the candles had all been blown out, so the wind was not just in my mind's eye. I felt a bit dazed and dizzy, and started to fall to one side, but was caught by Deiric.

"Are you alright?" His voice wavered a bit, a tinge of worry and panic lingered in it.

Eimear was next to me a few moments later.

I yelped as my left hand burned where I'd cut it for the ritual. I looked down to see there was no longer a cut there. For a moment it looked like the palm of my hand was on fire, and then the glow faded to reveal a tattoo of a raven on my palm.

A caw from behind us caused us all to jump a bit and turn to look. Before I even registered what I was doing, my right arm raised and the Raven flew down from the roof where it had been perched and landed on my arm. It paused for a moment and then leapt off my arm to the plate with the meat on it. We watched as it pecked at it and ate it.

I realized now that the goblet I'd used for my blood offering was empty and you'd have had no idea there was ever anything in it. The goblet of mead was also empty. I grabbed my sword and looked it over. The blade now had symbols carved into it, and the bloodstone that had been sitting next to it was a part of the hilt.

"Okay, would you like to clue us into whatever the hell is going on?" Eimear finally said. Her face was a mixture of horror and confusion.

The raven had finished its meal and now looked at me. *I am Macha.* I heard in my mind. *Lady Morrigan sent me to aid you. I am honored to be your familiar.*

I blinked, staring at it as though I'd seen a ghost. It's head tilted slightly, that dark black eye staring straight into my soul. *They cannot hear me. We can communicate in our thoughts, if speaking out loud to me makes you uncomfortable.*

You can hear me? I asked in my head.

Macha dipped her beak, a slight nod, but then added, *Yes*.

Deiric also heard me, and shifted me a bit where I was still leaning against him so he could look at me. "Are you alright?" His voice was a little more worried now. "Why are you asking if someone can hear you?"

"She didn't say anything." Eimear said.

"She thought it." Deiric added, glancing at Eimear before looking back at me. "Mira, what the hell is going on?"

I shook my head and rubbed my face with my other hand. Deiric helped me sit back up, but I was exhausted. I did not realize how much that would take out of me.

"She shielded me." I finally said. "She offered me her shield and her help."

"At what cost?" Eimear asked as if she could have heard the entire conversation, though I knew she hadn't.

"I have to give her offerings on every dark moon, and when our conflict or war is over I have to have a temple built in her honor." I said, staring at Macha, who continued to look at me blankly. "This- this raven was sent to me by her as well. To help me."

Macha looked at each of them for a moment, and then looked back to me, taking a few steps toward me.

"You were speaking to that?" Deiric asked.

I just nodded. "It communicates to me in my mind. She is my familiar, assigned by the Morrigan."

Macha's head twitched a bit, twisting around as she looked at them both again, and then back to me. *I will stay out here, but you may leave a window open if you'd like me to come in if you need me.* She finally said, before flying up and perching on the roof again.

"Let's get this cleaned up and get inside." Deiric finally said, and put my arm up around his shoulders to help me to my feet.

"I'm okay. I'm just exhausted." I said quietly.

"I'd guess so." He said as we walked toward the house. "You were glowing the entire time, from the moment that you bowed to her."

"She shielded me even then, hiding my powers from them. If I've understood her correctly, I am entirely shielded from them now, and they will not be able to track me at all." I half laughed and smiled. "Hell, they might even think I'm dead if I've entirely disappeared."

"We could hope so." He mumbled as he walked me past Zane, Aris, and Leo, who were pale as ghosts.

I sat my sword on the dresser once we'd gotten upstairs.

"Those are symbols for her, I assume." He said, gesturing toward the sword.

"I would assume so, yes, but I don't recognize all of them." I sat on the bed. "She asked specifically for blood offerings. I wonder if I'm meant to use the sword for that. She didn't specify."

"You should get some rest." He said, and helped me get off my corset, skirt, and blouse. "I'll be back in a few minutes." And he turned to leave.

"Would you open the window for Macha?" He looked at me funny for a moment. "The raven."

He nodded, walked over and opened the window so she could fly in if she wanted, and then headed out the door and back downstairs to the others.

I laid back in the bed, and it didn't take very long for me to slip off to sleep. I dreamt of all sorts of wild images that night, ravens, battles, bloodshed. I don't think I'd classify any of it as a nightmare. It was as though I was looking through the Morrigan's eyes as she walked the battlefields of wars long past, carrying the souls of the dead to the afterlife.

Chapter 26

Mira

I was jolted awake just before sunrise the next morning by a caw right next to my face. I practically jumped off the bed.

"Fuck." I shouted.

Deiric, also jostled awake, practically leapt on top of me before he realized it was Macha. "Son of a bitch." He grumbled, resting his face into the pillow over my shoulder from where he was now partially on top of me. He sighed and rolled off of me onto his back.

"What the fuck Macha?" I said as I rubbed my face and stared at her.

Macha cocked her head at me from where she was perched on the bedside table.

"You just did that to fuck with me?" I asked, out loud, because there was no reason to speak in my head.

You need to be more aware of your surroundings. She said.

"We are in a house that is warded and shielded to the high heavens, surrounded by death dealers and at least one other witch. I hardly need to be concerned while sleeping *here*." I snapped.

I could practically feel her sigh, despite that a raven is obviously not capable of that sort of gesture. She sat there for another brief moment before she flew back outside. I flopped back down on the bed and stared at the ceiling, still processing the fact that I was now abruptly awake because of my familiar.

Deiric huffed a laugh and rolled onto his side to look at me. "Things not going so well with your newfound friend?" He propped himself up on his right elbow.

I rolled my eyes and glanced over at him. "So we're just going to skip over the fact that you launched yourself on top of me?" I jabbed at him.

"Look, I protect first and ask questions later, *I'm sorry.*" He added a sarcastic offended tone to that apology and waved his arm in feigned annoyance.

I grumbled and rolled over, or rather flopped over onto my side to look toward the open window.

He hooked his arm around my waist and pulled me back into him. "Go back to sleep." He whispered into my ear. "We don't need to be up this early."

"I don't even know if I can now."

He sighed and gently kissed my neck. "It doesn't hurt to try." He snuggled into me and laid his head down again.

All I could do was lay there and stare toward the open window. I'm sure I'd learn to love this helper she'd given me, but right at this moment it made me want to scream.

*

Later that morning, Leo, Aris, and I were preparing to head out to Valla to offer to take care of the Chupacabra for them.

"This is a two to three day trip on foot at your pace." Leo commented. "If you're willing to let one of us carry you, we can get there much faster."

"I'd rather *not* be carried, but I can respect that it will get us there faster." I paused for a moment, getting used to the feel of having all of my weapons strapped to me again. "Have you ever considered getting or using horses?"

Aris scoffed. "We're still faster than horses on foot if we don't have to move at a *normal* pace." He gave a half smile. "You could always just shift us there though."

I sighed. "Do you realize how long it's been since I've even attempted to shift *anywhere*?" I considered it.

Macha perched on my shoulder, which made me jump a little. *You can shift places now. The Morrigan's shield will protect you.*

I glanced over at her. *I haven't done it in so long. I'm not even sure if I can, especially not with other people.*

Of course you can. She said softly. *Just because you're out of practice doesn't mean you're totally incapable.*

"I'd guess about nine years or so at this point." Aris shrugged. "It's not like you can royally screw something like that up."

I sighed again. "Fine." I glanced over Aris and Leo for a brief moment. "Are we ready then?"

They both nodded.

I didn't give them a chance to brace themselves, before I shifted us to a road just outside of Valla.

"Shit, some warning would've been nice." Leo snapped.

I glared at him. "You said you were ready. Was that not warning enough?"

He looked a bit green. "No, not really."

Aris just smiled. "See, I told you you could do it." He handed me a cloak, much nicer than the one I had when I first came to the manor. "We got you a nicer cloak. It will cover your tattoos."

"Do you think it's necessary to cover my tattoos at this point?" I asked, taking the clock and wrapping it around my shoulders anyway. It was a beautiful black material that glimmered in the sunlight, similar to the cloak I'd seen Eimear wear that day I'd run into her in the other town.

"We don't want to take too many chances. We'll explain who we are, but we don't need to advertise it excessively." Leo answered for Aris. His face was finally returning to a normal color

I nodded, "Let's get moving then."

Macha shifted on my shoulder. *Let me have a look first.*

I glanced at her. *For what?*

To make sure there aren't any mercenaries or assassins there. She said plainly.

I nodded and she flew off.

"She's going to scout it out for us first." I explained to Aris and Leo who looked confused.

Several minutes later, she came back and perched on my shoulder again. *There doesn't seem to be any Solas mercenaries or other unsavory characters there at the moment. There are wanted posters for you though.*

I nodded and looked at Leo and Aris. "We're good to head in."

Leo stared at Macha like she was a lion ready to pounce and nodded.

"She isn't going to eat you if that's what you're worried about." I commented and he finally took his eyes off of her and looked at me.

"I'm sorry, the fact that you suddenly have a Raven following you around is just going to take some getting used to. It's… unsettling." He said quietly. "It will probably look creepy or suspicious if she is on your shoulder when we walk in too."

I nodded and gave her a sideways glance. *Head back to Valla and stay vigilant. If you see something we should be worried about, come to me right away.*

Understood. She said as she took to the skies again.

"Shall we?" I asked, as I turned and motioned toward the village.

They nodded, and fell in step behind me as we strode toward the village. I put my hood up, since that was how I traditionally traveled before I had met any of them. Some people stopped talking or whatever they were doing and watched us pass by on our way into the village, and others just gave us sideways glances then continued about their day.

We kept walking until we'd made our way to the same tavern that Leo had met Aris in. I walked in first, and they followed right behind me, taking up their places to my right or left as soon as they cleared the narrow door.

We didn't get very far into the tavern before two men stood up and blocked our path.

I removed my hood to reveal my face and their faces went ghostly pale.

"You- You're Scáil?" One of them stammered. He was pudgy, certainly not starving. His clothing was old and tattered, and he was probably in his forties or fifties. He had dull hazel eyes and parts of his disheveled hair and beard were graying.

"Yes." I answered. I gestured back toward Aris and Leo. "My friends tell me that you've been looking to hire me to handle your problem."

"Their kind are not welcome here." The other man spat, and I shifted my gaze to him with a raised brow. He was tall and thin, and may have been related to the older man. He had short brown hair, equally old and tattered clothing, with a small hat on his head. His eyes were the same hazel as the man he stood next to.

"Their kind?" I asked.

"Vampires. Death Dealers." The first one said, rather coldly.

"Interesting. They told me that they'd been served in this tavern before. What has changed?" I asked calmly, aware that everyone was now turning to look at us.

"We didn't know what they were when we asked them to help us." The younger one spat.

"Well, if they're not welcome here then I would presume I am also not welcome." I said matter of factly. "Best of luck with your Chupacabra." I turned to leave and took a step toward Aris and Leo. Their faces were unreadable and hard as stone.

"Wait-" The older one started. "We need your help."

I stopped and half spun toward them again. "My death dealers are a part of the package now. If they are not welcome here, then I am not going to help you." I made eye contact with the older one as I spoke, and held it firmly.

"They sent these monsters, why on earth would we allow them in here?" The younger one spat, and I shifted my gaze to him, which caused him to shift slightly on his feet.

My eyes were cold. Cold as death as I fully turned to face them. "Death Dealers, or anyone from the Oíche coven for that matter, do not command or create these beasts. They've hunted them for millennia for you ungrateful pricks. For free, I might add. I took over in their place when you all slaughtered half of their upcoming ranks."

They both stared at me with a mixture of fear and confusion on their faces.

"So I repeat. If they are not welcome here, then we have no interest in helping you. Best of luck." I smirked, the only real expression I'd given them thus far, and began to turn to leave again.

"Wait, please." The older man reached for my arm and Aris stepped to the side and drew his sword before he could touch me. I scolded him with just my eyes. He relaxed and sheathed his sword. I turned around again.

"You have to understand, the Solas coven told us that the Oíche sent all of these monsters. We are hesitant to trust anyone from Oíche and to let any of that coven help us." He stammered.

"No. I do not understand." I glanced between him and the younger man now. "Tell me, do the taxes you're forced to pay actually do anything to help you with these beasts like they claimed they would?"

There was a murmuring from the growing crowd, and I glanced around at them for a moment. They all stumbled back as my gaze fell upon them.

"Have the Solas mercenaries or forces *ever* showed up to offer you any help at all?"

Silence. A heavy silence filled the room.

"If the answers to those questions were yes, you wouldn't have to scrounge around for coin to pay mercenaries like myself." I said simply. "And, much to your dismay, I am a part of the Oíche coven as well."

They stumbled back a step. "You're a sorceress."

I scoffed. "That scares you more than a death dealer?"

They stared at me blankly. Finally, the younger one spoke. "There is a hefty bounty on your head. What makes you think you can walk in here and offer to help us and that we won't just take you to the Solas coven for the coin they're offering for your head instead?"

"Threatening the sorceress with two death dealers, when you're nothing but a room full of useless humans who can hardly hold a sword let alone fight?" I looked around at the people now slowly backing away or pushing themselves back against the wall and bar. "I'll admit I'm impressed. Impressed at the bold stupidity of it, but impressed nonetheless."

"You bitch." The young one snapped.

"I'll lay it out for you then, shall I?" I was growing tired of this little game we were playing. "Here is our offer. We will kill the Chupacabra, bring you its head as proof, and in exchange you will spread the word among the people, discreetly of course, that the Oíche coven is gathering their forces and working to support and help the people again, *for free*." I added some emphasis and a low snarl at that, as if the idea of working for free made me sick.

"With that, you will *not* under any circumstance tell anyone related to the Solas coven who helped you when they come to collect your taxes. Or, you can deal with it on your own and we'll move along to the next village that needs our help. If it were me, I'd go with the first option, but if you'd like to continue to lose livestock and villagers to that beast, be my guest."

They stared at me blankly again.

"You have until sundown to make your decision. We will wait at the village limits for you to come tell us what you decide. If you accept the offer, the beast will be dealt with before sunrise."

The older one nodded.

"It was a pleasure." I said with a wicked smile, turned, and walked away. Aris and Leo continued glaring for a few moments at the two men we'd spoken to, before turning to follow me. They kept their hands on their blades threateningly, as though they'd need them at all.

"That was a little bit harsh, don't you think?" Aris commented as we made our way to the edge of town.

"I think you forgot who I am supposed to be." I mumbled.

"You were a lot colder than I've ever seen you." Leo seemed to agree with Aris.

I glanced over my shoulder at them. "I am a mercenary. I don't speak kindly to anyone that pays me. I set a price, I give them a choice, and then if they decide it isn't worth the price I move on." We reached the village limits and I turned to face them fully. "Neither of you really knew me when I was just a mercenary. You've seen the side of me that is *me,* or at least the version of me I choose to share with you. This is an entirely different facade. You'll get used to it."

Aris frowned. "I'm not sure that I'd like to."

I scowled at him, a little harsher than I intended. "I'm not a helpless 15 year old girl anymore, Aris. There is a lot that has changed since then. If you expect these people to respect me the way they did when I was a mercenary, I have to keep up that facade."

His jaw tensed and he went quiet, looking down at the ground in front of him.

"It was a good show at least." Leo commented. "Now we see what they decide."

Macha appeared on my shoulder. *They're coming. They will accept your offer, but they do not have good intentions. They plan to turn you in after you've completed the task.*

I nodded, and she shot off to the skies again.

"That's still going to take some getting used to. You look like some sort of death bringer." Leo said, his face contorted with a bit of disgust.

"Really, death dealer?" I quipped, with a half smile.

He half laughed. "Okay, fair point."

"They're coming." I said.

Leo and Aris turned around to face the village now. The two men rounded the corner and were headed toward us. Their entourage from the tavern hadn't followed them.

The older chubby one spoke first. "We'll accept your offer."

"We'd like to meet you here in the morning to confirm the job is done." The younger one added.

I nodded. "Very well. We'll get started on tracking it."

They started to turn to walk away.

"I'm not done."

They halted and turned to face me again. "I want to make something very clear. If you go back on the part of this deal that forbids you from contacting the Solas coven about us, I will come back here and personally make sure that every single person in this town is slaughtered just like my parents, my friends, and my family were all those years ago."

Their faces paled. "And I will make sure that you two are the last to die, so you get to watch the suffering your betrayal caused. Do you understand?"

They nodded.

"I want you to repeat our deal, and what I just said."

The older one cleared his throat. "You will kill the Chupacabra, bring us evidence that it has been killed, and we must discreetly spread the word that the Oíche coven is going to begin helping us take care of these monsters again. For free. We won't contact the Solas coven."

"Or?" I clarified.

"If we contact the Solas coven, our entire village will be slaughtered." He stammered.

"Good." I smiled. "Now go tuck yourselves away somewhere safe while we rid this village of that beast."

They turned and almost ran this time.

"Was that really necessary?" Aris was more annoyed this time.

I turned and faced him again. "Yes. Macha overheard them and they were planning to turn us in first thing in the morning after we'd completed the task."

Both their brows raised.

"They're not going to risk us ransacking this village. And if they do, I will hold true to my promise."

"Mira, that's not who you are." Aris said softly, reaching out to me for a moment.

I stepped back, avoiding his touch and stared at him coldly. "This is war, Aris. They slaughtered innocent people years ago. Women, children, and coven members without magic to defend themselves. If they choose to break a deal that we made, they are no longer innocent people. They've conspired against us."

He stared at me speechless for a moment.

"She's right." Leo finally broke the silence. "War is cruel. Their actions all those years ago were far worse than her threat." He looked back at where they'd run off to. "They killed for sport years ago and targeted people when they were at their weakest, killing women and children all the same as the actual warriors with no mercy. We clearly spelled out the consequences of betrayal. It is entirely different."

We walked out in silence as the sun began to set. Listening for the sounds of the beast in the area we thought it tended to frequent.

After a long while, a rustle in the bushes behind us caused the three of us to turn our backs to one another, watching in all directions, primed in fighting stances.

A low snarl came from the bushes in front of me, and its eyes glimmered back at me. It stood from where it had crouched in the bushes, its jagged teeth barred.

I tossed away my cloak and held out my sword, prepared to go on the defensive. In the blink of an eye it launched into the air, charging the three of us. Aris and Leo stepped back slightly behind me as I swung at it, slicing its face. I jumped to the side and rolled out of the way of its pounce. It hissed and charged me again. I got up to a kneeling position, then dodged left and slashed at it again, getting its front leg this time.

Without giving it the chance to pounce again, I lunged forward and went to leap onto it and stab the back of its neck, but it spun and swatted me as I leapt into the air. I slammed into a nearby tree. I collapsed to my hands and knees gasping for a moment because it knocked the wind out of me.

Aris jumped in front of me as the beast charged me again, despite that I was already rising to my feet to make my next move. He let it charge him straight on and stabbed his blade right through the middle of its head, not even flinching as the teeth sliced his arm.

"As entertaining as it would be to watch you battle this bastard *without* the healing, speed, and strength we have, I can't watch you get the shit beat out of you just because you're too stubborn for your own good."

I scowled at him. "How do you know that *wasn't* my next move?"

He glanced at his arm, shredded, but already healing. He didn't even appear to be in pain, but I am sure he felt it. "Because *this* would've killed you."

He walked over and offered his other hand to help me to my feet. I took it reluctantly and looked over to see Leo cutting the head off to take to the villagers.

"It was a valiant effort." Leo said, stabbing the head with his blade so he didn't have to carry it with his hands. "But Aris is right. I'm sure you would've killed it with a few more minutes to go back and forth with it, but we aren't going to just standby while you get your ass kicked." He looked over at me with a smirk. "Or it'll be our heads on a stick if Deiric finds out." He lifted the beast's head to prove a point.

"Fine." I said as I brushed the dirt and bark off my shoulder, which was scuffed and scraped up from the tree. I walked over and picked up my cloak from where I'd chucked it before all hell broke loose. "Let's head back then."

We made it back to the edge of the village as soon as the sun rose, and Leo chucked the head off of his sword at the villager's feet.

"As promised." He said.

"We'd like to apologize." The younger one stammered. "We had intended to deceive you and turn you in, but the entire village discussed what you'd said yesterday." His voice trailed off and he looked down at the beast's severed head. "Not the threat I mean, but the rest of what you said." He looked up at me again. "The Oíche coven truly doesn't send these beasts?"

I kept my face blank and unreadable. "The Oíche coven wouldn't send beasts to terrorize anyone. All we want is to be able to practice our magic in peace. Our exchange has always been to offer protection for the ability to practice in peace."

I looked around at all of them. "The Solas coven just got greedy and power hungry. They sought to wipe us out so they could thrive on your weakness and turned you against us. After those brutal and savage attacks, where half of our coven was slaughtered, women and children right alongside true warriors, we went underground to save whatever remained of us."

"Women and children?" A woman in the group of villagers behind them stepped forward and asked. She was horrified to hear that. They probably didn't know anything about those days unless they were directly involved.

"Yes. They showed no mercy. They attacked manors that were not heavily warded or protected. There were only two survivors from one of the houses." My voice hitched at the end of that statement, and I looked away. I took a steadying breath and cleared my throat. "We are working to rebuild, but we need the support of the people, because we are now severely outnumbered and disconnected."

The older man spoke at last. "We will spread the word. The Oíche coven was never to be feared."

The woman took a few more steps forward, past the men, and locked eyes with me. "You were one of those two survivors weren't you." She asked, her face filled with sadness and what I would guess was pity. "You must've just been a child then, or a teenager at best."

I held my lips in a tight flat line, and simply nodded.

Aris stepped up next to me and cut in. "She and I were the only survivors, aside from a witch who had to be turned to save her." He glanced at me before he continued. "I hardly consider that witch a survivor, because she *did* die to become what she is now."

It hit me then and I don't know why I didn't see this before. They'd determined I was a sorceress because we never turned women into vampires. Because *every* death dealer I'd ever met was a man. That was why all those years ago my father was forbidden to tell me what I was and forbidden from training me. They just didn't know he'd already done that. We kept it a secret, from *everyone* but his inner circle. A small amount of anger flared in me for a moment. I was always bothered that the leadership was mostly men but it was far more than that.

"We need to move on." I cut in, and glanced at Aris, who stepped back to his position behind me again. "We have other villages to aid and cannot waste any time."

I did not wait for a response from the villagers or Leo and Aris before I turned and walked away. Leo and Aris hesitated for a moment, before following me down the road out of the village.

When we were far enough out of the village Macha circled down to us and landed on my shoulder. *They've kept their word. They have not sent for Solas, but they did send messengers to the neighboring villages to let them know that the mercenary Scáil is back and that Oíche is not a coven to fear.*

I nodded and turned to Leo and Aris. "They've kept their word."

"Deiric will want a full report." Leo pointed out.

I shifted us back to the house.

"Fuck's sake Mira." Leo breathed the moment we were at the house. "I asked for more warning."

I shrugged. "Sorry." Macha flew up to her usual perch.

Deiric appeared at the front door.

"I assume you ordered them to stand in, anyway." I walked up to the porch and removed my cloak. I was already a bit sore from getting slammed into that tree.

Deiric cleared the space between us in a flash and examined my shoulders, mostly healed but still red and inflamed from the scrapes and cuts I got when I hit the tree. I was sure my back was bruised pretty badly. "Clearly they didn't step in fast enough." He sent a sideways glance to them.

"If we jumped in right away she'd have killed us herself and you know it." Aris said, and then walked past us into the house.

Deiric just frowned a bit.

"Would you be willing to let me fight my own battles if you turned me?" I asked, probably a bad moment to ask that question, but it had been burning in me the whole time.

"Yes." He answered without even giving it a second thought. "You'd be less likely to get your ass kicked if you could move a little faster." He led me into the dining room where tea and a plate of food were waiting for me.

"Sit, eat, and relax." He said softly.

I obeyed.

"I don't understand why you didn't just use your magic now that you're shielded." He added when he sat down across from where he motioned for me to sit.

I scoffed and sat down. "Honestly, I've gotten by so long without it I didn't even think to use it."

"Clearly." Leo said. He sat down next to me at the table. Then, realizing he actually spoke the word out loud, he froze and glanced around at all of us. He cleared his throat and muttered, "sorry."

I chucked a grape at him. "Look, I pride myself in the ability to kill these things *without* magic. Don't you dare sit over there and judge me when you only saw me fighting one for less than a minute. I've fought far worse things than that."

"Oh I don't doubt that, but I still can't stand by and just watch. It's just not in my nature." Aris commented.

I rolled my eyes at him.

"We'll see what comes of all of this over the next couple of days before we pick the next town for you guys to travel to. We have another meeting with Silas, Garrick, Killian, and Lazarus in three weeks." Deiric looked over at me. "If you decide you're ready to be turned, all you have to do is say the word. There's no reason to wait, but no reason to rush it either."

I just nodded and set my focus on the food he'd given me. I was still mulling over the fact that women were rarely high in the ranks of the coven and not ever turned into death dealers. The women who were born without magic were just turned into natural healers, herbalists. They could've been so much more if we allowed it.

Chapter 27

Mira

I woke the next morning frustratingly sore, but knew if I didn't move it would get much worse. Deiric gently rubbed a salve Liala had given me on my back.

"Do I even want to know how you got hit this badly?" He commented as he was finishing up.

"It slammed me into a tree when I had jumped to try and deal a better blow to it." I said, looking down at the crow tattoo on my palm. "I was getting up to go after it again when Aris stepped in."

Deiric sighed, and gently tugged on my shoulder to turn me to face him. "You don't have to fight these beasts anymore, you know. You can let us handle it and just do all the talking."

I met his eyes, they were soft, caring, but also clouded with worry. "I refuse to sit on the sidelines while everyone else fights. I was forced to sit out the fight while my family was killed. I will not make that mistake again."

His thumb brushed my cheek and his jaw tensed for a brief moment. "I'm not asking you to sit on the sidelines. I'm just asking you to allow those who are better equipped to fight right now to fight for you."

I pulled out of his touch and scowled. "I am perfectly capable of fighting. I may break easier than you all do, but that does not make me any less qualified."

"That's not what I meant and you know it." He snapped.

I just sighed and looked back at my hand again.

He came around and kneeled in front of where I was sitting on the bed. He took my face in his hands and made me look at him.

"You are the most powerful sorceress in these lands. We don't need you to fight beasts. We need you to lead the fight against Solas so we can free the people of their rule. You are no good to any of us, beaten and broken, because you insist on fighting a Chupacabra or some other beast by yourself."

He paused, studying my face for a moment. "You are going to lead us to a better world. A better group of leadership that will keep things in order much better than we ever did years ago." He smiled now. "Don't beat yourself up just because you couldn't help years ago. Everything happens for a reason, and you are here now because the people are finally *ready* to accept that we were not evil in the first place."

I didn't know or care if he had been reading my thoughts all this time to have known precisely what to say. I slipped down onto the floor with him and wrapped my arms around his neck. I didn't have words to say what that meant to me, so all I could do was hug him.

After a few moments he pulled back from me. “I do need to get ready. Silas and Elias will be here shortly with a report on the villages near them.”

I nodded and we both stood up. He went over to his dresser to finish getting dressed and I walked to mine to start rummaging through the drawers and dress for the day.

*

I wandered into the kitchen a few hours later while Silas, Aris, Leo, Deiric, and Elias were discussing their reports and the status of the villages around them. Liala was over by the counter, cleaning some of the dishes that were in the sink. She looked up as I walked in.

“I can make you some lunch if you’d like.” She offered with a small smile.

I looked at the dishes in her hands, and glanced back at the guys at the table for a moment. “I’m okay for right now.” I locked eyes with her. “That’s not why I came in here.”

She stopped washing the dish she held in her hands, and lowered them to the edge of the sink, giving me her full attention. “Did you need something else?”

I hesitated, glancing again at her hands holding that dish, then met her gaze again. “Actually, yes.” The guys were still chatting behind us, seeming to not even notice I’d entered the room. “I had a question for you.”

She sat the dish down in the sink and wiped her wet and soapy hands on her dress. “Out with it then.” She said and she turned to face me fully.

"Would you like to train, and learn to fight like the rest of us?" I asked plainly, studying her face and her eyes for her reaction as I spoke.

Her eyes flashed something I couldn't read for a moment, and she just looked at me a bit surprised. I realized in that moment that all conversation at the dining room table had ceased and there was an uncomfortable silence.

"Women don't traditionally train for battle." Was all she said.

I continued to stare into her eyes, not flinching. "I didn't ask you what women traditionally did. I asked you if you'd like to learn."

She hesitated, and glanced to the dining table where they were all watching us intently. I glanced over for a brief moment as well and sighed. A flick of my wrist sent a wall of shadows up between us.

"I also am not asking them. I am asking you." I persisted and her eyes met mine again.

"I'm not sure that I'd be very good at it." She finally said quietly. She looked over at the sink full of dishes. "I've only ever done housework and some simple spells and charms for people." I remembered she was one of the lower level witches. She was not very powerful but had enough magic to do simple enchantments.

"You're a death dealer now, or at least you could be. Would you like to train?" I pushed.

Those gray eyes found their way back to mine, now filled with some cautious optimism. "I suppose it wouldn't hurt to see what I could do. It looks somewhat fun when you guys are all sparring."

I smiled. "Fantastic." Another flick of my wrist had that wall of shadows hurtling toward us, and she flinched, but when she opened her eyes and looked down, I'd used those shadows to dress us both in the same leather armor I'd seen Deiric, Leo, and Aris wear normally. My sword had also appeared, strapped to my hip like it was normally.

She gasped, and patted her clothing for a moment like she couldn't believe it was real. I'd also braided her hair, up and out of the way.

I glanced over at the table, where they all either sat or stood now staring at us in utter shock. Silas's brows were raised and his jaw was practically on the floor. Leo and Aris were surprised, but their faces didn't show it as exceptionally as Silas.

Elias was the only one who seemed a bit unamused or unphased by it. Deiric had an approving smile on his face, but those eyes suggested he was imagining ripping these leathers off of me later. I just smirked and motioned toward the door as I glanced back at Liala. "Shall we?"

She looked at them, looked at me, and then glanced back to the sink of dishes.

"Leave it." I waved my hand and they all disappeared. "We've got a war to prepare for." I smiled at her.

War. We were actually preparing for war. I said the word before, but it didn't really sink in until right then, and hit me right at my core. This wasn't just combat training. We may very well be fighting on a real battlefield at some point.

She returned my smile and walked toward the door, then out to the open grassy area in front of the house. Clearly that statement hadn't landed with her the same way it now landed with me.

"You can pick your jaw off the floor, Silas." I commented as I wandered past them and followed her outside. My voice was colder now. Solemn.

Aris offered me his sword. I nodded my thanks and accepted it. It would work for today, but Liala needed her own blade.

I sat Aris' sword down on the stairs. "We'll get to that, but for now, we need to work on a fighting stance first."

Liala nodded and took a stance that somewhat resembled what she'd likely seen us do when sparring. I chuckled. "You're close, but let me finish explaining first."

I took my own stance for a moment. "Your fighting stance can be wider or narrow, but it needs to be steady and strong." I walked over to her as she held the stance she'd taken. In two swift movements, I'd knocked one leg out from under her and had her almost falling over, but I held her up.

"You are too light on your feet and not grounded in your stance. You don't want to be up on your toes. Keep your heels planted." I released her and she tried again.

I tried the same movements I'd just done and she held firm this time. "Better." I walked around so I was in front of her again. "Once you master a solid stance, you can start to work on building on that to be able to move quickly, while still staying solid on your feet.

I spent the next thirty minutes walking her through stances and movements until she'd gotten them pretty solidly.

"Now let's try these with a blade." I demonstrated how to hold it. She took Aris' sword, worked through the stances a few times again.

"Good." I said. I was a bit impressed already, she was a fast learner.

I demonstrated a few ways to attack and defend, watching her closely as she mimicked them. I spun my sword and faced her. "Now, I want you to apply all of that and come after me."

She looked at me like I was nuts. "I've barely learned how to stand correctly and you want me to attack you?"

"You've watched us train many times, haven't you?" I asked.

She nodded.

"You will only pick up on this and get smoother with it if you actually apply it in a real fight." I smiled. "Don't worry, I'll take it easy on you."

It was almost as if that last comment set a fire in her because she scowled a bit and came at me. *Good.* I thought. I wanted to channel some of that inner rage she had. She was quiet and calm, but I knew there was a fire in there.

Sure enough, I didn't have to take it as easy on her as I thought. She watched me spar with the guys many times over the last few weeks. She learned some of my movements, and began to apply what I just taught her pretty flawlessly.

I saw movement out of the corner of my eye as we continued, our blades crashing together occasionally as we battled it out. The guys had all filed onto the porch and were watching us closely.

"Is that all you've got?" I jabbed at her when she stumbled a bit.

Her eyes were on fire with determination now and she lunged at me again, with more ferocity this time. I wasn't holding back anymore, and she was keeping up, step by step.

A few moments later, she used one of my favorite moves against me and spun my sword right out of my hands.

It went flying toward the house, stabbing in the dirt just before the steps.

She smiled and held her blade flat, pointed right at my throat.

"Nice work." I smiled. "But-" I slammed the back of my forearm up into the side of her sword as I swung around and kicked it out of her hands. "Now what?" I took up a fighting stance with both of my fists up by my face. Her sword skidded across the ground near mine.

She stared at me in complete shock for a moment before lowering into a stance herself.

I waved one of my hands again and a strap of knives appeared across her chest. My knives.

She glanced down, then looked at me. "You don't have any." She said with a little hesitation.

"Prove to me that I need them." I smiled wickedly.

Without a second thought she grabbed two of the knives from the strap I'd put on her, and came at me.

I admit, I was impressed, because we hadn't done anything like this yet, nor had we discussed it. I wondered for a moment if she'd actually fought back that day all those years ago.

Each blow she tried to deal to me I blocked. Each time I reached for a knife from the strap on her, she blocked me. After several minutes she finally managed to land a blow to me, resulting in a small gash on my cheek that had me spinning backward for a moment.

"Fuck." I spat and she paused for a moment.

"I'm sorry, I-" she started to say.

I wiped my face, healing my cheek as I did so. "Nice shot. I think you can do better than that though." I jabbed at her again. We were both a bit out of breath now.

Her jaw tensed, and she came at me again. We continued for several more minutes, before she finally managed to break my stance, spin me around and hold a blade to my throat.

I was breathing hard, both hands on her elbows. Her left arm had wrapped up under my chin and held my head back while her right hand was holding the knife at my throat. I tapped her elbow. “Alright, I yield.”

She released me and I stumbled forward a step, rubbing my throat and trying to catch my breath. I turned to face her and she had a massive smile on her face, her eyes like fire.

I bent over for a moment, bracing myself on my thighs. My hair was a mess, stray pieces all over the place, some stuck to my face with sweat. In between somewhat gasping breaths I finally managed to say. “That’s enough for today. We’ll go again tomorrow.” I stood up and brushed the stray hair back out of my face. I looked over at Aris with a smile.

“Aris, you’re up tomorrow.” I chuckled. “I’ll enjoy watching you get your ass kicked.”

He leaned against the post he stood next to and crossed his arms with a sly smile. “It was quite fun watching *you* get your ass kicked just now.”

“Fuck off.” I spat, still catching my breath. I looked at Deiric, who had the shittiest grin on his face.

“I take it this means you’re going to start campaigning for us to turn women as well.” He crossed his arms and raised a brow.

“You read my mind.” I said plainly, my breathing finally slowing a bit.

Silas walked toward me and put a hand on my shoulder. “It’s about time we shook things up a bit.” He smiled. “Nice form, little wicked one.”

I went to swing at him, a playful punch rather than a real one, and he caught my fist. “Oh no, you’re not going to land another blow on me. Not today anyway.” He released my hand.

“Challenge accepted.” I breathed with a slight smile.

“In the meantime, I’ve given Deiric a list of the villages by our manor who have been plagued with various different beasts. You can take your pick and my men will be at your disposal if you need them.” He glanced back at Elias. “We should get back.”

Elias nodded and walked out to Silas. “We’ll be back in a few weeks.” Was all he said to me before the two of them disappeared.

“I see you’ve remembered how to use magic finally?” Leo jabbed at me after they disappeared.

I scowled at him. “I hadn’t *forgotten* how to use magic. I had just gotten accustomed to not using it.”

He rolled his eyes. “Same difference, to me anyway.”

I turned my focus back to Liala, who was putting the knives back in their holsters, and walked to pick up Aris’ sword. I walked over to her as she stood back up with it and admired the blade.

“I may not *technically* have the authority to do this, but-” I walked around to glance at the tattoo on the back of her neck which barely peeked out over the edge of her armor. “I can change your tattoo if you’d like?”

She raised her brows at me. “To what exactly?”

“Well, you’re not a witch anymore. The only ranking we have for vampires other than elder is a death dealer.” I said quietly. “I could either replace the mark you have with that of a death dealer, or I can add the death dealer mark below it, to honor your past.”

She glanced down at her sword. “I’m hardly trained.” She said softly.

“But you will be.”

She traced her free hand down the blade for a moment. “I’d like to keep my mark, but I would be honored to have the mark of a death dealer also.”

I nodded. I held my hand over her neck and upper back. She winced slightly as I added the swords to the bottom of her tattoo.

Aris came over to us, and reached his hand out to her. She took it, and he pulled her into a half a hug. He patted her shoulder and then pulled back. “I will be honored to fight alongside you one day.” He motioned to the sword, and she handed it back to him. “We’ll get one made for you.” He smiled.

Leo and Deiric followed suit. Deiric looked over at me and smiled. “I told you. You’re going to lead us to a whole new way of thinking.”

I returned his smile. “I think we’ve all earned a drink.” I raised a brow in question to Deiric.

He seemed shocked for a moment, then smirked. “Fine. I’ll dig out another bottle from my stash.” He turned to walk to the house, but then paused and glanced over his shoulder at me. “You better not overdo it again though.”

I laughed. “I’ll try not to.”

We all followed him back inside for a drink.

Chapter 28

Mira

A couple of days later we decided to go to a small village on the edge of the area Silas and his legion covered. From what Deiric had explained, his legion was far larger. I still traveled with two of Deiric's men though. This time, Zane and Renwick were to accompany me, so that each of them had the chance to assist me.

Once we were ready, Zane and Renwick stood close to me, and Macha perched on my shoulder while I shifted us there. We were cloaked in shadows for a moment, before they disappeared to reveal a road ahead of us. I had dropped us a few miles from the village.

Renwick staggered from us and vomited in the bushes. I turned and Zane looked a bit green also, but seemed to be able to keep it down.

"You get used to it." He mumbled, his voice a bit harsh as he glanced over at Renwick. "It's still awful though."

"You've been shifted before?" I asked, raising a brow.

"A long, long time ago, yes." Zane mumbled.

"Let's get moving. Alaric is supposed to meet us at the edge of town." As if I'd told her to scout out, Macha launched off my shoulder and up into the air toward the village.

This village, Eldra, was a bit larger than the last village we'd been to. When we neared the village Alaric stepped out of the trees and took a spot next to me as we walked.

He was tall and slender, his long black hair tied back in a plain ponytail at the base of his head. He didn't wear armor, but instead wore a formal dark gray tunic with silver trim, similar to what I'd seen Silas wear, with plain black pants and boots.

"The village leadership is not expecting you, but they have heard the rumors circulating that the mercenary Scáil has returned, among other things." He commented as we continued toward the village. "I see you've already brought backup with you, but our men are at your disposal should you need them. We believe that it is some kind of cursed Elk. They walk into the woods in a trance and are never seen again."

"Interesting. Where are we to meet the leadership?"

"They'll likely be near the town square at this time of day. They'll recognize you and approach you on their own. We've scouted the area and there aren't any Solas mercenaries or devotees." He stopped when we were less than a hundred feet from the village edge. "Will you be needing anyone from our legion to assist you?"

"I think they'll be able to handle things, but if you'd like to lurk nearby just in case I don't have an issue with that." I said flatly.

He nodded. "Send word if you need anything," and in the blink of an eye he was gone.

I turned and continued walking into the town, Zane and Renwick just a step behind me. We made our way toward the village square, where we passed a small board with posters and bulletins on it. I glanced over and noticed one was a sketch of me, a wanted poster. I stopped, approached the board and grabbed the paper.

"That is a pretty hefty bounty on your head." A male voice commented from somewhere to my left. I lit the paper on fire in my hand and turned to face him. The ashes of the paper blew out of my hand back toward Zane, who stood still and unflinching.

"It is." I commented quietly. My face was still mostly covered with the hood of my cloak. He was tall, somewhat muscular and very blandly handsome. He was well dressed, for a commoner, so I presumed he had to be the village leader Alaric was referring to. His plain brown hair was a bit wavy, and fell to his shoulders. He looked young to be in a leadership position, but I wasn't going to question it.

"I assume you've come to rid us of our beast?" He asked.

I removed my hood finally and stared him down for a moment. "If you would like help with it, yes, I have come to offer my services."

"And your death dealers, what purpose do they serve?"

"They've sworn fealty to me, and travel with me in case I need any assistance. Will their presence be an issue for you?" I asked calmly.

"No. I've heard the rumors. Tell me, is it true what they say, that the Oíche coven does not in fact send these beasts?" He asked.

"Yes. We have no reason to send them to harm or terrorize people. We do not create them or control them. We help destroy them because our abilities make it easier for us, where other mercenaries might fail or be killed because they are too slow or not strong enough."

He nodded, considering for a moment. "What are your terms for your help? A fee as hefty as your bounty?"

"We require no money. We are seeking peace, and requesting that for our services you will aid us in spreading the word that we are not what Solas claims we are." I paused for a moment while he surveyed Zane and Renwick.

"We also require that you do not report us to them. We want things to go back to the balance we had before Solas took over."

"You expect me to trust you, after all that Solas has told us about you?" His face was blank, except for a single raised brow.

"I do not expect anything from you, except the chance to prove that we are not what they say." My voice had an edge to it, that he read right into.

"They say that you are a Dhampir." He looked again at Zane and Renwick before finally settling his gaze on me. "Is that true?"

"Yes." I crossed my arms. "We have nothing to hide from you." Though that wasn't a detail I was eager to blast from the rooftops.

"And if I accept your offer, you will kill the beast and just move on?"

"Yes. We have people in the area to let us know if any other beasts surface, but once we've removed this threat we simply move on to the next." I glanced around at the few villagers who were watching.

"We are trying to prove we can be trusted. We don't *have* to help you. The fact that we've shown up here should be proof enough that we have no ill intentions. Otherwise, there is no sense in risking being turned into Solas for the price on our heads."

"Very well. We will accept your offer." His voice was soft, but contemplative in a way that made me a bit suspicious.

That felt too easy, but I nodded. "We will bring you proof by sunrise tomorrow."

"What of the death dealers that have been lurking in our village? Will they also be moving on when you've finished your task?" He asked when I started to turn to leave.

I stopped and turned to face him again before I replied. "The death dealers that lurk here will not leave. They are tasked with keeping tabs on all threats to the people for us. You can rest assured if another beast finds its way to this town that they will either take care of it, or they will send for us." I glanced around again. "If you prefer they leave, you will be left entirely unprotected."

"Solas protects us." A villager snapped.

I snorted and shot a glare in that villager's direction, unable to control my somewhat amused reaction. "Solas has left you to deal with this beast on your own. They will not step up if another takes its place. Their protection stops at protecting you from us, which they've never had to do in the first place."

I turned my gaze from that villager back to the leader who I'd been speaking to. "If you wish for them to leave, simply say the word when we've brought you proof and I'll see to it that it is done."

He nodded and I turned to leave. We had plenty of time before sundown to make a plan and find this cursed beast. I needed to create shields for myself, Zane, and Renwick to prevent us from being put in a trance.

Before we began tracking or searching for it, I put a shield up around all three of our minds, blocking the ability for the trance to be used against us. We headed out to the last place a villager was seen walking into the woods. Eventually I picked up on the track where they'd walked through the woods and followed it to a small cave that tunneled deep underground.

"Surely going in there is *not* a good idea." Renwick commented.

"It certainly isn't what I'd advise." I commented, peering down into it as far as I could see. A moment later I saw a glimmer of white as the skull of a massive elk came into view, with antlers stretching as wide as I was tall. The massive and grotesque beast came charging up from the hole.

I tried to back up and was not fast enough as it flew from the cave and grabbed me by the throat with one of its hideous claws and pinned me to the ground about twenty feet back from where I'd been standing.

Zane shouted and Renwick charged it. The beast turned its attention to Renwick just as he was within striking distance and swung its massive rack of antlers at him.

Renwick screamed as he was stabbed and then blasted back with enough force to rattle the tree he hit.

I got to my feet and held my sword out to distract it while Zane crept up behind it. I threw a knife into its left side, and it turned to me, charging forward with horrifying speed. I put up a shield of wind in front of me which it slammed into. It only seemed slightly dazed.

Renwick had risen from where he'd been slammed against the tree, slightly unsteady, but he went to charge it again just as Zane launched himself from where he'd been creeping up behind it and stabbed the beast right in the back.

It let out an awful howl, but did not completely go down. It thrashed where Zane still held on, withdrawing his sword to stab it again. With its focus on Zane and Renwick I ran toward it and slid underneath it to get to the sensitive spot below its rib cage and stab it in the heart.

I didn't notice until after it died and began to fall that I'd sliced my side on one of its talons as I slid underneath it.

"Shit." I gasped as it landed half on my legs and I was pinned gripping my side, which was now gaping open and bleeding.

Zane was at my side in a matter of seconds. "When the hell did that happen?" He asked, staring at the gash.

"I must've hit one of its talons when I slid under it to kill it." I grumbled. "Can you get it off me so I can move?"

Renwick was next to me a moment later and he drug me out from under it while Zane lifted it off my legs. He laid me down gently and came around to my side to try to help me, but I was already working on healing it.

"What the hell is that thing?" Renwick asked, realizing I would be fine in a few moments.

"Does it matter?" Zane asked. He went around and broke off an antler. "This will make a fine piece of proof." He commented. "I'm half tempted to use it as a trophy myself."

I scoffed, sitting up now that my side was at least healed enough that it wasn't killing me. "You didn't deal the killing blow, so that would be my trophy."

Alaric appeared from the trees. "Is everyone alright?" He seemed genuinely concerned. I lifted myself up to my feet and he looked me up and down. "Are you alright?"

He stared at the blood and my tattered clothing. Half of me was covered in the black sludge like blood from the beast and the other half was my own blood.

"I'm fine." I said, but he was already next to me and looking me over, confused when he didn't see a source of the blood. "I healed myself."

His eyes finally settled on the slightly red area where the gash had been. He nodded. "I see you found the beast. Faster than I would've thought." He looked over at Zane and Renwick.

"I've had lots of time to practice tracking these sorts of things. This is the first one of its kind I've seen. It did take all of us to bring it down though." I stared at it, it was massive. "I'm not sure I could've gotten this one on my own." I was not afraid to admit it. It was three times the size of any of us.

"Would you like some fresh clothes?" Alaric asked.

"I will, but I'll worry about that later." I didn't need to use more magic than necessary when we were outside of the shields and wards of the house, regardless of the Morrigan shielding me. "We can probably make it back to the village before the sun even goes down." I looked back at Zane and Renwick who merely nodded in acknowledgement.

"You are welcome to come to our manor when you're finished." Alaric said with a small smile. "I am sure the rest of our legion would appreciate meeting you. Silas can have a change of clothes waiting for you there, as well as a meal, if you'd like."

I glanced at Zane and Renwick, who merely shrugged. "We will come to your manor afterward, but we'll be returning home before nightfall."

Alaric nodded, "Meet me at the village limits when you're done." He disappeared.

*

We walked into the town square just before sundown. One of the villagers went to retrieve the leader we'd spoken to earlier in the day. After a few minutes he was walking up to meet us. Zane tossed the rack of antlers to the ground between us.

"As promised, here is a part of the antlers of the beast that was lurking in your woods." I said flatly.

He examined them and looked me up and down, my dress and corset were shredded, and my cloak also had been tattered and torn. The blood had dried some by now.

"Are you alright?" He asked.

I glanced down at my shredded clothing. "We are alright."

"We will permit the death dealers to remain here, as long as their only purpose is to monitor for future threats." He said, still carefully examining the damage to my clothing, and that of Renwick's armor.

I nodded. "You have my word. They are only here to keep an eye on the safety of the village."

"Thank you." He said, and it felt like his words were actually genuine for once.

I merely nodded and we headed out to the edge of the village to meet Alaric.

Alaric was waiting patiently in the road where we'd met him earlier in the day, and then led us to a large manor about a mile outside of town and far more than a mile away from the road. It was significantly larger than Deiric's home, my home, and clearly housed more than vampires. When we walked through the large entryway there were several people in the foyer, which rivaled that of a castle. Some of them glanced at us in confusion and intrigue.

Alaric turned to Zane and Renwick. "Vlad will show you to a room to freshen up." His gaze shifted to me. "Follow me."

I glanced back at Zane and Renwick, who were a bit reluctant to leave with the man Alaric had motioned to, but I nodded that I was okay, and they followed him.

Alaric led me to a room down a hall just off of the main entryway. It was a small bedroom. "Silas left a change of clothes for you. When you're changed and cleaned up he would like you, Zane, and Renwick to join all of us in the main dining room. Esther will show you to the room when you're ready." He glanced around the room. "There is a small bathing room in the corner." He said, before he left the room and left me by myself.

I glanced around, my change of clothes had been left on the small couch in the middle of the room. I walked over to find a black sparkly dress made of the most exquisite silk, and nothing more. I scowled a bit. I'd never worn a formal gown, and this appeared to be far more formal than I was used to.

I cleaned off my face and any other dirt that lingered on me in the bathing room before I put on the dress. It was soft and stretchy, but fit me like it was made for me. It had a neckline that wrapped around the back of my neck leaving my shoulders exposed, with the front dipping so low that it went to the middle of my chest, between my breasts. The back was completely open, with it finally wrapping around me just above the base of my spine, revealing the entirety of the moon phase tattoo down my back, as well as my scars. It had a small train on the back.

There was a light knock on the door, I opened it to find a woman, slightly shorter than me with long auburn hair staring back at me. She smiled.

"My name is Esther. I see the dress fits you quite well." She admired it for a brief moment. "Silas picked it out himself. He has exquisite taste, don't you think?"

I examined her slowly. Her clothing was far more plain, simple. She wore a blush pink dress, floor length, sleeveless, that hugged her curves tightly but was flowing and loose below her hips. "It is far more formal than I expected." I observed.

She brushed past me into the room and motioned for me to sit in front of a small vanity along the wall. "Your hair is a mess. Allow me to help you with it?" She asked.

It felt more like an order than a question, but I walked over and sat down. She gently brushed out my hair, frowning occasionally when she pulled out something that had likely gotten into my hair when I'd slid under the beast earlier. I hadn't put the effort into washing or cleaning my hair.

When she finished brushing and was satisfied, she put it into a very simple long braid down my back. A relief I supposed, since that is what I traditionally did myself.

"They're waiting in the dining room for you." She said once she'd finished the braid. "Follow me."

She led me to the dining room in silence. The entire manor was rather ornate in nature, the dining room was no exception. It was huge, probably the size of our house. Silas sat at the head of the table. Zane and Renwick were already seated along one side of the very long table, and I was gestured to sit at the other end of the table.

They sat to my immediate left. The looks on Zane and Renwick's faces were indescribable, as they had not seen me in anything other than a plain skirt, corset, and blouse or some form of armor. I at least didn't feel entirely out of place, because everyone in his manor seemed to be dressed rather exquisitely as well.

"Welcome to my home." Silas said, waving his arms to welcome me as I walked to the chair Esther had directed me to. "That dress looks even better on you than I would've thought." His smile was absolutely wicked. "Please, sit. Have a drink and enjoy the food."

I did as I was instructed, but did not touch my drink.

"I hear you were injured in today's hunt." Silas said from the other end of the table, watching me intently.

"I sliced my side on one of the beast's talons while delivering the killing blow." I explained.

He smiled. "You were able to use your magic to heal yourself I see."

I glanced up from the food he'd provided. "Yes, I've found a way to shield myself to allow me to use my magic."

"Interesting." He said softly. "Yet Deiric has insisted you travel with at least two of his men." He gestured toward Zane and Renwick, who sat awkwardly at the table unsure which of us to focus on.

"Yes." I said quietly. "It's a good thing too because this beast was not one I could've killed on my own."

"I seriously doubt that."

"If I relied solely on my magic I may have killed it on my own, but it was hardly worth trying to do that." I maintained a steady eye contact with him now. "Did you invite us here simply to discuss that, or was there another purpose to this visit?"

"You are all business aren't you?" He smirked. "Deiric told me that you'd be entirely uninterested in anything beyond business. I had hoped I might crack that hard facade you always have on if I wined and dined you a bit."

"Surely you're smarter than that."

Alaric practically choked on his drink next to me. Silas sent him a glare.

I took this moment to glance around at the table. Elias sat to Silas' right, and I assumed the rest of the men on that side of the table were warlocks or sorcerers, since they had food in front of them as well. Except for Zane and Renwick of course.

The other side of the table just had glasses in front of them with what I assumed to be blood or liquor. I glanced at Alaric, who merely nodded as if he'd heard me thinking. Fantastic, another mind reader. He smiled slightly confirming that thought.

"If you were trying to impress me, you'd have been better off going for an interesting knife or sword than a fancy dress." I looked at Silas again. "But you knew that already."

He scoffed. "You really have no interest in things that are more feminine? Jewels, gowns, and whatever it is other women would enjoy?"

I scowled at him. "I am a mercenary." I said with a hint of annoyance, as if that furthered my point that riches and finery weren't going to help his case.

"You are a sorceress. You became a mercenary out of necessity. Surely at one point in your life you were more interested in something other than weaponry?" He also raised a brow, that wicked smile remaining on his face.

"Oh, there's plenty that interests me more than weaponry, but I doubt you can provide any of that to me." I decided I'd bait him. There wasn't much beyond weaponry he could try to charm me with.

"I'll accept that challenge." He swirled whatever was in his glass. "How do you like the dress anyway?"

I looked down at myself again. "It's a bit much for my taste, but I suspect you knew that already too."

He scoffed. "I even went for the least fancy out of all of the dresses I could find. I suppose it was foolish of me to think I could win you over when you've already chosen an elder for yourself." He quipped, finishing his drink.

"A valiant effort." I said, with a half smile. "Deiric didn't win my affection with gifts. He won it with respect.. Among other things."

Renwick shifted in his chair. Zane remained stone faced, and cold.

Silas's eyes were like fire. "Really? Do tell."

"The intricacies of my relationship with him is none of your business." I said bluntly.

He frowned. "You haven't touched the mead. Is it not to your liking?"

I glanced up at him. I'd begun idly eating the food he'd provided while we spoke. "I prefer whiskey."

Zane chuckled a bit, which prompted a small smile from me.

Elias waived his hand and the goblet disappeared, leaving a short glass in its place with whiskey. "From Silas' private reserve." He said simply.

I raised a brow at Elias and he just shrugged.

"You probably want to be careful with that." Silas added with a sly smile.

"She knows that already." Alaric said with a smirk, before I had even had the chance to take a breath to speak. I frowned at him for dipping into my thoughts again.

I reached for the glass and carefully took a very small sip. It was just as smooth as what Deiric had. When I set the glass back down, I looked over the group of men in front of me again before settling my gaze on Silas. "Is there a purpose to this dinner, other than trying to shoot your shot with me because you're a little jealous of Deiric?"

"You took care of a problem for one of my villages in the name of bringing some power back to this coven. Consider this my thank you."

I half laughed. "Should I expect this after every problem I take care of for you?"

Silas snorted. "Perhaps."

"Perhaps next time then you'll find more appropriate attire for me." I raised a brow and smirked.

"Oh I like her." One of his death dealers commented, while the others were snickering a bit and struggling to hide their amusement.

He hissed at them, but then looked back at me. "I do enjoy these little games of ours." He smiled slightly.

"It's hardly a fair game. You make it far too easy to insult you."

Both brows raised, and even the sorcerers and Elias had a laugh at that comment.

"I've certainly underestimated you."

"Don't take it personally. Most people do." I glanced at Zane and Renwick, who were both smiling slightly as they watched silently. "We should get going. I'd like to get back before sundown."

"Oh certainly. I wouldn't want to keep Deiric waiting for you." That wicked smile returned to his lips. "Be sure to let me know what he thinks of the dress I've chosen for you."

I rose from my seat, tossed back what remained of my drink, and gave him a wicked smile of my own. "I'm sure he will appreciate how easy it is to take off."

Even Silas, despite his jabs and general enjoyment from this little game with me, was not prepared for my response, and was left a bit speechless. The look of surprise on his face was quite priceless. Renwick had choked on his drink. Alaric was beaming and tipped his glass to me. Some of the others were desperately trying *not* to laugh. Elias had covered his face with his hand and was looking down in his lap.

"Shall we?" I looked at Zane and Renwick, who rose at that question. "Thank you for dinner."

Silas cleared his throat, finally finding his voice. "I also had this made for you." He said, and Elias waived his hand at the moment he finished speaking.

A sword appeared on the table in front of me, where my plate had been. The sheath was an ornate black leather, and the hilt had a very soft black leather grip with equally ornate designs as the sheath.

"I anticipated you wouldn't appreciate the gown, so I had this made as well." I glanced at him briefly to see that sultry smile on his lips, but returned my attention to the sword.

I picked it up, pulling it from the sheath to fully examine it. It was light, perfectly balanced and smaller than the blade I typically carried. I offered him a small smile.

"It seems you do know me a bit better than I thought." I said as I slipped it back into the sheath.

His sultry smile turned into a wicked grin. "I'll accept that as a thank you, I suppose."

I waved my hand and my weapons appeared in it, summoned from where I left them before dinner. "Until next time." I smiled and turned to leave.

The table went eerily silent. I realized as I took a few steps away, that none of them, including Zane and Renwick had ever seen anything more than my shoulders. They had not seen my scars from my many battles before meeting them and finding a way to use my magic. The scars certainly weren't anything horrifying or overwhelming, but there were enough of them that anyone might cringe or feel a bit awful at the sight of them. I stood tall as we walked out of the dining room and then out of the manor.

Macha landed on my shoulder when we descended the stairs and I shifted us back to the house.

When the shadows cleared, I was just steps in front of Deiric, who was casually sitting on the stairs and watching Aris and Liala train behind us.

Liala and Aris stopped when they saw us.

"You're back sooner than I would've expected." Deiric said as he stood up and looked me over. Macha flew off of my shoulder to perch on the roof. "You're a little over dressed for hunting monsters. Who do I have to thank for this?" He smiled as he came up closer to me to examine the dress.

"Silas thought you might like it." I smiled.

"Silas also gave her some of his personal reserve of whiskey." Zane said as he walked past us. "I give her twenty minutes before she's drunk out of her mind."

"She actually handles her liquor quite well." Deiric said, without taking his eyes off of me.

"I told him you'd probably appreciate how easy the dress would be to take off."

Deiric laughed. "I'm sure that made him regret his choices pretty quickly."

"It was fun to watch him squirm. He even gave me an audience to embarrass him in front of."

Deiric grabbed my weapons from me and slipped his hand to the small of my back. "Let's get you inside before you *do* start to feel that drink." He paused for a moment when he took in the sword Silas had given me. "I assume he had this made for you as well?"

I shrugged. "He is desperate to impress me, I guess."

Deiric just huffed a laugh.

I let him lead me inside and up the stairs to the bedroom. "This does look incredible on you, by the way." He said when we were finally alone. "While I realize he didn't choose this for my benefit, I do like it."

I slipped my arms up around his neck. "Is this your way of saying you'd like me to dress up more often?" I said with a small smile.

"Maybe." he returned my smile and his hands slid to where the dress rested at the base of my spine.

"Join me for a bath?" I asked, and I waved my hand to the bathing room, where I filled the tub with nice hot water and some of those salts and oils that Liala had given me when I'd first sparred with them.

He answered by pulling on the neckline of the dress to get it up and over my head, and let it drop to the floor. "I'd love to."

I pulled off his shirt and grabbed his hand to drag him with me to the tub.

Chapter 29

Mira

We decided we would go to Deilginis next, where they seemed to be having issues with a Lanzani. This time, Deiric and Xander would accompany me.

Deiric was still sleeping soundly against me with his arm wrapped snugly around my waist. I lay there quietly for a few moments just enjoying the calm of the house before anyone stirred. I could hear the birds chirping outside of the window, and it was so peaceful.

I don't think I'd ever taken the time to just lay still and listen before. I usually woke and got right out of bed, but if I moved I'd surely wake Deiric, so I was forced for a few moments to either try and fall back asleep or to lay quietly and just take it all in.

After a while, I slid my arm down slightly so I could interlace my fingers with his where they were resting against my chest.

He took in a slightly deeper breath and squeezed my fingers, and then me, for a breath before he relaxed again. "Good morning." His voice was still groggy with sleep.

"Morning." I said softly.

He didn't move, just laid there in silence for several minutes almost like he was starting to drift off to sleep again. "We don't have to go to Deilginis today." He kissed the back of my neck. I sighed and pressed myself into him in response. "We could just lay in bed all day," he whispered. He kissed down along my shoulder.

I turned my head to look at him, and he had a sleepy smile on his lips. "We don't have to go, but we *should* go." I smiled back at him.

He sighed. "Where's the fun in that?" His eyes traced down my body and then back up to meet mine. "We could go tomorrow instead."

I turned myself so I was laying on my back now, looking up at him. "You're insufferable." I said with a small smile. "While the idea of laying here all day with you is very enticing, I think that the people of Deilginis would like to be able to safely wander outside of their village."

He grumbled. "Fine." He leaned down and gently kissed me, before letting his hand start to wander.

I grabbed his hand before it got too far. "Are you just doing this because you are worried I won't let you and Xander take care of the beast for me?"

His face was still inches from mine, and I could've sworn I saw surprise and a little bit of disappointment in his eyes. "I'd rather you let us take care of it, but whether we went today or tomorrow wouldn't change your opinion or mine." He paused, pulling his hand free of my grasp and sliding it down my thigh. "I would just prefer to have one day with you all to myself." He gave me a sultry smile. "Is that too much to ask?"

I slipped one of my hands up and into his hair and smiled at him. "No, it's not too much to ask, but *I* would rather not put this off another day." I pulled him into a soft and gentle kiss, despite that I now also really wanted to throw myself onto him. "Perhaps we can spend the day in bed tomorrow instead?"

"Hmm." He grabbed my thigh now and rolled onto his back, pulling me up on top of him. "That's not what you're thinking about though."

I pushed myself so I was sitting up straight, sitting just above his hips now, and just smirked down at him. His hands rested on my hips. "You know I hate it when you do that."

He had an amused grin on his face now. "I hate when you *insist* on being all business."

I rolled my eyes and tried to get up off of him to get dressed, but he held me firmly in place. I leaned down into him and slid my right hand up to his throat, as though I'd hold him there and choke him. His smile only widened.

"Go ahead, I might enjoy that." He stared up at me, his eyes on fire with excitement and amusement.

I scoffed. "You are *absolutely* insane." I went to move to get up again and this time he let me, but he watched me walk to the dresser with that excitement and amusement still lingering in his eyes. "You should get up and get dressed too, you know." I said flatly.

After watching me put on my underwear and bra he finally slowly climbed out of bed and wandered over to the other dresser to get dressed himself.

*

The day went by rather quickly. Eimear had decided that she was going to go out to a few of the villages nearby for a few days, saying she wanted to get out of the house a bit before our next big meeting and maybe catch up with a friend or two. I helped her pack a bag to hold her over for a few days while she traveled and then saw her off.

Shortly after I'd finished my dinner, Deiric and Xander came in to get me so we could be on our way to Deilginis. I strapped on my knives and my sword, which I had brought down with me and laid on the table that morning, and we all shuffled outside. Macha landed on my shoulder and I shifted us just outside of town.

We walked into town and didn't get very far before a woman came up to me and stopped right in my path.

"You're Scáil?" She asked, quietly.

I nodded.

"Follow me." She glanced behind me at Deiric and Xander with a tinge of fear in her eyes before she turned and led us through the town to a manor far more extravagant than the buildings surrounding it. When we approached the door it opened as if they were expecting us and a man was standing just inside, holding the door open with a smile on his face.

"Ah yes, the infamous Scáil!" He said excitedly. "We've been expecting you for some time." He was dressed rather casually, his white shirt partially unbuttoned but tucked into his leather pants. His hair was golden brown and curly. It fell to just beyond his eyebrows and would've covered his eyes if it hadn't been so fluffy with the bounce from his curls.

"I assume you're here to handle our Lanzani problem?" He stepped to the side as he spoke, allowing the woman to walk inside past him. He motioned for us to follow, but I stayed on the front steps.

"Yes." I said coldly. "I assume if you're expecting us, then you already know our price."

His smile widened. "Yes, I'm very aware of your terms. It's about time that we see some changes!" He glanced behind me at Deiric and Xander, who simply stood stone faced and silent on either side of me, just one step back. "And these must be two death dealers. Daywalkers." He specified. "A pleasure to meet you."

He seemed far too excited, but who was I to judge? "Do you accept our terms then?" I asked.

His attention turned back to me. "Of course!" He offered a slight bow. "I don't require proof. I trust at this point that you'll just come tell me when it's been done and be on your way. However, if you do decide you'd like to stay, our innkeeper would be glad to give you a room at no charge, and I'm sure you'll find the folks in the tavern will be quite welcoming as well."

I raised a brow at that. "You seem far more excited than most to be working with us."

"I've never been a fan of those pompous pricks. Quite honestly I'm excited to be involved in some kind of revolution. The people here will be glad to be rid of the Lanzani at any price, so I thank you for taking the time for us."

I offered a half smile, and then nodded. "We'll return when we've taken care of it."

He merely smiled, nodded, and then said "best of luck" before closing the door.

I turned to find Deiric and Xander's faces had switched from that stone cold look to that of a bit of shock. I smirked. "It isn't *usually* that easy."

Deiric looked at me in confusion. "That was almost *too* easy."

"Well, you said yourself that some people are tired of them. Clearly he is overly excited to work with us, so I'm sure word is traveling quickly." I glanced above us to where Macha was slowly circling. "If we had anything to worry about, Macha would notice and tell us."

Deiric nodded, but just barely, and I walked between them to go back down the stairs and into the streets. "Shall we?" I asked and motioned toward the edge of town.

Deiric and Xander followed me out to the edge of town and then into the woods.

"We should split up." Xander said quietly. The sun was setting behind us. "It will attack regardless, but if we are slightly spread out, we'll have a better chance of surprising it when it goes after one of us."

Deiric looked at me, his eyes showing the little bit of worry his face didn't convey. "He's right." I said softly. "But we won't put too much distance between ourselves."

I turned and headed out straight into the woods while Xander flanked to the left and Deiric flanked to my right.

It took half the night of searching before I finally heard a rustling ahead of me, slightly to the right. I stopped and listened closely, trying my best not to make a single sound.

There was a deafening growl followed by a massive beast, at least twice my size coming flying from the brush in front of me headed straight for my face. It could've resembled a bear, if it didn't look so absolutely rabid and massive. Its jagged teeth glimmered in the moonlight and its claws were huge. Similar to the Chimera I'd battled not long ago.

Anticipating it to be similar in strength to the Chimera, I held my ground and swung my sword at it, but I vastly underestimated the force with which it flew at me. I had sliced both of its front legs, but it didn't falter in its advance.

I tried to duck or dodge. I was not fast enough, and it bit down on my shoulder and left arm before I could get out of the way.

I screamed in pain and it jerked its head and threw me to the side like a ragdoll, slamming me into a tree. My sword went flying somewhere behind me, further into the trees toward Deiric.

I was gasping for air, the wind knocked out of me and my left arm was almost useless, dripping in blood from the massive wounds to my shoulder and upper bicep. I tried to roll and prop myself up but I only managed to roll onto my side to face the beast.

Deiric was there less than a second later, followed by Xander. The Lanzani charged for me again, but Deiric charged as well and slammed into it from the side, stabbing it with his sword and shoving it further away from me.

Xander was next to them now, slitting its throat before it turned to go after Deiric, but it still thrashed and hissed.

Deiric withdrew his sword and lunged for it again, though it was dying anyway, and stabbed at its chest. After a few moments, it finally stopped thrashing, and died.

Xander ran over to me first, finding me laying on my side in a pool of blood, still gasping and trying to catch my breath. I couldn't move. Every time I tried my shoulder and arm were lit on fire with pain.

Deiric arrived less than a second later, right in front of me, kneeling. "Mira." His face was wild, ragged with worry. "You should have yelled for one of us." He scolded as he tried to assess the damage.

I winced and yelped as he lifted my arm and evaluated it. "I didn't… have the chance." I gasped. I could feel the color draining from my face.

"Shit." Deiric cursed. I saw him tearing at his armor by his wrist. A moment later he held that same wrist to my lips and the metallic taste of blood filled my mouth. "Drink Mira." He demanded.

I was delirious, barely conscious now, but I did as I was told.

He withdrew his arm and breathed a sigh of relief as my arm and shoulder mended themselves in a matter of seconds.

I took a deep breath finally and started to lift myself onto my elbow. I was still breathing raggedly for a few moments until I got my bearings.

I looked around, and didn't realize how much blood I'd lost until then. I was laying in it, my hands were covered in it. Xander was still looking down at me in horror, but had taken a few steps back. I could see him fighting to keep himself under control for a few moments until he was a bit farther away.

"You could have *died*, Mira." Deiric finally said, still kneeling next to me, in my blood. His eyes were distant, some relief lingered there, but so many other emotions as well that it was hard to read.

I pushed myself up to a sitting position, then onto my knees, before I finally said, "I didn't have the chance to yell. I heard it, and then it was launching itself at me."

"Why on earth didn't you use your magic?" He was furious now, I realized.

"I didn't have the chance to even think of using it." I said too quietly. "I acted based on instinct, which I've trained myself *isn't* magic first."

He sighed and rubbed his face with one of his blood covered hands. Then, realizing that he now had blood all over his face, he half laughed. It was one of those laughs, where it was almost concerning and entirely unnerving, given the circumstance.

My face must've said what I was feeling about that, because his expression softened when he looked at me. "This is why I don't want you doing this without one of us." His tone was serious, but no longer angry. "You would've died if you came alone. Hell, you may have died if it wasn't *me* here."

"I guess we *should've* stayed in bed all day today." I tried to joke with him, but the half smile he gave me didn't reach his eyes.

"I'm sorry." I said softly.

He sighed again. "It isn't your fault. You're human." Then he rose to his feet and offered a hand to help me up.

I stood, and scowled down at myself. I was soaked in my own blood, and so was he. I waved my hand and cleaned both of us up.

"Let's head back to town." He mumbled. We all stalked back in the direction of the town. The sun was coming up already. By the time we got back to town it would be nearly lunch time, we'd wandered so far into the woods.

Chapter 30

Mira

We arrived at the town limits just after noon. The woman who'd approached us the evening before was waiting outside of the manor when we finally reached it, and looked genuinely worried.

"We were worried something had happened." She said, breathing a sigh of relief.

Deiric remained silent, but I would imagine that his face wasn't as stone cold as it had been the day before. Neither of them were putting on very good faces, it seemed, because the woman looked at both of them and then studied me carefully.

"It didn't go exactly as we'd planned, but it is dead." I said flatly.

She offered me a half smile and nodded. "Thank you." She glanced back at the two of them again, before she said, "his offer still stands. You're welcome to stop by the tavern, and you'll likely be welcomed with drinks, or a meal." Her eyes settled on me as she said that.

"Thank you. We'll likely be moving on though." I said simply.

She just nodded and turned to go into the house to deliver the news.

I turned to walk away and met eyes with Deiric briefly. His eyes and the look on his face very plainly said '*it didn't go exactly as we planned'* was an understatement. I walked between them to head out to the edge of town. Macha circled above us, discreetly. I didn't know where she'd been while we were tracking it. I didn't feel it necessary to ask.

Deiric and Xander fell into step behind me as we worked our way back out to the road that led out of town. I wasn't really paying attention to anything around me, when a familiar voice stopped me in my tracks.

"Scáil?"

Deiric and Xander stopped just as abruptly as I had.

"Cedric?" I said, as I turned to my left to look at him.

He looked relieved to see me. He wore that familiar leather jacket, his lute slung over his shoulder on his back, and had a black tunic with silver embroidery. His hair was a bit messier than I remembered, but otherwise he looked the same.

He smiled now. "I hoped I might catch back up with you eventually." He glanced at Deiric and Xander briefly before his eyes met mine again. "I thought you'd been captured or killed, until I heard murmurings about your latest adventures," his gaze shifted to Deiric and Xander again who had moved so they were both behind me again, as I faced Cedric, "with two death dealers."

Their expressions must've changed at that comment, because his face now seemed to have a tinge of fear in it.

"Captured twice." I said, with a small smile. "They have a tendency to underestimate me."

He smirked, his face relaxing a bit. "I'd be glad to buy you drinks so I could hear those tales."

Deiric stepped closer to me, subtly. I didn't turn my head, but glanced at him out of the corner of my eye, at the same moment Cedric did, then I looked back at him. "Unfortunately, we need to be moving on." I said as I met Cedric's eyes again.

Cedric gave me a sultry smile, ignoring Deiric's proximity to me. "Are you sure?" He reached into a hidden pocket inside the top lapel of his jacket and pulled out a piece of paper. He opened it, "Until next time. I look forward to hearing your songs." He raised a brow. "I'll be playing in the tavern shortly."

My cheeks heated. He'd kept the note, a reminder of that evening, I guess.

"I'd like to hear the songs." Xander spoke up.

Deiric and I both looked at him incredulously. He returned our looks with raised eyebrows and crossed arms.

"What?" He glanced sidelong at us. "It'd be nice to hear about a *successful* tale after that shit show back there."

I scoffed at him. "Thanks, asshole."

Deiric finally let out a small relieved laugh.

I looked back over at Cedric who looked completely confused. "So… you're coming to the tavern then?" He tucked the note back into his jacket and stepped toward us, waving his hand and pointing his finger around at us. "All of you?"

I smiled, and looked over at Deiric. He had a slightly bemused look on his face, and merely crossed his arms and shrugged.

"Sure." I looked back to Cedric. "I suppose we do technically have time." I gestured with my chin. "Lead the way."

He hooked his arm on my elbow before I could move away from him and excitedly began tugging me in the direction of the tavern.

Deiric's eyes met mine as I was tugged past him. His brow furrowed, eyes narrowed, and his lips pressed into a firm line.

I just smirked at him, waved my hand to say not to worry about it, and fell into step with Cedric.

"I don't think he likes me." Cedric commented after we were a few steps ahead of them as they followed behind us.

I glanced at him and he had a devilish grin on his face. "He isn't a fan of you because he knows precisely what happened the night I told you those stories." I gave him a slightly devious grin of my own.

He raised a brow. "I'm not sure if I should be flattered or insulted."

"Nervous is the word you're looking for." Deiric commented from behind us. His tone was only mildly threatening, with a slight tinge to it that suggested it was a joke. I knew it wasn't.

Cedric glanced back at him, and I am guessing the look on Deiric's face reiterated the threat, because Cedric's head snapped around quickly and he relaxed his grip on me a bit. "You could've explained that a little better." He muttered.

I chuckled. "You didn't exactly give me the chance to." I looked ahead to where we were going. "I'm sorry."

I could see him studying me out of the corner of my eye for a moment, and then glancing back at Deiric again.

"I'm happy for you." He said, much quieter, knowing Deiric could likely hear it anyway.

I could see the tavern up ahead. I glanced over at him.

"I can read between the lines Scáil." He said plainly, locking eyes with me for a moment. I opened my mouth to speak, but he stopped me. "We had one *very,*" he smiled, "fun night." He looked ahead to the tavern now. "I hoped to run into you again for no other reason than I wanted to make sure you were alright *and* I couldn't have you go and die before you heard the absolute masterpieces I created from your stories."

I knew that he was partially lying. I could see the slight pain in his eyes even though he looked away. I walked the rest of the way in silence.

When we reached the door he held it open for all of us. The barkeep smiled at me when I walked in.

"What are we all drinking?" She shouted from behind the bar.

I glanced back at Deiric. He was looking at Cedric, a slight look of amusement on his face as Cedric shuffled away to go set up to play. He looked at me finally, and then looked beyond me to the barkeep. "Whiskey." He said flatly.

I looked back just in time to see her smile and turn around to prepare drinks for us. I spun around again to look at Deiric, who was right in front of me now, forcing me to look up at him.

"You slept with *him?*" His eyebrows were raised, and the bemused look on his face made me want to slap him. That thought resulted in a smirk from him.

I gently punched him in the chest. “Don’t you judge me.” I smirked as I turned to find somewhere for us to sit.

He had a grin on his face that was dripping with amusement when I sat down at a table close to where Cedric was setting up and I looked back up at him again.

“I’m just trying to see what you saw in him is all.” He mocked. Xander walked around to sit on the other side of the table, while Deiric sat next to me, his arm resting on the table behind me. “Were you just that drunk?”

I jabbed him with my elbow. He feigned pain for a moment, then smiled wickedly at me. “He’s quite charming actually.” I said plainly. “He might not have the allure of the dark and mysterious death dealer, but he’s certainly attractive in his own right.”

Deiric rolled his eyes. The barkeep brought our drinks over and smiled.

“This round is on the house, as a thank you.” She said plainly. “Enjoy the entertainment, and best of luck in your travels.” It was like she knew we wouldn’t be staying very long.

“Am I missing something here?” Xander finally spoke up behind us.

Deiric glanced over his shoulder at him. “She seems to enjoy bards. In more ways than one.” He smirked.

Xander practically spit out his drink.

I turned to face him with a quick glare. “*You* don’t get to judge me either.”

He put his hands up and looked down at the table, brows raised a little bit in amusement and defeat. He wasn’t going to push his luck.

We all turned and watched as Cedric set up, and then eventually began his set for the afternoon and evening. He made sure to make a grandiose gesture toward us, or rather, toward me. The guest of honor, who he'd sing about this evening. I simply raised my glass to him in response.

His responding wink made Deiric clear his throat and shift in his seat. I jabbed him with my elbow and caused him to almost spit his drink out. My sidelong glance was enough to tell him to drop it.

Chapter 31

Mira

We had just finished our drinks when two men burst through the door, dragging someone with them.

Deiric and Xander immediately jumped to attention, but didn't rise from the table. I watched cautiously as the men came over to us and chucked who they were dragging in front of us.

The man wore a long navy cloak, which covered his face until they'd chucked him to the floor. I recognized him immediately. He was the man who shot me with those arrows. I shot right to my feet.

"We found him lurking on the edge of town. The Lord had us interrogate him, and we found out he was a Solas mercenary. We thought you'd like to handle him." One of the men said.

Cedric had stopped playing, and everyone had stopped and stared at us. Rage boiled in me, as I glared down at him.

There was nothing but fear in his eyes as he stared up at me.

"You." I seethed.

Deiric rose now, also glaring down at him. "Did you get anything else out of him?" He asked of the two men that delivered him to us.

"Other than that he was lurking here because he thought *she* would show up, no." The other man said.

I watched him as he looked at Deiric, the two men that drug him here, and then behind me at Xander, who I assumed had also risen to his feet. His eyes met mine again, and I knew he was going to run.

He started to scramble to his feet to make a dash for the door, and I pulled one of my knives out in a swift motion and slammed it into his left shoulder, right where the arrow had been in mine. Then I took another knife and hit his thigh in the same place he'd struck mine. He shrieked in pain and crumbled back to the floor.

"Oh, I'm sorry. Is that painful?" I barely recognized my own voice, but I was overjoyed to get my revenge at last.

"You bitch." He spat.

I knelt down next to him and twisted the knife that was still in his shoulder and he screamed.

"If you're going to kill me, just get on with it." He spat.

"And save you all the torment and pain you caused me?" I mused, a murderous grin finding its way to my face. "Now that just won't do." I twisted the knife in his thigh this time and he just ground his teeth and grunted, refusing to give me the satisfaction of hearing him scream again. "Tell me, how does it feel to have someone kick you when you're down and bleeding?"

He snarled at me in response.

"I thought so." I pulled both of my knives out and stood back up. I looked at Deiric, whose face was a mixture of shock and pride. "Dispose of him in whatever way you find most entertaining. It doesn't have to be quick."

A murderous smile found its way to his face, but he looked at Xander. "You can have this one." Then he looked back at me. "We'll be back shortly."

I nodded, and they grabbed him and drug him back out.

Everyone in the tavern was still staring at me. Some had a look of fear, some were simply too shocked by it all, and the men who brought him to me had wicked smiles on their faces.

"Thank you for bringing him to us. I apologize for the mess." I waved my hand and the blood disappeared.

"Of course m'lady." One of them said with a slight bow.

I looked over to the bar, where the barkeep just stared at us, frozen for a moment with shock. "Would you be so kind as to get these two men a drink?"

She blinked, and looked from me, to them, then back again.

"I'll pay for it of course." I offered. "Whatever they'd like."

I met their gazes again and they smiled and nodded in thanks, then made their way to the bar. Another wave of my hand sent the coin over to the bar where they stood, more than enough to cover whatever they might like to drink.

I returned to my seat and looked over to Cedric, who was still staring at me.

"You asked earlier for the story of how I was captured." He nodded. I smiled. "He shot me with a poisoned arrow, right in the gut. I ripped it out and turned to run. He hit me with another in my shoulder, then one in my thigh before I finally went down. I used the one in my shoulder to slash at him, and cut his leg. I had pulled the other one from my thigh to swing again before I blacked out because he kept kicking me where he'd shot me with the first arrow while I fought him off."

Cedric's eyes got wider. Everyone in the bar was listening now. "I woke up on the back of a horse, bandaged, but not shackled except a single metal band on my wrist to block out my magic. When he stopped in the village, I snuck off, reopened my wounds while running from him, but got out. A witch I'd managed to run into, literally, while I was fleeing came to find me and heal me, and one of the death dealers I'd met and worked with prior to this incident caught up with me. He broke off the band that blocked my magic, and I've been traveling with two of them ever since."

Deiric and Xander came back into the tavern now. I looked at them as they walked over to me, both looking entirely unamused but confused as to why everyone was still so quiet.

I looked back at Cedric. "It was hardly a story worth a song, until now." I let a small smile creep to my lips. "Now, he got what he deserved."

Deiric and Xander sat down silently. Everyone slowly went back to what they'd been doing before the disruption. Including Cedric, who took a few extra moments to stare at me, as though he didn't recognize the cold person he'd just witnessed torture a man without a second thought.

We stayed for another song or two before I decided it was time to leave. I walked up to Cedric when he took a brief break between songs.

"Perhaps one of these days, we can have you play at a party for us." I smiled. "When we finally level the playing field anyway."

He smiled slightly, hesitantly. "Perhaps."

I stepped closer to him and pulled him into a hug before he could resist.

He sighed, returned the hug, and then whispered. "I'm glad you got away, and that you're safe."

"I know." I whispered. "I'm glad to see you're doing alright too."

We released one another at the same moment and I stepped back to look at him. "Until next time." I smiled.

He huffed a laugh. "Until next time."

Chapter 32

Mira

I shifted us back to the manor. It was about the time I'd usually have dinner. Macha flew off of my shoulder and took up her usual perch on the porch roof.

Xander wandered into the manor without saying a word.

I stood and just stared up at Macha for a few moments.

Deiric stepped around me and blocked my view of Macha, forcing me to look at him.

"Something on your mind?" He asked.

I had been completely silent from the moment I said goodbye to Cedric. We all had.

"I think I'd like you to turn me." I said flatly. "It seems like I would be far more useful and be in less danger if I weren't so fragile. So *human*."

"Are you sure you're ready for that?" He studied me closely.

"Yes. I think I am." My voice was quiet, almost too quiet I guess.

"I hope this isn't because I made that comment out there, when you…" His voice trailed off and he looked away for a moment, then met my eyes again. "I didn't say that to sway you into deciding to turn before you're ready."

"That is the closest I've ever come to actually dying." I said softly. "In all my years of running, of fighting, I'd never been so close. And it had never happened so quickly." I looked down briefly, then met his gaze again. The intensity behind those eyes was overwhelming. "I want you to turn me before you're forced to. While it is still a choice I get to make myself."

He nodded. "It will take you a few days to get used to everything. If you want to be turned *before* the next meeting, and not feel like killing everyone in attendance, we'd want to do this sooner than later." He said simply, and held my gaze. "Even if we do it tomorrow, you'll still be a bit on edge at the meeting."

The look in his eyes suggested that I would be more than on edge, but I was sure I'd be able to manage it.

I nodded. "I think I can handle it."

"You can also just wait until right afterward. There really isn't a rush."

"The longer we wait, the more likely it won't be a good time for the transition because I *won't* have time to adjust well. I don't want to put myself in a situation where I might kill someone because I don't have a handle on myself yet."

Something shifted in his eyes that I couldn't place. They were far away and cold now.

"Tomorrow then?" I asked.

He lifted his hands to hold my face gently, and brushed his thumb across my cheek. “If you’re really sure.”

“I’m sure.”

He kissed my forehead. “I’ll let everyone know they’ll need to find somewhere else to be tomorrow.”

“You act like I’m going to go insane.”

He just chuckled. “I think you underestimate how much you’ll be able to hear once you’ve transitioned completely. It’s better to have the house empty and quiet so you can adjust gradually. I’m not worried about their safety so much as I’m worried about you.”

I nodded.

He gave me a half smile, then turned to walk into the manor. His hand slipped into mine so he could drag me along with him.

*

I woke up the next morning just as the sun was rising. Deiric had already gotten up, or maybe had been up all night, I wasn’t entirely sure. The house was quiet and still. Macha sat on the windowsill watching me. I sat up and stared at her for a moment.

Are you sure you’re ready? She said gently.

I would rather do it while I’m prepared for it than when I’m forced to for some other reason.

Her head cocked to the side. *I will be here when you wake up.* And with that she flew out the window.

I got up and began to get dressed. Just as I was braiding my hair Deiric came through the bedroom door.

“Are you sure you still want to do this?” He asked gently, walking over to where I stood at the dresser.

I finished tying off my braid and turned to face him. "I'm sure."

He nodded. "I've sent everyone out for the day. I already have blood prepared for you to feed when you wake up."

I nodded. "I know I have to feed within a day or I'll die."

He looked a bit shocked. "You know the process already?"

"It was explained to me a *long* time ago. Before I even fully understood what I was. I have to drink *your* blood, die with it in my system, and then feed to complete the transition."

He traced my jawline gently, and then slipped his hand behind my head, interlacing his fingers in my hair. He stared into my eyes for a few moments, studying me for any sign of hesitation. "I'll be downstairs when you wake up, just to make sure no one comes in until you're ready."

I nodded. He stepped back, and bit his wrist, before offering it out to me. I pressed my lips to his wrist and drank until he pulled it away gently.

He leaned into me, pressing his forehead to mine. "I love you." He said softly. He kissed me, and before I could say I love you in return he snapped my neck in one swift motion and I crumpled lifeless into his arms.

*

I jolted awake and sat up in the bed. The smell of blood filled my nose and I looked over to the bedside table to find a glass already full and a pitcher next to it filled to the brim. I glanced around the room and I was alone. He'd said he'd be down stairs, I remembered.

A hunger, or I suppose rather a thirst that I'd never felt before took over me before I'd really even had the chance to think of anything else. It was like I'd been in a desert for a week without water, and I *needed* a drink.

I reached for the glass, the metallic taste of the blood curbing that hunger that ran so deep through me that I could hardly stand it. When I'd finished the glass, I poured another, half tempted to drink straight from the pitcher but having enough control that I was at least more civilized than that somehow. Despite the savage part of me that just wanted to dump the entire pitcher down my throat, the *human* part of me that was as stubborn as the day is long demanded that I pace myself.

I had almost finished the entire pitcher and it was like the world caught on fire for a moment. I could hear *everything.* I could smell *everything.* It was overwhelming.

Macha appeared on the windowsill just as she'd said she would. The scratching of her talons on the wood was something I never heard or noticed before. Now the noise danced through my ears, overwhelmingly obvious.

She cawed, and my ears rang. I let out a small yelp and covered my ears, bringing my knees up to my chest as if curling up into a ball might relieve the cacophony of sounds now bouncing around my skull.

Deiric was next to me in an instant. "It's okay." His voice was barely a whisper but it felt like he was screaming. He was gently stroking my back with one hand and had the other arm around me. "You'll get used to it."

I gasped, relieved he was there and I wasn't figuring this out on my own but too overwhelmed to even speak for a few moments.

I'm sorry Macha said, but that didn't make my ears scream. It was almost soothing in a way.

We sat in silence for a few minutes, until the sudden rush of noise seemed to even out and I settled into it a bit. "I can hear *everything.*" I finally managed to whisper. I almost didn't recognize my own voice.

"It gets easier to handle after a while. It is a lot to take in." He said softly.

"It is so *loud.*" I stammered. "I can hear the wind rustling the leaves on the trees, your heartbeat, Macha's heartbeat, your breathing, *everything.*"

"I know. I promise, you will get used to it."

I relaxed and let my legs slide down off the bed, so I was just sitting normally next to him for a few moments. He hooked a finger under my chin and lifted my face so I was looking at him. His eyes filled with concern, but also something else I couldn't place.

"I love you." I breathed. And the concern seemed to fade as his eyes began to sparkle a bit at that. "You didn't give me the chance to say that."

He half laughed, his thumb stroking my cheek while he held my face for a moment. "I'm sorry."

I realized for a moment that I hadn't even tried to use my magic yet. I held my hand out between us, palm up, and summoned a small flame. Just as a test. It ended up being slightly larger than I'd intended and prompted us both to jump back a bit. "Sorry." I stammered.

He chuckled. "You're going to have to get used to that I guess. A little more power than you're used to?"

I smiled, "probably a lot more. I only wanted a little flicker of a flame."

He raised a brow. "Just try not to burn the house down when you're practicing." He smiled.

I nodded, then I froze. "Someone is here." I heard footsteps on the stairs outside.

He looked away, listening. There was a light knock on the door. "Stay here." He breathed, and then he was gone.

I heard the door open slightly downstairs as he answered it.

"Are you going to let us in or not?" Silas.

"It's not a good time." Deiric said.

I walked to the top of the stairs, much faster than intended, but was completely silent as I moved.

"We have a report for you. I'd rather not have to wait and come back again another day." Silas said. His irritation and impatience dripped from his voice as he spoke.

Deiric reluctantly stepped back and opened the door, and both Silas and Elias walked into the entryway. "I'm telling you, it is *really* not a good time." Deiric persisted.

Silas looked around, realizing no one else was home. Finally, he looked up the stairs, right at me. His brows rose as he took me in for a moment.

"Elias, you should wait outside." He said flatly.

Elias and Deiric both followed his gaze up to me. Deiric frowned, probably a bit frustrated that I didn't listen and stay in the bedroom like he asked

Elias' eyes widened, as I presume he realized why Silas told him to go outside, and he quickly went out and shut the door behind him.

"Has she completed the transition?" Silas asked simply, as though I wasn't standing right in front of him and could hear every word.

"Yes."

"How long ago?"

"Well, probably about 10 minutes ago now. Your timing couldn't have been worse."

Silas smiled as he looked me up and down again. "I'm impressed she didn't come flying down here to rip Elias's throat out."

I was right in front of him in the blink of an eye. I almost ran into him actually, but managed to stop myself in time. "I'm not a monster." I insisted, standing almost nose to nose with him, scowling.

He huffed a laugh. "That depends on who you talk to, I suppose. Regardless, it takes most new vampires days to control their hunger." He said, his eyes like fire as he stared down at me. "I'll admit I'm impressed, but you're so new I imagine you're still getting your bearings and didn't even register Elias' scent yet."

I snarled at him.

Deiric gently grabbed my arm and pulled me closer to him, wrapping his arm around my waist. "Easy killer. He's right. You are still getting your bearings." He gave me a half smile when I glanced at him.

"What have you come to report?" Deiric looked back at Silas now, who was still eyeing me up like a brand new toy he might like to play with.

"We've gotten reports from a handful of other villages in our area and the surrounding areas that they have other, smaller beasts that need to be dealt with. Now that I see her current state, I don't suggest we send her to deal with them for quite a while, lest she lose control and become the problem."

I snarled at him again. "Don't underestimate me. I have more control over myself than you think."

"Oh I don't doubt that, but I'd rather not take any unnecessary risks." Silas mocked.

"Was that all you came to report?" Deiric snapped.

"So edgy today." Silas taunted. "I also came to find out when you planned to turn her, but I suppose this answers that question. Given the way things are going, with the people seeming to support us in record numbers lately, and some of the rumblings I've heard that we'll discuss more in next week's meeting, we'll be on the verge of finally making our move."

"I wouldn't be so on edge if you had chosen *any* other day to show up to discuss this." Deiric's voice was cold. Colder than I'd ever heard it.

"I think she should be repeating her snap at me to you. Don't underestimate her. She's handling herself quite well right now all things considered, and managed to run down the stairs without tackling me on her first attempt at speed, so sending everyone away for the day feels like overkill." Silas looked at me, then back to Deiric.

"I sent everyone away as a precaution. It isn't like we've had many female vampires to compare or understand how the transition might affect them differently." His grip around me tightened just a bit.

"Besides, even if she ended up having total control of herself right away, adjusting to her heightened senses can be the worst part. Sending everyone away was the easiest way to make sure this house was as quiet as it could get." His voice softened some.

Silas shrugged. “She seems quite confident she’s got control.” A wicked smile appeared on his face. “If you can keep a hold of her perhaps we should allow Elias to come back in here?”

Deiric took a step back, pulling me with him, and nodded. Silas opened the door. “Elias, would you mind coming inside for a moment?”

“I don’t appreciate being the test case, but if you’re certain she won’t get free and kill me, I’ll humor you.”

Silas just chuckled. “Deiric’s got a good grip.” He opened the door. “I think.”

I snarled at him, resulting in a slight squeeze from Deiric. “Don’t tempt her Silas. I’m pretty sure the only person in this room she would like to go after right now is you.”

Elias walked in and stood slightly behind Silas, looking me over, then staring at the arm Deiric held tightly around my waist.

Now that he’d entered the room and I was closer, his scent overwhelmed my senses. He smelled like cedar and tobacco, something I’d never noticed despite being in close proximity to him before. I could hear his heartbeat, a bit faster at the sight of me.

Something primal in me took over for a moment, and I realized I could feel the fangs now. I could feel the hunger they’d described, and every single part of me wanted to fly across the entryway and sink my teeth into him.

He stumbled back a step when his eyes met mine, but Silas and Deiric didn’t move, except to tighten his grip on me. “Breathe.” He whispered into my ear.

I tried taking a deep breath, but made the mistake of breathing in through my nose, which made me lurch forward just for a moment. Deiric braced himself behind me, preparing for me to pounce. I took another breath, through my mouth this time, and relaxed just slightly.

"Interesting." Silas said, and my focus shifted to him, my fangs still out, eyes still no doubt black as night as I fought every instinct to try to feed on Elias. He seemed more amused than impressed, but there was still a bit of surprise on his face that Deiric didn't have to fight me any harder than that.

I took a few more steadying breaths, as my gaze fell back to Elias. Finally, after what felt like an eternity I managed to stifle that primal need to feed and my fangs retracted.

"I'll admit I'm impressed." Silas mused. "Although if Deiric didn't have a hold of you I'm sure this would've gone differently."

My focus shifted back at him and my fangs were out before I could even register what I was doing as I lurched for him. The rage that boiled at his mockery was more intense than I felt when I was human. The movement caught Deiric off guard but I didn't get more than a step closer to Silas before he'd steadied himself again and stopped me.

"I did warn you the only person in this room she seemed to want to kill was you." Deiric said and he pulled me back again to add some distance between us.

"She is going to be a handful." Silas laughed. "I'm glad *I* am not in charge of her for the next week, or for the meeting. Best of luck with that." He said as he looked me up and down one more time. "Let's leave them to it, Elias. We'll see you at the meeting." He turned to leave, and once Elias had walked out the door he glanced back at me. "I look forward to seeing how you progress, little wicked one."

I snarled and lurched forward again, this time knocking Deiric off balance more than the last, but Silas and Elias shifted before I got too close. The moment he shifted I relaxed.

"You really don't like him do you?" Deiric laughed, completely releasing me at last.

"He knows exactly how to strike a nerve with me." I snarled at where he'd been standing.

"Bold to challenge an Elder like that." He said, and I looked over at him in confusion. "I shouldn't be surprised though. You're barely a day old and you're already snarling at an Elder like he wouldn't absolutely kick your ass."

I scoffed and closed the door. "You forget I kicked his ass weeks ago."

"He also didn't use any of his strength or speed on you. You do have superhuman strength and speed now too, but he's got six hundred years on you. I don't recommend pushing your limits too much. He can take a joke and certainly enjoys taunting you, but if you threaten him like that in front of his men I doubt he would let you get away with it without proving a point and retaliating."

"If he's going to taunt me like that, then he's got no right to retaliate if I react." I snapped.

"That's not how he's going to see it." He evaluated me for a moment. "Anything you felt before you were turned is going to be even more intense now. Is there anyone else you even had a mild distaste for?"

I considered it for a moment. "Not really. It isn't even that I necessarily dislike him, I just don't appreciate his jabs at me." I looked back at the door, at where he'd been standing. "I have always been a little extra pissed when people doubt me because I'm a woman or because they just underestimate me in general."

Deiric laughed. "This meeting next week is going to be fun." He considered for a moment. "Maybe you should sit this one out?"

I scoffed. "What, you don't trust me to keep myself composed?"

He merely made a face that I swear could've said, *did you see yourself just now* and I couldn't help but laugh.

"Look, I've got a week to sort that out. Just give me a chance. If I think it's too much I'll leave the meeting before it gets out of hand."

He nodded. "I will have Aris sit next to you though. If anyone is going to stop you before you *do* kill someone, it would be him or me so one of us needs to be close enough to catch you."

"I can accept that." I smiled. "So what now? We get the house to ourselves all day."

"You are under control now because you just fed. You'll be craving more before you know it. The first couple of days the hunger is overwhelming."

"So we'll have to go hunting?" I asked.

"We'll get to the hunting at some point, yes. There are other options though in the meantime."

The confusion must've been evident on my face because he came up a little closer to me and smiled.

"You can feed on more than just humans and animals you know." He slipped his hand around my waist and pulled me into him. "I've also asked Zane and Aris to hunt and collect some blood *for* you while they're out over the next couple of days."

"What, you don't think I can handle the hunting right away?" I leaned back so I could see his whole face, and not just get lost in those fiery blue eyes.

"I'm certain you'd handle it just fine, but I would rather keep you in here in case any of the local villagers wander too far into the woods and I can't catch you before you do any damage you *don't* want to do."

I nodded, and his free hand slipped up into my hair as he leaned in a little closer. "We could go outside and fight, let you experience what speed and power you have that way, or we could do other things that are probably vastly more exciting."

I smiled, slipped my arms around his neck and grazed my lips against his. I understood in that moment exactly what he meant when he described how the mating bond slipped into place for him. It hit me like a slap to the face. I wanted him, right then, and right there. More than I'd ever wanted anything else. I slammed him against the wall faster than I'd ever moved before. "You're mine." I whispered.

He gasped out a small laugh and the hand that had been gently playing with my hair now grabbed a fistful and tugged as he pulled my head to the side to kiss down my neck with a ferocity beyond what he'd ever done when I was human.

I groaned when he bit my neck and spun us around to slam me into the wall instead.

"And you're all mine." He snarled as he kissed me.

My hands were in his hair now, grabbing and pulling at it as he kissed his way down to my breasts and pulled at my blouse with his teeth. I pulled him back up to meet my lips and he slid me up the wall until his face was between my breasts again.

He grabbed my thighs and yanked my legs up around him, ripping my skirt slightly in the process.

Then we were in the bedroom. The movement was so swift and smooth I didn't even notice it. He laid me down on the bed, and I reached up and ripped off his shirt, not even bothering to pull it over his head. He just smiled and ripped off my corset in a similar fashion. Then I flipped us around so he was laying with his head on the pillows and I was on top of him.

He was smiling up at me, a hunger and ferocity burning in those eyes that I'd never seen, not in all the times we'd made love prior to this. This was different, fierce, like we were both burning in pure desire. I leaned down to kiss him and bit and pulled at his lower lip. He sat up into me and ripped my blouse off now. He kissed his way down my neck again and bit me.

I moaned, that fire inside me ignited again by the feeling of his teeth on my neck. I grabbed at his hair and pulled his head to the side before I sunk my fangs into his neck.

He made what I can only describe as a growl mixed with a moan and shuttered against me. His hands firmly gripping my hip and my back as he clawed at me while I fed on him, hardly able to hold myself back.

After a few moments he flipped us around, pulling me off of him and then pinning me to the bed with my hands over my head. "Easy, love." He breathed and leaned down to kiss me. "Don't get too carried away." He said into my lips. "It's my turn." His free hand traced my body from my shoulder down to the waist of my skirt, leaving me squirming and breathless at the tickle that hand left in its wake.

He kissed down my neck before sinking his fangs into me and feeding on me. He at last released my hands and I clawed at his back and arched up into him.

I tried to flip us around again but he braced against me, feeding longer than he ever had when I was human. When he'd finally paused for a moment he lifted himself up and looked down at me, my blood dripping from his lips.

"I love you." I breathed. He leaned down and kissed me, the metallic taste of my own blood now on my lips.

"I love you too." He whispered against my lips. Then his lips trailed down my body, licking any drop of blood he'd left as he made his way to the waistline of my skirt. He yanked at it, and shredded it as he ripped it off of me, then continued kissing even lower, ripping my underwear off with his teeth.

I waved my hand and his pants disappeared, the underwear too. He just looked up at me with that wicked, sexy smile on his face before unleashed himself on me. He didn't stop until my legs were trembling and I was groaning and clawing at the sheets. When I thought I couldn't possibly take it anymore he was on top of me again and plunged himself into me.

I moaned and clawed at his back.. He kissed up and down my neck, biting occasionally, while he thrust into me in a ferocious rhythm that made my world spin. Release found us both at the same moment and we were left gasping for air for a few moments as he lay on top of me before pulling himself out and collapsing next to me.

I rolled over to stare into those beautiful blue eyes while we both tried to slow and steady our breathing. "You failed to mention just how much better *that* would be as a vampire." I breathed.

He just smiled, slid his hand into my hair and kissed me. "I can't reveal all the secrets right away. That takes away the fun of it all."

"I didn't take too much did I?" I asked, glancing at his neck where I had bitten him, already healed.

His eyes glimmered as he stared back at mine. "No. I wouldn't have let you take too much." He stroked my hair for a few moments. "You'll figure out what your limits are eventually. It takes time." He said softly.

I snuggled into him, laying my head against his chest as he settled onto his back and continued to stroke my hair gently.

Chapter 33

Mira

Later in the day, we'd ventured outside, confirming that I in fact do not need a daylight ring to walk in the sun. Macha sat perched on the roof over the porch, watching us quietly.

"The most important thing we need to work on is getting you used to how fast you *can* go and moving normally as much as possible." Deiric said as he spun his sword and turned to face me. "I want you to start off coming at me without holding back, then gradually try to slow yourself down."

We both wore our armor, which realistically didn't offer that much protection against the swords, but it was better than my usual attire for this. "Are you sure that's a good idea?" I asked, drawing my own sword and preparing to launch at him.

"I can take it." He smirked. "Just try not to go for my face."

I smiled, and lunged for him, moving with a speed I wasn't accustomed to. And in one quick movement, a combination of a block and a blow in and of itself, he sent me stumbling and rolling almost ten feet from where we'd collided. It knocked the wind out of me, and I rose to my elbows gasping for a moment.

He chuckled. "I told you I could handle it."

I grumbled and lifted myself up, blowing a piece of hair out of my face. "Dick." I spat at him, which only made his smile larger.

"You can do better than that." He teased, and I lunged at him again, a little more careful this time, but just as quickly as the first time. Again he blocked me and sent me flying. This time I slammed into a tree at the edge of the clearing in front of the house and dropped to a knee.

"This is more fun than I remembered." He laughed.

I practically growled at him. He just motioned for me to try again. "Come on then. You've got to land at least one blow today."

We went back and forth like that for hours. Each time I thought I'd finally figured it out I'd get a little closer and he'd blast me away from him again. After a while, the others started getting back to the house, either because they were finished whatever it was he'd sent them out to do or the sounds of our swords clashing signaled to them that it was okay to return.

They casually gathered on the porch to watch, which was mildly humiliating, but I imagined all of them with the exception of Liala likely went through this at some point.

We clashed swords, face to face for a moment. "There you go." He breathed, but then shoved with his sword while he swept my feet out from under me and dropped me to the ground again, his sword pushing gently on my chest to hold me down.

I just looked up at the sky for a moment, gasping for air because I'd given it my all for far longer than I would've ever normally thought possible. He lifted his sword, releasing me, and reached down to help me up. I took his hand and he pulled me to my feet.

"That's enough for today I think." He smiled.

"You could've taken it a *little* easier on her." Aris said from where he sat on the steps. He smirked as he rested his head on his hand, his elbow propped on his knee.

"What's the fun in that?" Deiric asked, glancing at Aris for a moment before settling his gaze back on me. "Can't let her get too overly confident." A playful smile found its way to his lips.

If I had any energy left, I'd have punched him for that, but I just raised a brow and gave him a half smile as I still tried to catch my breath. "Safe to say you've kicked any confidence I had straight out of me today."

"It wasn't exactly a fair fight." He gently patted my shoulder. "I didn't hold back at all."

"What he's trying to say is, you just pretty successfully held your own against an elder who has six hundred years on you. So you *should* at least be a little proud of yourself, but don't let that go to your head." Aris said with a smile, before standing up and walking into the house. "You owe me twenty silver pieces." He mumbled to Zane as he walked past him.

"You were *betting* on me?" I practically shouted at them.

Aris stopped and smiled back at me over his shoulder. "Don't be pissed at me. Zane bet that you wouldn't last more than an hour before you gave up. Renwick wisely opted *not* to place a bet, while Xander seemed to think you wouldn't last more than a few minutes."

I glared at Zane and Xander who started rummaging through their pockets to pay up.

"And what did *you* bet?" I snarled at Aris.

"He bet that you would keep trying until *I* finally decided we'd done enough for the day." Deiric said, before he could reply.

"You *knew?"* I just stared at him.

"Deiric bet that you'd surprise us all and actually land a blow. I came *very* close to losing 10 gold pieces on that." Aris mocked, and then took the coins from Zane and Xander and walked inside as he shouted over his shoulder. "I expect you to pay up by morning."

"You bastard." I snapped.

Deiric just smiled and slipped his arm around my waist. "That's hardly how you should talk to the person that bet you'd kick his ass."

The mixture of emotions that rushed through me was hard to describe. I felt *everything* more intensely now. I was frustrated, but grateful he had more faith in me than anyone else. I wanted to hit him, but I also wanted to kiss him, and I couldn't really tell which I wanted to do more.

"You could've saved yourself ten gold pieces by letting me land a blow." I finally said, when our faces were just inches from one another.

"I could have, but I wanted it to be a real hit." He smiled, the fire behind his eyes was mesmerizing. "And you came damn close a few times." His eyes danced across my face for a moment, before he gave me a quick peck on the cheek and pulled me along as he walked toward the house. “Let’s have a drink shall we?”

I wasn’t sure if he meant whiskey, or blood, but I wasn’t turning down either.

Chapter 34

Mira

The next morning Zane, Aris, and I spent time sparring. Deiric had gone out to hunt, assuring me that he'd take me with him tomorrow. Around noon, we were all sitting in the dining room sharpening and cleaning our swords and knives.

I heard someone approaching the house outside, but since it was likely to be Liala, Leo, or Xander I didn't bother looking up as the door opened and they hurried into the house. It wasn't until she rounded the corner that I realized it was Eimear. She smelled sweet, like Jasmine, I wondered if she'd always smelled that way and I'd just never noticed it. I looked up to see her arms full of bags, food, I realized, probably for me because she wasn't aware I transitioned. I froze.

She smiled when she saw me, but then frowned when she saw we were all busy cleaning and sharpening blades. We'd grown to become great friends, despite that I didn't see her terribly often lately.

"I thought I'd arrive a few days early and bring some fresh items from the village market for you." She walked over to the counter and sat everything down. I found myself fighting against all of my senses, and every part of my body now telling me that *she* was my next meal and not the bags of food in her arms. "I figured no one here except maybe Liala took the time to actually get you things to eat, and since you only really wander out to go on monster hunting trips I thought I'd come check in on you and we could train some with your magic."

Zane and Aris were watching me like hawks, as I tried to stay intently focused on the knife I was sharpening. They didn't move though, didn't say a word.

Eimear walked over and went to touch my shoulder as she started to say, "aren't you hungry?"

I dropped the knife I was holding and darted across the room, to where I was as far from her as I could get, putting Zane and Aris between us. I was horrified I'd lose control and I was not ready for her to even remotely be that close to me, just in case. Zane and Aris, to their credit, didn't even flinch, like they'd read my face and body language to judge that I was moving away rather than toward her before I even made the conscious decision myself.

Eimear's face paled and she stared at me. "You-" She backed up a step.

I was leaning back into the wall, fighting with myself in silence.

"Neither of you thought to stop me at any point and tell me?" Eimear snapped at both of them.

"We weren't expecting you." Aris said flatly. "It was a good test for her at least."

"And you would've stopped her before she got to me?" She gasped, her voice laced with fear.

"Yes." Zane said quietly. "We are both faster than her, and given that she knows you, she's more likely to fight against it than harm you anyway."

She looked back at me, her face unreadable with what I could only guess to be a mixture of shock and hurt. "When did you transition?"

I relaxed some, finally realizing I had more control over myself than I would've thought. "Yesterday." I said softly. "We weren't expecting you for another day or two." I managed to say.

"I guess I didn't need to bring all of this then." She motioned back toward the various fruits and other foods I could see spilling out of the bags.

"I'm sorry." I couldn't think of what else to say. I started to take a step toward them and Zane shifted slightly where he was sitting.

Eimear didn't take her eyes off me. Aris shifted his gaze from Eimear to me as I took another step, cautiously evaluating. I felt like I had a decent grip on myself, and slowly continued to make my way back to where I was sitting. Eimear retreated a step or two as I sat down and picked the knife back up to resume sharpening it.

Zane relaxed some and returned his focus to his own knife.

"You seem surprisingly in control of yourself." Eimear finally commented as she dared to turn her back to me and return to the kitchen where she began unpacking everything and putting it away.

"I have to be." I said plainly, finally satisfied with the knife I'd been working on. I sat it down on the table.

"Most new vampires aren't allowed near any of us until they've had an entire month to adjust to everything." She said quietly, now working on putting something together for her to eat.

I looked over at Aris, who merely nodded as if I'd asked out loud for confirmation.

She came over and sat down directly across from me. "I assume you asked for this, so what made you decide to do it so suddenly?"

I straightened in my seat, still uncomfortable with that sort of proximity to her. "I knew it would be an adjustment, and I didn't want to be in a position where I did it out of necessity and didn't have time to adjust before I would have to interact with others." I said softly.

"Deiric, or one of you lot should've sent word out. What if I had arrived and she was here alone?" Eimear looked at Zane and Aris now.

"We didn't have any plans to leave her here alone, and again, we were not expecting you for at least two more days."

"You expected her to have this much control even in two more days?" She snapped. Her doubt in me was a bit infuriating, but I understood her concern.

"We weren't sure what to expect. If we found it to be an issue we would've sent out word to move the meeting or we would have sent her somewhere else." Aris looked at me now. "I had a feeling though that her stubbornness would make her a bit better at having more self control than the rest of us. Besides, she was *half* vampire by blood. There was always the potential that the transition wouldn't be quite as hard for her."

Eimear scoffed. "That's a hell of a risk to take don't you think?"

"It was her decision." Zane snapped.

"Yes, but you could've said no and waited for a better time." Eimear snapped right back.

"Is there ever truly a good time for this?" I jumped in, unable to keep my annoyance from finally pouring out.

She caught my gaze and something in my face must've told her to back off, because she chose her next statement very carefully. "I suppose there isn't really a *good* time to do this at any point, but there was possibly a *better* way to make sure no one unintentionally put themselves in harm's way like I just did."

I wanted to snap at her again and remind her that she's the one who just waltzed into a house full of vampires without even knocking, but I decided against it. "Well, you're here now and clearly I didn't harm you so there's nothing left to debate. I suppose you should be thankful that my answer to your initial question was no."

I could see a small smirk on Zane's lips out of the corner of my eye. Eimear saw it too because she glanced at him and snapped "wipe that smirk off your face, asshole."

Even Aris tried and failed to stifle a laugh.

"Walking into a house full of vampires and asking one if she's hungry is probably the most ridiculous thing I've ever seen someone do." Zane was not just smirking but actually smiling now, the amusement plastered all over his face.

"How was I supposed to know she turned?" Eimear's cheeks were flushed red.

I half laughed, and realized I'd just finally relaxed completely. It wasn't as hard as I thought I guess, being around people, as long as I'd made sure I fed beforehand. I imagine if I hadn't fed this morning this would be a different ball game entirely but I could manage this. "You couldn't have known, but it is still pretty funny."

She chucked a grape at my face, and I caught it without even flinching.

"Show off." She smiled, and went back to eating the lunch she'd made for herself.

Chapter 35

Deiric

I woke up insanely early, and couldn't get myself to fall back asleep. Our next meeting with Garrick and the other elders is tomorrow, and all I can think about is what might happen if she's not ready to handle being around that many other people.

I rolled onto my side and slipped my arm around her waist. She shifted slightly and leaned back into me, but seemed to still be asleep. She has been adjusting so well, I couldn't entirely believe it. Every other death dealer we turned had been an absolute mess for at least a month, and here she was only five days in and already able to handle herself well around humans.

I suppose it made sense. She managed to train herself out of the habit of using her magic for years. Why shouldn't she be able to fight this too?

I don't know how much time had passed before she seemed like she started to wake up.

"Morning." She mumbled, and slipped her hand around mine where I was still holding her.

"Good morning sunshine." I whispered into her ear and kissed her shoulder.

She arched back into me, letting out a soft sigh. "You're up early."

The sun hadn't even risen yet. "I could say the same for you." I said softly and propped my head up on my elbow so I could look down at her.

She rolled onto her back now, not releasing my hand and looked up at me. Her eyes were still a bit glazed with sleep. She blinked a few times, studying my face for a moment. "What's wrong?"

"Nothing." I said flatly, but not convincing enough to stop her questions.

Her brows furrowed. "I don't have to read your thoughts to tell that something is wrong." She readjusted her head on the pillow. "I can see it all over your face."

I sighed. I thought I had better control on my face than that.

She chuckled. "You don't realize just how *little* control you actually have over what shows on your face."

I shot her a small glare. It took me a moment but I realized she heard my thoughts. I hadn't mumbled that out loud.

She had a huge smile on her face now. "It's a handy little trick."

I didn't think she inherited that gift from me. She hadn't mentioned it at all. I suppose it made sense, given that I turned her, but it was very rare. I wondered what else she'd heard over the last couple of days.

Her face softened some. “It comes and goes. My ability to hear thoughts I mean. But your eyes give everything away, even if your face doesn’t. The others don’t see it, but I do.”

I just studied her face for a few moments.

“Spill it. What is on your mind?” She said finally. Her face was devoid of emotion now, maybe slightly concerned, but mostly flat.

I sighed again. “I’m worried about our meeting tomorrow.” A vague answer, but it wasn’t a lie.

“That’s not all.” She was wide awake now, and there was an intensity in those bewitching violet eyes that cut right through me.

“I’m worried about you.” I finally mumbled.

Her face contorted into confusion and disbelief. “Why are you worried about me?”

“I’m worried about you, because I can’t understand how you’ve been able to resist the urges I know you have sometimes.” She wasn’t going to stop in her persistence to know what bothered me, so there was no sense in holding it back now. I hesitated for a moment, watching as her face softened while she listened to me and waited patiently for me to continue.

“You are suppressing something that is an instinct, and doing so with a perceived ease that makes no sense to me. I am worried because I know that at some point whatever reserve you’re pulling that strength from will run out and I don’t want you to be put in a position where you’ll snap and do things you’ll regret.”

Her expression was unreadable now. Her eyes glimmered a bit in the dim light of the room. “I’ve spent years suppressing who I am for my own safety. This is no different." Her voice was unnervingly steady.

"You don't have to do that anymore." I said softly.

She shifted slightly so she was more turned toward me, but didn't fully turn onto her side. "No, I don't have to suppress my magic or *me* anymore, but I *do* have to suppress this new side of me for other people's safety." Her eyes danced around as she studied my face for a reaction. "Everyone is depending on *me*. I can't falter now."

For a moment, I had to wonder how *she* was sleeping soundly at night, with that kind of weight on her shoulders.

She smiled. My confusion must've been evident in my face, because she reached up and gently slid her thumb across my cheek before her hand rested on the side of my face.

"I sleep soundly because when I'm in here with you I'm not the powerful sorceress everyone is depending on to save the coven. I'm just me." She paused for a moment, her eyes seemed to stare straight through my soul. "I'm just the version of me I don't have to hide from anyone else. The happy, authentic, and genuine version of me that had forgotten what it was like to be *truly* loved by someone else, regardless of my flaws or *what* I am.

"I sleep soundly because when I'm in your arms I can forget everything else. This place, you, everyone here, feels like home. I didn't know where I *belonged* until I met you and came here." She paused again. Her hand slid up into my hair now, gently running her fingers through it while she stared up at me.

"Don't keep yourself up at night worrying about me. I've been through far worse than this, and can weather the storm if it means we get many, many more moments like this."

I couldn't come up with words to convey what I felt after everything she'd just laid out in front of me. It was probably the *most* genuine I'd seen her in all our time together. I could feel tears welling in my eyes, and she just snuggled into me in response, pulling me into her and nestling her head into my shoulder.

"I love you." She mumbled.

"I love you too." I whispered into her shoulder while I wrapped both arms around her and squeezed her tightly to me. Those words hardly felt like enough to convey how I felt about her.

We laid like that, wrapped in each other's arms long enough that she dozed back off to sleep, and I finally did too.

Chapter 36

Mira

Deiric and I had just gotten back to the house from a short hunt that morning when Silas and Elias arrived. Early as always. Elias froze when he saw me, just for a moment.

"Interesting choice in attire for the meeting today." Silas commented, looking me over. "We're not being subtle about the transition then I suppose?"

I was wearing my armor because we'd been hunting. I waved my hand and shadows enveloped me for a moment, modifying my armor into a plain black dress, no corset this time, and nothing exceptionally fancy.

"Better?" I raised a brow and curled my lip a bit in annoyance.

"Dramatic, but yes." He glanced at Deiric. "Do you plan to tell them about her transition?"

"If it becomes relevant, yes. Otherwise I'd prefer to keep it to ourselves or they'll likely be irritated that we've invited them here with her being so new."

He nodded. “Alright. Clearly she’s capable of being around Elias, so I assume she’ll do fine with the others.”

“I’ve been around Eimear most of the week. I’ll be fine.” I snapped. “You can stop talking like I’m not here.”

Silas just smiled. “After you, little wicked one.”

If looks could kill, I’d have killed him a hundred times over by now. However, I guess this is a game we’d always play. I walked past him and up the stairs into the house where Eimear and Liala were preparing for everyone else to arrive. We had about thirty minutes before we expected any of them.

Killian and Lazarus arrived a few minutes later, together, with one of the sorcerers that had come with Garrick at the last meeting. I wondered for a few moments if they could tell I transitioned. They both watched me cautiously. Aris and Leo came into the dining room next, standing against the wall on either side of the window I sat in front of, just like I had done during the last meeting.

Macha appeared on the windowsill and cawed at me. *I’d like to listen. I have some updates of my own.* I opened the window for her.

“A raven?” Elias asked.

“Yes.” I didn’t glance back at him, but kept watching Macha, who now perched in the open window and surveyed the room. I was surprised they hadn’t noticed her any other time they’d been around us lately.

“Your familiar?” He seemed somewhat bothered by her presence.

“Yes. Is that a problem?” I asked as I glanced over my shoulder at him for a moment.

"I just wasn't expecting that." He said flatly, carefully. The look I'd given him must've been too cold or threatening somehow. He seemed nervous.

Garrick arrived a moment later. He had shifted directly into the dining room this time and sat down with the sorcerer he brought with him. "Shall we?" He asked. Straight to business.

Deiric updated him on our trips out to handle some of the creatures terrorizing local villages, and Silas gave him updates on the way the people seemed to view the coven currently. All positive things. No one mentioned me at all, other than the parts I played in taking care of the threats.

"There is a new magister coming into power in the Solas coven, my sources have told me." Garrick finally started his part of the report.

This is what I needed to tell you about. Macha started.

"They are hosting a party to celebrate in a few days before he is officially sworn in." Garrick continued.

His name is Devlon. He is someone who will serve as an ally to us. He disagrees with a lot of what the Solas coven has been doing, but he doesn't advertise it except to his most trusted sorceresses and sorcerers. Macha said. *You'll want to find a way to chat with him and join forces.*

"We may be able to use this as an opportunity to send someone in and do some more internal spying. He tends to be easily distracted by sorceresses at these events. We could send one of our own in to distract him and also listen in on anything they may discuss in those parties."

You should go. You can enchant a piece of jewelry to disguise yourself and with your senses heightened you will hear more than a human sorceress would. If you can get him alone, you can persuade him to join you. She cocked her head at me. *It will not take much.*

I nodded, stood and turned to face the table. Deiric locked eyes with me, his face a mixture of concern and intrigue. He could tell I had an idea but likely had no idea what I was about to say. "I'll go."

"With all due respect, they know exactly what you look like. We can't send you in there." Garrick said dismissively. "Even if we *could,* it is far too much of a risk."

I scoffed. "You could enchant a piece of jewelry to alter my appearance so they wouldn't recognize me. Make me look like whatever it is he seems to fancy."

He looked at me, and met my gaze now as I glared at him. "It is best to keep you here where you'll be safe until we need you."

Rage sparked up in me and I fought it back down. I had to remain calm. "My sources tell me he will be an ally, and I am likely far more experienced in charming a man to get him alone than your sorceresses are." I said coldly.

"Your sources?" Garrick scoffed.

I waved my hand back at Macha.

His eyes narrowed. "How did you manage to get a familiar, or more specifically, a raven of all things?"

"I have my ways. I'm not interested in sharing that right now. However, she tells me that he does not share the same beliefs as the rest of that coven and would likely make a great ally if we can get close enough to him."

I paused, looking over at Deiric who seemed horrified by the idea of me trying to seduce another man. "Besides, I will be able to hear far more of their discussions than a human sorceress would anyway."

"There's no way you're ready for that." Silas said, and without hesitation, he'd sliced Elias's forearm with one of his knives to prove a point.

"You son of a bitch." Elias shouted.

Silas grabbed his hand and stopped him before he could heal himself. "Wait." He growled.

The smell of the blood felt like it set me on fire. The tight grip of control I had on myself faltered a bit, but I turned away and darted to the window, where I gripped the sill like my life depended on it. I couldn't stop the fangs from coming out, but I'd be damned if I was going to let myself lunge for Elias. Macha had flown away before I reached the window.

"You've turned her?" Garrick stood from the table, furious. "Why on earth would you invite us here if she is so new. Are you trying to get us killed?" He shouted at Deiric.

"You've proved your point Silas. Release his arm so he can heal himself." Lazarus snarled at Silas. "Sit down Garrick."

I took a few steadying breaths before I turned back around, just in time to see Garrick take his seat and Silas glaring at Lazarus as he let go of Elias' arm and he reached over to heal himself. My eyes had returned to normal, and I'd managed to withdraw my fangs before I faced them.

"How long has it been since she's fully transitioned?" Lazarus asked, looking over at where I still stood leaning against the open window.

"It's been a week." Deiric said and met my gaze, with a shimmer of pride in his eyes and a small smile.

"Impressive." He looked me up and down as I sat down and relaxed. The smell of blood lingered in the air from what had stained and soaked his clothes, but I fought like hell against every part of me that said I needed to go into a frenzy. "I don't think I've ever had one of my fledglings get control over their hunger so quickly." He smiled.

"Tell me, Silas, why do you think she's not ready to do something like this? The likelihood she'll actually encounter someone actively bleeding at an event like that is very low, and despite that you just sliced his arm open, she's managed to calm herself down in less than two minutes. If she's managed to have this much control in just 7 days, I don't see any reason why she *shouldn't* be the one to do this."

I stared at Lazarus, unable to hide the shock on my face that he had actually seemed genuinely impressed. The last time we'd run into each other he seemed to hold nothing but hatred toward me, and now he looked at me with so much more respect.

Silas scoffed. "If someone *does* get injured or happens to be bleeding she'd give herself away immediately."

I looked at Silas now. I was about to open my mouth to speak when I swear I heard Deiric say *Fuck, she's going to rip his head off,* and it made me stop and look at him. We locked eyes. *Please don't snap on him. Not here*. His lips didn't move. I was hearing his thoughts again.

Fine. I thought back to him. I settled down into my spot by the window.

"Oh fantastic. She seems to have inherited some of Deiric's abilities as well." Lazarus' voice dripped of amusement.

"What?" Silas now looked between Deiric and I. Deiric still stood staring at me. I sat calmly staring back at him.

"They seem to have exchanged more than glances just now. It wasn't hard for me to see she was about to bite your head off before she glanced over at Deiric and settled a bit." I saw Lazarus smile out of the corner of my eye. "She'd be the perfect person to attend this party. She'll be able to tell if this new magister has any reservations about an alliance with us."

"I don't-" I started, but Lazarus cut me off.

"Surely Deiric can teach you how to control your abilities over the next few days leading up to the party. Managing that is nothing compared to managing your hunger, which you seem to have done in record time."

I just stared at him blankly.

"Garrick, find a piece of jewelry and enchant it to change her appearance and disguise her voice. She's going to that party. Create two other items for myself and Elias to wear. We'll go with her in case anything should go wrong." He smiled.

"You don't give me orders, Lazarus." Garrick snapped.

"Do you have a better idea?" Lazarus turned to Garrick now, who opened his mouth to speak, but then closed it and said nothing. "I didn't think so."

"It's settled then." Killian said, the only one who had yet to speak for the entire meeting. "If she can build us an alliance within the coven, perhaps we can avoid a bloody battle after all. We could take them down from the inside out."

Macha appeared on the windowsill again. *You will not avoid a battle.* I looked up at her. *You will have allies that will fight with you, but you cannot avoid a real battle, no matter what you do.* Her voice was a bit different now, I realized it wasn't her voice I was hearing. It was the Morrigan. She had the gift of seeing all time, including the end of days. She knew exactly what would happen.

"We won't avoid a battle." I said quietly, still looking up at Macha. "We may be able to avoid a larger, bloodier battle, but we won't avoid a battle entirely."

When I looked back at the table they were all staring at me, a bit of concern on their faces.

"Does anyone else have anything to add?" Deiric said after clearing his throat. The table was silent for a few moments.

"We will come to collect you before the party, and will set up to arrive in a plain coach. I will pose as your attendant, and Elias will pose as your father. We'll provide you with a dress and the ring to change your appearance when we come to collect you."

I nodded.

"Thank you all for your time." Deiric said, and the meeting dispersed. Garrick and his sorcerer disappeared almost immediately. Lazarus and Killian both approached me as soon as everyone was dismissed.

"You are quite fascinating." Lazarus said as he once again evaluated me. "What made you decide to ask to be turned so suddenly?"

"It just made sense to do it now, rather than wait until I might have to at some point." I said flatly. It didn't seem relevant to mention what happened on our last outing that officially changed my mind and convinced me it was time.

"You have a level of control that I've never seen at this stage." Killian said.

"She's as stubborn as an ox. She always has been." Aris came up to the three of us with a small smile on his face.

"That explains why you didn't react to Silas' antics. Did you know she would keep herself under control?" Killian asked.

"No." Aris said quietly. "I did want to give her the chance to figure it out for herself, though." They clearly realized that his and Leo's presence this time was just to keep an eye on me. Leo had already walked off somewhere.

I looked beyond them and Silas was still steaming at the table with Elias, who looked less than thrilled. "How will Silas feel about the fact that you've decided to use his archmage?" I looked at Lazarus.

He merely scoffed. "Silas was my second until we needed an Elder for another legion in that area. He doesn't get a choice. I still outrank him in age at least." He glanced over at Aris for a moment. "You should be an Elder, should you not?"

"It's not a title I'm eager to hold." He said regretfully. I've heard that before. "I'd prefer to stay under Deiric, if that would be alright with everyone else."

"I suppose we can allow that for now, but we will need to replace the legion that ran that area eventually."

"Understood." Aris nodded and walked away.

"Once you've managed to either secure him as an ally, or get whatever information you can, we will leave immediately. We are not spending more time there than we need to." Lazarus looked back at me.

"I understand."

"Good." He smiled and walked to the sorcerer that had shifted them here, motioning for Killian to follow. "I'll see you in a few days then."

They shifted out, leaving just Deiric, Eimear, Elias, and Silas. Celeste opted not to attend this time. I walked around the table to stand next to Deiric, keeping him between Elias and I. Silas was glaring at me. I looked at Elias.

"I am sorry about your arm." I said, and I meant it. Even if Silas wasn't going to say it.

"You have nothing to be sorry for. This prick likes to make a spectacle of everything. You handled it quite well, all things considered." Elias said, with a small half smile.

"I told her to simmer down, even if I didn't *realize* she would hear me." Deiric smiled at me.

"You're a bastard." I said to Silas. "If I hadn't heard Deiric's thoughts, I might've said far worse to you right then. That was entirely unnecessary."

"It needed to be tested eventually." He said and crossed his arms.

"Perhaps, but you didn't have to slice his arm to do it."

He scoffed. "Let's get going Elias." Elias shifted them out without another word.

"That went well didn't it." Eimear finally said, and I couldn't help but laugh.

"Well, I didn't kill anyone, so I'd call it a win."

Deiric smiled over at me. "Was the bar that low?"

I returned his smile. "When he cut his arm, I wanted to kill Silas, *not* Elias. So, yes, the bar was actually that low for me."

"I admit I hate the idea of you trying to seduce this other magister, but I think you'll do just fine." He smirked a little. "Just try not to go beyond seducing him or I may have to kill him."

He said it like a joke, but I knew he was not kidding. I just shrugged. The thought of doing anything more than seducing him enough to get him alone made me want to puke, but I'd do it if I had to.

Chapter 37

Mira

Lazarus and Elias arrived mid-afternoon to bring me the dress and a ring to alter my appearance. It was a beautiful emerald green dress with a low back, similar to what Silas had given me that time I had my clothing shredded when we killed the Elk-like creature.

Once I put on the dress I slipped the ring onto my finger and looked in the mirror. It was insane to see someone else staring back at me. The ring turned my long black hair blonde, and my eyes were now a glimmering hazel. My tattoos and scars were hidden, leaving me utterly bare.

Deiric walked in a moment later and stopped in his tracks. "I don't know what I expected, but it certainly wasn't this." He said softly.

"You don't like me as a blonde?" I turned and he locked eyes with me.

"You look lovely, but I prefer those beautiful violet eyes and your natural hair much more than this." He gave me a half smile. "Are you ready?"

I nodded and we walked downstairs together. Eimear, Aris, and Leo were off to the side in the dining room. Lazarus and Elias stood by the door, having donned their disguises too, I couldn't recognize them. I could only tell who was who based on their height.

"You'll be attending as a sorceress named Selene." Lazarus said.

I nodded.

"Shall we?" Lazarus asked as he opened the door for Elias and I. That was his purpose tonight.

"Ladies first." Elias said, and I walked out the door, glancing over my shoulder for a moment to see that Deiric, Eimear, Leo, and Aris were all watching, their faces were riddled with worry, likely thinking the worst of this idea.

Elias shifted us to where we would meet up with the person they also had under cover that would drive the coach with us to the party.

"His name is Devlon." Elias finally said. "You won't be able to miss him when we get there. He's got light brown hair and emerald green eyes. There is a reason he's usually found with women." Elias said with a half smile.

I just nodded. I needed to focus on my mask, who I needed to be tonight. A heavy feeling of dread filled my stomach. I had to walk into a room full of people who likely wanted me dead, or worse and I had to act like I was elated to be there.

"Are you sure you're up for this?" Lazarus finally said softly, and I looked over at him. I wondered if he could *see* my dread and the underlying fear beginning to take over me.

"Yes. We're not going to get another opportunity like this."

He nodded. There was a bit of genuine concern on his face for me. Like he knew just how badly this could all go if we were discovered. I assumed that was likely why he volunteered himself to go. I gathered by this point he was the oldest of the elders at all of our meetings. I wondered if he knew the original Dhampir all those years ago. No one ever explained to me what happened to him in the end.

We arrived, and were welcomed with open arms into the party. No one bothered to check us for invitations or even asked our names. It was a bright and cheery party with lots of food and drink.

Lazarus played his part and retrieved drinks for both Elias and I, though we barely sipped them as we milled about and made small talk, introducing ourselves briefly to some as I scanned the room for my mark. After what felt like an eternity, the lights dimmed and music began to play.

I saw Devlon enter just as the dancing began. He was dressed in a red long coat with gold trim, very formal. A pair of plain black pants and boots accompanied it. I understood now what Elias had meant. He was certainly not hard to look at. He had very refined cheek bones, and a well sculpted jawline that would've had most women swooning. Not exactly my type, but I could appreciate that he was very classically handsome.

I observed some of the dancing for a moment, learning the movements so I didn't look entirely out of place, and then made my way to the edge of the dancefloor.

After a few moments Devlon's eyes fell to me, while he was wandering around looking for a partner. He gave me a soft smile and offered his hand. I gave him a brief curtsy as I'd seen other women do, and accepted his hand.

We danced in silence for a few moments before he finally said, "I've never seen you before. What's your name?"

"Selene." I said softly.

He smiled. "I am guessing you already know mine." He said. I had a part to play. I let my cheeks get a bit red and I nodded.

His smile only grew at that. The music changed and we ended up in a much closer dance, close enough that I could finally whisper in his ear. I was not hearing any specific thoughts from him.

"If I may be so forward as to ask, I've been told that you have a slightly different vision for this coven. Is that true?"

Shit. I heard him think. "I do have some plans." He said softly. Vague. I struck a nerve.

"I think that we could use some fresh perspectives." I tried to be casual. He spun me around as a part of the dance and I now had my back to him. His lips grazed my neck as he leaned in to continue to whisper to me.

"Is that so?" He said softly, his hands wandering a bit more than I'd have expected them to. I must not have struck a nerve too deep, if he was still so focused on taking me to bed with him.

Another spin and I was facing him again, my head slightly leaning on his shoulder. I let my hand wander up into his neck and my fingers gently toyed with his hair. I needed to get him alone first, make him think I wanted *him* too.

He leaned in, "This is hardly the place for this."

"Perhaps we should find somewhere more private then?" I whispered back.

This was far easier than I expected. He thought. "I might know of a place." His hand slipped down to my ass, and I had to remind myself again *not* to react like I was absolutely disgusted by it.

"Lead the way." I whispered.

He kissed my neck lightly and took my hand. He led me to a door along the edge of the room. I saw Lazarus and Elias out of the corner of my eye, watching us.

"Be sure I'm not disturbed." He said to one of the men standing beside the doors.

The man looked a bit disgusted, but stepped to the side and we went through the doors, down a long hallway to a bedroom off to the left. I guessed, given the reaction we got, this was a common occurrence for him.

Once we were alone, his face went cold. "Why are you really here?"

I stared at him, genuinely shocked for a moment.

"You are not one of my emissaries, and yet you acted just the same as they would. Have the magisters sent you to try to see if I'm planning a coup?" He snapped. "I've put a shield up around this room so no one outside can hear us, so get on with it."

"Straight to the point then." I finally turned off my act. "You have your emissaries pose as your lovers?" I questioned.

He raised a brow, but didn't falter much beyond that. "You're not with the magisters of Solas then?"

"No. I'm not with Solas at all. I am here because I heard that you have a very different viewpoint than the rest of the Solas coven, and that you might be seeking to rebalance things the way they were years ago."

"And if that is true, what exactly are you here to ask or offer?" His face returned to a neutral and unreadable expression.

"Is that true?" I persisted.

"Yes." He was curt and flat with his response. Not willing to budge beyond simple answers and give me his *real* viewpoint.

"I am here on behalf of the Oíche coven to seek an alliance."

He couldn't hide the shock on his face. "The Oíche coven? You don't bear their mark."

"It's hidden by an enchantment." I explained.

"And I'm just supposed to blindly trust you?" He stepped closer to me, waving his hand in feigned annoyance.

"How am I to trust you when your entire coven likely wants me dead?" I countered.

"Why send an attractive woman to do the dirty work then?"

"I think that answer is obvious but I would ask you again why you have emissaries that pose as lovers." I was growing tired of this dance we were doing.

"What is your real name then? I imagine they wouldn't have sent you in here and used your *real* name for this little ploy." He was studying me, just as much as I was studying him. His mind was not giving me any clues to suggest he was lying, just genuinely concerned someone was out to get him.

"Alesmira." I said, "but you may know me as Scáil."

His face paled. "The mercenary they're hunting."

"Yes."

"The Dhampir." He said. *Shit, shit, shit.* Those thoughts were loud and clear. He was starting to panic.

"Would you be interested in an alliance with the Oíche coven to rebalance things the way they used to be?"

"I- Are you insane? What the hell are you doing here?" He looked at me with genuine concern in his eyes.

"Answer my question." I persisted. "We don't have much time."

"Yes. I would be interested. Do you have a plan?"

"We are working on it, but I'd like you to meet with our leadership, discreetly." I stepped toward him now.

"Do you have a meeting day and time?" He was still looking at me like I'd gone entirely insane, but was getting back to business.

I heard footsteps. "Someone's coming."

Before I could think or even react he launched himself on me. "Play along." He whispered as he forced his lips on mine and his hands slid into my hair.

I wrapped my arms around his neck and played along. A moment later the door swung open.

"I said that I didn't want to be disturbed." He spun around to the man now standing in the doorway.

He had black hair, and was dressed in a very fancy blazer, all black. I would've sworn he belonged to the Oíche coven in that outfit, but I didn't recall his face or seeing him at the party either for that matter. His piercing gray eyes looked me up and down for a moment.

"You know I don't follow orders." The man said.

"Tellus." Devlon snarled. "What do you want?"

"Just a quick word with you, if your lady friend doesn't mind." He glanced back at me, my hair now disheveled and god knows what else messed up.

Devlon motioned over to a powder room off of the bedroom we were in. I went in there and worked on fixing my hair, quietly.

"You are a very hard person to get alone." Tellus said as he shut the door and walked around Devlon.

"Out with it Tellus. I was in the middle of something."

Tellus scoffed. "Yes, of course, your flavor of the week, or the evening rather. Perhaps I could have a go when you're finished. She was quite exquisite."

I could have barfed.

"What do you want?" Devlon asked again.

He sighed. "I want to discuss your plans for the coven. My sources tell me that you've been having some discussions that might be of interest to the resistance."

"The what?" Devlon seemed genuinely surprised.

"Oh please Devlon, don't act so surprised. The *resistance.* You know, those of us who are sick and tired of these old bastards pining for ruling the people? Who would like to see things go back the way they used to be and to stop hunting down fellow sorceresses and sorcerers?"

I was incredibly still now, listening, not making a sound. Tellus realized I wasn't making any noise anymore and the door snapped open.

"Eavesdropping is not a nice trait in a lady." He snapped and reached to grab me but Devlon stopped him.

"Relax. She's on the same team. Sort of." He mumbled. "You both apparently planned to pursue me for the same reason this evening."

Tellus glared at me. "Who is she?"

"She belongs to the Oíche coven."

"She doesn't bear the mark."

"She's done some kind of enchantment to hide it." Devlon explained. "She wants to set up a meeting with their leadership and ours."

Tellus just looked me up and down again. "And how do you know we can trust her?"

"Because I'm crazy enough to come in here and risk my life when everyone in your coven is hunting me." I snapped. "And we don't have a lot of time before people get suspicious of us all back here so you should shut up and listen." I snapped.

Tellus raised his eyebrows. Devlon shrugged. "She was just finishing discussing this with me when you walked in."

"I don't have a meeting time or place yet. We wanted to make sure this was even possible first, and we'll be choosing a neutral location." I had to choose my words carefully. "If you are in, I will go back and make arrangements, then send messengers to you to confirm."

"Messengers?" Tellus asked. "How are you going to do that without suspicion?"

"I will send ravens with a note. Send them back with your answer."

"Ravens?" Devlon asked.

"Yes." I responded, looking them both over. Their thoughts had yet to give me any concerns of loyalty. "Do we have a deal?"

They both looked at each other, considering for a moment. "Yes." They both said in unison.

"Great." I brushed my hands down myself and straightened my dress. "Then let's get back to the party."

"I'll be slipping out the back, but do enjoy the party." Tellus said with a sultry smile, and left us.

Fine, that was better anyway.

"Come on. We've got an act to put on then." Devlon said as he hooked his arm around my waist.

"I'm leaving shortly after we've rejoined the party." I said.

"That's fine. We at least have to act like we like each other until then."

We walked back out through the same doors we'd disappeared through on the way in. No one seemed to miss either of us, except possibly Elias and Lazarus.

Within a minute or two of us returning and making our way back toward the edge of the dancefloor Elias came up to me.

"If you'll excuse my intrusion." He said to Devlon. "We need to get back on the road. We've got a very long ride home." He smiled, and held out his hand to me.

Devlon nodded, and I took Elias's hand. He led me out to the coach, which Lazarus had already summoned. Lazarus held open the door while we both climbed in, and then climbed in himself and shut the door behind us. The coach lurched forward immediately, and we were on our way home.

"Well?" Lazarus asked when we'd been sitting in silence for several minutes.

"They've agreed to a meeting."

"They?" Elias asked.

"We were interrupted by someone else who was also seeking Devlon's alliance. He seemed to be the leader of *the resistance* as he called it. I guess there are a lot more people who disagree with the magisters than we thought." I explained softly, still on edge a bit until I knew we'd completely made it out.

As if Lazarus could tell, he put his hand on mine for a moment. “We made it out. We're far away and no one suspected a thing.”

“I will feel much better when we’ve actually made it home.” I said, and a moment later the coach stopped. We all stood up, and Elias shifted us back to the house.

I let out a breath of relief and within moments Deiric and the rest of the crew had come outside to greet us.

“How did it go?” Deiric asked.

“We need to pick a meeting place.” I said quietly, removing the ring from my finger and finally relaxing a bit.

“We don’t want to use any of our warded locations.” Elias said.

“No.” I said coldly. The idea hit me like a blow to the gut. “I know exactly where we’ll meet them.”

“I don’t like the sound of that.” Lazarus said, after he removed his enchanted ring as well.

“We go back to where it all started. Where the first attack happened.” I looked past Deiric at Aris and Liala, who’s faces went pale.

“That will certainly make a statement.” Lazarus said.

“Are you sure you want to go back there?” Deiric brushed my hair out of my face and just stared at me for a moment. “No one has been back there since the attacks except to have buried everyone who was lost.”

“Yes. We’re going to meet with them to finish this where it all started. It is neutral territory now, and we can set up wards and shields ahead of time.”

“I will check with Garrick.” Elias said. “In the meantime, everyone lays low for a few days until we get an answer. As soon as we get his approval, we’ll choose a day and time.” He paused for a moment.

"We will need to pick something soon though. They are trying to locate all of us to wipe us out completely. I overheard some of the other Magister's talking at the party about it." His voice went cold now. "They've been fashioning many weapons to accomplish that effort."

I turned to look at him. "You didn't mention that on the way here."

"You had just attended a party where every single person who worked to set up those attacks, and likely ordered them, was dancing casually around you. You had to pretend to be someone else to avoid being discovered in a room full of people who want you dead. I could see the fear in your eyes after we'd started to leave. There was no reason to add to that until we were somewhere we were all safe." He gestured to the house.. "Go have a drink. You've more than earned it and it will take the edge off your nerves."

Lazarus placed a gentle hand on my shoulder. "It takes some balls to walk into a room full of people who would kill you on sight and stay on task as well as you did." He chuckled. "And, you didn't even think about killing your mark when your lips were less than an inch from his neck in there. When I transitioned, I couldn't even look at someone's neck from across the room for a month without wanting to rip their throat out. I cannot *wait* to share that part of the tale with Silas. His head will explode." He gave me a genuine smile. "Nice work." Then he and Elias shifted away.

I couldn't hold myself together anymore. The shock, stress, fear, and the relief of making it home to my found family hit me all at once. Coupled with the fact that if we didn't act soon it would all be for nothing.

Deiric must've seen it on my face, or heard it in my thoughts, because he had put my arms up around his neck and his arms wrapped around my waist before I even realized my legs were starting to buckle beneath me.

I clung to him like I'd never clung to anyone before. Everything hit me at once. The grief I'd tucked away for so long, the fear of constantly running to stay ahead of the mercenaries that tracked me down, the relief of getting out of the crazy situation I'd just put myself in so I didn't have to run anymore. I broke down completely.

I don't know how long he stood there, just holding me, before I calmed down, the sobbing stopped and my breathing started to return to normal. "I'm so sorry." I finally stammered into his tear soaked shirt.

"You have nothing to be sorry for." He said quietly, and squeezed me tighter to him for a moment.

"I'm sorry for this. For breaking like this."

"You are allowed to break sometimes. You don't have to be sorry for finally letting someone be there for you when you can't hold yourself together anymore." He paused, and one of his hands slipped up to gently stroke my hair. "You are one of the strongest people I've ever met, and I've been around a while." He kissed my forehead. "Let's get you inside."

I realized at that moment that everyone else had still been outside when I'd practically collapsed into him.

"They all went inside right away." He whispered. "If you want to have a drink, we can stop in the den with them and sit for a while. If you'd rather just go upstairs, no one is going to be bothered by that either."

I just wanted to hold onto him and not let him go. I wasn't ready to face anyone else yet. Not after they'd seen me break that way. He didn't say a word as he scooped me up into his arms and carried me inside and upstairs, where he laid with me and held me until I fell asleep.

Chapter 38

Mira

I woke up the next morning still in Deiric's arms. We hadn't even changed from the night before, so I still wore the emerald gown, and he was still wearing the same shirt and pants he'd had on when we got back.

He was already awake, but hadn't moved. I realized the sun was already up and had been for a while.

"Good morning." He whispered, and squeezed me gently before he pulled away slightly to look at me.

I opened my mouth to speak, and before I got words out he kissed me.

"Do *not* apologize again." He gently brushed his thumb across my cheek as he held my face for a moment. "We can stay in bed all day, if that's what you need, but we should probably at least get you into something a little more comfortable than that." He glanced down at my gown for a moment and then back to me and smiled.

There was a gentle knock on the door. "Elias is here for you." Eimear said from the other side.

Deiric glanced over at the door, "I'll be down in a minute." He looked back at me. "You don't have to come down with me. I'll be right back up."

I grabbed his hand and stopped him before he had gotten very far. "I'll come down with you."

He stopped mid-turn and looked at me. "Are you sure you're up for that?"

"I'm okay." It felt like he was staring through my soul and the doubt on his face was clear. "I'll be okay." I assured him. "I can't hide in here forever. And I've told you before I'm not going to sit any of this out, no matter how much it might break me."

He looked down for a half a second, then looked back up at me. "Well, at least get changed."

I waved my hand and we were both in fresh clothes. I'd switched myself to a plain blouse that stopped just above my navel and a black skirt that was just as soft and simple. No slit up the side this time, just a floor length skirt. Then I sat up and climbed out of bed to freshen up and follow him downstairs.

Elias stood just inside the entryway, staring up at us as we walked down the stairs. "Late start?" He said gently.

Eimear peeked in from the dining room before I could say anything. "We all had a few drinks last night. They deserved the option to sleep in." She winked at me, and then went back to whatever it was she was doing. A lie, but I was thankful that she thought enough to cover for me.

"Garrick has approved the meeting location and sent some of his sorceresses and sorcerers to set up the wards. We will meet outside because we do not feel the need to waste our magic to clean up the house just yet." He paused for a moment and locked eyes with me. "I do not recommend going inside when you get there."

"I've seen it already." I said sadly. "A long time ago."

His brows raised for a moment, but then he continued. "They'd like to do this tomorrow or the following day at the latest. Solas will not find our manors thanks to the wards, but he doesn't want to wait too long before taking the fight to them. He believes it will be best to do it right after Devlon is officially sworn in. An ambush will give us the best chance."

I nodded. "I will send out the messages right away."

"I will check in later today to see if you've received word." He glanced back at Deiric. "He wants you, Eimear, Leo, and Aris at the meeting whenever we decide it will be. The Magister is to be sworn in in three days."

"Three days?" I breathed.

Elias' gaze shifted back to me. "Yes."

Deiric squeezed my hip gently, out of view of Elias. "We'll prepare."

Elias nodded, and he was gone. We had to prepare for a battle in *three days*.

"You don't have to be there-" Deiric started to say.

"I will not sit this out. Not again. Not with so many people I care about at risk, *again.*" I snapped at him. A little harsher than I intended to be. That now familiar rage was already building inside of me. "They will pay for what they've done."

He stepped back for a moment, a little bit shocked. I realized it was because I had summoned fire to my fists without even thinking about it.

Eimear jumped in. "Maybe we should spend a little more time training with your magic before this. I wouldn't want you to light the entire field on fire." She started, but then considered for a moment. "Then again, that might work to our advantage I guess."

I pushed that rage back down a little bit and the flames disappeared. "I need to send the messages out." I said, and walked past Eimear into the dining room to the open window, where Macha appeared almost immediately as though I'd summoned her.

I just need to remind you that today is the dark moon. She said gently.

I nodded. *I will arrange to make an offering tonight. Can I have you make sure these messages are delivered?* I held my hand out with two rolled up notes in it that I'd summoned just a moment before.

I will see to it that they are delivered and then returned to you. She reached out and took both of them from me, clutching one in her talons and the other in her beak. *They will be delivered when they are alone and it is safe.*

I nodded again, and she flew away.

"Is she alright?" I heard Eimear whisper to Deiric, likely forgetting I could hear them.

"She will be." He replied quietly. "She can hear you, you know."

"Eavesdropping is not very nice." Eimear whispered, and I knew that it was directed at me.

I walked back over to them. "It isn't like I'm *trying* to eavesdrop. Enhanced hearing and all." I waved my hand up to my ear. I put my steely eyed mask on again. They may have seen me break down last night but I wasn't going to let them in on anything more than that.

"We need to go hunting so you can feed before you do any training today." Deiric said after a few moments of awkward silence between the three of us. "It will be a few hours I'm sure until we get any responses."

"I'll train with you a little bit when we get back." I said to Eimear.

"We'll focus on controlling that apparently untamable rage of yours." She said with a smile as we turned to leave. And for a moment I considered what she'd said a few moments ago.

Releasing it would certainly give us the upper hand. I shook the thought away as we walked out to go on a hunt. I know Deiric heard it, though, because he squeezed my hand for a moment and gave me a knowing look

.

*

When we returned from our hunt Macha sat patiently waiting on the windowsill. *I've received word from both Devlon and Tellus.* She motioned to the papers on the sill next to her with her wing.

I picked them up and opened them. Both of them had agreed to the meeting time and place for tomorrow. They'd bring some of their trusted higher ranking members with them.

"Good news I hope?" Deiric glanced over my shoulder at the papers.

"Yes. They've agreed to the meeting place and are bringing some of their other members that have the same views as them." I said flatly. "They're willing to meet tomorrow." I hoped we hadn't made a mistake in trusting them. I felt like I was fire itself, walking on the thinnest ice and just praying that it didn't melt beneath me.

"It will be okay." Deiric tried to assure me. "Your sources, which are far more all knowing than any of ours, were confident about it, weren't they?"

Macha shifted on the sill as he looked over at her. *My sources do not lie. They will not betray you. These are a few trustworthy people. They will stand with you on the battlefield.* Her voice changed slightly toward the end of that. *Do not forget my offering*. That was the Morrigan's voice again.

I nodded, calming myself a bit, though even with her reassurance it was challenging to not worry even just a little bit.

"I need to do an offering for the Morrigan this evening."

Eimear appeared inside the window behind Macha. "I'd like to give her an offering as well, if that would be okay."

"We all will." Deiric said.

Chapter 39

Mira

Elias had arrived later in the day and returned to Garrick with word that the meeting was on for tomorrow. The wards had been completed shortly before he came to check in with us.

That evening, after sunset, we all gathered to give an offering to the Morrigan. We'd poured some of our best mead into a goblet, and brought a bowl out to put our blood offering in. Using my sword, which she'd adorned with symbols and the bloodstone, each of them added to the offering bowl. I did so last, trying to stay away for as long as I could to try and keep myself in check. Somehow, I did not have any issues.

I lit the candles, whispered a quiet prayer to her, and bowed in front of the offering. Everyone else kneeled behind me with their heads bowed as well.

As it had the first day I'd summoned her, a rush of wind blew past and blew out the candles. When I looked up, our offering had disappeared before us and we were left in the dark, everything around us deathly quiet.

A weird wave of energy that I can only describe as relief washed over me. I assumed that meant the offering was appreciated.

*

The next morning we all prepared for the meeting. Everyone who was staying behind seemed a bit restless, but said they'd be sparring and training in our absence.

I wore my armor, so did Deiric, Aris, and Leo. Eimear had put on a slightly more formal dress, which I imagine she rarely tended to wear. It was black and glimmered like a starry night sky. It was strapless, but did have long flowing sleeves that hung just off her shoulders. It just barely brushed the ground as she walked.

We all gathered together in the clearing in front of the house where Zane and Xander were preparing to spar, while Liala sat quietly watching.

"Ready?" I asked. They all nodded and I shifted us to the house. My first home.

As the shadows cleared around us, the house, or I guess the better term would be manor, stood tall and empty, abandoned as the earth had begun to take it back over. Vines grew up the sides of it, and it looked like it hadn't weathered well over the years.

I hadn't realized how long I'd stared at it until I felt Deiric tug gently on my arm.

"Don't dwell on that too long. We don't want to keep them waiting." He whispered into my ear as we turned away and headed to the group that had gathered at the bottom of the large staircase that led to the front door.

Garrick, Elias, Lazarus, Killian, and Silas were already there, along with several other sorcerers and sorceresses that I didn't recognize, but determined they were with the Oíche coven based on their attire, which was very similar to Eimear.

As we approached, another group had shifted in next to us, and I glanced over to see Devlon and a group of sorceresses. We locked eyes for a moment and his eyes went wide. He recognized me for who he *knew* me to be now, not the woman he'd met a few nights ago. I didn't wear my enchantment today.

His gaze shifted to Deiric, sizing him up and settling his gaze on his hand on my arm for a moment before looking toward the larger group we were both walking toward now.

"Devlon, I assume?" Deiric said quietly, his hand releasing my arm and falling to his side. We had to be more formal here.

I nodded. I looked ahead and Silas met my gaze for a brief moment before he turned and continued talking to one of the sorcerers I didn't recognize. His face was unreadable.

Another group shifted in just then, off to the left ahead of us. This time it was Tellus and another group of mostly women. Sorceresses and sorcerers I'd assumed, but it was odd to see that the women seemed to outnumber the men in their groups. A refreshing surprise I guess.

Garrick waved his arms and a circle of chairs formed around us as we all finally congregated in the center of the clearing in front of the house, right in the middle of what would've been a gravel road had nature not taken that over as well.

"Thank you all for coming." Garrick said, very formal. "Please have a seat." Garrick looked at me and motioned for me and everyone with me to come sit next to him.

I was placed at his left hand, and Lazarus sat on his right. Deiric took the seat to my immediate left, followed by Aris, Eimear, and then Leo.

Elias sat next to Lazarus, then Killian, Silas, Alaric, and several of the others who I had yet to meet. Devlon and Tellus sat next to one another directly across from Garrick and I, and their collective groups filled in to the right or left of them until there were no chairs remaining.

"We understand that there is a plan within the Solas group to move forward with wiping us out entirely. Were you aware of this?" Garrick asked Devlon. No small talk then, we were getting straight to the point.

"I just heard of it this morning, yes." Devlon replied, rather diplomatically.

"We intend to take the fight to them first." Garrick continued.

"That's certainly a wise choice." Tellus cut in. "What exactly is your plan?"

"We would like to make our move the moment that Devlon is sworn in as a Magister." Garrick said plainly. "All of the important parties and their highest ranking members would be in attendance for that, so it is the perfect time to strike."

"Given that they don't seem to view you as a threat they're not likely to have any wards or shields setup." Devlon commented plainly. "It's bold, and doesn't give much time for preparations, but it might work."

"We've been preparing for far longer than you realize." I cut in. I could see a slight smile from Lazarus out of the corner of my eye. Devlon's eyes flickered for a moment, a mixture of shock and intrigue.

"Will you be a part of the attack?" He asked.

"Yes." I replied before anyone else could speak up. I wasn't letting myself get cut out of this.

Devlon merely nodded. "We will fight alongside you. We have not had much time to prepare, but we are ready to fight for what we feel is right." He glanced around for a moment at the people with him, who all nodded or mumbled their agreement. "What exactly is your plan if we are able to take them down?"

"We'll need you to take over and appoint new Magisters who align better with our coven's working together once more. Do you have anyone in mind?" Garrick asked.

Tellus smirked. "We've brought our future Magisters with us." He said, motioning with one hand to the women and men on either side of them.

Garrick raised a brow at that. "Are there more of you than just what you've brought here that will fight with us?"

"We have hundreds, some under the other magisters as well." Devlon replied. "They are a part of the resistance I didn't realize was growing under Tellus. What is your plan for the current Magisters? They will likely not want to partake in the battle. Are you intending to kill them?"

Garrick had opened his mouth to speak, but I had my own ax to grind, and there was a reason I wanted to attend this meeting, so I spoke before he could.

"Killing them would be far too kind." I said plainly. The entirety of the Oíche coven members in attendance turned to me. I couldn't look to see all of their faces as I held Devlon's stare, but I could *feel* their eyes on me. "I will bind their magic and they will serve time for what they've done."

"You will bind their magic, all by yourself?" Devlon's tone was steady, no trace of the doubt I was sure everyone else had. "That usually takes multiple magisters to accomplish."

"I've got a few tricks up my sleeve that I'm not interested in revealing just yet, but yes. All by myself." I let a wicked smile find its way to my lips, as I revealed my fangs and a few of them shifted in their seats. "I'd like them to have to watch as we rebuild everything they destroyed." I casually gestured to the withering manor behind me.

I felt Deiric stiffen in his chair next to me. This was not the broken girl he'd held last night. This was the most powerful sorceress to walk these lands seeking her sweet, sweet revenge for all the wrongs done to her. I relaxed and let my fangs slip back and away, and glanced at Garrick finally, who sat gaping at me.

"Unless of course, you had a better plan?" I leaned toward Deiric a little as I looked at Garrick fully.

He cleared his throat and shifted in his own chair. "If you're confident that will work, I think that is a fine idea." He paused for a moment, looking back at Tellus and Devlon before looking at me. "If it doesn't work though, they will be executed."

I merely nodded, and we both looked to Devlon and Tellus, who looked at each other for a moment, considering, before nodding in unison.

"What time will the ceremony be complete?" Garrick asked.

"Likely just after five in the evening." Tellus said flatly.

"I can make sure that a notification of some kind is sent out, mind to mind, to one of you so you can shift there." Devlon offered.

"You can notify me and I will make sure to get the word out to everyone else. We will shift in, with all of our forces, as soon as I receive word." Garrick gestured around to the rest of us there. "These are just my higher ranking members and those who have helped with this effort. There are many, many more."

Devlon smiled. "Good. Perhaps we'll outnumber them." He glanced at me. "We'll certainly have the element of surprise, in more ways than one. The dark hair suits you far better than the blonde you used in your disguise."

Deiric shifted next to me. A movement that Devlon no doubt noticed.

"It will be an honor to fight with you." He looked back at Garrick. "Is there anything else to discuss? We should be getting back before they notice we've been away."

"No. We will see you on the battlefield." Garrick said simply.

Devlon and Tellus nodded in unison again, and in the blink of an eye, they were all gone.

"You could've shared your plans with the rest of us beforehand, you know." Garrick said as he looked at me again.

"Where's the fun in that?" I just smiled. "You played along quite well."

"I think he was too shocked to speak up." Lazarus chuckled.

"The idea came to me shortly before they asked. A gift from the gods, so to speak." I smiled.

Garrick's face went grave. "The raven, that was also from the gods?"

I nodded.

"I underestimated you. No one has worshiped the old gods in a very long time. I'm surprised that it even occurred to you, to seek them out."

"You can thank Deiric for the idea. He didn't even know he'd given it to me at the time."

Garrick smiled now, and peeked around me to look at Deiric with a subtle nod.

"Ready all of your forces. We will shift them all there just before five o'clock tomorrow." And with that, he'd shifted himself and all those who had arrived with him away.

I looked at Lazarus for a moment, who merely smiled. I swear his eyes glimmered in something resembling pride, and then Elias had shifted the remaining group away as well.

Chapter 40

Deiric

She stood and turned toward the manor. I hadn't ever been here, and had no idea what it would've looked like years ago. It looked run down and ruined now.

I stood up and turned with her. I saw Aris rise out of the corner of my eye as well.

She slowly made her way around the chair she'd been sitting in and started up toward the manor. I didn't dare stop her. Instead, I trailed behind her, motioning for everyone else to simply wait outside.

The front doors swung open on a phantom wind, likely emanating from her. She walked in silently.

The inside of the manor was horrifying. There were old dark stains of blood on nearly every surface. Otherwise, the inside had weathered the elements much better than the exterior, except for any places where a window was cracked or broken.

She stalked over to the stairs on one side of the main foyer, and proceeded up them without a word. I continued to follow her silently, determined to be there if she needed me.

When we reached the top of the stairs she headed down the hall and turned into a room on the left. It had another door on the opposite side which opened into the other hall. This manor was nearly triple the size of ours.

She halted above a rather large stain of blood on the wood floor.

"This is where they killed my mother." She said softly. She glanced to the far corner. I guessed that is where Aris had pulled her to. I could almost picture it. The man in the doorway ahead of us holding the cross bow, her and Aris cowering in the corner. I shuddered at the thought.

She turned to her right, and a large old book lay open on a stand along the wall. It was covered in a thick layer of dust. She blew on it, and dust filled the space. Her fingers gently traced the pages for a brief moment before she closed it and tucked it under her arm.

It was a grimoire, I realized. Likely her mother's if I had to guess given its location the day of the attack.

She turned and looked back at me. "Let's go home." Her face was cold and unreadable. Her favorite mask, that she usually didn't put on for me anymore.

"Mira." I said softly.

She met my eyes for a very brief moment. The pain behind them almost broke me, but then she blinked and it was gone. Replaced by some cold hatred I barely recognized.

She brushed past me and began to head back outside. As she did so, shadows began to fill the space around us. I quickly caught up with her, not wanting to be left in the wake of whatever this magic was from her.

She filled the entire manor with them, and it wasn't until we reached the front steps and began making our way back to the rest of the group that they finally disappeared.

I turned back, and the manor looked brand new. Within the doors we'd just walked out of, I could see the blood had all been cleaned up as though it had never been there. They slammed shut on the same phantom wind that had opened them.

We reached the bottom of the stairs and she shifted us home.

"That was fast." Liala said. Zane and Xander had been sparring when we arrived but stopped abruptly.

"That was almost too fast." Zane commented.

"We launch our attack shortly before five o'clock tomorrow. They will fight alongside us, and will appoint new magisters when we win." Mira said coldly.

"If we win?" Xander asked, like he'd heard her wrong.

"When we win." She said, way too swiftly.

"That's a little overly confident isn't it?" Zane commented.

She glared at him. "We have two options here, either we come out victorious or we are all dead. We don't have an option except to win." She glanced around at everyone. "They're not going to take any prisoners."

His face went rather grim.

"Go back to sparring." I snapped at him. "And include Liala too. We have all been summoned to the field tomorrow."

They just nodded and Liala got up to join. Aris and Leo also headed over. I doubted Liala was ready for battle, but we would need all the help we could get.

"You should take it easy today." I said softly to her. "You'll want to save all the strength you can for tomorrow."

She simply nodded, but she wasn't really listening. She was far away in her mind, so far that I couldn't even hear what she was thinking.

I caught her arm when she started to walk past me and turned her to face me.

"We *will* win tomorrow. We have to." I said softly.

She locked eyes with me. Her eyes were so distant even their usual vibrance seemed to disappear, and then she turned and walked into the house without another word.

I knew better than to follow after her at that moment. She didn't want to be around anyone, not even me. She likely thought she had to shoulder all of this alone, even though the attacks would've happened regardless of her existing or not. She didn't cause them. All that she could be blamed for was accelerating their push for power.

I finally turned to watch the rest of them spar and sat on the stairs, but found myself lost in my own thoughts just as much as she was. One chance. We had *one chance* to fix it, or die trying.

Chapter 41

Mira

We all spent the day mostly in silence. A lingering dread hung in the air around the manor. Even Deiric was more solemn and quiet than usual. We had dressed in our armor at the start of the day, despite that we didn't need to be ready until the evening.

Our entire lives depended on the outcome of this battle today. One final bloody fight to give us the chance at being free again. At not having to hide in the shadows.

Deiric had nothing but concern for me in his eyes, which made me worry for him. I hoped he wouldn't be distracted by trying to protect me on the field this evening. He'd need to be focused on surviving it himself. I at least had my magic to protect me. We hoped they wouldn't have any of their vervain soaked weaponry, given that this would be more of an ambush.

It wouldn't stop them from summoning those weapons after we arrived, I realized, but I hoped, hell, I *prayed* they wouldn't. Macha tried several times to assure me that everything would happen as it should, and it would be okay, but even knowing that the messages were likely coming from the Morrigan herself did nothing to calm the chaos in my mind.

I finally rose from where I was sitting when Garrick sent word, mind to mind, for us to make our move. "It's time." I said flatly.

We'd been gathered outside for a while already, in silence. They all stood and I shifted us into the field just as Devlon was turning to stand and face the crowd, the other Magisters standing in a line behind him, having just completed the ceremony.

The magisters didn't notice us right away. Within seconds the rest of our groups had shifted in, and the magisters as well as some in the crowd had finally noticed our arrival and turned to face us.

Devlon nodded at us, and every single one of his allies shifted their clothing to look like our armor so we would not mistake them for the enemy. We drastically outnumbered the remaining Solas members now, which was a pleasant surprise.

"Show no mercy." Garrick shouted and our lines of warlocks, witches, sorcerers, sorceresses, and vampires alike surged forward. I took my place at the back, as several others did to block the magical attacks sent to the vampires while they advanced through the crowd. There were no titles, no rankings today. We all fought as one unit. As equals.

No one was prepared for battle but us, so this was an absolutely brutal ambush. Still, armed with their magic they were able to do damage to us without much effort.

I had to keep my head on a swivel as I blocked for Aris, Leo, Zane, and Deiric. Then turned to block a blast of flames for Xander as he charged toward a sorcerer.

To my left, Garrick and his group had managed to make it halfway to the magisters, who merely watched in horror at the bloodshed occurring in front of them. They had their own shields up, but did not aid their people. I wouldn't have expected anything less. Devlon at least was fighting alongside all of us.

Lazarus joined Aris in fighting against two more powerful sorcerers and I blocked the onslaught of ice shards that came flying at them.

Someone lunged at me from where I now stood in the center of all of this chaos, and Zane slammed into them, knocking them back before driving them through with his sword with terrifying ease.

We may have outnumbered them, but they had the high ground, quite literally in fact as the magisters stood at the top of the small hill in this field and their people had been lined up not far from them, on the gradual slope.

I turned and blocked again for Aris, as another mage or sorcerer stepped in and sent lightning shooting at him.

We were not advancing anymore. They were holding their ground. They had taken to breaking the wooden chairs and benches laid out for this ceremony to use as stakes for the vampires.

I spun around, hearing the struggle behind me to find Xander and Zane surrounded now, and put a shield up around them. I heard a caw to my left where Macha flew above, trying to bring my attention to where I was needed.

I looked over just in time to see Deiric take a shard of wood to the gut and fall to his knees, his sword nowhere to be found in the chaos around us. His assailant was now charging at him with another shard.

I acted on an instinct I didn't know I had, and shifted myself in front of Deiric. I grabbed the piece of wood that this warlock intended to use to stake Deiric from him in a movement so swift he didn't see it coming. I unsheathed and slashed my sword across his chest.

He cried out in pain and dropped to his knees. There was nothing but fear in his eyes as he watched me step closer to him to grab him by the throat.

By this point my fangs were out and I wanted nothing more than to rip out his throat. Instead, I drove that shard of wood through his heart, before I let him drop to the ground.

I heard shouting to my right and glanced to see Leo struggling with another sorcerer. I sent a wall of shadow to blast the sorcerer back and give Leo the chance to recover. Then I glanced over my shoulder toward Deiric.

Lazarus was now kneeling next to Deiric and trying to remove the ramshackle stake so he could get back to his feet and keep fighting.

I turned to face the battlefield ahead of me. Our people were faltering, we were falling back as they continued their advances against us. Each more brutal than the last. We were losing too many people, on both sides.

"*ENOUGH.*" I shouted. My voice shook the ground, and every single person fighting against us held their ears for a moment before they dropped to the ground, unconscious. I wasn't totally aware of what I was doing, but something took over me and this magic just spilled out as a result. An unconscious instinct to protect the people I loved.

The shields protecting the magisters shattered at the same moment. Before they could react, I had plumes of shadow and darkness surrounding them and holding them in place so they couldn't shift out of this.

I didn't bind their magic. I *took* their magic. Ripped it from them like it was a simple trinket they'd been wearing around their necks. I returned it to the earth, to the very source of where all of our magic came from.

They crumbled once the shadows and darkness released them. Alive, but unconscious.

Everyone on the field was watching me now, in shock and awe as I let the shadows around me creep out to touch all the wounded, healing them at least enough to hold them over until our healers could get around to work more on them. Then I shifted in front of Devlon.

He stumbled back a step, and stared at me.

"I trust you are prepared to swear in your new magisters now that the bulk of your coven's leadership has been demoted." I muttered.

His eyes were filled with a mixture of fear and admiration of the power I'd just displayed. He shrunk away from me a bit farther. Shadow still slithered around me, slipping off of me like smoke.

"Y-Yes." He stammered. "I can swear them in now."

"Good." I said resolutely. "The floor is yours." I shifted back to Deiric, kneeling in front of him where he was still slightly buckled over on his knees in the blood soaked grass. He held himself up with one arm while clutching his stomach with the other.

"He ripped it out on his own, but he's not completely healing because it was splintered and broken." Lazarus explained. "We need to get the splintered pieces out." He was still kneeling next to him.

I dropped to my knees in front of him, so I was face to face with him. He tried to hide the pain behind a stone cold expression, but I could see it in his eyes. I reached toward his wound, and shadows extended from my hand, carefully removing all of the remaining shards and splinters.

He had looked away, but as I healed him, he looked back up at me, and relief washed over his face now.

"Thank you." He breathed, as he sat up straighter now. He took me in for a heartbeat before throwing his arms around me and yanking me in for a hug.

That embrace finally calmed me, chased the remaining shadows away and I relaxed into his arms with a sigh of relief. My fangs had finally retreated as well, and I just clung to him for a few moments.

"I guess that mated bond goes both ways now." Lazarus commented.

I had closed my eyes as I let myself almost fall into Deiric, but I opened them and looked up at him. Deiric's grip loosened slightly.

Lazarus had a small smile on his face. "Despite your reputation, I didn't think you had that kind of ferocity in you." He motioned to the warlock behind me, then the field beyond. "I was coming to save his ass, but you beat me to it, and I have to say I'm impressed."

I took him in fully now, as Deiric and I rose to our feet. He appeared uninjured, but his armor was torn in some places and he had blood splattered all over him, including his face. I didn't even notice the smell of it, with everything else overwhelming my senses.

I finally turned to look at the warlock who had been charging Deiric. Ferocity was one way to put it. I barely even knew what I had been doing. I acted entirely out of rage and instinct.

Macha appeared and landed on my shoulder a moment later. *You did what you had to do.* She said softly, ruffling her wings as she settled into a comfortable perched position.

My face must've shown my general disgust, and distaste in what I'd done, because Deiric said softly, "if you hadn't intervened, it would've been the same result, just by someone else's hands."

I met his gaze. He slipped his arm around my waist and offered me a gentle smile that didn't quite reach his eyes. Those eyes were riddled with concern now, for me.

"Are you alright?" His voice was calm, despite the look in his eyes.

The adrenaline, the drive I had in those last few minutes was wearing off. I felt my knees starting to give out as the exhaustion finally started to hit me. I'd never used that much power before, never done anything like that in my *life.*

Deiric's grip on me tightened, and he caught me before I started to truly crumble. Macha flapped herself off my shoulder and landed on the ground next to us. I had reached out with my left arm and wrapped it around his neck and shoulders the moment I felt myself falter, and clung to him with everything I had, which wasn't much by this point.

"Are you alright?" He asked again, supporting my entire weight now, but holding me so that no one could tell.

"I- I don't know." I barely recognized my own voice. I was hoarse like I'd been screaming for hours.

"She needs to feed." Lazarus said quietly. He was right in front of Deiric and I, mere inches from us, but he was looking around to the others as they walked around to check on friends, allies, and even those who lay unconscious around us. "She used too much power."

I felt faint, and I could've sworn I started to see stars as he said that. My eyes fluttered closed and my head swayed toward Deiric's shoulder as my grip on him began to falter as well.

The next thing I knew, something was pressed to my lips, and the metallic taste of blood jolted me into a bit more alertness. The instinct to feed brought me back, and I realized that it was Lazarus' wrist I was now holding onto, drinking from. I tried to pull back from him, but he held my head so I couldn't move.

"Drink." He demanded. Deiric was watching around us, and I was mostly hidden from view from everyone nearby with them both crouched on either side of me.

I reluctantly obeyed, and continued to drink until he stopped me.

"Alright, up." Lazarus ordered. He rose first, followed by Deiric, and the two of them yanked me to my feet. I was swaying for just a moment and held on to Deiric for some stability.

"What the hell happened?" I looked at Lazarus, then at Deiric.

"You used too much power." Lazarus hissed. "You need to be more careful so you don't use up *all* your energy on a single strike." He was scolding me, but there was a gentleness in his voice that I hadn't ever really heard from him before. He looked at Deiric. "If she looks like she's fading again, find someone else for her to feed from. You can't handle losing any more blood than you already have." He glanced around again. "We cannot have anyone here seeing her that weak." His tone was no longer gentle. Those last few statements were an order.

Deiric nodded, and looked around us for a brief moment before he locked eyes with me as Lazarus walked away to help his men. "Are you alright?"

"That's the third time you've asked me that." I said softly.

He smiled. "Well, at least you remember the first two times. You looked paler than a ghost for a few seconds there." He paused for a moment as he looked me over. "We should get you home as soon as we're able." He said softly.

Macha still stood a few feet from us on the ground, standing next to the warlock I'd killed. *You will need to feed again soon.* She said softly. *Lazarus is right. That was a bit too much for you.* She turned to the warlock and pecked a bit at him.

Gross. I thought to her. She merely cocked her head at me slightly and then went back to snacking on him. I guess she had a point to give me that look. I didn't really have room to talk given that I practically fileted him for her.

Chapter 42

Mira

Garrick walked over to us, as the others had started to gather around Deiric and I.

"That was certainly a remarkable display of power." He seemed genuinely fascinated. "What did you do to all of them?"

I stared at him blankly for a few seconds, then looked around at the field ahead of us, where everyone still lay unconscious. "I knocked them out." I explained.

"And the magisters?" He asked.

"I took their magic."

"Took it?" I locked eyes with him again. His face had gone pale, and that was indeed fear I saw in his eyes.

"Yes."

"How?" He stepped back slightly as he asked that.

"Honestly? I don't know how. I was acting entirely on instinct, or by some guidance beyond myself." I said, and looked down at Macha again, who didn't even look up for a moment.

"The raven?" He asked. Macha looked at him now and he recoiled another step.

"No. She notified me Deiric was in trouble just before I did that, but she didn't offer me any other guidance." I looked up at him again.

"I don't *have* their magic. I gave it back to the earth." I gestured toward the ground.

He just stared at me for a few moments, utterly speechless. "How did you come to have the Raven as a familiar? I know you said you prayed to the gods, but how or rather, who sent it to you?" He finally asked after a few moments of awkward silence.

"I prayed to the Morrigan." I said coldly. I stood a bit taller, no longer needing to lean on Deiric at least for the moment. "I need to erect a temple in her honor. It was a part of our bargain."

His eyes went wide again. He looked at Deiric, Macha, and then back at me again before his face finally softened some into an unreadable look. "We'll assist in the creation of the temple in whatever way we can."

"Thank you." I mumbled, then looked beyond him to where Devlon was still organizing his magisters.

Garrick followed my gaze. "We have magisters of our own to swear in, but we can handle that another day." He said while he watched the process with me.

I looked back at him again. "We should be doing that today as well. If we're intending to have things balanced, we must have all of our magisters assigned right away."

He turned to me with a raised brow. "Do you have any suggestions?"

I gestured over to where Devlon and the new Solas magisters were standing. "Well, for starters, we can include women."

"I already offered a position to you." He retorted.

"More than just me." I cut in before he could continue with his thought.

"So you'll accept the title?" He asked casually. He stood as still as a statue this whole time, his body language still a bit cautious.

"I will accept the title, I suppose. Although I think a new title may need to be created for someone who is effectively immortal *and* a sorceress."

He raised a brow and finally relaxed some. "Do you have a suggestion?"

I smiled, and glanced at Deiric who simply looked at me a bit confused. "Well, actually, yes." I looked over at Garrick again. "I don't think that I'm nearly old enough for it though."

Deiric huffed a laugh, realizing what I was about to say. "Technically, if it is a *new* title, it can have its own rules." He mumbled. "And you are the *only* one of your kind."

Garrick looked at Deiric, who did not meet his gaze, and then back to me. "Out with it then."

"I am thinking Elder Mage might be a bit more fitting, since I am distinctly more powerful than any other magister, and I would be better suited to maintain the balance between the two covens rather than be a part of the leadership in one." I looked beyond him again to where Devlon was now walking over to us. "We'd probably want to include Solas in this discussion, so I could be formally recognized by both sides."

Devlon shifted in front of us just moments after I finished saying that. "Do you need any help healing anyone from your coven?" He was looking at me as he asked, rather than Garrick.

I glanced at Garrick.

Summoned to speak again, he looked over at Devlon, who met his gaze. "I think we're alright. I believe that more damage was done to those who didn't ally with us than anything else."

Devlon nodded. "We'll take care of them." He looked at me now. "Thank you for healing them at least enough to give us time to get around to all of them." He looked me up and down for a moment. "That was quite impressive."

"It seems you've walked up at the perfect moment." I said with a small smile. "We were just discussing my title within the coven." I gestured to Garrick with a jerk of my chin. "He had suggested Magister, but I think that I have a more fitting role in mind."

Devlon raised an eyebrow. "There isn't anything at that level aside from a magister or an archmage."

"It would be a new title." I explained. "An Elder Mage, the only elder mage, I suppose. I would oversee everything and keep the balance between our covens."

Devlon smiled. "It would be nice to have someone who is solely dedicated to keeping the balance so this doesn't happen again. A liaison so to speak." He glanced at Garrick, then Deiric, and then back to me. "I like 'Elder Mage', it is ancient and alluring."

Deiric stepped closer to me, likely an instinct before he even realized he'd done it.

Devlon glanced at him. "Relax, Elder." He smirked. "I saw enough to know that she wouldn't have reacted the way she did just before she ended this battle for anyone other than a mate."

I raised a brow and he locked eyes with me when I cocked my head in surprise and confusion. "You know more about us than I would've expected."

"My father was a sorcerer in the Oíche coven, but my mother is in the Solas coven. I learned plenty about both." He said simply. "Did you think some random Solas sorcerer would *really* care that much about balance between the covens if he didn't have something to gain or some kind of history between the two covens?"

I almost smiled, but then I realized he said *was,* not *is,* in reference to his father. "*Was* in the Oíche coven?"

"He didn't survive the attacks."

I frowned. "I'm sorry. That's something we have in common I suppose"

He shrugged. "I worked like hell to get to this position so I could try to find a way to rebalance things myself. It doesn't bring him back but it helps prevent others from experiencing the same kind of loss."

"How did you manage to hide your connection to our coven? I imagine the magisters never would've considered you for that spot if they knew about it." I had to know.

"That is a story for another time, but my mother made sure that secret stayed buried. Until now at least." Devlon smiled. "Keep me posted on the status of the rebuild on your side of things." He turned and began walking away before he finally shouted back. "I look forward to working with you, Alesmira."

Chapter 43

Mira

I turned to Garrick. “I trust you’ll get the new magisters sworn in today?”

He nodded. “We can make your title more official at the meeting to discuss the treaty between the covens.” Then he turned to walk back to the rest of the sorcerers and sorceresses several yards away who were slowly gathering in small groups as they finished healing one another.

“Are you able to shift us home?” Deiric said softly.

Before I could respond Elias appeared in front of us. “I’ve been informed that you all may need some assistance in getting back to the manor.” A small smile found its way to his lips for a moment when he glanced at me.

I nodded and he shifted us without another word, including Macha, who merely squawked in response to being removed from the person she’d been snacking on.

“We’ll check in once everyone has dispersed and things are more organized.” Elias said, and then he was gone.

"We need to go hunting." Deiric said as Eimear walked around us and was about to say something. "Go in, get yourself cleaned up. We'll be back eventually."

She nodded and turned to walk into the manor.

Aris appeared next to me now. "Are you alright?" I turned to look at him and his concern was written all over his face. "I saw you collapse."

"I'm better now." I said. My voice was still a bit hoarse, but I didn't feel like I'd faint at least.

Aris nodded and then headed for the manor himself. The others slowly followed suit, leaving Deiric and I alone outside.

I looked over at him for a moment, and locked eyes with him. "Are you sure that *either of us* can actually handle hunting at the moment?"

He smiled. "We're not going after an animal this time, so yes." He paused for a moment, and brushed a loose piece of my hair out of my face. "There is a village not far from here. I'm sure we can find someone suitable."

I stared at him a bit surprised. We hadn't ever hunted *humans* up until this moment.

"Just trust me." He pulled me along with him, his arm slipping from my waist to my hand as he walked toward the woods in the direction of the village he mentioned. "It'll be far better for you than whatever I could catch out here anyway."

I followed him for what felt like forever. We finally reached the village when the sun had already set, and I was exhausted again.

"Wait here." He said quietly, before he turned and headed into the village.

He came back several minutes later, dragging a rough looking man behind him, still conscious and alert, willingly following him.

My confusion must've been clear on my face, because he gave me a small smile and said, "I've compelled him." He shoved him toward me. The man stumbled a bit and then stared at me sort of blankly. "He's a menace, a criminal, and will not be missed. He's all yours."

I hesitated, and just looked between Deiric and this man, then back to Deiric. Deiric sighed, then he grabbed the man, and was in front of me in the blink of an eye. "There's a bounty on his head, dead or alive." Deiric said flatly. His fangs were out now, eyes dark and he had a sinister look on his face. He held his head to the side to expose his neck as he pushed him into me. "Think of him like one of your marks and drink him dry Mira."

Deiric's lips curled up into a smile when I grabbed the man from him and sank my fangs into his neck. Deiric turned and walked back to the village.

He didn't struggle, or fight back. It was almost too easy. Deiric returned a few moments after I'd finished him off, and looked like he'd found someone for himself to feed on. He still had blood dripping from his mouth.

That sinister smile found its way to his lips again. "Shall we go retrieve our bounty, my beautiful lady of the night?"

A similar smile found its way to my lips. He cleared the distance between us in the blink of an eye and slipped his hand up into my hair, letting his other arm slide around my waist. His face was inches from mine. "Just when I thought I couldn't fall more madly in love with you, you have to go and look at me like that." His eyes met mine, black as night, that sinister smile shifting into something with more hunger, something more sultry.

My hands slid up and around his neck, into his hair and I pulled him in closer, until our lips were almost touching. “I could say the same about you.”

He gently pressed a kiss to my lips, before he pulled back slightly and his fangs finally retreated, eyes returning to that beautiful blue. “We *should* go turn him in before we get too distracted.” He had a sly smile on his face now.

I let my own fangs retract. “I suppose you’re right.” My hands slid down from his hair, across his jaw line and wiped some of the blood away with my thumb. “We can finish *this* later.” I said with a sultry smile.

He stepped back and heaved the man over his shoulder, then motioned for me to follow after he finished wiping off his face with his sleeve.

I wiped my face on my sleeve as well, and followed him into the village to retrieve our bounty.

Chapter 44

Mira

I woke the following morning to the sound of someone clearing their throat. I was sprawled across the bed and Deiric, with my head resting on the middle of his chest and my right arm wrapped around him. I sighed and started to move when his grip around me tightened and he yanked the sheet up over me with his other hand.

He let out a low snarl. "What the hell are you doing here Silas?" His voice was still groggy with sleep, but the anger still gave it the bite it needed.

I opened my eyes, and Silas was standing right at the end of our bed, smirking. It was probably mid-morning, but we had been up very late last evening, and didn't anticipate being bothered with anything today.

"Mira has been summoned to the meeting they're having to discuss the terms between the covens today." Silas' voice was dripping with amusement as he stared down at us.

"And you had to come in here personally to wake us up?" I snarled before Deiric had the chance. I used the arm that had been wrapped around him to pull the sheets closer to my chest when I lifted myself up to glare at him.

He scoffed. "Would you rather I sent someone else?" He raised a brow and leaned in toward us, with his arms crossed.

"I would have rathered you knock on the fucking door." Deiric snapped.

Silas straightened, shrugged, and brushed invisible dirt off of his shoulder. "The door was cracked, so it would've swung open anyway." His tone was entirely dismissive. "The meeting is just after noon. Lazarus also requested you, Deiric, and Aris. Teron's manor needs an elder."

They had said it was something that we would need to discuss. I suppose it made sense for Aris to take over that manor in my father's place.

"Is that where they're holding the meeting?" I asked, but continued to glare at him.

"Yes." Silas said, very matter of factly, and then turned to walk out of the room. He stopped just as he reached the door and glanced back over his shoulder. "Oh, and I trust you'll wear something formal. This is an *official* meeting. You'll want to look the part." Then he left, not bothering to close the door behind him.

Deiric sighed and his head dropped back to his pillows. I was still stuck on the word *formal*.

Deiric lifted his head and looked at me and I turned to look back at him. "Formal dress is usually what you've seen *him* wear when he comes to these meetings, for us anyway. Or, we wear our armor. It generally depends on the nature of the meeting. You'll have to wear a dress similar to what Eimear wore the last time we were at the manor."

I considered that for a moment. A semi-formal gown, of course. I found myself thinking back to my time in that manor when I eavesdropped outside of the meetings in my plain clothes. I would've hated being paraded around in formal attire if I had been allowed in them. I never paid attention to what my father or Aris wore.

"The dress Silas gave you would actually be perfect." Deiric finally said softly. "Though I hate to admit that." He had a small smile on his face. "I'm guessing he anticipated this one day happening. He may be a prick on a good day, but he does have far better political foresight than I do."

I laid my head on his chest again. We still had time to lay around and be lazy a little longer before we *had* to go. I suddenly dreaded this, despite that yesterday I was welcoming a new title for myself. I hated those meetings. I hated the magisters that had run them back then even more.

"You never explained *why* you hated those meetings so much, aside from your lack of inclusion in them." Deiric kissed my head and laid back on his pillows. "Aris explained *some* of it, but refused to go into detail."

I considered it for a moment. "Is it awful that I sort of hope the magisters I remember from back then were some of the ones lost in the attacks?" My voice was cold and distant.

Deiric squeezed my shoulder. "I'd feel better answering that question if you gave me a better understanding of *why* you feel that way."

I sighed. "I am sure that Aris said I wasn't supposed to know *what* I was, did he not?"

I felt Deiric nod his head.

"Well, I wasn't supposed to know *what* I was because they never intended to have me transition. Their plans were always to keep me ignorant of what I was and hide me from

Solas, and anyone outside of the coven." I paused for a moment, remembering some of the arguments I overheard. My father was always furious when he came out of those meetings.

"Honestly, I'm not sure how they thought I *wouldn't* figure it out eventually given that I would live far longer than any of the other sorceresses my age, and age *incredibly slowly* once I reached maturity but they didn't seem concerned." I huffed a laugh. "My father never knew or noticed that I eavesdropped. Aris did though, and would talk me through it when we snuck off to train at night."

Deiric laid quietly while I explained, his hand now lazily tracing circles on my back.

"I knew women weren't allowed in the meetings, but I don't think I ever understood *why* they wouldn't want me to transition until just recently. It finally hit me that we didn't have a single *female* vampire or death dealer anywhere except Liala when we went to Valla and they immediately picked me out as a sorceress. I guess me being born a *girl* was probably a frustrating disappointment."

"I am *sure* that your parents didn't feel that way." Deiric cut in before I could say another word.

I scoffed a little. "I was an accident." I said flatly. "I don't think they had any idea *what* to expect. But from what I gathered eventually my father found himself in deep shit when the coven found out about me. Especially when they found out I *did* have magic."

I finally turned and rested my chin on Deiric's chest so I could look up at him. "Do you know what happened with the first Dhampir to make them hate me so much?"

He lifted his head again and met my gaze. "I was new when the first Dhampir was killed." His voice was soft, contemplative even. “I don’t know much about him. Lazarus would be able to tell you more. I don’t think they *hated* you, but I know that they didn’t ever want another to be created.”

He reached up and tucked my hair behind my ear. “I only heard that you existed years ago and nothing more. They were very cagey on all the details back then. If a decision was made to *not* turn you, I can almost guarantee that didn’t come from us. The magisters would’ve made that decision all on their own and shut us out no matter what we said in protest.”

He paused for a brief moment. “We have never been *against* turning a woman. I just can’t imagine that there are many women who would want to hunt monsters for an eternity.” A small smile found its way to his lips. “But we also haven’t ever asked.”

I smiled up at him. “Perhaps we *should* ask the female nightmages. Give them a choice like we do the men?”

“I guess you can bring that up at one of our private coven meetings.” He said softly. “But I think we should get moving now, so we’re not late to this one.”

I sighed again, and slowly started to sit up and make my way off the bed to get cleaned up and get ready.

Chapter 45

Mira

I shifted Deiric, Aris, and myself to the manor. It seemed they decided we were having the meeting in the foyer. The front doors were open and I could hear them all inside.

When we walked in, everyone was split into two groups, with all nine magisters from the Solas coven on one side and all nine from the Oíche on the other. I was surprised to see everyone there already. We arrived just before noon, to make sure we weren't late.

Lazarus walked over to us, from where he was lurking off in the corner of the room behind us. "I assume we have you to thank for cleaning up the place before we got here." He had a slight smile on his face.

I met his gaze, which quickly fell to look over my dress, but then rose back up to meet mine. "I couldn't stand to see it in such shambles when we were here for the last meeting." My voice was flat.

"They all arrived early in anticipation that they'd have to clean it up before the Solas magisters got here, but were pleasantly surprised when they found it clean already." He nodded to Deiric and Aris, finally acknowledging their presence. "We'll need to chat after the meeting is over." He said to Aris.

"Are we waiting on anyone else?" I cut right to business, donning my familiar mask. I glanced around and saw Killian walking over to us now, but no other death dealers. No sign of Elias either.

"No." Lazarus said quickly. Noting my confusion he continued, "Silas and Elias are not necessary. Deiric, myself, and Killian are here for you. Otherwise we would not be necessary either."

I raised a brow. "For me?"

"You should not attend these meetings without a few of us along with you." The tone of his voice said enough. They were here for my protection, if I needed it. It seemed odd, given that I didn't feel I needed *any* protection, but I wasn't going to argue with him.

"Understood." I looked beyond him back to the main area of the foyer. There was a long table in the middle of the room with nine chairs setup on either side. At the head of the table was one chair, and behind it were four others, two on either side, likely arranged by Lazarus for them to sit with me. I looked back at Lazarus just briefly before motioning toward them.

I began to make my way to my seat for the afternoon, and Lazarus, Deiric, Killian, and Aris followed.

Garrick and Devlon finally took notice of our arrival as we strode through the foyer, and began ushering the rest of the magisters to take their seats.

I took my seat at the head of the table. Deiric and Aris took the chairs to my right while Lazarus and Killian took the chairs to my left. When everyone had finally settled, it was Garrick who spoke first.

"We need to set the terms for our alliance, or peace treaty of sorts." He said. "I'm hoping we can keep this short. I don't believe it needs to be a very long and drawn out discussion."

I glanced at Devlon. "I believe it should be fairly straightforward." He started, glancing at me while he spoke rather than Garrick. "First and foremost we have the matter of Mira, who has suggested the title of Elder Mage for herself." He looked around the table. "This position will require her to act as the mediator between our covens, and keep the balance at all times. She will be our swing vote."

I nodded.

"She should also be included in all of Solas' private coven meetings as well. In order to keep the peace between us, she will need to be aware of what *both* covens have going on within them." He paused briefly and looked at all of his magisters. "Do any of you have any issue with welcoming her into *our* coven?"

My jaw dropped for a moment, but I gathered myself quickly and returned my face to a neutral expression. Not before Tellus noted my reaction and smirked, though. Not a single one of the magisters spoke up against the idea. This was certainly *not* what I expected from this meeting today.

Devlon turned to look at me. "Would you be willing to be initiated as a part of our coven as well?"

I wanted to glance at Garrick, or any of the magisters from *my* coven, but I could imagine the looks they were likely giving me right now. I was sure this had caught them just as off guard as me, despite that I guess this is the obvious choice to make.

"I would be honored." I said with a subtle nod of my head.

"Wonderful." Devlon said, with a small smile finding its way to his lips. "For the purpose of this alliance, or treaty, however you prefer to refer to it, Mira will sign as a member of both covens."

I finally turned enough to see Garrick's face, along with several of the others and they didn't seem as surprised as I was. I assumed this was discussed on the battlefield yesterday, after I had left.

"There is no initiation ritual, unlike your coven. We don't mark our members." He smirked.

I just nodded and returned his smirk.

"All bounties set out by this coven will be canceled, effective immediately. Should there ever be an issue with one of the members of either of our respective covens it should be dealt with by the coven that they belong to, or agreed upon between us before a bounty or punishment is spelled out if needed." Devlon began the negotiations for the alliance now.

I had forgotten there was still technically a bounty on my head and shifted a bit in my chair, but otherwise didn't react.

"We should also dictate that any feuds between members of our respective covens will be dealt with on a case by case basis and brought before all of us here to resolve." Garrick added, I presume anticipating that there was still a fair amount of animosity among all of the lower ranking members.

"The king and the people will go back to governing themselves without our influence and all of the previous taxes we set out for them will no longer be in effect." Tellus said. He glanced at me now. "Death Dealers will resume their previous tasks of handling any threats to the villages as they did before the attacks if they're able."

Lazarus spoke up from beside me. "We will need time to rebuild our ranks, but Mira has at least taken care of some of our concerns already."

Tellus nodded. "You can return to those duties as slow as is needed to allow for new members to be trained and safe to be around humans."

"Any attacks on any member of either coven will be dealt with swiftly and harshly. Attacks made on manors of either coven will stand as a declaration of war." A female magister whom I had yet to meet from our side spoke up. She stared boldly at the Solas magisters.

"Do you have a specific punishment in mind?" I found myself speaking before my mind could fully catch up to the words now falling out of my mouth.

Her gaze shot to me, as did most of the others. "I hadn't considered a specific punishment, no." Her eyes and body language gave nothing away, but I could *smell* the fear as her gaze lingered on me.

"The punishment should fit the crime." I mused. "An eye for an eye so to speak." A few people shifted in their seats. "If the conflict or attack is within one coven, the magisters of that coven will determine the punishment. If it spans across the covens, then this group will decide." I glanced around at all of them. "There's no reason for extra bloodshed over a minor disagreement. I'm sure we can all agree on that?"

There was a heavy silence.

"Does anyone else have anything to add?" I asked.

I waited a few moments for people to speak up, when no one did I continued speaking. "We should meet regularly, to discuss any issues within the covens. We can do so with everyone in this room or we can appoint one magister to speak for the rest for each coven in a smaller meeting. Is there a preference?"

Devlon and Tellus whispered to one another briefly, as did the four magisters who had survived the attacks on our side. They all seemed to have a similar conclusion though they hadn't spoken it beyond a whisper yet.

"It's settled then." I said with a small smile. "We'll hold a smaller meeting with just the appointed magister."

There was a lot of shuffling and murmuring. They had forgotten what I was, and that I could hear them even when they whispered. I noted they also likely didn't all know about my ability to hear thoughts, something I planned to keep a secret as long as possible.

I waved my hand and a long scroll of paper appeared on the table in front of us, outlining everything they'd brought up in a good bit more detail including my role in everything.

"If there is nothing more to add, please take the time to review this and sign it." I glanced around at everyone one more time. "Every single magister from each coven must sign it." I specified.

Devlon reached for the scroll first, scanned through it slowly, and eventually signed it. He passed it to Tellus, and it made its way around the table. We all sat in silence while each person took their time reading it over.

When it had finally made its way around the table and was signed by Garrick I took it and signed it. A wave of my hand put a copy of it in Garrick and Devlon's hands. The appointed magisters that would work with me in our monthly meetings.

"Thank you all for your time." I said.

Devlon spoke up before everyone could rise to leave the table. "Before everyone disperses, we'd like to propose a gathering, a party of sorts to celebrate our alliance." He mused. He had a wide grin plastered on his face as he looked at me.

I raised a brow. "A party?" I tried not to act entirely disgusted by the idea, when in reality I truly loathed parties.

"Yes." Tellus said. "It seems only fitting since this was made possible by your infiltration of a very shitty party thrown by those old pompous pricks."

"Plus, we'd like the people to see that we are on good terms now." Devlon added, with a small smirk.

I huffed a laugh.

"I think that sounds like a wonderful idea." Garrick smiled, but it didn't meet his eyes. I could see some of the skepticism there, despite the signed treaty in his hands.

"We already took the liberty of making some arrangements this morning." Tellus added, and some of the other magisters in their group offered smiles of reassurance. "We have already sent word to the King of the reorganization among the covens, and he has agreed to host a ball in honor of our peace agreement. It will be a way to get word out quickly to the people as well, since the lords will be in attendance, or at least invited."

"They will likely want to discuss having some of the Oíche members assigned to their court as we had for our coven as well, but we can handle that another time so you have time to rebuild first." Devlon added.

A ball. I loathed parties, and a *ball* of all things. I heard Deiric stifling a laugh behind me. He leaned closer to me, just enough to whisper in my ear.

"Not a fan of parading around in a ball gown I take it?" He mused.

I snorted and shot him a look. It didn't go unnoticed by Devlon, who smirked when I met his gaze, seeing my distaste written all over my face.

Garrick stood and reached across to Devlon and Tellus to shake each of their hands. "Please let us know if there's anything we should assist with."

Devlon and Tellus also rose from their seats.

"We've taken care of everything." Tellus smiled. "Spread the word to your coven. The ball is scheduled for Friday evening starting at eight o'clock. All are welcome. There will be plenty of space and food for everyone."

Devlon glanced at me, and waved to Deiric, Aris, Lazarus, and Killian still sitting behind me. "Death dealers are welcome as well, there will be plenty of whiskey and mead available for everyone."

I offered him a small smile and nod, despite that the idea still made my skin crawl a little bit, before I too rose from my seat.

Deiric, Lazarus, Killian, and Aris rose from their seats at last, as well as most of the other magisters who got up and began to chat amongst themselves. They were shaking hands and making casual introductions with each other.

"We've also taken care of the entertainment already." Devlon's smirk got a little larger. "It will be a fun evening."

Something about his comment made me a little *less* excited to find out what their entertainment might be, but I shifted my focus to the guys behind me. The four of them all had rather amused expressions on their faces.

"I never knew you had such a problem with parties." Lazarus said. "You seemed to have no problem attending that party days ago."

I glared at him. "That was work. If you gave me a choice, I wouldn't have attended that out of my own free will either."

He raised a brow. "And yet you offered to go." There was a light questioning tone to that statement.

"You know precisely why I offered to go. That was the *first* formal party I've ever attended. I loathe dressing up. I'd much rather drink in a seedy tavern somewhere and dance around there than take part in those absurd ballroom dances."

"You managed to find a gown for this gathering today." Killian said with a small sly smile.

"Silas gifted this to me. I don't own any gowns aside from this."

Aris chuckled and put a hand on Deiric's shoulder. "You're going to have your hands full with her. Best of luck my friend."

Lazarus smirked at me again, and then motioned for Aris to follow him a few steps away so they could discuss him becoming the elder for this manor. A title he certainly earned.

"We'll have to find you another gown I suppose." Deiric's voice dripped with amusement, and strangely something else that I couldn't put my finger on.

"I'm sure Silas could help." Killian offered, earning him a snarl from me.

"I'll find something on my own, thank you very much." I snapped.

Killian shrugged. "He does have exquisite taste."

Chapter 46

Mira

It took me a while, but I managed to find a gown I didn't absolutely hate, to my surprise. It was made of glimmery black satin fabric, with a skirt that hugged the tops of my hips and dipped in a low v-shape in the front a few inches below my navel. It was floor length and had a slit up the right side, which was only visible when I walked or moved. The top piece of the gown had a neckline which dipped down between my breasts and connected up around my neck. It cut off just below my chest wrapped around my back with a delicate silver chain where the top connected to the skirt. My entire back was exposed because the skirt dipped low there as well and rested just above the base of my spine.

Deiric only disliked it because of how revealing it was, but to his credit didn't push back too much when it was the first one I decided I didn't hate. He wore a black and silver tunic, with intricate embroidery one could argue was fit for a king. It was far fancier than anything I'd ever seen him in and matched the gown I'd chosen perfectly.

Everyone else had similar black or dark navy tunics of varying levels of adornment, while Liala and Eimear wore gowns that were equally as sparkly as mine but covered far more of themselves. Liala's was a soft lilac color, and Eimear's was a beautiful royal blue.

I shifted us there, just outside of the palace walls, where the coaches were arriving for the lords, and the palace was like nothing I'd ever seen. The stone walls towered over us. We were ushered through to the gardens and eventually a massive open courtyard. It was decorated with flowers, candles, and floating balls of light I assumed were powered by some of the Solas sorcerers magic.

The king, queen, and some members of their court were seated at a table opposite to where they had set up a stage of sorts for whatever this evening's entertainment would be. They were chatting with some of the magisters from Solas who lingered up by them when we arrived.

We began to make our way through the crowd of people and found Lazarus first, who already had a glass of whiskey in his hand.

He smiled as we approached. "I see you found a gown." He looked me up and down for a moment. "I certainly wouldn't have expected it to be so risqué."

Deiric glared at him resulting in an eyeroll from Lazarus and me.

Lazarus lingered with us, seeming to have arrived by himself. He and Deiric were both still on edge and keeping a careful eye on me. It only added to the questions I had about the first Dhampir, who by my understanding was not around long enough to make an impact. Tonight wasn't the time for that discussion though.

Devlon spotted us from across the courtyard and shifted in front of us in the blink of an eye. He handed Deiric and I each a glass of whiskey.

"Welcome." His lips curled into a wide grin. "I hope you'll find this to your liking?"

I took the glass, as did Deiric, but neither of us took a sip.

Devlon frowned just for a moment. "You *do* like whiskey don't you?"

"We do." Deiric said curtly.

"The last time I had a drink in the same room as someone associated with Solas it didn't end very well for me. You'll have to forgive us if we're a bit hesitant to drink, even with the treaty." I added, which got me a look from Lazarus.

"*You* are a part of Solas too now, you know. Still, I can accept the hesitation." Devlon said, barely batting an eye at our lack of interest in the drinks. "Still, I hope you enjoy the entertainment we've lined up for the evening."

"Some lovely orchestra to play those bland ballroom melodies I'm sure." I said the words before I could stop myself.

Devlon actually laughed at me. "That's not the entertainment I'm referring to. Although there *will* be some of that as well." He turned and gestured for us to follow him. "This way."

He walked over to the other side of a large courtyard where there were tables and chairs scattered about, all just as lavishly decorated with flowers, table cloths, and centerpieces as the rest of the courtyard and gardens had been. He had reserved a table for us, for some reason, despite that we wouldn't be eating.

"Please have a seat." He smiled. "The first part of this evening's entertainment will begin shortly."

We all took our seats, Lazarus sat to my left and Deiric to my right, while the rest of our crew shuffled around us to fill the remaining seats at the table. I looked over to where the "entertainment" he mentioned would be setting up for the evening, and shrunk back in my seat.

"What?" Deiric asked, before following my gaze. He couldn't stop himself from laughing. "Oh for fuck's sake."

There, setting up at the stage was Cedric. He wore a lavish navy tunic, dressed to the nines for this event. There were *several* other bards milling about close by. Bards I recognized almost immediately and I could have died right there.

"What?" Lazarus asked, entirely confused by whatever it was Deiric found so amusing. Within moments, the remainder of our crew was giggling or chuckling right along with Deiric.

"And here I thought this would be dreadfully boring." Zane muttered behind me.

"You keep your mouth shut." I snapped back at him. I turned to face the table and glanced at them. Aris just sat with a shitty grin on his face.

"Watch it, Zane. You know damn well she'll make sure you're paired up with her for sparring tomorrow and kick your ass." Aris muttered.

I casually emptied the whiskey from my glass under the table only to summon a decanter of Deiric's whiskey from the house and pour myself a very tall glass. I also summoned glasses for the rest of them, should they decide to drink with us.

"I'm clearly missing something here." Lazarus said, doing the same thing with his drink.

Deiric calmed himself down enough to *also* empty his glass onto the ground and refill it with the whiskey we trusted before he finally said, "Oh, don't worry you'll find out soon enough."

I looked over at Lazarus who was still immensely confused, sipping his drink. "It's better that you *don't* understand what they've found so entertaining." I turned to face the open courtyard and stage again.

"Oh I highly doubt that." He said with a smirk and a brief chuckle.

Almost as if on cue, one of the bards, Beitris, locked eyes with me from across the courtyard. Her face lit up and she darted over to me. She wore a beautiful violet gown, long and flowing gracefully around her. It glimmered with each step. The top of the gown clung tightly to her curves and perfectly accentuated her features.

She looked far more formal than she'd been the last time we saw each other, but still just as beautiful. Her long golden hair was done up in a braid around her head and wound tightly into a bun. Her lips were a brilliant shade of red.

"Scáil!" She was beaming at me. "I didn't think I'd ever run into *you* again." Her voice was bright and cheery, despite the emphasis she put on the word you as she spoke.

Deiric almost choked on his whiskey. The bastard.

"Beitris." I said softly. "How are you?"

She snorted. "I suppose I should be flattered that you remembered my name. I'm doing quite well. I hear you've been busy lately."

I let my eyes wander for a few moments, taking her in again. "Do you really think you're that easy to forget?" A sultry smile found its way to my lips. I could feel the look Deiric was giving me now without having to see it. *I told you I'd look, but not touch. Calm down.*

Deiric scoffed beside me and casually sipped his drink.

Lazarus was eyeing her up now, I could see him out of the corner of my eye.

"Don't bother Lazarus." I glanced at him for a moment before I met her gaze again. "She doesn't swing that way anyway."

She snorted. "That you know of anyway." She gave him a brief glance and a smile.

Lazarus chuckled and leaned back in his chair, at least beginning to partially understand what everyone found so entertaining. "Oh this is just glorious." He clinked his glass with Deiric's behind me. "I'm not sure we have enough whiskey." He commented.

Deiric leaned back in his chair and slipped his arm nonchalantly around my shoulders. "No, we certainly don't."

I ignored them. "They must be paying quite handsomely to have all of you here." I gestured toward the group of the other bards who were gleefully chatting away and hadn't noticed that I was in attendance yet.

She didn't even glance behind her. "These parties *always* pay handsomely, but you never decline a request from the king." She glanced at the rest of the crew around me, who were now observing us quietly. "Are these all of the death dealers I've been hearing about?"

I nodded. "Some of them."

"Are you going to introduce me?" She smiled.

I smirked, sipped my drink, and gestured to Deiric. "Deiric," I gestured to Lazarus, "Lazarus," I waved my hand behind me and named them off in order. "Then we have Zane, Liala, Eimear, Renwick, Xander, Leo, and Aris. Eimear is a witch. Deiric, Lazarus, and Aris are elders." I assumed the classification of elder meant nothing to her but it felt worth mentioning.

Her eyes traveled around the group behind me, but doubled back in what I thought was Renwick's direction. "Renwick?" She asked, like she'd heard his name before, or knew him and hadn't noticed him until now.

My jaw hit the floor. "Renwick!" I spun around excitedly and his face was bright red. He was desperately trying to sink into the floor. I chuckled and spun around to look at her again. The sultry smile on her face filled in the shred of doubt that I had. "I take it back, I guess she does swing that way." That also explained how he learned that song.

Her gaze shifted to me again. "Well, this is certainly more interesting than I expected the night to get." Her cheeks flushed a bit. "I should get back and get ready." She spun around and headed over to the rest of them without giving me the chance to reply.

"She was fun." Renwick said, his voice barely a whisper.

"Oh yes she was." The sultry smile returned to my face as I remembered the night I spent with her.

Deiric mumbled something under his breath.

"You get me for an eternity, don't sit there and sulk because I had a little fun before you." I mumbled to him. He merely sipped his drink again in response.

After a few minutes, Cedric started to play. Some of the songs were about my various conquests, but not all of them. I summoned more whiskey, which we all casually drank as we sat back and watched people mill about around the gardens and the dancefloor.

I recognized several of the lords who wandered among the crowds, and I saw Garrick and Silas at one point, but none of them noticed us, despite that we were sitting very close to the stage.

Tellus wandered over when Cedric had finished his set and Beitris began to get herself set up. "I hope that you're enjoying the party?"

I raised my glass in response. "It's lovely."

"I especially appreciate the entertainment." Deiric added with a cocky grin, seeming to be back to enjoying how their presence made me squirm a bit as I prayed none of the rest of them ventured over here.

Tellus smirked. "We hoped it might be appreciated."

"Oh, you have no idea." I mocked, my voice laced with sarcasm.

He cocked his head a bit in confusion, but the smirk remained. "I take it you are not one for dancing then?" He raised a brow at me.

"I dance." I said defensively. I saw the look I got from Lazarus out of the corner of my eye, knowing my disdain for this party. "In taverns mostly." I finally added.

Tellus huffed a laugh. "Well, perhaps as the night goes on you'll loosen up some." He glanced out onto the dancefloor where people were beginning to sway and spin around to the music, finally feeling the effects of the liquor.

I snorted, but didn't deign to reply.

He shrugged and wandered off to join the dancing.

I finished my glass and went to reach to refill it when Deiric caught my hand, and finished his glass.

"There's no sense in sulking in the corner all night. I don't see anyone here who seems to be a threat." He stood and pulled me to my feet with him. "Care to dance with me?"

I gave him a look to suggest he was out of his mind, but he sighed and pulled me along with him anyway. Zane, Liala, Renwick, and Eimear rose and followed. Leaving Xander, Aris, and Lazarus at the table, content to sit and watch.

"I am not nearly drunk enough for this." I commented.

Deiric spun me into him before I could say another word. "You weren't any more drunk that night at the manor than you are now. You just don't want to dance and let loose around this many people." He whispered into my ear, then spun me back out again.

I sighed. He pulled me closer to him as the music slowed down some.

"We won. It's over. Relax and have a little fun." He said softly.

Beitris started the song she'd written about me. The one Renwick sang that night, almost as if on cue.

I smiled, tried to relax a bit, and we danced and spun around just like we had that night. The rhythm and energy around us finally started to bring my tired and weary soul back to life again, a little bit at a time, with each new song.

Chapter 47

Mira

We were dancing around for quite a while, through one more bard, before the sound of a raven's caw above my head caught my attention. I knew it wasn't Macha, because we had left her at our manor for the evening, but it snapped me right back to being on guard.

Deiric and I locked eyes at the moment we both heard it, but didn't even slightly falter in our dancing. Our faces were both still masked as though we were blissfully unaware.

There are three men, armed with stakes now lurking in the party. They are human assassins. We do not know who sent them yet. Macha's voice was faint, far away in my mind, but still audible. She must have eyes everywhere.

I created shields around every single death dealer I knew at the party, myself included. Then I sent out my own message to all of them, including Deiric.

There are three assassins lurking among us, armed with stakes. Be on alert.

Deiric and I proceeded to dance in a way that would allow us to spin slowly, scanning the courtyard for anyone suspicious. Lazarus rose from the table and began to scan the crowd casually as well.

I spotted Devlon not far from us, chatting with one of his magisters. A blonde woman who looked strikingly similar to how I had when I donned my disguise at the last party.

His eyes met mine for an incredibly brief moment, but he must've noted something within my eyes or my face that prompted him to head in our direction. He pulled the magister with him as though they were coming out to dance.

"You've finally decided to join in the dancing I see." He said when they reached where we were dancing.

"It is certainly a lovely evening for it." Deiric's voice was colder than I think he intended.

We paused our dancing for a moment to stop and face Devlon and this woman.

"Mira, Deiric, I'd like you to meet Quinn, one of our newest magisters." Devlon motioned to her. "She was one of my best emissaries."

I gave her a polite nod. "It is good to officially meet you." My voice also came off a little bit colder than I intended, as I continued to cautiously scan the crowd behind her while I spoke. Deiric's arm stayed protectively around my waist.

"Are you looking for someone specific?" Devlon asked, noting my wandering eyes.

"I'm just enjoying seeing everyone so happy and carefree." I smiled and tried to keep my voice more light and cheery, though it hardly worked. Mind to mind, I spoke to him instead so I didn't alarm any of the people around us.

I'm told there are three assassins here, I assume for me. I would hope that they aren't here on behalf of someone within the coven.

The brief look of horror on his face said enough. He was not aware of these men. He quickly plastered a mask on his face though, and smiled. "Perhaps it's time we retire for the evening?"

Quinn jumped just slightly at those words and her brow furrowed for a moment until she looked from him to me, and then back again. "I suppose it is getting rather late." Her face was unreadable.

I wondered if this was some form of code between them, and if he had also sent her a message the way I had to him.

"If you'll excuse me. It was nice meeting you." She smiled and quickly scurried off to the edge of the courtyard where she spoke with someone else very quickly and I lost sight of her.

Devlon looked around us, and seeing nothing amiss he stepped closer so he could whisper to me. "That's always been our *shit has hit the fan* phrase." His smile was nervous now. "Tell me what you know." He motioned for us to follow him over to get some refreshments.

"I already did. I have no other information at the moment."

He nodded as we walked calmly to the table with drinks and light snacks.

A caw to my left prompted me to turn my head. A raven sat atop the garden wall and just beneath him stood a man all by himself that appeared to be scanning the crowd. I reached up and gently touched Devlon's shoulder, trying to keep my movements casual.

He glanced back at me and I motioned to the wall with my eyes. He dipped his chin in response, but didn't say a word. We'd need to take them down quietly, before they made their move if we were going to get any information from them about who sent them.

We reached the table and Devlon handed me a glass of wine.

Behind you. Macha's voice was ragged and quick this time, closer than she sounded before. She must be flying here.

I spun immediately and dumped my wine on a man approaching behind me. I grabbed his wrist when I bumped into him, and with it the stake he was dropping from his sleeve to his hand.

"Oh I'm so sorry. I didn't see you there." I said quickly, using my free hand to brush his tunic as though it had been an accident.

His expression didn't give anything away, but his eyes gave away all the fear that now simmered within him. My grip on his wrist got tighter, so much so that a little more pressure might have simply broken the bones in his arm. I would take pleasure getting answers out of him.

Tellus shifted next to him. "My apologies, Mira has had quite a bit to drink this evening." He smirked at me. "Allow me to help you get cleaned up?"

The man stared at me for a few more moments before he looked at Tellus, who already had a hand on his shoulder.

"It is in your best interest to go with him." Deiric snarled. "I can promise you that if you're left to me you won't need to even worry about the wine stains on your tunic."

I grabbed the stake with my other hand now, and released his arm so Tellus could shift him to wherever it was they were rounding them up. I shifted the stake away from us.

A small nod from Tellus and they were gone.

"That leaves one." I observed.

"I can promise you, they were not sent by us. I don't even recognize him. There must be someone else who is out to get you, and I'll take great pleasure in finding and ending them myself." Devlon's voice was probably even more threatening than Deiric's had been, if that was even possible.

There was another caw, over at the tables closest to where we had been sitting. Lazarus heard it and turned to see the raven circling above the man that was lurking in the shadows over there.

Devlon shifted, following my gaze, and grabbed him before Lazarus even made it to him.

That was the last of them. Macha said. *I am almost there and I will keep watch for other threats.*

Devlon appeared next to us again moments later. "If you'll follow me." He motioned across the courtyard and began walking swiftly in Lazarus' direction.

Deiric and I quickly matched his pace and followed him over to Lazarus.

"You'll want to follow me as well." Devlon said to Lazarus as we proceeded past the table to an opening in the hedges at the edge of the courtyard.

I checked my shields again, and we all followed him down a pathway to a different area of the gardens. After making it through the maze of tall bushes and plants, we finally came to another small courtyard where Tellus, Quinn, Garrick, and another one of the Oíche magister's now stood.

The men that they had caught were bound and sitting on their knees next to a large and extravagant fountain in the center of this space.

"I thought you might like to participate in our little interrogation. None of them seem willing to speak at all." Tellus commented as we approached.

Devlon walked over to stand with them.

I stopped a few steps away from the one sitting in the middle of the group, who I'd dumped my wine on. Shadows slithered out from me, and surrounded them. They squirmed some, but otherwise didn't react.

"What is your purpose here this evening?" My voice was cold and flat.

His response was to spit at my feet.

I smiled. A shadow wrapped itself around his neck and began to slowly constrict.

"I'll ask you again. What is your purpose here this evening?"

His face was hard as stone. He glared at me as though he thought I was bluffing. I had no problem resorting to less desirable methods to get my answers.

"I could just compel him." Deiric offered, coming to stand to my right with his arms crossed.

I considered it for a moment. "I suppose that would work." I sighed a bit. "It's far less fun that way."

Lazarus chuckled behind me. "It's far less messy too."

I motioned for Deiric to proceed with compulsion.

Deiric approached him. My shadows found their way around his mouth so he couldn't spit in Deiric's face.

"You will tell us who sent you, and what your purpose was here this evening." Deiric said, his voice steady and calm. "You will answer every question she asks without hesitation, and give nothing but the truth."

The man nodded and I released my shadows. Deiric retreated to my side again. The rest of them stood silently watching.

"Now, what is your purpose here this evening?" I finally asked again.

"We were sent to assassinate you." He said flatly.

"By who?"

"We don't know who sent us the assignment. We received a small pouch of gold pieces with a note on our doorstep." He spoke freely now. "We would receive the rest of the payment when they confirmed you had been staked."

"Do you still have this note?"

"No. It disintegrated the moment that we accepted the task." He said.

"Interesting." I looked at the other two, who were now trembling. "Do you make a habit of hunting vampires?"

"We hunt whatever we are paid to hunt."

"Are there more of you?"

"No."

I looked over at Devlon. "A note that disintegrates when they accept the job suggests that whoever sent it either *has* magic, or is working with someone who does."

Devlon nodded. "We'll do an internal investigation."

"We will as well." Garrick added.

"What should we do with them?" Lazarus asked from behind me.

I stared down at them, and they all seemed fearful now. "They were just hired to carry out a job. They were disposable, and likely not expected to succeed." I said boredly. "If the person who hired them thought they would be successful there would be no reason to hide behind a mysterious letter."

They were human, sent to kill a vampire *and* a sorceress. They likely depended on the element of surprise or the fact that I would be intoxicated at a party, otherwise it was a suicide mission. In some ways, I admired their bravery.

I looked up and looked around at all of them. "This was a test. Whoever sent them is likely watching. They are probably here now."

Devlon, Lazarus, and Deiric did not appear phased by that statement, but Tellus, Quinn, Garrick and the other magister, whose name I had yet to even learn, were all horrified.

"Do you really think someone would be so bold to be at the same party where they ordered a hit?" Quinn asked softly.

I envied her innocence. "Of course they would. You underestimate the cruelty and general wickedness some people are capable of."

"I prefer to think the best of people." There was a slight snarkiness in her tone that cut through me like a knife. Especially when she stuck her nose up just slightly when she said it.

I felt the surge in my shadows, despite that I tried to stifle it when she struck that chord with me. Her eyes went wide for a fraction of a second and she stepped back.

I sighed, and my voice was as cold as ice. "You think that way because you haven't experienced the cruelty this world has to offer. Count yourself lucky and pray that you never do."

"That sounds vaguely like a threat." Tellus stepped slightly in front of Quinn.

"I don't make vague threats." I lifted my chin. "If I intended to threaten you, you would know. In a way I am envious of her ignorance to it all."

Tellus relaxed some, but didn't move away from her.

"While they seem to have a distaste for vampires, or at least for *us* they didn't come here for any reason other than the payment they were promised. You all can decide their punishment." I gestured to all of the magisters.

"You were about to torture them for answers and now you could care less what we do with them?" Quinn was utterly flabbergasted at my lack of interest in them now.

"I wanted to find out who ordered them here." I shrugged. "They can't give us that answer so they are no longer of use to me and they are hardly a threat." I stared at her for a moment, her distaste written all over her face. "If Deiric hadn't been here to compel them for answers, what would *you* have done? Asked them nicely?" I let my lips curl into a wicked smile.

Fire formed at her fists and I swear I saw smoke rise from her head.

"There it is." I chuckled. "I knew it was in there somewhere." The fire seemed to intensify. "Remember that feeling Quinn. It isn't quite the same as the rage and frustration you'd feel if you spent most of your life hunted simply for existing, but *that* is a small taste of the frustration you might feel if you couldn't enjoy more than forty-eight hours of peace before someone makes a move to kill you again."

Like I'd blown out a candle, she extinguished herself and just stared at me blankly.

"So yes, I couldn't care less what you do with them." I said, rather matter of factly. "Thank you for assisting in disabling them and getting them back here so we could interrogate them. I, unlike those who hunted me prior to this, have no desire for *power* so you can choose what you'd like to do with them. I would simply like to return to *enjoying* this overly fancy party you've thrown for all of us."

Devlon snorted and smiled. "So you *were* enjoying the party?"

"The bards were a nice touch." I offered him a small approving smile. "Now, shall we decide their punishment so we can get back out there and *maybe* see if there is someone who looks disappointed that I'm not dead?"

"We'll leave their punishment decision to the king." Devlon said. "Tellus, Quinn, and Liam, if you'd be so kind as to grab them and bring them out with us. I'm sure the king will have somewhere to keep them for the evening."

They nodded and each went to grab one. I called back the shadows that still lingered around them.

"Shall we?" Garrick finally said, as he walked through all of us. "This is not how I would like to spend the rest of my evening."

I turned and followed him, with Deiric and Lazarus close behind me. Devlon followed next and they drug the men back out with us.

Macha landed on my shoulder the moment we cleared the gardens and entered the courtyard again. *We've been scanning the crowds. I have not determined who may have ordered the hit yet.*

Thank you for keeping an eye on things for us. I reached up and gently ruffled the feathers at her neck. *I'll be sure to find you a meal fit for a queen.*

She responded by inching closer to my head and rubbing her head gently into my cheek.

Deiric offered me his arm. I took it and allowed him to lead me back out onto the dancefloor while Devlon and the magisters headed over to the king.

He smiled at Macha. “I think she’s going to scare away everyone around us.”

I glanced over at her, and she didn’t seem to have any intention of leaving my shoulder. I smiled. “I think I’m okay with that actually.”

Once we really started to dance she did finally fly off to our table, where she perched on my chair next to Lazarus. He seemed to have no interest in dancing or straying far from the table for the evening. I kept all of our shields up for the rest of the night, and was thankful to find that we had no further disruptions.

We didn’t ever determine who paid the assassins. We would have plenty of time to stress over that problem later, but tonight, we would celebrate our freedom. I had a feeling we were in for an eternity of being hunted, and I understood now that this ensured an eternity of working with and honoring the Morrigan as well.

Perhaps that was the plan all along. She had said she was expecting me. Perhaps, all this time, I actually had her to thank for my very existence. The Nightmare Queen, Queen of the Slain, creates a would-be creature of the night who has to die to be reborn as an immortal who will stand as a reminder to honor and worship the fierce Lady of War forever.

Chapter 48

Deiric

Tonight was the dark moon, and it was the perfect moment for what I had planned. Mira was still downstairs with Liala and Eimear, which gave me plenty of time to find the dress Silas had made for her. I slipped into the small closet where she stored the handful of gowns she had. I sorted through them until I found the one I was looking for, pulled it out of the closet and hung it on the door.

She would know something was up when she came into our room and saw it hanging there, but she wouldn't get the chance to question me before I could ask her. I stripped out of my fighting leathers then changed into a nice white tunic with my finest black and silver embroidered vest and a pair of plain black pants. I heard her light footsteps ascending the stairs and waited by the door for her to walk in.

She nearly jumped when she almost ran into me, then spun around to shut the door behind her. "Were you waiting there for me?" She smiled, then took in what I was wearing. "What are you–"

I pulled her into me with one hand at her waist while I cupped her face with the other to stop her with a kiss. She let out a soft laugh and smiled against my lips before she pulled back to look at me again.

"Okay, I'm not complaining, but *what* is going on?"

I smiled. "Well, you've done me an incredible honor by being my mate, but I thought it was time we might make that more official and I asked you to be my bride."

Her smile didn't falter, but she blinked in surprise. "I– Yes." She stammered. "Yes, of course I would." Her arms linked up around my neck. "So long as you don't make me go through with some large and elaborate ceremony."

"Nothing big." I leaned in so our lips were nearly touching. "But we can't skip the ceremony entirely."

"And what exactly did you have in mind?"

Despite her wish *not* to do a ceremony, her eyes seemed to sparkle with excitement. I brushed my lips against hers in the slightest kiss before I made a show of thinking it over and then smiled. "I was thinking we'd do it tonight *and* that you could wear that." I gestured toward the dress behind me with a nod of my head.

She glanced around me to see the dress hanging on the door. She narrowed her eyes at me, smile never faltering, and then slipped out of my grasp to walk toward it. "Fine." She reached up and pulled it down off the door. "But, if I find out you've got something extravagant planned I will *kill* you."

I rolled my eyes and smirked, but prayed that what I'd setup wasn't too *extravagant* for her while she began to change.

"Let me guess," she tossed over her shoulder while her skirt and corset dropped to the floor. "You already have someone lined up to *do* the ceremony somewhere. I just have to shift us there."

"Something like that." I leaned back against the dresser behind me and watched her pull her blouse up over her shoulders. Her bra fell to the floor next before she finally stepped into that gown.

"Better?" She asked, spinning around in it and smiling at me.

"Much."

Macha flew in and landed on her shoulder. I hoped the raven either didn't know of my plans, or didn't tell Mira if she did. "We should go to the Morrigan's temple first. Wouldn't want to be late for her offering."

"Of course." I smiled, walked over to her, and linked my elbow with hers. "Shall we?"

She eyed me suspiciously, but then smirked and shifted us just outside of the temple. We walked up the stairs of the large marble building together. When we reached the threshold, a flutter of black baccara petals rained down on us. Her confused, but excited laugh echoed in the large round chamber of the temple.

Silas handed me a single rose. I nodded my thanks and turned to hand it to Mira with a smile.

She took it, and seemed too stunned to speak. Silas just smirked, and walked in front of us to continue to toss the rose petals in a straight path to the altar where Lazarus stood waiting for us.

I'd have arranged for someone to play music, if you wouldn't have killed me for the extravagance.

She huffed a laugh. *I may still kill you anyway for bringing Lazarus* and *Silas into this.*

It'll be worth it.

We walked up to Lazarus together where he stood behind the altar with an uncharacteristically large smile on his face. Silas stopped to Lazarus' left, so he was standing to my right when we reached the altar.

"I'm surprised she agreed to this." Silas said with a knowing smirk.

Mira shot him a glare. "I'm surprised *you* are helping."

Silas shrugged, like it was really no big deal, and then Lazarus cleared his throat.

"We'll skip the 'if anyone objects' bit and get straight to business." He lifted up the white, black, and gray handfasting cord that he had braided together by my request. "Please entwine your left hands, binding your spirits, uniting your lives for eternity."

We joined hands, or wrists, actually, over the large marble bowl on the altar. Lazarus began to wrap the cord around our joined hands and tie it, while he said a very short blessing.

"With this material, I bind Alesmira and Deiric to the vows they make to each other. The binding is not formed by this knot, but by your vows. You hold in your hands and hearts the making or breaking of this union. Just as your hands are now bound together, so too are your lives. May you be forever one, sharing in all things, in love and loyalty, for eternity. May your marriage be blessed with patience and dedication, forgiveness and respect, love and understanding."

He finished the knot as he finished speaking, then he glanced between us. "I imagine you don't have any vows prepared." We both shot him a withering look. He smiled. "A blood oath then, before we exchange rings?"

We both nodded, and I started to open my mouth to say I didn't have rings either, but Mira smiled. *I'll take care of that.* I gave her a look asking what she meant, but she didn't elaborate.

She sat the rose she still held down beside the offering bowl beneath our tied hands, and called her sword to her hand. She passed it under her outstretched arm to Lazarus.

"A dagger would be far more practical." He commented as he lifted it up and motioned for us to offer up our other hands.

"We're in the Morrigan's temple, and likely going to seek her blessing. Shouldn't we use the sword she *personally* blessed for me?"

He made a face that said she had a point before he brought the sword up toward our hands. "Do you both know the blood oath?"

We nodded and he sliced both of our palms in one swipe. We joined our hands and I was surprised that neither of our hands seemed to heal like I would have expected. It was as if some kind of magic prevented it.

"You are blood of my blood, bone of my bone. I give you my body, that we might be one. I give you my spirit, until our life is done." We spoke in unison.

"I call upon the Morrigan to bless this union, if the Goddess of Death finds it favorable." Lazarus said, offering both of his hands up and outstretched toward us.

Wind blew into the temple, swirling the rose petals Silas had tossed on the floor up toward us while our hands continued to bleed into the bowl. The candles and torches blew out, leaving us in darkness until the wind receded. When the torches and candles lit again our hands were no longer bleeding and there was no blood in the bowl. In its place were all of the rose petals.

"Now for the rings."

Shadows swirled around our bound hands before slithering into two fine bands and encircling our ring fingers.

"Tattoos?" Silas asked, peaking over my shoulder.

"Someone didn't plan ahead and get rings made." Mira smiled.

Silas elbowed me. "Idiot."

I shot him a glare. "This is better anyway."

"If you say so." He settled back into where he had been standing behind me.

"By the power of the earth, sea, and sky, I now pronounce you bound in heart and spirit." Lazarus said, then began to carefully unbind our hands.

When our hands were finally free, I didn't give him the chance to say that we could kiss, before I spun her into my arms, dipped her down, and kissed her. I would never forget the absolute sparkle of joy in her eyes when I pulled back and gazed down at her.

"I love you." She breathed.

"I love you too, anamchara."

Silas patted my back. "Yes, we're well aware. Now, how are we going to celebrate?"

Mira laughed at the annoyed look on my face as I lifted her back up to her feet. "I vote we find the closest tavern and get sloshed."

I raised my brows at her and she laughed again. "What? No one is going to recognize us. Not for one night."

She gestured to Macha, who now perched on the offering bowl. "She can keep an eye out for anything suspicious."

"Fine." I smiled, still holding her close to me. "A tavern it is then."

Nearly an hour later, we were all drinking and dancing while a bard none of us had ever heard of sang all kinds of wild ballads about ancient battles and warriors. Even Lazarus, despite his usual lack of merriment, joined in.

Coven Hierarchy Explained:

Items grouped together (without an extra line break) are at the same level as far as authority in the coven.

Elder Mage - Vampire/Sorceress - only one of its kind.
Magister - Overall Leaders of Coven - 9 in total per coven.

Archmage - In charge of relics and enchanted objects, finding and training sorcerers/sorceresses.
Castor - Chosen by the spirits/gods and gifted with unique abilities.

Sorceress/Sorcerer/Mage - Abilities with a certain element (or multiple elements depending on power level). Can enchant objects, tattoos, etc. more powerful than a witch.

Elder/Master Death Dealer - The leader of a legion of vampires similar to a general in an army. Also the oldest vampire in the legion. Will always have a daylight ring. 300+ years old.

Witch/Warlock - Lower level member who can do simple spells for the public, healers.
Death Dealer - Vampires that report to the Elder. The "soldiers" of the coven, handling deadly beasts and battles. Only given daylight rings as needed.

Nightmage - Has no magic but born of a magic bloodline. Usually natural healers, create potions, etc. Can be turned to Death Dealers if they choose to.

Acknowledgements

I am not sure where to start, because honestly I never expected to *actually* write this book. I had so many creative ideas as a teenager, and after I got my first job a lot of my creative pursuits got pushed aside while I chased other dreams and worked myself half to death. I was a people pleasing workaholic who worked to avoid her emotions, there's no other way to say it. The chaotic rollercoaster that is my life finally slowed down a little bit this year, and I read a different romantic fantasy series recently that reignited my imagination and this book idea came back with it!

My idea for this book was originally *very* different, however the basic conflict and original main characters remained the same, and was morphed by how my life and my own story changed. A lot of the strength in this female main character is a reflection of the strength I found in myself over the years, taking the time to heal from my own traumas. With that, I am thankful for every single person who came into my life that helped me heal, shape a life for myself, and see a real future. It has certainly been a rough ride and I'm thankful to have a very special support system behind me.

I'd like to thank my husband, for helping me through some of my darkest moments so I could get to a point mentally, physically, and emotionally to feel confident enough to put these words on paper and pursue this. He should also get a special mention here for being my go to person for vampire lore, because while I knew a lot on my own he certainly influenced a lot of the book by being a vampire lore expert! He also took great pleasure in pointing out any plot holes I left, which I am immensely thankful for.

I'd like to thank several of my friends for being the first people to read this book, and giving me their honest feedback, which to my surprise was a lot more positive than I thought it would be! It was terrifying to be vulnerable enough to share my weird creative thoughts with anyone, my husband included. Specifically, I'd like to thank Mandie and Abbey who were the very first two people to finish it, but there were several others who were equally excited to read this when I deemed it ready and were *literal* cheerleaders about the whole thing. The reassurance of both Mandie and Abbey that this book was in fact *enjoyable* to read is what finally sealed the deal on my decision to publish it.

The cover art itself is a simple sketch I made to put my idea for the cover on paper so I could explain to someone what my vision was when I commissioned them to design it. The reactions that Mandie and Abbey had to it, combined with the reactions of several of the other friends that I mentioned and several people who watched my TikTok about it inspired me to just use that sketch as the cover art. Much like the female main character of another romantic fantasy series I've recently fallen in love with, my love of art, drawing, and painting returned through the faith and support that my friends had in me. My own "found family", most of whom found me in my mid twenties, with the exception of Abbey who's been by my side through it all.

I'd also thank my entire spirit team for guiding me in this effort, because I know that there was a lot of influence in there from them. My spiritual journey has been interesting (let's call out that religious trauma am I right?). One of the things that someone I think of as a mentor always says is that you should daydream to help grow your psychic abilities. The first time she said that I felt defeated, because I didn't really daydream at all anymore. Then I started reading fantasy/fiction again and it all came back in a flood of sudden clarity that I cannot even begin to explain. I wrote this book in less than a month, because I just couldn't turn it off. I would wake up with the scenes for the book playing in my head and I had to go and immediately write them down so I wouldn't forget them.

Everything happens for a reason, and I'm thankful I *didn't* write this in high school. I needed to heal and grow so my characters could too. I hope you enjoy reading this series as much as I enjoyed writing it. And yes - I am already working on the second book. Maybe a prequel too, for Lazarus' backstory, but we'll have to see where the second book's adventures lead me first.

Oh and how could I possibly forget. "Draga" the little red bay mare in the beginning of the book I added because of my own little red bay "dragon" that I regularly ride and compete in my other passion - Eventing. In real life, I call her my little red dragon, but her name is Fondue.

www.ingramcontent.com/pod-product-compliance
Lightning Source LLC
Chambersburg PA
CBHW030810310726
48980CB00006B/443/J

* 9 7 9 8 9 9 2 9 1 8 2 9 8 *